ADVANCE PRAISE
MAJOR

MW01028557

"Dan Harary's book *After They Came* is an entertaining and upbeat work of sci-fi that cleverly incorporates key parts of the UFO phenomenon's lore and backstory - a delightful tale of wonder and hope."

—Nick Pope, UFO Expert,
Contributor to "Ancient Aliens" TV series;
UK Ministry of Defence, Ret.

"*After They Came* is a captivating novel of benevolent alien contact, incorporating author Dan Harary's vision of how to solve humanity's most intractable problems in order to create a world of abundance and peace. While exploring the impact of alien contact on the people of Earth, Harary, a skilled writer, offers-up a thought-provoking example of identifying just what, in his judgment, really needs fixing."

—Richard Dolan,
Author of A.D., After Disclosure:
When the Government Finally Reveals
the Truth about UFOs

"As a key witness myself to the awe-inspiring and non-threatening 'Phoenix Lights' mass UFO events in 1997, I feel that author Dan Harary's *After They Came* offers a welcomed and novel approach to an often much maligned topic. His book presents a fictional odyssey of one man's intimate connection to benevolent beings who gift him and humanity with a stellar 'Wish List' by which to help save our world in crisis. Along the way, Harary concurrently gifts the reader with information about ancient artifacts located around the globe, long-held lore about the alien/UFO phenomenon, and even historical UFO data."

—Lynne D. Kitei, M.D.,
Author/Award-Winning Filmmaker,
Phoenix Lights Network

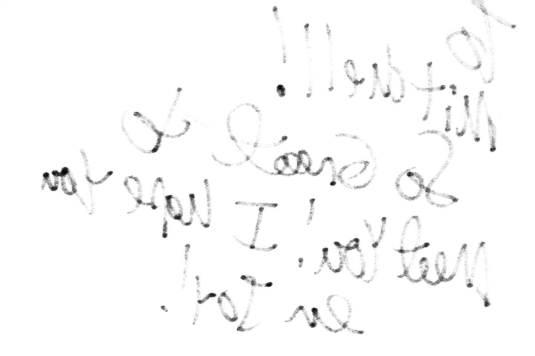

After They Came
Copyright © 2023 Daniel Harary

Published by:
Genius Book Publishing
PO Box 250380
Milwaukee, Wisconsin 53225 USA
GeniusBookPublishing.com

ISBN: 978-1-958727-02-7

230124 Trade

For my father

"The Lord went before the Israelites by day in a Pillar of Cloud to lead them along the way, and by night in a Pillar of Fire to give them light, that they might travel by day and by night; the Pillar of Cloud by day and the Pillar of Fire by night did not depart from before the people."

—Exodus 13:21, 22

PART ONE

"Wonder Man"

"What kind of world do you want? Think anything.
Let's start at the start - Build a masterpiece.
Be careful what you wish for.
History starts now."

—John Ondrasik

CHAPTER ONE

The evening Jonathan Michael Tuckerman chose to end his life would soon become known around the world as "The Night They Came." Not only did THEIR arrival interrupt his long-planned suicide, but it also quite inadvertently made Jon, without question, the most famous and significant human being on Planet Earth.

"JT," as his parents and childhood friends called him, had been planning his suicide for three years, as he was no longer interested in continuing the endurance contest he called a life. Interminably unfulfilled, JT was the survivor of a traumatic existence which held no joy for him. He had accidentally killed his first wife in a car accident. His twin children, now adults—his son, Isak, lived in Iceland as a computer tech for a large oil company, and his daughter, Lauren, was living in Paris as a bohemian artist—rarely, if ever, spoke to him. They were too busy with their own lives to return his phone calls, emails, texts, or holograms.

Compounding his problems, Jon's business—formerly a multi-million-dollar event planning and production company in Los Angeles—had failed spectacularly following the death of his business partner. He was massively in debt and felt he "owed the world" money.

Equally unlucky in love, JT did somehow manage to get married a second time. However, that coupling only lasted two years. When the money ran dry, so did wife number two. And, even today, during the truly rare occasions when he was able to interest an actual woman into having sex (following an expensive dinner date he couldn't afford), his penis no longer obeyed his commands. Like everything else in his life, even his "Johnson," his closest and dearest friend, had become an evil betrayer.

With a major birthday milestone rapidly approaching, JT had begun to put his affairs in order. He updated his will, leaving his meager possessions to his unresponsive kids, discarded his childhood treasures long held in storage, touched base through social media with every former co-worker or distant friend he'd ever known (essentially to say 'goodbye' without them knowing), and, perhaps most painfully, shed his long-prized pornography collection. (Since the age of twelve, he'd been squirreling away copies of *Playboy* magazine, and had since amassed virtually every issue in existence—except for the very first... the priceless copy that featured Marilyn Monroe on its cover.)

Finally, the date he'd been awaiting for three years, his seventieth birthday, had arrived: November 22, 2033. Jon Tuckerman spent the day running errands (purchasing the largest bottle of vodka he could find; refilling his three antidepressants at the corner drugstore, gassing up his shitbox car, and studying the route he planned to drive up (from his shabby neighborhood to the secluded Malibu beach he'd preselected years earlier as the site of his demise).

Now, he had just one step left... he'd waited until the last day to craft just the right suicide note—one that would explain his actions to those few (if any) individuals left behind who might actually give a flying fuck. "To whom it may concern," it began. "If you're reading this note, it means that I am now 'on the other side of no tomorrow,' to borrow a phrase from Donald Fagen. While I have had some moments of pleasure and joy here and there during my seventy years, most of that time has been an endurance test of unbearable loneliness and solitude. I no longer wish to simply exist without meaning or purpose. Anything I was put on this planet to accomplish I have already accomplished. Now, I just seek the peace and quiet of sweet eternal sleep. I am not ending my life to hurt anyone. My actions tonight are solely those of a man turning seventy who wishes to bestow upon himself the ultimate birthday gift... peace of mind."

Night fell and JT took one last look around his underwhelming apartment. His OCD still flagrantly in charge, Jon straightened the placemats on his dining room table, rearranged the pillows on the couch, and picked up a few stray pieces of lint ("white things," as he'd always called them) off his carpet. He then placed the vodka and the prescription bottles into a plastic grocery bag, and the suicide note in his pocket. With keys, jacket, and bag now in hand, he turned off the lights, walked through the kitchen, and descended the back stairs. His car awaited him in its usual parking spot, just at the bottom of the building's rear exit.

The drive to Malibu was uneventful. Pacific Coast Highway wasn't terribly busy on a November night at 8:00 pm. After twenty-five minutes, JT arrived at the seaside restaurant and bar he had preselected. Adjacent to the property was a small, tight alleyway. He drove as close to the sand as possible, stopping his car at a chain link fence on a bluff. He retrieved his invaluable grocery sack and strolled down onto the beach in silence. He marveled at the remarkably bright full moon that illuminated the majestic Pacific Ocean seemingly asleep before him.

Jon sat on the sand about ten yards from the point where the surf kissed the shore. The waves were mild and foamy. Looking around, he saw neither another car up on PCH nor another human being anywhere. The powerful moonlight was the only source of brilliance massaging his eyes. JT unscrewed the vodka bottle and began to guzzle, as though a thirsty man in the desert who'd come upon a lovely oasis. Pills were popped like candy—many quickly swallowed, some chewed—anything to ensure a speedy process.

Jon looked up at the moon and smiled. His heart began pounding, and he could almost hear the adrenaline pulsing through his veins. A sense of peaceful bliss overcame him. He began to gently cry, not from sorrow or fear, but from enormous gratitude and relief.

He opened his phone and began scrolling through his digital photo collection. Most of the pictures were of Isak and Lauren, taken during the weekends they had spent together at the park when the kids were quite young. Pushing them on the swings. Playing kickball. Eating ice cream cones from the truck stationed there every Saturday for years. Those times—those wonderfully enjoyable, fleeting minutes, were now thirty years gone. JT never found another person, activity, or passion that could replicate the simple loving hours he had spent with his children that way, so very long ago.

Realizing the suicide note was still in his jacket pocket on the passenger seat, JT stood and made a mad dash to his car. Tripping up the incline along the way, he smacked his forehead on a rock. "Fuck, really!?!" he said out loud, wiping a small piece of skin and some blood from his face with his shirt. He opened the front passenger door and carefully placed the note, now featuring a few bloody fingerprints, onto the dashboard, and tossed the jacket onto the back seat. He wanted whoever would eventually tow his car away later to know that this—his most heroic of acts—was not merely the scene of some random criminal activity or mysterious murder.

Slamming the car door closed, JT made his way down the beach... back to his stash of chemical bravery. Pissed about his bloody head, he picked up the vodka bottle while still standing, and began to guzzle with abandon once again.

Falling to his knees, JT next emptied the remainder of pills from his three bottles into his hands. He gang-banged them into his mouth, then swilled as much vodka as he could consume. He continued in this manner for at least fifteen minutes—far longer than he'd anticipated.

Jon stood. The world began to spin, as though he were stuck on a demonic merry-go-ride from Hell. Realizing his moment of truth had arrived, he ripped off his shirt, pulled off his socks and shoes, then fell unceremoniously face first into the sand. Like a fish out of water, he wriggled out of his pants and underwear, and began laughing hysterically when he realized he'd made a giant "sand angel." The moonlit Pacific now called to him. His future was clear and bright (although spinning a bit too quickly for his liking).

Standing once again, JT began the walk toward his destiny. The cool air felt refreshing against his bare skin. His thoughts no longer racing, and with his determination focused, he looked up at the moon and smiled.

Stumbling along, Jonathan Tuckerman, wasted as he now was, knew he had moved beyond the point of no return. The only direction "home" for him was straight ahead into the unforgiving, frigid blue sea. Through sheer force of will, he managed to eradicate his vertigo-like symptoms commonly known as "the spins." He knew that these—his final moments alive on Earth—needed to be fully embraced, cherished, and enjoyed. He simply had to experience his death in a manner equal to the symbolic importance he had fastened to it for so long.

Upright and smiling, he strode gingerly into the water, a man on a mission. He began laughing—as the cold waves reached his knees, his groin, his chest, then his neck. Never a strong swimmer, JT continued to jut himself forward, while trying to keep his head and hair out of the water for as long as possible.

Jon began to doggy paddle once he'd reached the point in the sea where he could no longer stand. He looked like a turtle. He stopped laughing, and began gasping for breath, as the effects of the drugs and the alcohol started overwhelming him. Closing his eyes, he tried to float— full body atop the water—for a moment or two, but his energy quickly abated. Now on his back, he began to sink below the surface, face up, inhaling salt water as he descended.

Looking one last time up through the water at the moon, Jon experienced what was sure to be his final thought: "Is it my imagination, or is the moon turning colors?" Drifting into unconsciousness, he realized he must have been hallucinating. He closed his eyes for the final time. The end—the sweet peaceful end he had desired for so many years was now merely seconds away.

The gigantic spacecraft that beamed JT up from the sea, naked, was later reported to be about the size of a Walmart. The massive, diamond-shaped "flying saucer" rotated as it silently hovered in the sky, emanating spectacular colors beyond description. Remarkably, the ship was seen by not one single resident of Malibu upon its initial revelation, having shot straight up into the sky from its hiding place somewhere beneath the gleam of the Pacific Ocean.

JT, now onboard a UFO, was, for all intents and purposes, deceased. Inside the craft, his rescuers, using only hand motions, placed his drenched, naked body on a table made of light. Suspended in air and rotating as though a pig on a spit at a Hawaiian luau, Jon's corpse was bathed in a variety of colors and textures more impressive than those found in a sixty-four pack of Crayola crayons. Essentially becoming "reborn," JT's body, which began to make a sizzling noise, was being relieved of the overdose of salt water, vodka, and mood-altering drugs that had consumed it just moments before.

The "Benevolents"—a term the world would soon bestow upon the extra-terrestrials who'd saved Jon's life—stood guard in silence as his cadaver regained its color, normal heartbeat, functioning brain activity and regular breathing. Even the fresh cut on his forehead had healed. When the table stopped rotating, Jon regained consciousness and raised one eyelid. Not recognizing his surroundings nor his newfound "friends," he attempted to speak, but could not. *"Heaven? Hell? Purgatory?"* he thought to himself. *"Where in the holy fuck of sweet baby Jesus Christ am I?"*

The taller of the Benevolents was a creature who could only be described as the most stunningly beautiful "Man" imaginable, with long, flowing, white-blond hair, sky blue eyes and pale white skin. His thick white robes glowed with an overpowering effervescence. His companion was an equally stellar "Woman"—comparable in appearance, also with long bright white hair, but a bit shorter, with intense, dark brown eyes. The Male raised his hand and placed his palm on JT's eyelids. No words were spoken, yet Jon clearly heard the word "rest" in his right ear and relaxed instantly.

Wherever he was now, or whomever he was with, he was no longer concerned. Jonathan Michael Tuckerman had never, in all his life, felt more rested, relaxed, or at peace.

CHAPTER TWO

The phones in police stations across Los Angeles County began ringing incessantly. Now flying through the sky on this historic night, the spacecraft was so bright, so large, and so overwhelming, the residents of Southern California were panicked beyond measure. While the U.S. Government—and countless other governments—had, of course, long known about the existence of extra-terrestrial life and flying saucers from across the universe (since retrieving four dead alien bodies in 1947, from two UFO crash sites... Roswell and Corona, New Mexico), none of them had yet taken concrete steps to disclose that life altering data with their fellow man.

Now here, on this night, a spacecraft so devastatingly "Not of This World" was hovering over Los Angeles. The airship silently swirled southeast from the coast of Malibu over Santa Monica and West Los

Angeles, and then due east across Century City, Beverly Hills, and the Mid-Wilshire district. Picking up speed, it careened over Koreatown and MacArthur Park, and ultimately appeared to be headed toward downtown Los Angeles.

Police cars, ambulances, fire engines, motorcycles, helicopters, and even military vehicles of all shapes and sizes suddenly assembled seemingly from nowhere. They began racing east as well, starting in West L.A., and chasing the craft down the city's major boulevards (Olympic, Pico, Wilshire, and Santa Monica) desperately attempting to keep pace with the massive UFO that was now illuminating much of the sky over la-la-land. Television trucks with elongated antennae were also screeching along the Southland, broadcasting live feeds of the magnificent spaceship which, after less than seven minutes in flight, had, through a global telecast, already captivated and captured the attention of almost every sentient being on Earth.

Perhaps because it was the largest open space within Los Angeles proper, the Benevolents chose to park their ship just above the infield at Dodger Stadium. There it sat patiently, swirling, its literally indescribable colors and light patterns bringing false daylight to the darkened home of the Dodgers. In no hurry, the craft now seemed to be awaiting its audience with military, police, fire, EMT, and other local law enforcement officials, not to mention the hordes of media members also arriving. Hundreds were frantically scrambling for position, as they anticipated the big event—this "Grand Opening Ceremony of The Third Kind."

The cacophony in the parking lot at Dodger Stadium was overwhelming, with cars, trucks, vans, choppers, tanks and other bizarre looking military vehicles, sirens blaring, all doing their best not to collide with each other. As the countless people arriving at the site began taking their places on the infield, encircling the craft that gently hovered perhaps two hundred feet above them, few spoke. Anxious trepidation was conveyed almost entirely through intense facial expressions.

Dozens of military and police personnel, with guns drawn, had begun kneeling. TV camera crews hustled for close proximity as well, while maintaining a respectable distance between themselves and those with exposed weapons at the ready.

After hovering for nearly half an hour, the ship stopped rotating and released a low, not unpleasant humming sound. A hush fell over the assembled masses on the field. Suddenly, a beam of bright, lemon-yellow tinged light shone down from the craft, just above second base. Three figures could be seen on the infield: the seven-foot tall "Male" alien; his counterpart, the rapturously gorgeous six-foot tall "Female," whose supernatural beauty might best be described as "offputting", and a naked Jonathan Michael Tuckerman. The Male and Female were now standing on the ground. Above them, JT was suspended vertically in the light beam, his arms extended, his nude body turning 360 degrees, as though on display in a department store window.

L.A. Police Chief Stanley Clark raised a megaphone, barking through the surreal scene. *"Who are you? Why are you here? Do you mean us harm? Where have you come from?"* Clark's team of sharpshooters stood around the entire perimeter of the ship. The Male alien raised his hand and smiled. Every weapon that had been raised and pointed at him and his companions fell to the ground. The police and military personnel were stunned—feeling as though their fingers and hands had gone numb, they were unable to hold onto anything.

A complete silence now filled the stadium. Even the sirens that had been blaring out from the parking lot suddenly fell silent. No one spoke. The wondrous aliens smiled and an ease fell over the crowd. One reporter would later describe the ambience as though "everyone in the stadium that night had suddenly overdosed on Xanax."

Without moving his mouth, the Male spoke first: "We have chosen to reveal ourselves to you—to mankind—on this night, because we felt the time had come for us to help. We have traveled a long way to talk to you. Man must learn that his real purpose here on Earth is to help his fellow man. We have been visiting your planet for hundreds of thousands of years. In fact, we helped craft your species to become the dominant force here. We have been monitoring your progress ever since. We feel that a sadness has befallen mankind... a sorrow of missed opportunity. You have not worked hard enough to solve the problems faced by so many. You have a lack of passion and compassion, an unwillingness to work together to find common ground. Your advancements in technology have only caused a further disconnect amongst you. You spend more time engrossed with your electronic screens than embracing each other in real life. Each of you has become an island. You are clearly a people whose destiny remains unfulfilled."

The Female raised her hand. "We have come to improve your collective condition," she declared, also without moving her mouth. "We have invested a great deal of care into your civilization. We no longer wish to remain passive and watch from afar, as many of your countries' leaders rule without offering aid to the plight of others. You have become comfortably numb. We are willing to share some of our technologies and abilities with you—not to be used for weapons, but so man may make advancements in easing the problems that cause so many of his fellows to suffer."

Silence continued, not only throughout the stadium but in homes around the world. Billions were now watching, live, this historic moment on their television, computer, mobile phone, and holographic display screens.

The Male once again took charge: "Our emissary to Earth—he who shall represent us, will be this man, Jonathan Michael Tuckerman. Just a short time ago, he nearly died—drowned in the sea by his own hand. We have saved his life and selected him to serve as a conduit between us and your best and brightest. Bring to him your ideas for improvements... speak with him about how our involvement can best serve and benefit man. We will work through him to solve as many of your woes as we are able. You should know, we have abilities far beyond your imaginations. Please note... you must treat Mr. Tuckerman with great care, dignity, and respect. This man is important to us. He and he alone shall be the sole means by which you may communicate your requests."

The Female added, "We must travel back to our home now—a place you would not understand. However, rest assured that we care about mankind, and that we love you, as we understand the meaning of your word 'love' to be. To give this man time to organize his life's affairs, we will return to Earth one human-month from today. Thereafter, we will continue to meet with him once per human-month, to address issues adversely affecting mankind, one at a time."

Each of the aliens gently touched JT's shoulders as he was lowered onto second base. Now standing with his arms at his sides, he stopped rotating. Clearly in a rapturous trance, it was obvious to all that he was not quite "with it." Suddenly, the light beam from above appeared once again, scooping up the two aliens. The spaceship swirled madly and within seconds flashed off and into the moonlit sky. Vanishing so quickly—as though it had never been there at all—the craft's sudden departure punched a hole through the clouds, throwing the stadium into darkness.

Now, with the only lights inside the stadium coming from TV camera crews on the field, throngs of military and police officers rushed to second base, to retrieve Jon Tuckerman. Having revived from his stupor, but realizing the chaos that was about to ensnare him, the naked subject of the world's attention decided just at that moment that now would be a most excellent time to faint.

CHAPTER THREE

For JT, the hours following the "Event" were little more than a blur. In an instant, he had become the center of the known universe. He would later learn that following the departure of the craft, he had crumpled into a fetal position on the ground, was secured by the military, and had been whisked away in a bulletproof army vehicle. His escort, comprised of more than fifteen additional security vehicles, had ensured his safe arrival at Los Angeles Airport a short time later.

A massive, camouflage green, C130 cargo plane, surrounded by countless flashing red, blue, and silver lights, awaited him at LAX... its enormous bay door having been lowered to the ground. JT's vehicle was driven directly into its belly. Three additional military cars joined inside. The plane then closed its door and began its ascent into the full moonlit sky.

On board, two doctors placed Jon onto a hospital gurney and began to examine the still very much disoriented fellow. Deeming he was a bit dehydrated, they hooked him up to an IV drip. Just a few minutes later, JT became aware of his surroundings.

"Better now?" Dr. Leon Murdoch asked as JT awoke and began showing a degree of interest in his predicament.

"Yes, thank you," he whispered. "But can you dim these lights, please? My eyes are killing me." Murdoch, a kindly man in his early eighties, glanced at the military officer apparently in charge and nodded silently. The plane's harsh white interior lights were dimmed to a more subtle bluish hue. For Jon, the ambiance on board now felt much less threatening.

A serious looking military man crouched at JT's side. "I'm Colonel Roberts. Dave Roberts. They said your name is Tuckerman, is that right?" JT nodded. "Who the hell *are* you, Tuckerman? You're clearly human. Why *you*? Why did aliens from outer space choose *you* as their liaison?"

It was only then that JT began to recall the spectacular series of events that had happened to him during the past ninety-minutes. He remembered how cold the ocean water had been. How exhilarated he'd felt. How he'd fully embraced his last heroic act—suicide—as the right decision. Then how the moon had suddenly appeared so much larger, brighter, and more colorful. He'd nearly been blinded during his frothy pas de deux with the salty sea water when the giant UFO sucked him skyward and into the annals of world history.

Jon flashed back to the moment inside the spacecraft when he realized he was no longer wet or cold. An overwhelming sense of calm, warmth, and love had embraced his body as it rotated in the light. He had tried to get his bearings on the ship but was incapable of making out the setting—it was just far too bright.

Someone—some "thing"—had taken his hand and soothed him. He'd sensed the presence of one, no two, "Beings" in the room. Scared to death and unable to speak, he had taken deep breaths while clutching his thighs so tightly his fingertips went numb. Foreign hands on his head—

one on each side, one from each of his captors—gently massaged his hair. Finally becoming so relaxed, he fell asleep and entered a dream state. His REM was so fast, it seemed his eyeballs were going to pop out of their sockets.

Jon's reverie quickly ended when Colonel Roberts grabbed him by the shoulder and shook him awake. "Still with us, Tuckerman?" he snarked. Jonathan came back to the moment, and realized he was no longer onboard a UFO with gentle, loving aliens. He was now in a very real, U.S. military aircraft, run by very real, hard-assed, military men.

"Yes, I'm still here. I'm trying to remember... it's all been just so very... very... "

"Remarkable?" suggested his second doctor... an extremely attractive woman working in tandem with Dr. Murdoch. "Your adventure this evening is nothing short of remarkable," she offered. "Many are calling it a miracle."

JT saw that the woman, this truly stunning brunette in her late thirties, was smiling at him—the first moment of magnetic male/female chemistry he'd experienced in longer than he could remember. "I'm Susan. Dr. Susan Parks," she said.

"So this is what it takes for me to get noticed by a beautiful woman? I have to be kidnapped by Martians?" JT did not mean to say those words out loud.

Dr. Parks' sweet chuckle surprised him. Clearly drawn to her newest patient—this odd UFO hitchhiker—Susan's warm, loving vibes lightened the weight of JT's waterlogged heart.

"Oh, ah, by the way... might I ask where we're going?" JT inquired. The Colonel replied, "You, my friend, have a hot date with the President of the United States. You've got some explaining to do."

JT nodded quietly. Sitting up, he suddenly realized he was still naked. "Ah, if I'm going to the White House, maybe I should be wearing some clothes?" he said sarcastically.

Apparently breaking the nearly morbid atmosphere, several of JT's attendants chuckled. "Sure." Dr. Parks smiled. "I believe we can find something around here that might fit you."

As the massive airplane, with its unprecedented cargo, continued to speed across the wintery sky that engulfed the United States, Jonathan Tuckerman, perhaps for the first time that night, began to understand the level of intensity and scrutiny his bizarre circumstances had presented to him.

"The President?" he asked. "What on earth do I have to say to her?"

"I don't think it's the 'On Earth' part she'll want to talk to you about," the lovely Dr. Parks answered.

CHAPTER FOUR

By later estimates, over 150 camera crews, reporters, photographers, and journalists, not to mention at least another 5,000 area-curious, had assembled at Obama International Airport in Washington, D.C., to greet the arrival of JT's military plane. During the course of the past six hours, the telecast of the Benevolents' appearance above Dodger Stadium had aired repeatedly, countless times, causing discussion and analysis from every media outlet in every corner of the civilized world. More eyeballs had witnessed Jonathan Michael Tuckerman's naked descent from a giant UFO—along with the pronouncements of his two companions— on live television than had witnessed The Beatles on "The Ed Sullivan Show" in February 1964, the Moon landing in July 1969, the attack on New York City on 9/11/2001, the Donald Trump-led riot on the U.S.

Capitol building on January 6, 2021, and the fall of the North Korean government in 2029, combined.

A fleet of security vehicles already assembled on the tarmac sped to meet JT's plane as it came to a halt. Scores of military personnel were on hand, ensuring the physical barricades they'd erected earlier would keep the media, and the massive hordes, from getting too close to Jon.

Colonel Roberts, Drs. Murdoch and Parks, and Jon were surrounded by a swarm of sharpshooters as they exited the plane and scurried into one of the larger awaiting ground vehicles. In a frenzy to get just a few images of the object of the world's attention—even just a fleeting snapshot of the man of the hour—several members of the media burst through the barricades, cameras at the ready. These over-eager journalists were thwarted, however, by dozens of deadly serious military men and women, guns nervously drawn, who were clearly acting within a "high alert" security status.

President Tameka Winfield, who had addressed the nation shortly after the "Event" at Dodger Stadium had concluded—to reassure the world that Mr. Tuckerman would be coming to meet with her—had ordered that the streets of Washington, D.C. be cleared in preparation for JT's arrival in her city. The tremendous military escort containing Jon and his handlers hastened from the airport and, with sirens blasting, drove toward the heart of American government. The entourage had clear access to the empty George Washington Memorial Parkway, then traveled across the Arlington Memorial Bridge to Constitution Ave. NW. They continued on 18th St. NW to H St. NW, then sped quickly into the direct path of the White House gates. A dozen helicopters following overhead broadcast live images globally, of every step of Jon's impending arrival to meet with the President of the United States.

When Jon's suite of vehicles screeched up to the front doors, the entrance to the White House was surrounded by armed guards. The security detail exploded from their cars and grabbed Jon so quickly his feet barely touched the ground. Murdoch and Parks ran closely behind their new patient, hoping to ensure that the confused man's physical and mental well being would not be overtaxed beyond what his still trembling body could handle.

Arriving at the Oval Office, Jon and his colleagues were greeted warmly by President Winfield, a striking, seventy-six-year-old woman, whose mere physical presence absolutely oozed charisma. With a somewhat puzzled look on her face, the president shook JT's hand heartily, motioning for him to sit on a sofa opposite hers. Encircling them—all standing—were Vice President Bradley Schoenberg, the Secretary of State, the Secretary of Defense, the Director of Homeland Security, and the heads of the FBI, CIA, and NSA, along with an assortment of other admirals, generals, and highly decorated military officials of virtually every size, shape, and color. Colonel Roberts, along with Drs. Murdoch and Parks, stood just behind the couch upon which Tuckerman was now seated.

"Well, I suppose we should begin," the president said. "Who are you, Mr. Tuckerman? How is it that you came to be here right now?" JT glanced around the stunningly well-decorated office. President Winfield's signature color scheme of magenta and mauve, showcased by the plush carpet, the drapes, and this very comfortable couch he was sitting on, was very pleasing to the eye.

Still quite overcome by the events that had taken place seven hours earlier, he cleared his throat.

"Today, or actually now yesterday, I guess, was my seventieth birthday," he began softly. "My plan was for my dead corpse to be decomposing someplace off the coast of Malibu about now or being eaten by sharks. But, instead, I'm in the Oval Office of the White House talking to the President of the United States." He shook his head in amazement.

"Please continue," the president said.

"My life has been a real shitshow, Madam President. A series of colossal disappointments and failures. I have been planning my suicide for about three years. All I really wanted was my life to end... for everything just to be over."

The president cocked her head to one side. "Surely things weren't THAT bad?"

JT smirked. "I'll give you the thumbnail of my life story. Then, perhaps, you can decide for yourself." He continued, "I was born and raised along the New Jersey shore. My parents were both extremely well-educated. My dad was an electronics engineer for the Army during the Cold War. He invented radar equipment and drone photography systems so we could spy on our enemies. When my parents first got married, my mother was his research assistant. After I was born, she became a high school science teacher. When I was eight, my dad told me I had been born with a twin sister, who died at birth."

Jon again glanced around the room, simply astonished at being with the President of the United States. "I was quite accident prone as a child, constantly injuring myself. I think I almost died a few times, but those memories are a haze. I had enough friends here and there, I guess, but I was a shy kid... the boy who always got picked last for sports. I never had a date in high school. I didn't even have the courage to ask a girl to my senior prom."

The faces of the assembled officials were stone. JT was being examined as though under a microscope by the most powerful woman and men on Earth. The moment was not lost on him.

"I went to college in Boston, where my parents met and got their degrees. I studied journalism. Those years were particularly painful. I was so shy. I could barely speak to anyone resembling a female. After I graduated, my father suggested I move to California. He always loved it and wanted to retire there himself. I got out to Los Angeles when I was twenty-four, with not a dime to my name.

I was qualified to do absolutely nothing. I found a series of temp jobs for a few years, until I made friends with a guy named Tobin Tanner. He'd inherited an event and party planning business from his father. I worked for him for three years, and then we became partners. Actually, I met my first wife, Janice, there. She was the bookkeeper. Tobin and I had a good run for a long while—generating millions—but then he got sick and died of liver cancer. I continued the business as long as I could, producing parties and events for people and companies large and small.

But the more money I made, the more I spent. I ran the business into the ground. Today, I'm about $240,000 in the hole."

"Not a very inspiring story so far," the president said. "You just attempted suicide, you are in massive debt, you had trouble with women, your business partner suffered with cancer, and your twin sister died. How does any of this help you befriend space aliens?"

"Honestly, I don't have the slightest idea, Madam President," JT replied animatedly. "Nothing about my life has been extraordinary. I haven't even told you about Janice's death in a car crash. My kids were two and four at the time. They're both in their early 40s now. They never forgave me. Said it was my fault... that I killed their mom!"

"Was it your fault?" the president asked.

"It was very, very late and I was really tired. Janice and I were driving home, back up to L.A. from a short vacation in San Diego. It started to rain—pouring rain out of nowhere. We were arguing. She told me our marriage was over. The car ahead of us stopped short. I slammed on my brakes. We skidded into a telephone pole. The car wrapped around it and Janice died instantly. The paramedics told me there was no way to explain how I was still alive."

"Your kids weren't in the car, I hope?" the president asked.

"No, thank God. They were at home in L.A. with their grandmother. As a single father, the next twenty years were really rough for me. Daycare and babysitters cost me a fortune. The kids and I had some fun times together, only they kept asking why I killed their mommy. My son lives in Iceland now, my daughter in Paris. They don't speak to me anymore. I married a second time fifteen years ago... to a writer named Barbara. But our family never blended. She was very cold to me—no love there. When I started having big money problems, she took off. I haven't had a real relationship with another woman in over twelve years."

Complete silence in the Oval Office. The Secretary of Defense leaned over the couch the president was sitting on and whispered into her ear. She nodded. "Yes, I agree, your life story is pretty sad, Mr. Tuckerman. Now, what can you tell me about your friends?"

"Friends?" a confused Jonathan responded.

"Yes…THEM!" President Winfield said, annoyed, pointing up to the ceiling. "Had you met them before? Why did they save you when you were drowning? Can you describe the ship's interior? What did they tell you?"

JT began to squirm. He'd never enjoyed being in the spotlight under any circumstance, and now this whole scene was so far beyond belief he could barely determine if he was awake or dreaming.

"Listen," he snapped angrily. "I went to Malibu Beach. I drank a bottle of vodka and took a shitload of pills. When I felt ready, I took off my clothes and walked into the ocean. The water was really cold. All I wanted to do was fall asleep. As I was dying, I looked up through the water, and thought the moon was changing colors. It was SO bright. God, I thought maybe I was entering Heaven."

"Suddenly, I was no longer cold, or even wet. I was on some kind of table—a light table—that was rotating. It was blinding in there. I felt the presence of some people, or whatever they are, but I couldn't see them. I did hear them talking to me... but their words weren't spoken out loud. I could sense them talking directly to me... like a telephone cord was hardwired into my ears and my brain. I felt very relaxed—very peaceful and calm. I did not have the feeling they meant to harm me."

The Secretary of Defense, clearly fed up, shouted, "Come on, Mr. Tuckerman! Enough nonsense! There *must* be a reason they came for you! How could they possibly have known to retrieve you from the Pacific Ocean just at that exact moment in time? Surely this is no coincidence or accidental rendezvous. You *must* know something more!"

Jon was becoming highly agitated. "I'm telling you the truth! I have no idea who they are or why they helped me! All I can say is that I was very comfortable on that ship. My depression was gone. My body was warm. Even the smells inside there were refreshing. I know I was dead— or nearly dead, and that aliens from outer space came to resurrect me. I know that's insane! But I'd never seen or spoken to them, ever before, in the 70-year history of my life!"

JT looked around the room at the faces of the assembled. Most seemed skeptical. A general shook his head in disgust. Jon could sense that some of his government's leaders felt he was either lying or holding something back.

He jumped to his feet. "Look! I didn't ask for this—for any of this! I see how you're looking at me. You think I was keeping my little extra-terrestrial friends from Pluto a secret? I just wanted my life to be over, that's it. I had no interest in continuing the agony of my shitty existence, living alone, a tremendous failure. Why they came for me, what they want me to do now, I have NO FUCKING IDEA, okay? I do *not* know why this is happening to me!" His cheeks were turning red.

The president rose. "Now, Jon, please calm down. We believe you." She scanned the room, realizing she was likely the only one. "Well, I believe you, anyway. And now that we've met, I will have to talk with my colleagues here about what intentions these aliens may have for making themselves known to us at this point in time. And, of course, we'll have to figure out just how *you* will fit into that scenario moving forward."

Exhausted, Jon Tuckerman took a step forward, then fell to his knees. Crumpling into a heap, he wound up plopping atop the presidential seal on the gorgeous magenta carpet. Springing into action, Colonel Roberts and Doctors Murdoch and Parks raced to his side, lifting his arms onto their shoulders. After a hospital gurney made a miraculous appearance as though from thin air, JT was placed upon it and whisked out of the building.

The planet's newest superstar began snoring madly.

CHAPTER FIVE

Nearly a week had passed since Jon Tuckerman's historic meeting at the White House. He had been resting at Bethesda Naval Hospital, where doctors had run a score of tests on him. Two hours after her meeting with JT in the Oval Office, President Winfield held a talk to the nation. During her address, she assured America—and the world—that she and her administration were excited about the now unquestioned existence of extra-terrestrial life—beings far more advanced than us—having come to visit Earth. She declared that she would do everything in her power to ensure the safety of Jon Tuckerman. While she did concede that "no one knows why Mr. Tuckerman was chosen, not even Mr. Tuckerman," she stressed that he was critically important to establishing a friendly relationship with these remarkable creatures from elsewhere. The president also announced that she and her staff had every intention of cooperating with the visitors, as long as their intentions remained noble, helpful, and peaceful.

JT was now the most famous man on Earth. A photo of him revolving in mid-air above his friends over second base at Dodger Stadium, all three bathed in yellow light, had, during the course of his hospital stay, appeared on the cover of virtually every piece of print journalism in the world. It had been played tens of thousands of times on television and been posted on the home pages of pretty much every news, religious, and lifestyle website in existence. The executives running Bethesda had to hire four additional, full-time staff members just to handle the overwhelming influx of cards, letters, flowers, gifts, and phone calls pouring in from every corner of the planet, intended for their extra-special patient... this newly minted global superstar.

JT had spent his time that week reading the book *Chariots of the Gods* by Erich Von Däniken, which had been written way back in 1968. Von Däniken had been the first author to propose an "Ancient Alien Theory." He alleged a variety of extra-terrestrial races had been visiting Earth for tens of thousands of years, interacting with, and influencing, the lives of humans on every continent. His theory hypothesized that these aliens helped to seed, shape, and guide the destinies of all races of human beings throughout man's early history, then left the planet. Considered a kook in the late '60s, JT realized that Von Däniken had been decades ahead of his time, and right all along.

On his last day at Bethesda, when both of his doctors, along with Colonel Roberts, visited him for the last time, Dr. Murdoch told his famous patient, "It's all good news, Jon. All your vitals have been completely stabilized. Everything is normal or better for a 70-year-old man. Your heart, lungs, kidneys, gall bladder, colon, intestines, liver—all good. No cancer, infections, diseases, or even arthritis. Bodily fluids all normal too—blood sugar, electrolytes, hemoglobin, white cells fine. Your blood pressure's right on the mark for a man your age. We did find your sperm count is quite high for someone your age... well above normal. I'm surprised you only had two children," he chuckled.

"Doc, a man needs a partner to procreate. My luck in that department hasn't been all that stellar lately, to say the least," Jon replied.

Dr. Parks gave him a flirty smile, pretending to be a bit embarrassed by his self-deprecating humor.

Murdoch continued, "We did discover something a bit peculiar in your body. We found a tiny piece of metal in the fleshy part of the 'webbing' between your ring and pinky fingers on your right hand. We've removed it, and our lab is studying it now. So far, they haven't been able to determine what kind of metal it is. They're thinking it's not something found on Earth. Their first inclination is that it might be a tracking device."

"Yeah, I was going to ask you about this," JT said, holding up his right hand and pointing to the three tiny red stitches in the webbing between his two outer fingers.

"If I had to venture a guess, Jon, I would say it's possible that slice of metal has been in your body since childhood—possibly even during your fetal state. Your new friends may have had their eyes on you, quite literally, your entire life."

The three stood in silence for a moment. "That does sound logical," Dr. Parks agreed.

JT sat on his bed. "So, what now? Did the president tell you what I'm supposed to be doing from here?"

"Oh, yes," Murdoch answered. "I'll let her tell you herself." He picked up the remote control to the large television in JT's room and began to play around with the buttons. "They said channel 617," he mumbled to himself.

Seconds later, President Winfield, wearing a warm, burgundy colored blazer, appeared on the screen, smiling. "How's our famous patient doing, doctors?" she asked.

"He's just fine, Madam President, medically speaking. All his vital signs are normal. Couldn't be better," Dr. Parks answered.

Murdoch added, "Agreed. Doesn't appear to be depressed... no longer suicidal, no more fainting spells. In fact, he was just asking us about his next steps."

The president wasted no time. "Mr. Tuckerman, we have studied the tape of you and your friends at Dodger Stadium. It's been reviewed and analyzed by our greatest minds, hundreds of times. The conclusion is that everyone here believes their message to be genuine. Therefore, we feel the best place for you initially would be at an office at the United Nations building in Manhattan. There you will be in a position to interact with spokespersons from around the world. You can listen to them talk about their countries' needs. You must listen to the problems they are experiencing in their homelands, then learn how to translate them into actionable solutions through the abilities and technologies the aliens may have available to help solve those issues."

"The United Nations… wow! okay, that sounds right, I guess," JT responded. The man whose event planning business had become an utter failure, who felt he "owed the world" money, whose own children had neglected him for years, was now being summoned by the President of the United States to spearhead an unprecedented conversation between dignitaries from the United Nations and an alien race from God knows where.

"Uhm, urrr… Madam President. There is something I'd like to ask you," JT said, clearly nervous and embarrassed. "As you know, I owe a LOT of people a LOT of money. What kind of salary would I be making at the UN?"

The president chuckled. "Jon, my friend. I've already had the Treasury Department review all of your financial obligations. They've reached out to all your creditors. Everything has been cleared up for you—you no longer owe a dime to anyone. Zero point zero! Also, your office at the UN will be fully staffed and fully funded. Congress and I signed an emergency appropriation measure of $175 million to launch your efforts. You won't need a salary. Anything you might request or require will be provided to you, indefinitely, without charge. I am naming you the world's first 'Inter-Stellar Ambassador.' Sounds fun, no?"

JT's head was swimming. Then he thought of something else. "Manhattan? How can I live in Manhattan without a salary?"

"Oh, I almost forgot," the president continued. "You'll be staying at my penthouse suite overlooking Central Park East. Since my Secret Service guys already have the site secured, it was the most logical residence for you. I'm sure you'll enjoy it. I certainly used to." She smiled.

"This is all just so much to absorb," Jon said. "I've never really done much of anything in my life to help anyone else. Just a small donation every once in a blue moon to some kids' charity... a few coins in a jar." He went silent.

"Oh, speaking of kids," the president interjected. "I have some people here in my office who would like to say hello." The camera from the president's video feed shifted. JT could now see two somewhat familiar faces.

"Hey, Dad," Isak said to his father. "So, what's new?" He laughed.

Then a beautiful brunette woman spoke. "Looks like you really stepped into the big shit, huh, Daddy?" Lauren chided.

Jon stood there with tears welling in his eyes. He had not seen, nor heard from, either of his two children in at least ten years. He nearly didn't recognize his bearded son or his voluptuous daughter. "Yeah, looks like your old man really did it this time," he tried to joke. "I only hope I can live up to the task the president and my friends from outer space are asking of me."

The video camera's POV shifted again, back to the president's face. "We're all here for you, Jon—myself, your children, your government, and your country—not to mention two good-looking Martians! Plus, you have no idea how many world leaders I've spoken to about you as well. They are all dying to meet you and work with you. You have far more fans than you could possibly imagine."

"Why me?" Jon said softly.

"Listen... we don't know, yet, why you were chosen—we may never know. Honestly, that's not even important," the president declared. "The fact is, Jon, you WERE chosen. You are one special man, Mr. Tuckerman. And while it's still far too soon right now to foresee how things may play out, everyone in the world has an opportunity here—through YOU—to enlist the talents of a supernatural race of beings who have come to help mankind. A new era has arrived for us all.

The fear and panic governments around the world had anticipated would befall human beings if and when aliens were ever to reveal themselves to us did not take place. Quite the contrary. We've received over thirty-four million emails from American citizens across every path of life asking us how *they* can help *you*! Everyone's on your team, Jon. We're all rooting for you!"

JT remained silent, the weight of the world on his shoulders.

"Smile for God's sake!" the president shouted. "You've been given not only the opportunity of a lifetime, but the opportunity of ALL TIME. Enjoy it. Embrace it. Have fun! People used to say, 'Life begins at forty.' Well, in your case, it looks like 'Life's going to begin at seventy!' A whole new world awaits you... one ginormous, wonderful opportunity. All you've got to do now is just grab it by the balls and shake it wide awake!"

"Yes, of course, you're absolutely right," JT said. "Thanks so much, Madam President, for this opportunity. I promise you I will do my very best."

"Your secret service detail should be there in your room any minute now to get you," she continued. "You'll be flown to New York and escorted to the penthouse. Your children will meet you on the plane as well. Bye for now!"

The president's video screen cut to the presidential seal. Dr. Murdoch grabbed JT by the shoulder. "Good luck, my man. You'll do just fine. You've got friends in big," he motioned his head toward the TV screen, "and even bigger places," he motioned his head toward the ceiling, "watching out for you."

Dr. Parks moved a bit closer to Jon. "Jonathan, my parents live in Brooklyn. I visit them quite often. If you think it would be alright, perhaps I could come visit you in the City—to ensure your health remains on track, of course." She winked.

"Yes, I'd like that. Sure," JT replied, stunned. Much to his very pleasant surprise, the sexual chemistry Dr. Susan Parks was clearly transmitting in his direction was obvious, erotic, and almost hypnotic.

For the first time in more years than he could remember, Jon Tuckerman felt the super-charged tinge of a real romantic possibility.

❧

JT's secret service team, which had given him the code name "Second Base," entered his hospital room. JT shook Dr. Murdoch's hand goodbye, while Dr. Parks gave him a quick, gentle, *so long… for now* hug. Feeling like a pearl inside a clamshell, Jon followed the four men out from his room, down the elevator and outside the main entryway. There, dozens of camera crews had been stationed for days, awaiting any fleeting glimpse of the world's new superhero.

"There he is!" a cameraman shouted. "Jonathan! Jonathan! Hey over here!" the media hordes began screaming his way. "Your fan club," a burly secret service agent wearing dark sunglasses blurted to JT. "Better get used to this, my friend. Your fame knows no bounds."

"And you are?" Jon asked as the men made their way through the throng.

"Mully. Donald Mulligan. Call me Mully."

Jon managed to give an awkward, five second wave to the media swarm, before being thrust into an armored military vehicle. Dead center within a seven-car entourage, JT's vehicle took off, while another two dozen military personnel remained behind to keep the media mob at bay.

Arriving at Obama International, JT's security detail drove him onto the tarmac and right alongside a magnificent aircraft with the presidential seal on its side. "Air Force Two," Mully said to Jon. "You're getting the vice president's plane today. Kind of a big deal!" All but carried into the craft, JT, now alone, walked down the plush aisle to find both his children seated, cold drinks in hand.

Isak rose first. "Hey Dad, nice to see you again," he said, approaching his father and extending his hand for a shake. Fighting back tears, JT extended his in return and the two men shook. Then, overcome with emotion, Jon grabbed his son and hugged him tightly. "I love you, boy," he said.

"Yeah, I guess it's been a while. Who ever thought that you—my suicidal father—would wind up becoming friends with aliens?" Isak joked.

JT, not especially appreciating his son's sarcasm, said nothing. He just smiled.

"You look pretty good, Daddy, especially for a dead guy!" Lauren interjected, rising next. Hesitantly, she approached JT and gave him an extremely awkward, five-second hug.

Jon stared at his two children in silence for a moment before he spoke. "You guys are adults! Isak, you're a man. Look at that beard! Lauren, you are…" he paused. "You are so incredibly beautiful. You look so much like…" he caught himself.

"Our dead mom? Yeah, I know. I see her face in the mirror every day," Lauren replied, a bit harshly.

"Look, I know that your mother's death can never be forgotten," JT said quickly, "but I'd really appreciate it if we could make the best of this new era in our lives. I've apologized to you both a million times for that accident. I wish I could go back and undo that night but I can't. I would just really like for us to now, at the very least, be friends. And maybe one day we can even become a family again."

Mully marched down the aisle and barked, "okay, family drama-time's over! Please buckle your seat belts. We'll be wheels up in five."

JT took a seat across the aisle from his kids. It was just then—seeing them again in real life after such a long separation period—that he realized his actual seventieth birthday present was this moment… this truly unexpected and extraordinary family reunion… with his long-lost, precious, and greatly missed children.

CHAPTER SIX

The penthouse overlooking Central Park East was magnificent, far surpassing anything JT or his children could possibly ever have imagined. "Dad, you've got some killer connections," Isak joked. Mully and his team ushered the three Tuckermans into the suite. "We've stocked the fridge with everything imaginable," he said, "But please note we do not allow alcohol—including beer and wine—or any drugs in here."

"Well, that sucks!" Lauren replied. "There goes the party I was planning for this weekend."

Mully shot the woman an evil sneer, then turned to Jon. "Mr. Tuckerman," he continued, "you'll find a broad array of clothing, toiletries, and amenities befitting a man of your newfound stature. You are not to have any medications up here, either. The president needs to ensure your safety. And, given the little 'birthday party' you threw for yourself back in Malibu, any medicine you might need during your time here will be given to you only when administered by a doctor."

"Dude, you need to get laid," Lauren snapped at the deadly serious agent.

Trying to ignore her sarcasm, Mully let the remark bounce. "I'm sure the three of you have a lot of catching up to do," he said.

As he turned to leave, two additional members of his security detail arrived, carrying large pizza boxes and a few six packs of soda. "Enjoy your meal, Mr. Tuckerman," one of them said.

Added the other, "We'll be here to retrieve you tomorrow morning at 8:30 am sharp, so please be ready to go."

"Okay, sure," JT replied.

At the front door, Mully turned around to face the room. "Oh, Mr. Tuckerman! Two very important things to remember. You are NOT to leave here this evening—none of you. There will be guards right outside this door and in the lobby, twenty-four-seven. Also, do not reach out to tell *anyone* where you now live. The president wants your new address to be kept secret."

"So we're prisoners?" Lauren complained.

"Yeah… really tough luck, miss, being trapped inside one of the most magnificent homes in Manhattan. Good night." Mully disappeared out the door, slamming it perhaps a bit more loudly than was called for.

For the next several hours, Jon and his children ate, talked, and showed each other photos on their phones of their personal exploits. Isak showed them shots of his jobsite in Iceland, him visiting oil rig fields, and his apartment, located near the main headquarters of his company. He also showed his dad and sister photos of himself with a tall, dark-haired, good-looking man who appeared to be a few years older.

"Who's this guy, your boss?" JT asked.

"God, Dad, don't you know?" Lauren interjected. "That's his boyfriend, Harold. Isak's gay!"

JT was truly shocked. "You're gay?" he asked his son in amazement.

"Yes, of course, Dad. I assumed you knew. I always thought you knew."

"Wow, I was really out of the loop on that one, huh?" JT sighed, glancing at his daughter. "So, what's Harold like?"

Isak proceeded to tell his father about his longtime significant other, an Icelandic native who worked as a holistic doctor in their community. They had been together for three years, lived together for two, and had four dogs.

"Good for you, son. That's great. Be yourself. That's all that really matters in the world, anyway," Jon said.

"And you? Are you gay too?" he asked Lauren.

"Good God no," Isak joked. "She's the hottest ticket in Paris."

"Nice, Isak! Thanks," Lauren mocked, pretending to be insulted. "Dad, you might say I'm rather popular with the fellas. Most of them are loser artists, musicians, or poets. But they're fun to hang with. They show me a good time, and I enjoy great sex. What can I say?" she chuckled.

A bit embarrassed by his daughter's bravura, Jon replied. "Have fun. Do what you want to do. Enjoy your lives. I never did. I never knew how. But if you two are having a good time, well, then, I guess I must have done at least something right."

The love JT had so nurtured, cherished, and enjoyed decades ago with these same two people on the swings at the park in Los Angeles began to ooze back into his soul. *"Maybe my kids still love me,"* he thought to himself. *"Perhaps they never really stopped."*

The next morning, chaos greeted the three Tuckermans, along with Mully and his security force, as the group was met by throngs of media, police, and thousands of New Yorkers in front of the penthouse building. Amidst the chaos, people held signs: "Jonathan Tuckerman Marry Me!" and "Take Me to Your Leader!" and even "JT Phone Home!" The mass assemblage was clear evidence that somehow the whole of Manhattan had learned where Jon Tuckerman was now based. Said one street cop to another while trying to maintain decorum, "My grandfather told me once about protecting The Beatles at the Plaza back in 1964. I think this might be even more insane!"

"YOU did this!" a livid Mully screamed at Lauren over the din. Feeling for the first time in his presence like a mouse, the normally overconfident woman said, "Uhm, ah, yeah, I guess so. Sorry! I only texted a few friends from college."

Mully and his team formed a human shield around Jon, hustling him into his awaiting vehicle, which was surrounded by the overly curious. "Dad!" Isak shouted, having become separated from his father. Lauren, too, was on her own. The pizza men (the two security agents from the night before) raced over to the younger Tuckermans and swept them up in their arms. "Come with us, NOW!" one shouted, taking them to a second military vehicle.

The anxiety in JT's car was thick. He sat in the back with Mully while two other agents were in the front seats. "That was SO NOT COOL, Tuckerman! SO VERY NOT COOL!" Mully hollered, shaking his head in disgust.

"My daughter," JT replied. "I have no control over her—I never really did. Hopefully she learned a lesson just now. I'll speak to her and make sure nothing like that ever happens again."

The security team awaiting JT's arrival outside the UN building was in full force. Dozens of police and military barricades had been erected, holding back the swarms of lookie-loos who had already assembled. "How did *these* people know I'd be here?" JT asked.

Mully replied, "The president issued a press statement last night while you were on the plane that starting today you'd be based at the UN. At least we were prepared for *this* mob scene."

The vehicles drove past the crowd and toward the rear of the building.

"We're not going to walk through them?" Jon asked, confused.

"No, sir. Sorry, no unnecessary risks can be taken with your life. We'll use the VIP entrance beneath the structure. There, you and your children will be greeted by UN Secretary General Kim and her minions."

JT's car arrived first, the second car with his kids right behind them. The Tuckermans and their security guards left their vehicles and made their way to an elevator bank. Quickly arriving on the 17th floor, the doors opened, and Secretary General Jana Il Kim, originally a native of South Korea, met the entire entourage.

"Such an honor, Mr. Tuckerman," she said, shaking JT's hand vigorously and smiling broadly at him and his children. "We are so excited to have all of you here! We have so much great work to do together! Let me show you to your office!"

JT and gang followed the tiny woman down a long corridor, arriving at a beautiful suite of offices that overlooked the East River. The view was spectacular. "All for you," Secretary Kim said, sweeping her arms through the air. Nine young men and women of various nationalities stood just inside the suite, clearly awaiting JT's arrival. "And this is your staff. Whatever you may need, they can and will make the arrangements for you. These wonderful people worked for me the past three years. As of today, they are now all for you!" The secretary beamed with delight.

Humbled and truly at a loss for words, Jon shook the hands of each member of his new team. "Thank you, thank you all," he said just above a whisper. "I'm not quite sure exactly what it is I'm supposed to be doing just yet. But as soon as I figure that out, I promise you guys will be the first to know." The staff laughed politely. Jon did not.

The next month of JT's life quickly became a nonstop whirlwind of activity. Thank God for his executive assistant, a twenty-nine-year-old woman named Meghan Marx, who was instrumental in running all things Jonathan Tuckerman. She set up his meetings, handled his phone calls, and arranged his daily schedule, while also reminding him when to eat, when to pee, and when to leave the office at night.

Meghan became JT's lifeline to the outside world.

Jon wasn't quite sure how to begin his new job. That first week at the UN, he primarily spoke only with those closest to him... his children, his staff, and the President of the United States, whose daily 3:00 pm phone calls he cherished. "Start big," the president had advised him. "Start big and work your way down. Who knows how long these aliens will be around to help, right? Create a 'hit list' of mankind's problems and concerns. Meet and talk with everyone possible who knows about those things. The more you learn, the more informed you'll become and the more intelligent you'll sound to your friends. You produced giant parties and events for your clients for years, Jon. Think of this challenge as producing the biggest event in the history of the world."

JT had Meghan wheel a large whiteboard on rollers into his office. He gathered his staff and children. "Just got off the phone with the prez," he told them. "She said we should start big. We should create a list of the world's most pressing issues, and study each of them extensively. I think that's the best possible advice. I'm going to write our ideas down, now, on this board. Let's just go around the room and call out what's on your mind. How can we make the world a better place?"

Isak spoke first. "No nukes," he said emphatically. "As long as the world has nuclear weapons, human beings can never be completely assured of their continued existence."

"Yes, good start," his father said, writing "No Nukes" as the first entry on the pristine giant board.

"Famine and the lack of clean drinking water," Meghan spoke next. Her comments were added to the list.

"Gun violence," said Lauren, adding, "school shootings, murders in the streets, rapes, sex crimes."

"All good," JT said, as he continued to scribble.

"Poverty in the land of plenty," added a male member of the staff.

"Discrimination based on sexual orientation and race," said a young woman. "More, keep going," Jon encouraged. Additional shout outs: "Cancer. AIDS. Drug addiction. Drunk driving. Religious fanaticism. Crimes against children."

"Climate change!" shouted Isak. All heads turned.

JT paused for a moment... the scope of that one overwhelming him.

"Even though I work for an oil company," Isak said, "it's time for the fossil fuel industry to end. It's given us air pollution, depleted the ozone layer, caused acid rain, and has been melting the polar ice caps. Maybe they can end global warming."

"All good," Jon replied, writing as quickly as Isak spoke. JT stopped and took a few steps away from the board. "What are we missing?" he posed to his audience.

Meghan: "War. Maybe the visitors can help us stop war?"

JT wrote "END WAR" on the board in all caps.

"Excellent start, you guys. Great list." JT examined the board intently. "Let's start with nuclear weapons. The president said to start big. That's pretty big. All in favor?"

Every hand in the room went up. "Good, looking good," Jon said. "All of you, start putting your heads together. Let's start researching every organization, society, and activist group out there that has been fighting for the end of nuclear proliferation. Compile the information and bring it to Meghan. Meghan, I'd like you to start setting up meetings for us as soon as possible with the leaders of those various outfits. Let's find out exactly what we're up against."

The staff stood and applauded. A product of sheer happenstance, JT had suddenly become a leader... a professor tasked with nothing short of eliminating all the world's mistakes with the help of magnificent extra-terrestrials. Hopefully, through his "connections" with these mesmerizing beings from another place and time, JT would be the one to bring an end to the long-simmering threat of a thermonuclear holocaust.

A few minutes after the members of JT's staff had returned to their desks, Meghan approached her boss. "Mr. Tuckerman, a package just arrived for you by messenger." She handed Jon a parcel, smiled, and returned to her desk.

Jon opened the package. Inside he found a small white jewelry box. Inside that, he discovered a sterling silver man's necklace with a small glass vial attached. He held the vial up to the light and could see a small sliver of metal inside. The accompanying note read: "Dear Jonathan... Thought you'd like to have this former piece of your body back. The techs were correct. It is some kind of tracking device... like a GPS system from the future. You should probably wear this every day so your pals in the sky will always know where you are. Thinking of you fondly! xxxooo." The card was signed by Dr. Susan Parks.

Jon placed the piece of jewelry around his neck.

CHAPTER SEVEN

Over the next several weeks, JT and his team met with members of top organizations from around the world to discuss the state of the Global Nuclear Threat. Scientists, biologists, chemists, humanitarian relief workers, and other experts informed Tuckerman's group about virtually everything there was to possibly know about nuclear weapons.

They were shown documentary films of Japan from 1945 following the aftermath of Hiroshima and Nagasaki and learned the secret history of America's "Manhattan Project." They watched old black and white interviews with members of the CIA from the 1950s discussing the Cold War with the former Soviet Union, and how that country had fought to catch up to, and surpass, the U.S. nuclear arsenal. UN-based experts from Asia described the more modern perils of the nukes that Pakistan and India had long threatened each other with, along with the ongoing instability of North Korea's fascination with their newer weapons, and Iran's long-held desire to start building their own.

Meghan had scheduled meetings with representatives from the Atom Project, the European Nuclear Disarmament Society, Friends of the Earth, Global Zero, the International Campaign to Abolish Nuclear Weapons, the International Atomic Energy Agency, the Arms Control Association., the World Disarmament Campaign, and the Federation of American Scientists... the leading experts in tracking the size of nuclear weapon inventories around the globe.

JT and his staff learned that, at present, nine countries in the world possessed a combined total of more than 15,000 nuclear weapons. Broken down by country: Russia 7,000, the U.S. 6,800, France 300, China 260, UK 215, Pakistan 130, India 120, Israel 80, North Korea 60—with Iran in the wings.

Jon's head was swimming. His brain had become so overloaded with data about the perils of a potential global nuclear conflict that he could barely sleep. He tossed and turned in bed every night, imagining the devastation that just one unfortunate error in judgment or a simple human mistake could potentially cause.

A giant "No Nukes!" poster from a famed 1979 rock music concert which Isak had purchased online was plastered across a wall in the Tuckerman UN office suite. It was the topic on everyone's mind there. The energy and enthusiasm being generated by Jon's officemates had given Jon a new lease on life... a new reason to wake up in the morning.

"Meghan!" JT shouted one day. "Please get me the president on the phone!"

In a flash, his superstar aide responded, "She's on line 3."

"Hi, Jon," the president said. "What's the scoop?"

"Madam President, I have an idea for you. I'm not sure how you're going to react to this, but I need to run it past you."

"Fire away, Mr. Tuckerman," she replied.

"Well... actually NOT firing away is the idea. What if I asked the aliens to simply deactivate every single nuclear warhead on the planet? I don't know if they can, but what if they *could?*" he posed. "What if, with one simple request, our world became non-nuclear?"

Silence greeted JT on the other end of the phone. Eventually, the president responded. "So literally, 'No Nukes,' huh?" she considered. "I think Congress would shit, Jon, not to mention the fact that the heads of the leaders of Russia, China, and Israel would explode."

"But if ALL the nukes were gone, then we're all on the same level playing field, correct?" JT implored. "We'd be back to pre-1945. No country would be a nuclear state. The threat of a nuclear accident vanishes. The one-upmanship that's been going on since the 1950s would be gone. I'd even ask them if they could monitor the world in the future, so that if anyone tries to build another nuclear weapon again, they would be unable to do so."

More silence. Then, "Jon, I really, really should run this past Congress, past the Joint Chiefs of Staff and the Pentagon. All the heads of our military. The CIA, the NSA, Homeland Security. I really, really, really SHOULD do all that," she said. Again silence. "But you know what? Fuck 'em! Let's do it, Johnny boy! Let's end the threat of nukes forever. Go for it! Do it with my blessing. If they actually do have that kind of power, let's make it happen. Oh, and while you're at it, ask them if they can also destroy every chemical and biological weapon out there as well. I'll get you our data on their suspected locations by tomorrow morning. I'll have it loaded onto an iPad for you, so you can bring it with you onboard their ship."

"Are we really going to do this, Madam President? Just imagine, you, me, and aliens from outer space ending the nuclear threat forever!" Jon said.

"That sure would look pretty good on our tombstones, Mr. Tuckerman," the president replied, adding, "Not to mention winning you the Nobel Prize! Do it, Jon. We're either about to make an enormous mistake or become the heroes of heroes."

The next morning, Team Tuckerman squeezed in a meeting with the Organization for the Prohibition of Chemical Weapons... the group's spokesman handing Jon a flash drive filled with additional data. As soon as that meeting ended, Meghan gave JT a package delivered by courier. Inside, he found the iPad the President had promised him. Playing around with it, he found charts, graphs, and statistics that filled nearly 400 MBs of data. As he fiddled with the device, a whirling noise that could not be ignored began to hum its way through the UN building. Faintly at first, then growing louder and louder, the sound became so intense, everyone in the building stopped what they were doing to wonder. A team of security men ran into the Tuckerman office.

"Mr. Tuckerman!" their leader exclaimed. "Your friends! They've come to see you!" Jon glanced at his desk calendar. It was December 22nd, exactly one month since he'd last seen them... one month since his seventieth birthday.

Meghan opened the blinds behind JT's desk. The view, normally one of the most magnificent of the East River in all of Manhattan, was a bit obscured by the gigantic aircraft—the now infamous "Dodger Stadium Special," as various newspapers around the world had nicknamed it right after its first appearance.

The giant airship hovered above the East River, about 600 feet in the air, swirling rapidly. "Mr. T, it looks like you've got a meeting today that I didn't have on your calendar," a clearly frightened Meghan Marx whispered. Normally JT's Rock of Gibraltar, the woman was now shaking.

Isak and Lauren approached their father's desk. "Good God, Dad, it's so much cooler in real life!" Isak said.

Lauren added, "Go get 'em cowboy! Go show those aliens who the real boss is around here!"

JT stood, iPad in hand. "Well, gang, looks like my ride's here," he said trying to sound nonchalant to alleviate the fears and concerns written on the faces of his young staff, while disguising his own. "It's alright everyone. We all knew they were coming back, right? Looks like today's the day!"

"Sir, I'm Sgt. Pike," said the hefty leader of the security detail. "Our orders from the Secretary General are that when they arrived to see you, we were to escort you up to the roof. Can you please follow us, sir?" JT quickly fell in line with the detail, which was comprised of eight heavily armed, muscular men, in bulletproof vests and helmets, carrying assault rifles.

"Would you like me to come up there with you?" a trembling Meghan asked.

"No... no thank you, Meghan. That's very sweet, but they're here only for me. I'm sure everything's going to be just fine." He then walked right up to her and whispered in her ear. "In case something horrible ever happens to me, would you please do me a favor?"

"Of course, sir. For you, anything," she answered.

"Please tell my children I said, 'Thank you for letting me be their father again,' and please tell President Winfield that it was the highlight of my life to meet her, okay?"

"Yes, for sure," Meghan replied.

"And Meghan, just so you know, I greatly appreciate everything you've been doing for me and for our little group here. You are the greatest personal assistant anyone could ever have." He gave her a quick peck on the cheek and she blushed.

Jon followed his military escort down the hallway, into an elevator, and up onto the roof of one of Manhattan's most iconic buildings. It was a clear, sunny, winter's day over cloud-free New York City. The group of nine men stood atop the building in awe... the colors glistening from the sides and bottom of the enormous aircraft were gorgeous and alluring. Hues so rich and deep in color and textures that several of the men, including JT himself, wiped tears from their eyes.

"Well, there's something you just don't see every day," Jon joked, trying to lighten the tense situation. Turning to Sgt. Pike, he said, "Sergeant, it's fine now. You and your men can stand down. I've done this dance routine before. I don't think they're going to evaporate me or anything."

The team backed off, taking several steps closer to the rooftop entry door. "Good luck, sir," Pike said. "The whole world is watching."

Jon walked toward the easternmost edge of the UN building and looked down. He could see that at least a dozen or more TV camera crews and photographers had already assembled below the site, recording the glorious craft for a global viewing audience.

A beam of light, seemingly brighter than daylight, aimed itself almost horizontally at the top of the UN building, encapsulating Jon in silver and orange hues. He took a deep breath. "Here we go again," he muttered to himself. As he became elevated, he couldn't quite "experience" the sensation of being airborne—he felt as though he were in some kind of suspended animation or dream state. He knew, mentally, what was happening, but his body felt like he was watching himself as a character in an old science fiction movie.

Aboard the craft, Jon was placed aside what he had originally described as a "table of light," but this time, he was standing. Recognizing his hosts from Dodger Stadium... the luminously beautiful "Male" and "Female" who'd saved him from drowning... Jon managed a weak smile. "Hey guys, long time, no see," he said feebly, his joke falling completely flat.

"What have you learned, friend?" the Male spoke first. "What are your people most concerned with? How can we help man? What would you like us to do first?"

JT could hear the words, loud and clear, as the Male alien communicated solely through telepathic transmission right inside Jon's head. Shaking, but determined, his voice quavering, JT said, "Nuclear weapons. There are far too many—more than 15,000 based in nine countries. Just one going off, even accidentally, would set off a chain of events that could become catastrophic in just a matter of hours. We've been living with this Sword of Damocles hanging over our heads since the 1940s. Even if one person somewhere along the way were to make just one mistake in judgment, global thermonuclear war could break out and eliminate much of mankind.

I spoke with our president. She agreed. So, on behalf of the President of the United States, my country, and all of humanity, I'd like to request that you destroy or deactivate or eliminate every single nuclear weapon that currently exists on the Earth. And, past that, if you can... please ensure that no nuclear bombs can ever be built in the future."

The aliens looked at each other—it appeared they were smiling. "Jonathan, we are most pleased that you would make this request first. Our mission here is not to alter or change the course of human history without specific requests for help or guidance from our carefully chosen contacts. Your planet's nuclear weapons fascination has been of great concern to us as well. We have been monitoring Earth since your 1945 far more often than we had before," the Male said.

The Female added, "Yes, we have the ability to locate and track every source of enriched plutonium and uranium used to build nuclear weapons on your Earth. We could have eliminated all of them decades ago, but we did not wish to intercede. Now that mankind has made an official plea to us, however, we will be glad to oblige that request."

Jon turned on his iPad. "The president provided this information to me for you to review. It shows the location of the world's nuclear arsenals, as well as where my government believes caches of biological and chemical weapons scattered around the Earth are being stored. Can you wipe out all those devices at the same time?"

Again, the aliens looked at each other, smiling. "How quaint," the Female said, referring to the iPad. She and her male counterpart each touched the small computer for just a moment, obviously downloading its data. Seconds later they removed their hands.

"We now have your president's information. We will cross reference it with our own intelligence," the Male said.

"That's great... terrific! Thanks so much!" Jon said, clearly excited.

His hosts smiled warmly at him.

"Can I ask you something personal?" JT added.

"Of course, friend. You may ask us anything you wish," said the Male.

"Do you have names? What do I call you? And where are you from?" JT inquired.

The Female responded first. "I am Kalyssa. This is Jorthon, my genetic father. We are a race some of our past contactees on Earth have called

'Nordics' or 'Tall Whites.' Our home is an interdimensional planet that you would not find on a star map, nor be able to comprehend. While it is very far from your Earth, our technologies and knowledge of wormholes in space-time have long enabled us to travel easily across galaxies and dimensions."

"Well, that explains a lot, I suppose," Jon said with a blank expression on his face, realizing how far beyond his mental capacity this new job of his demanded. "Well, thanks for introducing yourselves. I really appreciate that. Everyone's been asking me about you. By the way, when you guys start zapping out the nukes around the world, can you please start with North Korea first?"

Zip, bang, boom, bright lights, flash, zing, zap! Seconds later, and much to his surprise, JT found himself back behind his desk at the UN office. His fellow suitemates were astonished to see that he'd returned so soon, and without having walked in through the front door!

"Meghan! What's for lunch today?" Jon cried out. "For God's sake, I'm STARVING!"

CHAPTER EIGHT

Forty-eight hours passed. JT and the team were at their desks when the phones started ringing off the hook. Jon looked up at Meghan who was handling a call that was obviously quite intense. "Mr. T, line 2... SHE needs to talk to you, NOW!"

Jon, of course, knew who "she" was, and lifted the receiver.

"Jon, you have no fucking idea what's going down here! Holy shit balls!" the president shouted, clearly joyous. "They are absolutely freaking out! It was bad enough getting screamed at by the heads of Russia, China, Israel, and France last night, not to mention the King of England. Then, today, our guys at NORAD were losing their minds, too. Every nuke across our country, in silos from east to west, our biggest labs, even our submarines in every ocean, have all been deactivated. You did it, Johnny boy! *They* did it! *We* did it!"

JT sat in awe. "Really? You're not kidding me?" Jon asked.

"No, of course not! It's the real deal. The nuclear age is done. Oops, gotta go... the guys from the Pentagon are walking into my office right now to tear me a new one." Distinctive laughter from the President of the United States could be heard as she hung up the phone.

TV news broadcasts presented footage of the giant craft hovering over military installations around the world, blasting each of them with a variety of multi-colored light rays. The news clips also depicted the looks of astonishment on the faces of the military men and women, stationed at those facilities, as they looked up into the sky, helpless—the great UFO clearly in command.

"NO NUKES!!" screamed the headline in the next day's *New York Times*, featuring the largest typeface headline in the paper's 182-year history.

In a massive, front-page article by Max Weinstein, the paper reported:

> Apparently, Jonathan Tuckerman's friends in high places weren't fooling around when they claimed "We have come here to improve mankind's collective condition." In just the first month since their startling arrival and revelation to the world at Dodger Stadium, the "Benevolents"—as they've become known, have wasted no time getting straight down to business. After their first meeting since Mr. Tuckerman took on his unprecedented post at the United Nations as the world's first "Inter-Stellar Ambassador," his colleagues from wherever they're from have disabled every single nuclear weapon on Earth. Reports from the governments of Russia, China, Israel, France, the UK, North Korea, India and Pakistan have confirmed to this reporter that no nation on Earth now has the capability of wiping out another via nuclear option.

As for the United States, this reporter spoke at length yesterday with President Winfield, who, clearly pleased with this remarkable achievement, stated, "Yes, it is true, Mr. Weinstein. The United States is no longer a nuclear force. Mr. Tuckerman's aliens have indeed eliminated the use of every weapon within our collective arsenal. Every silo, every bomber, every submarine that held our nuclear might has been neutered. Commanders from NORAD and spokespersons for Los Alamos, Lawrence Livermore and Sandia Laboratories have all confirmed the same results. It's the first day of a new age, Mr. Weinstein. A new era for mankind."

It appears that nuclear weapons have now become a thing of the past, like manual typewriters, hula-hoops, disco, ponytails on men, Facebook, Twitter, and Google. No longer must one country, continent, or hemisphere hold its breath in fear that a governmental or military leader in another location might decide that that day is the day to wipe out millions. The chants of "No Nukes" from protestors in the 1970s and '80s, who rallied in the parking lots of nuclear power plants around the world, have been translated and acted upon by no less than an advanced race of creatures from another place and time— alien beings who chose to honor the request of just one man—one formerly suicidal man—named Jonathan Michael Tuckerman.

We must say an enormous "Thank you, Mr. Tuckerman" for your service to a grateful nation and a grateful planet. The world can sleep better tonight, knowing that you, and your remarkable new friends from the sky, have our backs."

However, Weinstein's article concluded with this ominous forecast: That is, of course, assuming they are not here to extinguish all of mankind. For if so, they may have just destroyed our sole means by which to combat them.

CHAPTER NINE

The chaos caused by the hundreds of visitors to Jon's office each and every day for the rest of that week was ceaseless. He shook more hands in three days than he'd shaken in total throughout the course of his entire lifetime. Throngs of people assembled in front of the UN building with giant signs: "Jon Tuckerman Plus Space Aliens Equals No Nukes!" read one. Isak and Lauren were ecstatic. Their father, so sad, so forlorn, so depressed for as far back as the two of them could remember, was now the man of the hour... the most heralded hero of this, or perhaps any previous generation.

As JT continued to receive accolade after accolade, embrace after embrace, from his colleagues at the UN, and visiting dignitaries from every corner of the globe, he kept beaming. His children couldn't remember the last time they'd seen the man smile—and actually mean it.

Neither could he.

Unfortunately, that last line of the Weinstein/*New York Times* article triggered a great deal of controversy for both President Winfield and Jon from suspicious citizens around the world. The president was scolded by numerous senators and members of Congress, along with several right-wing TV news anchors and media analysts, many of whom suggesting she should be impeached for agreeing to give up America's nukes without Congressional approval. Small groups of protestors living in "red states" throughout the U.S., as well as in London, Paris, Rome, Madrid, Berlin, Buenos Aires, Lima, Sydney, and elsewhere around the world, drew sizeable crowds waving signs in protest. One read, "Thank you President Winfield and Mr. Tuckerman for Allowing Space Aliens to Sign Our Death Sentence!"

Regardless of those activities, the president believed in her heart that she and JT had done the right thing. She acted to reward Jon with some personal gifts. The first of these was securing two separate, and quite beautiful, two-bedroom apartments in Manhattan for Isak and Lauren. By messenger, she'd sent keys to both of Jon's children, along with notes that read, "Thought it might be nice for each of you to get out from under your father's larger than life shadow!"

In addition, she also gave JT another gift—a person—an older Chinese man named Russell, who would serve as butler, chef, and personal aide to the world's new hero. "Jon, you will LOVE Russell," her note to JT said. "He makes a prime rib that melts in your mouth. He will spoil you rotten. Anything you need for your 'personal self,' he can find, build, cook, borrow, or steal. Enjoy him, my friend. He's a godsend."

Shortly after the No Nukes phenomenon had occurred, JT decided to take a day off from work, simply to decompress at the penthouse. Russell, now living in one of the two extra bedrooms just vacated by Jon's children, prepared his first dish for his new boss... prime rib, lobster tail, and potatoes au gratin. The meal nearly brought JT to tears. "Russell, you are MY hero," Jon said through a mouth dripping with butter sauce. "No matter what happens to me in the future, I'm keeping you."

Russell rarely spoke. Everything he needed to say was conveyed through his smile and his stunningly soul-piercing and wisdom-filled slate grey eyes.

Following the meal, it was all Jon could do to make his way into bed. The events of the previous month had been all-consuming and overwhelming. Brushing his teeth was a chore. He was bone tired. Crawling under the covers, his head hit the pillow so hard, he heard a small puff of air escaping from it. Chuckling to himself, he quickly drifted off to a deep restful sleep. It was only 9:00 pm.

Moments later, there was a gentle tap on the bedroom door. "Mr. Tuckerman, sir," Russell loudly whispered. "So very sorry to bother you, sir, but…"

"What's wrong, Russell?" Jon called from his bed.

"There is someone here to speak to you. A lady. Doctor Susan Parks. Shall I send her away?"

JT sat upright like a bolt of lightning had struck him. "Susan is here?" he shouted through the door. "Give me a minute, okay, Russell? Tell her I'll be right there. Please offer her a cold drink or something!"

"Yes, Mr. Tuckerman, of course. I will do that," the butler responded.

All but falling out of bed, JT suddenly found a stash of misplaced energy he didn't know he had. He quickly combed his hair in the bathroom mirror, rinsed his mouth with mouthwash, and double checked his eyes to pick away anything stray that might have formed during his solid forty seconds of rest.

"Hello, Susan, err, ahm, Dr. Parks. So nice to see you again," he said to himself in the mirror. "Dr. Susan Parks! What a nice surprise. What brings you here at this hour?" As JT practiced his greetings he realized his hands were shaking. "Relax," he said to himself. "You're the 'Friend of Aliens.' Take a breath, Johnny, she's just a girl. You'll be fine."

Now clad in a plush bathrobe over his pajamas and wearing fuzzy, warm slippers, Jon entered the living room.

"Why, hello there, Mr. Tuckerman, savior of man," Dr. Parks said, greeting him warmly. "How's the most famous human being alive doing this evening?"

JT couldn't help but smile broadly at this vision... his dream girl come to life. But then, quite unexpectedly, he let out a huge loud yawn.

"I'm sorry for the late-night intrusion. Were you actually sleeping? At nine o'clock?" she chuckled.

"Yeah, ah, sorry, I was, Susan Doctor, I mean Doctor Susan, err, ahm, Doctor Parks. I'm a lightweight I guess," JT replied.

Then, summoning courage from the soles of his feet, he added, "Had I known you were coming, I would have asked Russell to make us a romantic candlelight dinner for two." As soon as he'd finished the sentence, he made a face which read, "Where did THAT come from?"

Taking the bait, Susan jumped right into the pool. "Oh, romantic, huh? Next time, I'll make my dating intentions known to Russell well in advance. After all, he seems to be the man in charge around here."

A greatly embarrassed Russell Chimelong smiled, then silently began to slither away along the walls, wishing to be anywhere else at that moment.

"He really is an amazing guy," JT said. "So, what really brings you out tonight, Susan?"

Dr. Parks took a seat on the thick, deep blue sofa. JT sat across from her in a matching chair. "I've been thinking about you, quite a lot actually. Wondering how you're holding up... how you're feeling. What your emotions might be doing to you in light of all this... *misery*," she said, indicating the opulence of the penthouse. "I'm just concerned, Jon. After all, I am your doctor, right?"

The woman's eyes, face, hair, and smile literally took Jon's breath away.

For the first time in over a decade, Jonathan Tuckerman made a "move." Shocking even himself, he stood, approached the lovely woman, sat next to her on the couch, and held her hand.

"Susan," he whispered. "I really don't know what I'm doing. Everyone is expecting so much of me. I've got people from around the world coming into my office every day, looking at me like I'm some kind of Messiah figure. For some bizarre reason, aliens from Krypton like me very much, and they ended the nuclear age in a few days, just because I asked them to, okay. But THEY did that. I'm just a man, a lonely, simple, stupid man. A messenger boy who's had a troubled life for seventy years. For God's sake, I tried to kill myself, and I didn't even do that right! What if this whole intergalactic thing is a stupendous mistake? What do THEY see in ME?"

Susan leaned into Jon's personal space and kissed him. They each closed their eyes. It was clearly one of those once in a lifetime kisses—the kind every person dreams of—the kind made famous in 1940s movies. "Self-pity much?" she whispered before taking Jon's face in her hands.

JT began shaking, then actually started trembling.

"Are you okay?" Susan asked.

"I don't know what the hell's going on here, but I think, maybe, we might really be onto something big," he answered.

"You've got to stop doubting yourself and your situation, Jon," the doctor said. "Think of them as a gift. An unbelievable, supernatural gift from God. Out of the eight billion people on planet Earth today, highly intelligent beings from another planet chose YOU to represent them and all of mankind. Perhaps one day they'll tell you the 'why,' although that really doesn't matter, does it? Look at what you've already accomplished in just one month! Because of you, they let us know they exist, that they want to help us, and through you, they've already ended the nuclear age. And that makes you, Jonathan Michael Tuckerman, without any doubt in *my* mind, the most wonderful, sexy, and interesting man I've ever met."

"But I'm so much older than you!" Jon noted.

She kissed JT again. "Do you really think that matters to me?" she asked.

For a man whose pathetic sex life had been confined primarily to masturbating to porn for years, he was now in territory he'd pretty much forgotten how to navigate.

"So, do you think Russell would freak out if you and I threw a little pajama party in your bedroom... without pajamas, of course?" Susan whispered into Jon's ear. It was, without question, the sexiest single sentence he had ever heard in his entire life.

"Russell who?" JT joked. "Come on." The two stood, holding hands, and began walking toward Jon's bedroom. Passing Russell in the corridor, the three
exchanged guilty smiles and head nods. As Susan and JT made their way into Jon's inner sanctum, giggling like children, Russell gently closed the door behind them. "Goodnight and sweet dreams," the butler said softly.

Making his way back across the living room and toward his own bedroom, Russell smiled to himself. "Thank God, finally, this man is getting laid," he said out loud.

CHAPTER TEN

Jon spent the 2033 Christmas holiday weekend in the penthouse, where he introduced Susan to his children. The foursome enjoyed a relaxed few days together, with Susan and Lauren often sneaking out to go shopping along Fifth Avenue. The Tuckerman clan were invited to spend that New Year's Eve at the White House, where they celebrated the arrival of 2034 with the President of the United States, her daughters, her grandchildren, and a few of her closest friends.

Jon returned to his UN post on January 3rd. Starting late that morning, the phones in his office never stopped ringing, following the mostly positive feedback he received from around the world after the No Nukes events had taken place. While he still became nervous every time he entered his UN suite, JT was feeling a bit less stressed, given his first notable success with the nuclear weapons elimination, not to mention the mind-blowing sex he now was enjoying—often—with Susan.

Upon arriving at his office, JT's first act each morning was to meet with Meghan privately for fifteen minutes. (She made the best coffee he'd ever had.) They would discuss that day's compacted agenda and serve as each other's confidant. JT was in awe of her talents and skills in organizing the barrage of people who were now constantly demanding his time and attention. She ran his office like a Swiss watch, running everything on time to the minute—without a glitch—each and every day. Meghan would have been a remarkable general in a war, Jon thought to himself while watching the super woman in action. "Thank God for you," he said to her often. "I couldn't possibly handle any of this if you weren't here."

Team Tuckerman decided that Global Famine should be the next major problem to be tackled by the aliens. Meghan arranged meetings for the group with the World Health Organization, World Vision, Concern Worldwide, UNICEF, Action Against Hunger, CARE, the World Food Program, Mercy Corps, and Oxfam to determine the exact extent of this nightmare. UN delegates from across Africa—including South Sudan, Ethiopia, Kenya, Somalia, Yemen, Niger, Liberia, the Congo, Zambia, and Chad—also made their pleas to Tuckerman to speak to the creatures from beyond to enlist their help in feeding the starving millions in their homelands.

To each of the teary-eyed men and women who came through his doors to advocate the plight of their countries' hungry, JT would reply, "You have my word. I will relay your concerns to the visitors. I have no idea how they might go about solving this crisis, but I promise you I will make them aware of these humanitarian travesties. I only hope they might know some way to help."

Now, exactly one month since the giant UFO made its debut above the East River, the craft arrived again to retrieve its human guest star. The same protocols that had been in place the last time manifested once more, and Sgt. Pike and his men entered JT's suite. "Mr. Tuckerman, please follow us, sir," he said. Jon grabbed his iPad, now filled with data on the locations of the world's most hungry, and hustled out of his office, walking quickly behind his security detail.

Once again on the roof of the UN building, the men watched in wonder as the UFO, spinning and swirling as majestically as ever, never lost its eye-pleasing appeal. Said Pike, "It's just so, so…"

"Unbelievable?" JT filled in.

"Yes, sir, Mr. Tuckerman," Pike responded. "That really is the only word."

The light beam captured JT again and swept him quickly onboard the craft.

"Hello, friend, what have you learned?" Kalyssa asked. "Are your people pleased with what has been done with your weapons of mass destruction?"

"Yes, the world is very happy, very excited and thrilled," Jon answered. "Thank you so very much for that. Although there were some here and there who thought you did that to eliminate any chance we would have of defending ourselves against *you,* if *you* turned out to be malevolent."

Kalyssa and Jorthon looked at each other with puzzled looks. "Malevolent? Surely your associates must know we are only here to help?" Jorthon replied. "Your nuclear weapons would have no effect against us. If we were malevolent, we could easily eliminate all human beings in a few days' time."

Clearly a bit stunned, Jon said, "okay, good to know. Thanks for sharing."

Taking a deep breath, he decided to move the conversation forward. "We would now like to ask if you could please help us feed the hungry." He started up his iPad and showed his friends screen after screen of towns and villages across Africa, Asia, South America, Mexico, the Philippines, and elsewhere, most afflicted by severe famine. "This information points out the locations where millions of men, women, and children are starving. Their extreme poverty and the conflict between their governments and their militaries have led to this catastrophe of hunger. There is an ample supply of food for every human being on Earth, yet these poor souls do not have access to enough."

"How well do you know the story of Moses and the Israelites?" Jorthon asked.

"Ah, somewhat. They fled from Egypt, Moses parted the Red Sea, and they wandered in the desert for forty years. Why do you ask?" JT answered.

"Do you recall reading about 'manna from heaven'?" Kalyssa asked Jon.

"Yes, sure, a myth, a fairy tale, describing how Moses and his people survived all those years without food."

Kalyssa continued, "Not a fairy tale, friend. Our ancestors provided that nourishment to those travelers. Manna is real. The Israelites called it 'God's Nourishment.' But it was members of our race who provided that substance to keep them alive."

JT was stupefied. "Did your ancestors part the Red Sea too?" he asked, jokingly.

"Yes, of course," Jorthon replied. "Did you really think a human did that?"

Jon was quickly getting a class in Bible Study 2.0. His head was spinning.

"This news is beyond me," he whispered.

Kalyssa went on. "Our fellows dropped manna from smaller craft, which manufactured it on a daily cycle. Your people referred to it as a doughy substance that tasted like wafers made with honey. It provided enough of the basic elements required to sustain human life, indefinitely. That is, until a better solution could be affixed to the problem."

"YOU GUYS fed Moses and the Israelites in the desert for forty years with manna from heaven? You're blowing my mind," Jon declared, almost frightened.

Jorthon and Kalyssa looked at each other, not quite sure what to make of his pronouncement.

Pointing to his iPad screen, JT continued—"Is there any chance you could perform that same miracle again and drop manna onto the towns and villages on these lists?"

The two aliens touched the small computer with their fingertips for a moment. "We understand, Jonathan Tuckerman," Jorthon said. "We have your data. There is no need for hunger in your world where so many are so lavish and refuse to share their means with those less fortunate. We will work with you to ensure that all are fed."

Flash, zip, boom! And once again Jon was sitting behind his desk at his UN office.

"How'd it go, Dad?" Isak asked.

"Great! Hey... do you know what 'manna from heaven' is, son?"

Isak shook his head. "Nope, no idea. What does that mean?"

"In the next few days... hopefully, you and everyone else in the world will find out!" JT smiled.

Two days later, news coverage began monopolizing the television airwaves with reports that small flying machines, described as "resembling high school science projects," were seen hovering over each and every town and village around the world that had appeared on JT's list. Every four hours, each device—and it was estimated that there were tens of thousands of them—was seen dropping tons of a gooey, light brown substance in silver foil-wrapped balls—to the Earth.

Humans underneath the flying crafts, unsure at first what the blobs were, appeared hesitant, until the bravest among them began to unpeel the balls of foil, place their fingers into the globs, and then licking their fingers in pleasant surprise. Smiling wide, the pioneers in each town assured their companions that what had just been dropped from the sky was not merely edible... it was delicious!

The phenomenon was repeated in town after town, village after village, in country after country. Mothers holding their small, frail children with distended bellies would take very small pieces of the manna, roll it into tiny balls of dough, and gently feed their starving offspring. The children who still had the ability to chew on their own did so while humanitarian aid workers ensured that the sick, crippled, and elderly were equally provided with this gift from above. The manna was universally accepted within 48 hours of its first appearance among all those unfortunate enough to have had the need to receive it in the first place.

JT and his team kept a close eye on their large television screen.

The president called. "Jon, little buddy, looks like you and your pals did it again. We're getting calls from prime ministers, presidents, kings and queens, princes, and generals from around the world. They are beside themselves, thanking us for feeding their most impoverished. Some of them were crying. These magical aliens of yours are the greatest thing ever. I hope they decide to stick around for a while," the jubilant woman said.

The calls, emails, cards, holograms, and letters "Team Tuckerman" (a phrase coined by Isak) were receiving began overwhelming the office. They were getting thousands of thank you notes—from African, Asian, Mexican, and South American leaders, from American governors of various Southern states and mayors of small, rural U.S. towns scattered across the Midwest, and from humanitarian workers and other dignitaries, notables, movie stars, and celebrities across the globe. Meghan assigned two of the staff members to work full-time solely on cataloging, archiving, and responding to each and every piece of "fan mail" that was quickly flooding into the suite.

Meghan approached JT at his desk, wiping a tear from her eye. "What's wrong?" Jon asked. "Read this one," she said, holding forth a telegram.

"Thank you so very much, Mr. Tuckerman, for your wisdom, your empathy, and your friendship with the magical visitors from the sky. You and they have provided the most basic of life's necessities—something so many millions of our people had never dreamed possible. You are saving us—you are saving us all. May God bless you and your colleagues." It had been sent by the President of Ethiopia.

"Pretty cool, huh, kid?" JT joked to Meghan, who did not answer. She just stood staring at her boss somewhat starstruck, a special kind of love evident in her eyes.

Trying to gently detach himself from her adoration, Jon said, "But really, Meghan, *what did I do*? I'm just a messenger! *They're* the ones producing these miracles. I just made a simple request. I'm no hero. These cards and telegrams really belong to them. I'm just a big nothing."

"Mr. Tuckerman!" Meghan scolded, "you are NOT nothing! You are everything! You are the conduit... the reason that these great things are happening in the first place. Please don't ever negate yourself in front of me, or any of your staff, again. We look up to you. You are our leader—our inspiration!"

Jon felt sheepish.

"Clearly They chose *you* for a reason," the woman continued. "They wanted YOUR help. Millions of people are now benefitting from *your* relationship with these remarkable creatures. It really doesn't matter why you were chosen. You should learn to embrace the fact that through you, people around the world are beginning to see a new light in their lives. YOU, Mister Tuckerman, YOU are that new light!"

As she walked back to her desk, JT understood that Meghan had become his biggest fan. "Thank you?" he replied weakly, speaking to her back. "I suppose ending the nuclear age and feeding starving children around the world is something to be proud of," he whispered out loud, to himself. He said it, but the meaning of his words didn't really quite register. Despite his first two global accomplishments, JT still lacked any true sense of self-esteem. For far too long, he'd grown accustomed to the fact that his existence had held no meaning or purpose.

But now, really for the first time in his life, Jon Tuckerman was beginning to realize that, perhaps, he was no longer the king of the losers after all.

CHAPTER ELEVEN

Team Tuckerman chose Clean Drinking Water as its next big ask. Meghan invited spokespersons from the world's leading clean water initiatives to the UN to give presentations. These meetings included members of the Water Project, the World Health Organization, Water for People, Blood: Water, Water for Good, Water.org, and Generosity.org, among others. During these meetings, Jon and his staff learned that over two billion people—out of a global total of eight billion—did not have access to clean, safe drinking water. The problem was particularly awful throughout sub-Saharan Africa, including the Congo, Ghana, Nigeria, Ethiopia, and Uganda. Clean water was also hard to come by in large swatches of India, Pakistan, Bhutan, Nepal, and Cambodia. Jon was a bit surprised to learn that, much closer to home, dozens of towns and villages across Mexico were also experiencing the same desperate problem.

Like clockwork, one month later, February 22, 2034, the enormous flying saucer returned to Manhattan to retrieve its favorite guest. Sgt. Pike and his squad again accompanied JT onto the UN roof. The dazzling and wondrous craft spun before them. "Never gets old, does it, sir? Like looking into the face of God himself," Pike said.

A powerful ray of light, and once again Jonathan Tuckerman had been beamed aboard a giant spacecraft from outer space.

"Hello dear friend," Kalyssa greeted him, "What have you learned?" Jorthon added, "Are your people enjoying their manna?"

"Yes, very much so. We honestly can't thank you enough," JT replied. "Thanks to your kindness, so many impoverished in so many villages, small towns, and rural districts are no longer starving to death."

"What have you brought for our next assignment?" Kalyssa asked.

JT responded quickly. "Water—clean clear, water... for drinking, bathing, and cooking. More than two billion human beings do not have access to it. If you have the ability to provide them with clean water, I have the locations here (JT pointed to his iPad) that are most in need."

Jon presented his small screen to his friends, and again, they each touched the device for a moment with their forefingers.

"We can help," Kalyssa said.

"In addition, your own people can also aid with this problem at the same time," Jorthon said. "We have placed onto your device a blueprint for the design and construction of highly efficient water desalination machines. Show these plans to your scientists and engineers. These machines can easily be built adjacent to any large body of salt water. Within a few hours, they will have the ability to remove the salt from hundreds of millions of gallons of seawater and transform the extraction into fresh drinking water for human consumption."

"That's terrific! Thank you so very much!" Jon said.

"While you are pursuing the building of the machines, we will deliver a temporary solution for your water shortage, on a massive scale, to these stricken areas," Jorthon said.

"Can you tell me your plan?" a curious Jon asked.

"You shall see our solution soon enough," Kalyssa responded.

Zip, bam, boom, and Jon was sitting at his desk yet again.

"Dad? Are you actually smiling?" Lauren teased.

"Yeah, I think so. I think we're standing at the front door of a brand new world, kid. These aliens can do anything. They have a solution for every problem we've ever faced. They're like Aladdin's Genie. All ya gotta do is ask!"

Lauren walked over to her father's desk and gave him a hug. "Dad," she said. "I'm sorry we didn't talk for so long. My bad. I don't blame you for Mom anymore. To say the least, I think you're now more than making up for any screw-ups from the past." She kissed her dad on the cheek. "I'm very proud of you, Daddy," she whispered in his ear, then walked back to her desk.

Lauren's simple, loving act brought more joy to Jon Tuckerman's heart than any other moment he could recall, ever, in his entire life.

The next day, while meeting in his office with water engineers and scientists from New York, Washington, D.C., Philadelphia, and Boston, JT was instructed by Meghan to turn on the television.

Every channel was live broadcasting footage of thousands of forty-story tall, cylindrical, clear glass silos descending from the sky, and landing dead center amidst the regions that had been detailed on Jon's hit list. The silos were filled with clean water. Each silo had four spigots, facing north, south, east or west. Once stationed on the ground, the silos were hesitatingly approached by townspeople, marveling at their size, and having no idea, at first, what they contained.

On live TV, a young boy in Ghana touched a spigot, like a cat pawing at a piece of yarn. He flipped it up and fresh, cool, crystal clean water sprayed his face and body. He began to dance in the stream, singing a happy song, and beckoning for his family and friends to join him. The scene was so joyous, so filled with the young child's exuberance and pure ecstasy, that it was played and replayed on television many hundreds of times.

The video clip went viral—on a global scale—and immediately became iconic.

The phone rang. "They're calling your friends 'Mungu Wa Maji,' Jon," the president informed him. "It means 'The Water Gods.' They are singing songs in their native languages about the miraculous 'Water Gods' who came from Heaven to forever quench their thirst. These are people who haven't bathed in years, if ever. They have never known what clean water even tasted like! They are delirious beyond measure. It's all just so terrific, Johnny boy," she said. "Keep up the brilliant work, kid!"

Still on the phone, JT continued watching the scenes on his TV screen... jubilant people singing and dancing in the sprays of water, many smiling, many crying.

"Oh, hey, how's your meeting going on the desalination works?" the president asked.

"So far so good," he replied. "They seem to think that the plans we were given are a matter of simple construction. They're estimating the budget for each machine at about $3 million. They say each one could generate enough clean water—from any body of salt water—to be provided to hundreds of thousands of people, month after month, year after year. Now it's just a matter of funding."

"You leave that to me, my friend," President Winfield answered. "I'll make an emergency request to Congress for a $300 million bond. Let's build 100 plants right off the bat. If they do what they're supposed to do, we can share the water and the tech with every country that makes a request."

"Sounds good. Thank you, Madam President," Jon said. Hanging up the phone, he resumed his meeting.

Six weeks later, the first Tuckerman Water Project (TWP) was constructed and online. It was installed adjacent to Asbury Park, New Jersey, where Tuckerman had spent a number of summers as a child. The machine worked perfectly.

Media from around the world attended the opening ceremony of the first TWP site, during which the President of the United States and Mr. Jonathan Tuckerman each held one grip of a pair of giant, oversized scissors, as they cut a very large, ocean-blue colored ribbon.

"It's a new age for clean water for everyone," the president declared. "With this wonderful technology that our alien benefactors have shared with us, we and every other country now have the ability to provide a never-ending abundance of clean water for drinking, cooking, and bathing... enough for every human being on Earth, indefinitely. Never again will there be a water shortage. For as long as the rains continue to replenish the oceans, our source of new fresh water will never run dry."

Over the course of the following months, TWP's were constructed and activated in a hundred seaside towns across the United States, coast to coast. The alien desalination process proved so successful, it was quickly shared with—and adopted by—over seventy other countries, whose governments issued special bond programs by which to pay for them. In addition, each of the countries adopting the technology also committed themselves to sharing a percentage of the water they drew for their own citizens with those in other countries whose governments could not afford to construct TWP systems.

It had also been predetermined by both the president and JT that only glass bottles would be commissioned to contain the new water—not plastic—to help eliminate the widespread problem of plastic pollution. Concurrently, the glass industry boomed globally as well, since the "no plastic bottles" mandate had also been agreed upon and accepted by each of the participating water-cleansing countries.

By the time enough new water had been drawn from the seas by the functioning TWP plants, had been distributed to the masses, and had been stored for the future, the temporary alien silos had become drained. The visitors gently lifted them into the sky... floating them back up into the mysterious abyss in outer space from whence they came.

CHAPTER TWELVE

The hectic meetings at JT's UN office continued unabated, but now that he'd proven himself—to himself—for the third time, his self-confidence had elevated to new heights. Adding to his newfound self-esteem was the fact that he and Susan Parks had fallen madly in love and were having remarkable, breath-taking, mind-blowing sex at least three nights a week. Jon, for the first time in decades, no longer obsessed over the horrific circumstances that had overshadowed every waking moment of his life.

Team Tuckerman chose Gun Violence as its next assignment. Meghan arranged for sessions with the leaders of many anti-gun organizations, including the Brady Campaign, Moms Demand Action, New Yorkers Against Gun Violence, The Coalition to Stop Gun Violence, Americans for Responsible Solutions, and several others. JT and his staff listened intently as they were deluged with statistics about the proliferation—

primarily within the United States—of assault rifles and handguns belonging to men and women under the age of twenty-one, as well as by those deemed mentally unstable.

It was made painfully evident to all that the NRA's stranglehold on Republican lawmakers from "red states" in the U.S. Capitol made many members of the House and Senate hesitant to upset that powerful lobbying group. Those lawmakers remained compelled to acquiesce to the wishes of their hometown constituents whose commitment to preserving the Second Amendment—the right to bear arms—simply *had to be upheld at any cost.*

"Armed" with more data on this issue than any five human heads could contain or digest, Jon awaited his next visit from his friends in high places. Now a month later, March 22, they soared over the East River in their colorful spinning top. And, once again, Sgt. Pike and his men entered the Tuckerman suite.

"Theeeey'rrrre BACK!" Pike joked to JT.

Jon nodded, grabbed his iPad, and again followed the man and his team up to the roof.

"Never gets boring," Pike said, marveling for the fourth time at the sight of the famed flying saucer. A beam of light, and seconds later Jon was onboard the Dodger Stadium Special yet again.

"What have you learned friend?" Jorthon greeted him warmly.

Kalyssa quickly added, "Mr. Tuckerman, you look almost happy. May I ask to what you attribute this newfound satisfaction?"

"Well," JT answered, a bit sheepishly, "having become friends with the two of you and the President of the United States, of course." He paused, and then added, "Along with a tremendous amount of amazing sex!"

"Yes, we have long heard that sexual intercourse for humans is a powerful means of self-expression and satisfaction. We are glad to see you happy. We are not used to finding you in such good spirits," Kalyssa said, smiling.

"What would you like us to take on next, Jonathan?" Jorthon asked. "There are far too many guns in the United States—handguns and assault rifles," JT replied. "There have been terrible shootings killing innocent children at schools; mass shootings destroying people in movie theaters and supermarkets, inside places of worship, at music festivals, and in nightclubs. There remain countless robberies, one-on-one and gang-related murders, suicides, accidents, rapes at gunpoint... all being committed every day in some part of my country. I read that when we were at Dodger Stadium, you had the ability to cause the police and the military to drop their weapons against their will. I was wondering if you might be able to do something similar on a much grander scale?"

"That was just for show—a magic trick," Jorthon answered. "But first, what is the root cause of this gun violence against your own kind? Why do people do this to each other, Jonathan? What is the ONE WORD that explains this terrible problem?"

JT thought for a few seconds. He looked around the ship, looked down at his feet, scratched his chin, then finally answered, "Anger?"

"Yes, of course," Jorthon replied. "The root cause of human beings killing each other with guns or committing violent acts against one another is anger. Now, what if we simply were able to remove that emotion from the human psyche? What if we offered all of mankind a permanent solution... removing anger from the human equation?"

"You can do that?" Jon asked, far beyond astounded.

"Yes, in dramatic fashion," Kalyssa replied.

Jon began walking around in small circles.

Jorthon continued, "We can spray a chemical compound over your people... over every person residing on Earth. The result from their inhaling this material will be a permanent change in the amygdala portion of their brains. The thought or idea of violence of any kind will no longer be tenable. It simply will not be there. Think of it as an eraser. We can erase the mistake my Father, the Infinite Creator, made when He designed mankind, and remove the propensity for violence from human beings, forever, simply by altering one small portion of the human brain."

"Talk about playing God. I'm not sure I should be the person to make that kind of monumental decision," JT said.

"Perhaps you should speak with your president first?" Kalyssa suggested. "Yes, I really need to do that."

Jorthon added, "We will send you back to your office now. When you are ready, please come back up to the roof."

Flash, zap, pow!

JT was at his UN desk. "Meghan, I need the president NOW!" he shouted.

Moments later, his new best friend was on the line. "Heard you were onboard again," she said, "What's the latest, Johnny?"

"Madam President, we were discussing gun control—permanent, irreversible gun control. You're NOT going to believe this, but they have the ability to remove the emotion of *anger* from all human beings! They can spray us—all of us—everyone in the world, with a chemical that will eliminate any thoughts of violence, permanently. Just think of it, Madam President. Instead of gun control, it would be human being *impulse control!* They always say, 'Guns don't kill people... people kill people.' If we did this, guns would become obsolete. They would no longer be used or even necessary."

A long silence, then, "Jon, this is big. This is God big!" the president whispered. "What right do we have, really, to change the bodies of all human beings? Yet think of the consequences here. No more school shootings. No more gunfights in the streets of our poorest communities. Not just that... no more murders, rapes, stabbings, serial killers.

We'd be lab rats, but lab rats at peace with each other. A gentle, calm people without confrontation. Like John Lennon once sang, 'Imagine all the people, living life in peace.'" More silence, then, "Jon, we are surely over-stepping our bounds here... me as President and you as the friend of aliens. But my gut says yes, let's do it! After all, if this really works, no one will have the ability to get angry at us for having done it! Right?" Another silence, then, "Go for it, Jon. And please keep me posted," the woman sighed as she hung up.

JT returned to the UN roof, this time alone, and waved to the craft. He was beamed aboard instantly. "I had a talk with my president," he said softly. "She was hesitant, but she gave us her permission to proceed. First, though, let me ask you specifically, if you do this, *all* human beings will become nonviolent, correct? Will this affect other areas of daily life? Will your chemical make humans stupid or lazy or sick or impotent? Will we still be able to continue living our normal lives? Will this also prevent sex crimes, rapes, knife attacks, fist fights, and so forth?"

"Our material is organic to Earth, taken from a form of Pacific Ocean algae... there are zero harmful side effects. It will forever switch off man's amygdala to any thoughts of violence, nothing more. No other aspect of the human experience will be adversely affected in any way," said Jorthon.

"However," added Kalyssa, "the human emotion of hate will *not* be affected. A human may still feel hatred for another person or for a decision made by someone in authority above him, or even broccoli. But that is a different matter entirely, and if you wish, we can discuss that again at some point in the future."

"We only have the best intentions in mind for you and your people, Jonathan," Jorthon said. "Humans have been dramatically violent toward each other since we first placed them here. You know the story of Cain and Abel, I assume? The propensity toward violence is an error in human design. Yet we remained committed to not interfering with man's evolution until now. We look to you to make these decisions—the best decisions you can possibly make—to better the collective condition of your fellows. We can provide you with solutions but you, and you alone, Jonathan, must make these requests of us."

JT took a deep breath. "Do it. Spray away. Let's end the insanity once and for all." He looked up at his colleagues and they smiled broadly at him.

Bing bong boom! Jon was now sitting behind his desk once more. "Jesus, Mary, Joseph, and the little baby in the manger," he said out loud. "What in the serious fuck of life have I just done?"

☙

TV news crews around the world carried live footage of the Dodger Stadium Special hovering less than a thousand feet above the ground, spraying massive quantities of a bright pink chemical substance everywhere. People from every country, from every walk of life, came outside to watch. As neither the president nor Jon Tuckerman had made any kind of advance announcement about the procedure, no one knew what was going on. Dozens of men across the United States—fearing they were being poisoned—took shotguns and assault rifles onto their front yards and began firing at the craft... their bullets falling useless. But as soon as the pink spray became inhaled, all guns were dropped, people began smiling, and young children began dancing in the streets.

It took the spacecraft only seventy-two hours to spray every populated piece of land on the Earth. In the days that followed, gunfights between Israelis and Palestinian members of Hamas in the West Bank and Gaza Strip ceased. Soldiers across Iraq, Afghanistan, and Syria, including members of the Taliban, Al-Qaeda, and ISIS, as well as international peace-keeping troops from the U.S. and its allies, all lay down their arms and walked boldly into Middle Eastern town squares, where all congregants ate together, played cards, and shared war stories. Mexican drug cartels were so strongly affected by the spray, they began digging deep graves, where they began to bury all their weaponry!

Hunters across the South and Midwestern American states held gun burning parties. Police forces became the depositories for the guns—legal and illegal—that had been scattered across their communities for decades. Even the National Rifle Association, the powerful enforcer of every American's right to bear arms, released a statement: "In light of the newfound status we find ourselves in as the result of actions taken by the president, Mr. Jonathan Tuckerman, and his friends from the sky, we realize that now is the time for us to stand with all others who wish to destroy their weapons en masse. There is no longer any enjoyment in the use of a firearm. We have come to realize that guns no longer serve any discernible purpose."

"Jonathan Tuckerman, Messiah?" blasted the huge headline in that week's *New York Times* Sunday edition. The media had been reporting, ad nauseam, how JT and his alien colleagues had single-handedly ended the human flaw of violence. "Nothing short of God's personal interference could have caused this miraculous turn of events," the article read. "And with access to the powers of the most advanced race of beings in our universe, Mr. Tuckerman now, apparently, has the ability to quite literally play God—something he seems to be doing rather well. His accomplishments are already beyond legendary... they have become mythic. No Nukes. Manna from Heaven. Water for All. The End of Gun Violence. Let us praise and thank Mr. Tuckerman for his wisdom and accomplishments to date. And let us also pray that his powerful alliance with the 'Benevolents' never breaks bad. For, should that ever occur, we would surely all become doomed, very quickly."

೧

JT, Susan Parks, and President Winfield had begun a new tradition... once weekly luncheons at the White House. Continually besieged by media crews at the front gates, and by autograph hounds even within the White House and Congress itself, Jon Tuckerman never quite got used to the overwhelming fame his unparalleled situation had thrust upon him. Even President Winfield's grandchildren had asked for selfies with the harried celebrity, wanting to show the photos off to their grade school friends and teachers. He obliged, of course, shielding his annoyance.

Dr. Parks and JT had decided that she should move into the penthouse, following their 20th "liaison" there, with Susan and Russell having quickly become the closest of allies. JT and the doctor, clearly in love, had been featured on dozens of magazine covers around the world. As the lover of the world's most famous man Susan, herself was becoming legendary in her own right. Her medical practice, which she'd relocated from Maryland to Manhattan, was thriving—she had to hire half a dozen other doctors, along with a staff of eight, to manage and maintain the patient demand she now enjoyed.

Isak and Lauren had become quite famous as well. They both grew enormously fond of both Susan Parks and New York City, with the bond between Lauren and Susan representing an unexpected "gift" for JT. "My dad should have met you twenty years ago," Lauren would joke to Susan during their now regular shopping trips along Fifth Avenue.

"Thanks, kid," Susan replied. Your dad's a really special guy."

"One in eight billion, literally," Lauren observed rather poignantly.

CHAPTER THIRTEEN

Incurable Diseases were the next problem Team Tuckerman voted to tackle. Once again, Meghan jumped to the task, spearheading the group's study of some of the most prominent groups and associations dedicated to the eradication of all forms of cancer, AIDS, Covid (and its related coronaviruses), coronary heart disease, and Ebola, among others. In quick order, representatives from more than three dozen groups were presenting the facts behind these, the most stubborn of all human medical maladies, to JT and his staff.

Those who spoke were a diverse array of men and women from the American Cancer Society, Cancer.org, the Cancer Research Institute, the Leukemia Research Foundation, BeatLeukemia.org, the American Heart Association, the World Heart Federation, Doctors Without Borders, Africare, Save the Children, UNAIDS, AmFar, the Rucks Foundation, the Global Fund to Fight AIDS, the World Health Organization, and the Gates Foundation, to name some of the more prominent groups.

Charts, graphs, films, holograms, and testimonial videos played before Jon and his colleagues for weeks. Once again, he felt overwhelmed by the onslaught of the data—having never before realized how vast the most stubborn of human illnesses had been, and remained, for so many millions of people around the world. While Ebola was more prominent in African countries, it nevertheless remained critically important to keep those afflicted with that particular disease quarantined, so as not to spread the horror globally.

With more information than any dozen men could possibly absorb, Jon's iPad was again loaded up with this extensive data. He could feel the weight of the world on his much hyped shoulders but felt optimistic that his friends from the sky might have a cure for some, if not all, of these diseases. He made a point never to promise anything to any of the doctors, scientists, board members, CEOs, and humanitarian relief workers who came to his office, beseeching him to "please do his utmost" to convince his aliens to take on these herculean afflictions.

It was becoming more and more difficult for Jon to sleep soundly at night. While he loved the routine of coming home to the penthouse, and to a never-ending roundelay of remarkable Russell meals, he'd hit the sack as soon as he possibly could... occasionally even foregoing sex with Susan. Despite his fame and global successes, JT was still grappling to learn how to embrace true self-confidence, self-respect, and self-love.

On April 22, 2034, the flying craft from outer space appeared above the East River, calling upon its singular passenger. This time, JT shooed away Sgt. Pike and his team, insisting that they no longer needed to continue accompanying him to the roof. "I've got it now, boys," Jon told them. "It's all good. No worries. You can go back to protecting whoever else it is you protect."

Again on the roof... once more the light beam... and Jon was suddenly inside the great ship. He never grew tired of the beautiful colors and the luminous presence of Kalyssa and Jorthon upon his arrival. As soon as he looked into their faces, he instinctively felt their love penetrating his soul.

"Hello, friend, what have you learned?" Jorthon asked.

"We are ready for your next assignment," added Kalyssa. "What do you bring us?"

JT began explaining to his mentors the perils of the incurable diseases he had been briefed on. He showed them on his iPad the statistics and locations of thousands of known victims of the deathly illnesses he and his staff had studied in the preceding weeks. "Human beings have not yet cured these terrible illnesses," he told the aliens. "Our best research scientists and medical experts have been studying these ailments for decades, yet they remain unable to find a cure for any of them. I'm not expecting you to perform any miracles here, but is there something that can be done to alleviate the extent of these medical fiascos?"

"I'll be right back," said Jorthon.

Kalyssa remained and gazed deeply into JT's face. "You don't sleep well, do you Jonathan?" she asked.

"No, not really," he admitted. "I am so very appreciative of all that you two have done for me, but the responsibilities in trying to cure all of mankind's enormous problems have overwhelmed me. This job is so very intense, it's been causing me tremendous self-doubt."

"Just know you are important to us, Jonathan Tuckerman," Kalyssa said. "We have entrusted you for good reason to do these things."

Before JT could even ask the obvious follow-up question "What good reason?" Jorthon returned with a small glass vial of a dark brown liquid.

"May I see your screen?" he asked.

JT handed the wondrous creature his iPad. The Tall White typed in a few keys, then returned the device to Jon. "Take this vial and your screen back to your best laboratories," he instructed. "Have them mass produce this material. It's made from human stem cells that have been inactivated by radiation. When injected into newborn human babies—those no more than four hours old—it will prevent them from ever becoming afflicted with any of the diseases you mentioned... or any other which may show up in the future. Think of this as a means by which to reboot and inoculate the human race. Every newborn that receives this serum will enjoy perfect health for their natural lifetimes, and will be completely immune to any physical illnesses, whatsoever."

JT's mouth was agape. "Rebooting the human race? Isn't that playing God again?"

"We are not Gods," Kalyssa admonished. "We are born of the same Infinite Creator as are all other living beings, large and small. Our race is many thousands of years ahead of yours, Jonathan, and, as we've told you before, we are here now solely to aid mankind as best we can."

Thinking quickly on his feet, JT asked, "This is a wonderful gift for new children, but what about all the other people—young and old— already afflicted with these diseases? Is there anything that can be done for them?"

Jorthon answered. "You may inform your fellows that, if injected with this formula, any human being missing a body part will re-grow that body part, although it will take a bit of time. Also, anyone who is blind, deaf, cannot speak, is paralyzed, crippled, or deformed, will become whole. Any human currently diagnosed as terminal can also be injected with this fluid. However, it will not cure them... only stop the spread of their illness and eliminate their pain. After all, we are forbidden from changing the 'predestined death date' of any human being's lifecycle."

"'Predestined death date'?" JT was shocked. "Are you saying that every human being's life is predestined to end on a specific date on the calendar?"

"Yes, of course," Kalyssa said. "All life is predestined at birth. Humans, animals, plants—even our own people and the races of our friends from other planets, star systems, and dimensions. Lifecycles are not random games of nature. They are preconceived and determined upon inception."

"Wow! That's intense," Jon said. He paused and stared at the small vial in his hand. "Is there a name for this serum?" he asked his hosts.

"You may call it anything you wish," Jorthon said.

"Life Juice," Jon replied.

In less than a month, Jon Tuckerman's "Life Juice" had been mass produced and distributed by hundreds of laboratories and charities around the world. Television crews everywhere covered the first injections that were given to newborn babies in hospitals—and in homes—on every continent around the planet. Yet again, magazines featured Tuckerman on their covers, this time in a group photo with his staff.

Jon was sitting behind his UN desk when the phone rang again.

"She's on line 4!" Meghan shouted.

Jon lifted the receiver. "They're calling you 'Ajabu-Mtu,' Jon," President Winfield said. "It means 'The Wonder Man' in Swahili. There are tribes in Africa that post your picture on their trees! Your work has become invaluable, my dear friend. You are literally changing the future of mankind."

Jon now felt more empowered and emboldened than ever before in his entire life. There was a new bounce in his step, and a heretofore nonexistent smile that rarely left his face. The accolades from his fellow human beings staggered him... his popularity was stratospheric, literally. If the man had requested the title "King of the World," it was more than likely the delegates at the UN would have voted to elect him as such.

As JT was back at his desk, now watching newsfeeds on his computer, Meghan approached him with a strange look on her face. As he looked up, he noticed something was wrong. "Meghan?" Jon had never seen his right-hand woman this disturbed.

"I'm getting calls, lots of calls," she said. "While the serum they gave you was meant to eliminate physical illnesses, apparently, it was not designed to cure mental illness. We are getting overwhelming requests from dozens of organizations, begging us—you—to ask the aliens if they might have a magic cure for diseases of the mind as well."

Jon stood and hugged his colleague. "I should have included that in my last visit with them," he said. "They are very literal in pursuing solutions to the problems I present to them. They don't extrapolate an inch. It didn't occur to me to include mental illness. Let's get a bunch of mental health advocates in here ASAP. We'll make that the next assignment on our hit list."

Throughout the month, Tuckerman's group met with dozens of representatives from associations that had been battling mental illnesses for decades. The team learned that among the most prominent of these ailments were bipolar disorder, depression, schizophrenia, dissociative disorder, borderline personality disorder, eating disorders, alcohol and drug addiction, and anxiety. They were informed that untreated depression was one of the leading causes of suicide in the United States. Also, since his own mother was currently in the end stage of life due to Alzheimer's disease, the group placed that mental issue, along with dementia, in the basket too.

Jon loaded up his trusty iPad with data, which included these stats: Twenty to twenty-five percent of all Americans have a diagnosable mental disorder, five to six percent of American adults have a serious mental illness, and as many as ten percent of American children also have a serious emotional disturbance.

"These numbers suck," Jon told his staff. "I truly hope our friends have some kind of remedy for these terrible problems."

The whirling mass of wonder arrived again above the East River. Jon went to the roof... a flash. "What have you learned, friend?" Kalyssa asked her favorite human.

"First off, thank you both so much for the Life Juice," Jon began. "Virtually every country on Earth has been inoculating new babies with the stuff. People who've been blind their whole lives, military veterans, accident victims... many are sending us gifts and flowers. Once again, you've made an incredible impact on the world." The aliens nodded in silent acceptance.

"However, there is one problem," Jon continued, feeling rather ashamed. "I neglected to add something into my last request. We need your help, please, to combat the terrible condition of mental illness. There are various conditions that affect many of us whose brains do not work properly. People with depression are killing themselves, people with Alzheimer's disease and dementia no longer recognize their own loved ones, and people with schizophrenia make life terribly difficult for their caretakers—that is if they even *have* caretakers. I have all this data right here," Jon said, flipping open his iPad.

"Give me a moment," Kalyssa said, leaving the scene.

During her absence, Jon asked Jorthon, "Can I ask you something? Where do you two go when we're not together?"

The Tall White smiled and appeared to chuckle to himself. "We travel back and forth between your planet and our home, an opening into a dimension your scientists would say was located within the Pleiades star cluster. My home would take your people tens of thousands of years to reach. We are able to travel that distance in twelve hours of Earth time. Our people know the avenues and locations of wormholes in space. We can transport ourselves through them easily."

"Well, holy shit!" Jon said. "Can I go to the Pleiades dimension with you someday?"

"Do NOT rush things!" Jorthon scolded... his stern, out-of-character response taking JT quite by surprise.

Kalyssa returned, holding a small, tan-colored piece of what appeared to be rubber or plastic. "May I see your screen," she asked Jon, who handed her his iPad. She typed a quick entry, then handed the small computer back to him, along with the rubber item.

Kalyssa then told Jon, "Have your people manufacture this device... what you might call an ear plug. Provide the blueprints I have placed into your computer as open-source material on your Internet system. Any human who wears this ear plug will receive audio sound waves in synch with nature and the Infinite Creator's original intentions for the human brain. This device ensures a human brain will function as He designed it. Any human who wears this plug for just a short time will never experience any of the afflictions you have become concerned with. In quick order, all mental illnesses will be reversed and eliminated... normal human brain function shall be restored, permanently."

JT held the little plug in his fingers. "This tiny guy can do all that?" he marveled.

Added Jorthon, "The audio harmonic pulse it provides will attune the human mind to the correct wavelengths of the universe. No one who wears this shall feel confused or insecure, sad or anxious. No more will any human being be derided or mocked as 'crazy' or 'nuts.' It will deliver homeostasis to almost every human—however, there will surely be a few, rare exceptions to its effectiveness."

Moments later, Jon found himself back behind his desk, still squeezing the tiny, squishy rubber device. He looked across his desktop and gazed at an old black and white photo of himself in his mother's arms... the picture capturing the moment they'd arrived home from the hospital just after his birth. Wondering if this new wonder device might help his ailing mother, who'd been in a coma in a New Jersey nursing facility for many years, JT had Meghan deliver the plug by special bonded courier to his mother.

The next morning, Jon received a call from Mrs. Marion Cohn, the Executive Director of the home in which Jane Tuckerman had long resided. "So, sorry, Mr. Tuckerman," the woman told JT, "But your little ear plug had no effect on your mother's condition, nor did the 'Life Juice' vial of serum you sent us recently. She's still lying dormant on her bed, poor dear."

"Thanks for letting me know," Jon said, hanging up the phone, distraught.

While the Wonder Man was successfully curing people—total strangers—around the world, his efforts on behalf of his very own dying mother had led to no change whatsoever in her rapidly deteriorating state.

❧

An International Mental Health Consortium (IMHC) was quickly convened at the UN. Manufacturing companies around the world offered to mass produce the ear plug gadgets at minimal costs to consumers, with several of the larger corporations offering to provide up to 300 million of the plugs for free as a goodwill promotional gesture. Within a matter of weeks, the first ear plugs, which Jonathan named "Harmony Buds," were being delivered to doctors' offices, mental hospitals, clinics, asylums, prisons, drugstores, and psychiatrists' offices globally.

Once again, news crews assembled in every civilized nation to record the first people willing to insert the little plugs into their heads. The results seemed to vary little… within a matter of less than three minutes, users felt almost "instantly happy"—many of them crying with joy.

One TV report from the BBC was watched live by JT, his team, and President Winfield, who'd made a surprise visit to their UN offices. The BBC reporter, inside the corridors of a mental health hospital in London, was reporting live as dozens of longtime residents ("Lifers," as he'd called them) were being fitted with the Harmony Buds.

Almost every man or woman was seen to quickly change their facial expressions—some even changing their posture, as many who'd been hunched over began standing upright for the first time in years. Harmony Buds were inserted into a number of coma patients as well, with very impressive results… a few awakening with smiles, some after decades of living in vegetative states. A few, however, saw no change whatsoever.

"Well, ladies and gentlemen," the reporter stated, "it appears that our Wonder Man, Mr. Jon Tuckerman, and his friends from outer space have done it once again. Is there no end to the miracles these three extraordinary beings can perform for the rest of us? It appears not. So again may we say to Mr. Tuckerman and his colleagues, thank you so very much for your heroic feats. You continue fixing the problems of mankind that had, for far too long, remained beyond the wildest hope of any possible solution or repair!"

CHAPTER FOURTEEN

Issues of Poverty and The Unhoused were next up on the Team Tuckerman hit parade. Now working like a well-oiled machine, his staff, spearheaded by the ever-remarkable Meghan Marx, began arranging in-office meetings with advocates who had been working diligently for years to help alleviate those massive problems.

JT and his group met with representatives from the Institute of Global Homelessness, the Anthony Robbins Foundation, Depaul International, Citizens for Public Justice, the National Coalition for the Homeless, and even the UN's own Commission on Human Rights... led by a team of six men and women working just a few floors below Jon's office.

Team Tuckerman was staggered to learn the extent of the unhomed problem in the United States alone. Statistics presented to them revealed that nearly 600,000 people in America lived on the streets, with many of the country's largest cities holding the biggest numbers: New York City, 60,000; Los Angeles, 57,000; Chicago, 117,000; Washington, D.C., 7,000; San Francisco, Seattle, and San Diego, between 9,000 to 10,000 each.

On a global scale, the team was informed that estimates placed over a hundred-million human beings worldwide as being completely unhomed, while more than 1.6 billion people lacked what was described as "adequate" housing or shelter. Many of the statistics from impoverished nations dwarfed those from the United States. Mumbai, India, and Manilla each held the record at 23,000,000 apiece; Moscow, 100,000; Mexico City, 30,000, Jakarta, 28,000; Athens, 20,000; Rome, 17,000; Buenos Aires, 15,000; and Sao Paulo, 10,000, to cite just some examples.

Jon and Meghan worked closely side by side to compile the data into JT's now legendary iPad. "It's kind of funny, really," Meghan remarked, "that your friends, who are light years more advanced than us with their technology, are even able to understand our information on such a primitive device. To them, this iPad must be the equivalent of an ancient cave drawing." She and JT laughed in tandem, their fondness for each other having become quite familial.

June 22, 2034. The largest UFO the world had ever seen once again returned to the Big Apple, revolving above the East River, right on schedule. Jonathan stood on the UN roof alone once more, iPad in hand, ready to do battle against his latest designated enemy.

Onboard the ship, he heard the quite familiar, "What have you learned, friend?" from Jorthon.

"Where's Kalyssa?" Jon asked, noticing that Jorthon's companion was not there.

The alien responded, "She went to visit her genetic and biological mother, whose predestined death date rapidly approaches. She sends her warmest regards. Now what is the new project you wish to discuss with me?"

"There are eight billion people living today on the Earth," Jon began, "yet more than one and a half billion of them are either unhomed or living in squalid conditions. While the largest countries generate untold wealth for their top ten percent of citizens, the less fortunate struggle daily just to survive." Jon started up his computer and presented the data to his colleague. "I can't imagine you would have a magical spray or an ear plug to solve this one, but I'd love to hear what you think you might be able to do."

"One moment please," Jorthon said as he drifted off into another part of the ship. Jon never got bored inside the craft, ever fascinated by the gadgets, gizmos, and twinkling light boards that ran along the walls and ceiling... devices far beyond his comprehension.

When Jorthon returned, he was holding what appeared to be a leather satchel. "Please open your hand, Jonathan," he requested.

When JT did as instructed, Jorthon placed a baseball-sized, soft, golden rock into his palm. "Pure 24-karat gold," the Great Alien said. "My race first came to Earth eons ago in search of gold. It was a prized element for us. We used it within our propulsion systems to make them more efficient. However, once we learned how to replicate its properties synthetically, we were no longer in need of the original hordes we mined so long ago. Where I live, there are huge mounds of golden stockpiles... greater in size than your Rocky Mountains. I can supply to you—for use by all of your world's leaders—a massive abundance of gold. More than currently exists on all of the Earth."

"That's just incredible," Jon replied, yet again blown away by this alien revelation. "But how would we distribute it? And how much, in American dollars, would we be giving out?"

Jorthon gave pause for a moment to ponder JT's questions. "Take this idea to your leaders. Tell them that we will supply to the head of every government of every country on your planet the equivalent of $400 billion in gold, but only if they sign a pledge—a legal document—that ensures this donation will be used solely to provide new housing construction projects for those without proper homes. Plus, these funds must also be earmarked for food, clothing, medical supplies, and other items regularly required by the daily needs of those so impoverished. We will deliver the gold to you in massive containers... a fleet of large trucks will be required on your end."

Jorthon handed the satchel to Jon. "Use this as a show of good faith and as evidence that what I speak is true."

Jon emptied the satchel's contents onto the light table. A dozen gold nuggets appeared, their glitter so strong it nearly took his breath away. "How much is this *worth*?" JT asked.

"Your people would measure this small amount at about $4 million."

JT shook his head. "My God. Here, please take this back," he said, as he began replacing the rocks back into the sack.

"No, please, I do not need that." The Great One laughed. "This is now yours to keep. A gift. Do with it as you wish. Keep it for yourself or your family. Donate it to charity. Whatever you feel best."

Moments later, Jon was back at the UN in a daze. He stared at the satchel of gold now atop his desk. "Meghan!" he cried out. "I need her *right now*!"

In a flash, his aide replied, "Line 6."

"Madam President, grab hold of your socks, 'cause you are NOT gonna believe this one!" he began.

President Winfield listened to Jon Tuckerman's latest amazing story. "My God in heaven," she said, "what a gift."

"How do we proceed?" Jon asked.

A moment of silence. "You and I will address the UN together. I'll set that up," the president said. "Meantime, please work with a legal team to craft a legally binding contract... a pledge for the head of every country who wishes to participate... that the funds from your friends can and must be used solely according to their instructions, and not for the advancement of military forces or the personal gain of their leaders. After we speak at the UN, we can hold a signing ceremony... like our forefathers did when they signed the Declaration of Independence. I'll sign it first. Let's give it a name. You're good at that, Johnny. What can we call it?"

A moment of silence was followed by Jon's answer. "The Power of Gold Initiative," he said. "Very appropriate," the president responded.

President Winfield and her staff worked with Secretary General Kim to arrange for a special gathering at the UN in a few days hence. Meanwhile, JT and his team huddled with the senior partners of one of Manhattan's preeminent law firms to hammer out an ironclad legal document that would ensure not only that the gold would be appropriated correctly, but that a team from the UN would be allowed to monitor the construction of the new dwellings for the homeless.

Two days later, delegates from every country gathered inside the UN's great assembly room to witness what President Winfield and Secretary General Kim had promoted as "An Unprecedented Event Not to be Missed." A single television camera located at the back of the hall provided the live television feed of the proceedings, which was shared with every other major media news outlet on the Earth.

"Ladies and gentlemen," the president began, "today we welcome you with news of a remarkable gift. A gift that will soon be bestowed upon us all by the 'Benevolents,' who have been working with our beloved Jonathan Tuckerman these past months to help make the world a better place for all people. This unexpected—and truly extraordinary gift—which Mr. Tuckerman will explain to you, will provide new hope, new security, and new peace of mind to tens of millions of Earth's citizens across every corner of the planet. And now, without further ado, please welcome our very own Jon Tuckerman."

A standing ovation greeted JT as he hugged the president and approached the podium and its microphone. Nervous as never before, at this moment he realized this would be, without question, the largest group of people he'd ever stood in front of in his life. Trembling, and holding a legal-sized packet of papers in his hand, he glanced at his kids sitting behind him and to his right, next to the president. Isak gave his dad a "thumbs up" sign and Lauren shot him a wink. "Thank you all for coming today," he began weakly, his voice cracking. "It is my honor and privilege to announce to you—and to all human beings—a very special situation that is about to take place. As you know, I was selected by an alien race to serve as a liaison between them and my fellow humans. I do not know why I was chosen, but I was tasked with the assignment of working with them to help solve the enormous problems facing us all.

Today, I am very pleased to announce that the time has come for mankind to eradicate poverty and homelessness everywhere. We are a world of plenty, yet too many millions of us have been in desperate need of adequate shelter for far too long. I stand before you, today, to tell the world that our friends from the sky shall be donating to every country so interested, *a massive donation in gold*!

On their home planet, our visitors have an overwhelming abundance of gold they no longer need. To each and every world leader who signs this document," JT held aloft his papers, his hand shaking terribly, "a tax-free gift of gold shall be distributed for the construction of new housing shelters and meal centers for the poverty-stricken in the homelands of those leaders." Jon took a quick sip of water. "The amount of this gift, for each and every country that signs this document, will be $400 billion U.S. dollars."

A stunned silence befell the hall. Delegates, looking at each other, mouthed "billion with a 'b'?" Jon felt faint. After a ten second delay, everyone in the room stood... the standing ovation lasting four full minutes. Jon walked over to where President Winfield was sitting and placed the legal document before her. She signed it with a flourish and handed Jon the pen.

"Okay, who wants to read this?" she asked the crowd. A line of dignitaries stood adjacent to the president, awaiting their opportunity to read a copy of the contract, before rushing back to their offices to inform the leaders of their home countries about this unprecedented opportunity. It only took six days for the document (which was routed electronically around the world) to be signed by literally every president, prime minister, king, queen, prince, princess, emir, ayatollah, great leader, and dictator alive.

The day after his UN address, Jon had a vivid dream: Jorthon and Kalyssa appeared, telling him to meet them at Yankee Stadium on the

Fourth of July, at 10:00 am, with a fleet of massively powerful trucks by which to tow large containers of the gold they would be delivering to the world on that day. JT called the president, who arranged for the U.S. Army to send 193 (the total number of countries in the world) of its largest trucks to the site that morning. (A baseball game between the Yankees and the Red Sox had to be cancelled.)

As promised, precisely at 10:00 am on July 4, 2034, the massive flying diamond appeared above Yankee Stadium, as luxurious as ever. The world's media was on hand to cover the event. Special guests in attendance included President Winfield, the Pope, the King of England, Vice President Schoenberg, JT, his children, Susan, Meghan, two dozen other world leaders, and the twelve members of the newly formed UN Oversight Committee for the "Power of Gold Initiative," tasked to enforce the new contract in every participating country.

A powerful beam of light, much brighter and stronger than the one normally used to transport Jon in and out of the ship, beamed down, aimed at second base. The beam delivered a series of enormous crates, which appeared to have been constructed of thick glass, began to descend as though feathers escaping a pillow. As each appeared, those in attendance applauded. Cleverly, the aliens had secured each box to a four-wheel "dolly" so that the boxes were easily mobile. U.S. Army trucks the size of dinosaurs drove onto the infield, one at a time, attaching long tow cables to each box then driving back out across the field, through the stadium's parking lot, and toward JFK Airport. There, the boxes were to be sorted and shipped to each recipient's home country.

That night, and for days and days to come, TV news shows everywhere ran repeat footage of the huge boxes of gold floating gently down to Earth. Newspaper headlines around the world ran bold headlines, such as "The Power of Gold? Or the Power of Tuckerman?" and "Earth's First, Real Life Super Hero Helps Eliminate the Scourge of Global Poverty!"

CHAPTER FIFTEEN

The whirlwind of activity continued at the Tuckerman UN suite following the disbursements of the alien gold. One morning two weeks later, while Team Tuckerman was studying the causes behind their next assignment—Global Warming—Meghan rushed up to JT's desk, breathless. "Turn on the TV, quick! Winfield's having a big problem!" The giant TV screen came to life, with news programs carrying live coverage of President Winfield, Vice President Bradley Schoenberg, and the VP's transgender daughter, Cheryl Schoenberg, being confronted by hundreds of protestors who had been picketing Winfield's and Schoenberg's speeches at the opening dedication ceremony of a new community center in a prominently African American section of Birmingham, Alabama.

The protestors, clearly members of a local White Supremacist group, were carrying signs with intense, hateful racial slurs such as "This Nigger is NOT OUR President!" and "Rid the USA of Jew Communists" and even "Fags Burn in Hell."

While watching this horror unfold live on national television, Jon remembered Kalyssa's intriguing statement to him when she and Jorthon were explaining that the elimination of *anger* within human beings would *not* affect their other negative emotions toward people and things. They could still *hate.*

The scene presented a clearly terrified President Winfield, VP Schoenberg and his daughter, as the trio was being ushered out of the fairly small building by their Secret Service security teams, and into their awaiting limousines parked in front of the community center. Protest cries of "Fucking Nigger!" "Jews Will Not Replace Us!" and "Fag Lovers!" filled the air, as the two executives and the charismatic Cheryl were thrust into their cars and rushed away from the scene. Jon was furious. "Everyone," he addressed his team, "we are looking at our new assignment: Racial, Religious, and Sexual Gender Discrimination. Let's see what kind of data we can put together here quickly. I'll be meeting with my friends again in four days."

After extensive research, Team Tuckerman learned that there were dozens of hate groups that still openly existed across the U.S., more than fifty of them in just half the states. Over 30,000 Americans believed in the tenets of the KKK, that the white Aryan race was superior to all others, that blacks, Asians, Jews, Hispanics, and other ethnicities, along with members of the LGBTQ community, were considered "non-humans" and had no place thriving—or even merely existing—in any society. Not just an American problem, JT's group did its best to acquire information from around the world, based on published studies, byline articles, and speeches given by leaders of organizations committed to the end of all forms of human-against-human discrimination.

July 22 arrived, and right on cue, the flying saucer spun frantically above the East River. Jon zapped onboard and was most glad to see that Kalyssa had returned, along with Jorthon, to greet him. "What have you learned, friend?" She smiled glowingly at him. "What new problem troubles you?"

JT, clearly upset, laid out his case quickly to his friends: "Racial, religious, sexual, and gender discrimination, even in the 'Age of the Benevolents,' has failed to dissipate along with the violence and anger you so easily eliminated with your pink spray. As you anticipated, Kalyssa, hate remains a big problem."

Jorthon spoke: "Man's intolerance for his fellow man who looks differently than he does, or worships his God differently, or loves another in a nontraditional manner, or dresses in a unique way, was not anticipated by the Infinite Creator in His design of humans. When our ancestors helped to seed mankind on your planet many thousands of years ago, they had only the most humane and loving intentions. Yet, somehow, the Great One did not foresee that the diversity of human beings He crafted would have a difficult time accepting each other. This was not part of His plan."

Kalyssa interrupted. "Discrimination of one man by another is unacceptable. It is not what He hoped for. This behavior by His children must end immediately. Now that we have arrived here, there is no longer any room for intolerance between humans."

Jon steered the conversation back toward the current situation... the mistreatment of the President, VP, and Cheryl Schoenberg, which had so inflamed him days earlier. "Look, I know I keep coming to you two with these overwhelming issues because you are so wise. You always seem to have a logical solution to these problems, but I can't imagine there's a 'fix' for this one?"

The Great Aliens remained silent for several moments, far longer than normal, in fact. They began to walk in a circle around Jon, thinking. Chills ran up JT's spine. He'd never seen them do anything like this before. Finally, Jorthon spoke. "Arrange for us a live, global telecast... one that will be transmitted through every television, every radio channel, and every computer, mobile phone, digital and holographic device. We would like to address man all at once. Through our abilities, we shall deliver a solution which we believe will make a positive impact upon this unfortunate dilemma."

Jon was thrilled. "Are you serious? I can arrange that, sure. Are you going to lecture human beings on how to behave?"

"Not lecture... *persuade*," Kalyssa strongly interjected. "And in so doing, we will gently inform your people that discrimination of any form will no longer be allowed or tolerated in this modern era of your planet."

JT's head was spinning. "How can you do that? How can you possibly connect with everyone at once?"

Jorthon responded. "Kalyssa has a powerful ability to interact with human beings on a deeply emotional level. She is unique amongst our race. You would call her ability 'hypnosis.' She can change human behaviors through subliminal suggestions and thoughts that your people will not even realize are taking root deep within their subconscious minds."

Jon made a concerned face. "You want to *hypnotize everyone on Earth*? That's God big, again. I'd like to discuss this first with my president. Is that alright?"

"Yes, of course," Kalyssa said, zapping Jon back behind his UN desk. "Meghan!" JT screamed.

"I'll get her right away!" Meghan responded, realizing without further discussion that her boss was in need of the President of the United States. "Line six!"

"Madam President," Jon began, almost out of breath, "We can end racial, religious, sexual, and gender discrimination, easily and all at once. Here's how."

As he explained the idea of hypnotizing all of the civilized world at the same time through a mass media broadcast, the president listened in silence.

Finally, after JT had laid out the plan for her, the president responded. "Jon," she nearly whispered, "when I was a young girl, for years the white boys in school kicked me, threw stones, put gum in my hair, and called me a 'stupid Nigger bitch.' Both my parents worked for decades as cleaning people (a janitor and a maid), and neither could afford a college education. Growing up, I vowed to myself that if and when I was ever in a position to combat racial intolerance, bigotry, and deep-seated hatred, I would do everything in my power to do so.

When I became president, I did my best to pursue the end of those things through legislation. As you saw on TV the other day, however, they still persist." She paused. Silence on the phone—the longest period of silence JT had ever experienced with his president. "I don't have the power to change racist thoughts, Jon, but it seems your friends might. If they can change the hate-filled minds of small thinkers and negate man's intolerance for their fellow human who might look, or love, or pray differently, then I say go for it. Let's do it!"

Jon and his children personally phoned the heads of every major television, news, radio, and internet communications company, informing them that an "Unprecedented Media Event" was going to take place on August 1st from atop the UN building (the date and location the aliens had given him through another dream) during which Kalyssa wished to address all of mankind at once.

Every media concern said that yes, of course, they would be more than willing to share a "pool feed" from one primary digital camera placed atop the roof (a UN cameraman had been so assigned) and then share that signal via their outlets. The PR departments of each of those companies also spent days letting pretty much everyone on Earth know that the Great Aliens, the wonderful "Benevolents from the Sky," wished to speak to everyone, en mass.

President Winfield, VP Schoenberg, Cheryl Schoenberg, JT, his kids, Susan, Team Tuckerman, Secretary General Kim and an assortment of other governmental dignitaries and officials gathered atop the UN roof about thirty minutes before the great ship was to arrive. Jon approached the singular cameraman, who appeared to be trembling. "Don't be nervous, friend," JT reassured the man by gently touching his shoulder. "It's okay. They're here to make history. You're the guy that's going to help us do that. That should look pretty good on your resume, don't you think?" The nervous camera man tried to smile.

The diamond in the sky appeared once more above the East River, putting on what seemed like an extra-special light show for the camera. "Such a thing of beauty... what a thrill," the president said.

A sky-blue beam of light emanated from beneath the craft—seemingly connecting the ship with the UN roof. Appearing within the beam—in midair, suspended in all her glory—Kalyssa appeared, radiating gorgeously.

"People on Earth," she began crisply, and again as always, telepathically. "We are very distressed to learn of man's continued intolerance and discrimination of his fellow man, based solely on the color of one's skin, the prayers he delivers to his personal God, his manner of appearance, or with whom he chooses to express physical love. Each of us is a child born of the same Infinite Creator. The Creator of All. He made all of you on Earth. He made all of us who live on distant planets and other dimensions. Yet, unfortunately, your knowledge of the Creator—your understanding—is shallow. Your human minds are not equipped to understand the reality of the Creator's existence or abilities. But you must know that He has sent us to your planet to right any of the wrongs that continue to persist here."

Kalyssa's eyes began to glow a deep gold color. JT and the president glanced at one another—the only two people who knew that the "hypnosis show" had begun. President Winfield squeezed JT's arm. Kalyssa continued, "Every one of you has a role to play in improving relationships between yourselves and members of every race, creed, religion, nation of origin, and sexual orientation that appears within your path. For change to occur, every single man, woman, and child will BEGIN RIGHT NOW to adopt a new way of thinking. You will embrace a new life view... that a positive reverence for all life, both human and animal, is equally important. Each of you WILL NOW BE RESPECTFUL, CARING, AND LOVING toward each and every other one of you, regardless of your neighbor's differences. The Creator placed each of you here to ENJOY ONE ANOTHER, TO ADMIRE ONE ANOTHER, TO LOVE ONE ANOTHER. That is the answer to your riddle, 'What is the meaning of life'?"

The gorgeous alien's words were not only *heard* by all, both those standing on the UN roof and watching or listening to the broadcast at home, but could also quite literally be *felt* inside the human body... something akin to when the bass volume is too loud at a rock concert and one can internalize those vibrations within the gut and up the spine.

Now Kalyssa's whole face got more serious, more intense, turning a deeper hue of gold. Looking both angelic and a bit demonic at the same time, she continued. "The Infinite Creator WILL NO LONGER TOLERATE RACISTS, BIGOTS, OR BULLIES! He has informed Jorthon and me that He is no longer willing to accept racial divide amongst His people on Earth. These actions—so long a part of the human experience—SHALL NO LONGER BE TOLERATED OR ACCEPTABLE."

She paused for a full minute of silence. The dramatic effect was overwhelming.

"STARTING RIGHT NOW, ANYONE ON EARTH WHO ACTS CONTRARY TO THE CREATOR'S WISHES WILL BE DENIED ENTRY INTO HEAVEN UPON DEATH. AND YES, HEAVEN IS A REAL PLACE... AS LOVELY AS THE GARDEN OF EDEN DESCRIBED IN YOUR OLD TESTAMENT. BELIEVE MY WORDS, YOU DO NOT WISH TO BE BANISHED INTO HELL WHEN YOUR SOUL LEAVES YOUR BODY. DISOBEY THIS WARNING AND HELL WILL BE YOURS WHEN YOU DIE. AND JUST SO YOU KNOW, HELL IS ALSO VERY, VERY REAL!"

The beam of light retracted, Kalyssa returned to the ship, and the craft zapped away in mere seconds.

Silence blanketed the UN rooftop. Every single person there had become "enchanted," as Lauren would later describe the presentation. Kalyssa's hypnotic suggestion—clear, powerful, and intense—was embedded into the soul of every human being who saw or heard her speech live, as well as by anyone who viewed or listened to future repeat broadcasts.

"I only wish my parents and grandparents had been alive to see this day," the president whispered into Jon's ear.

"They are here, inside of you, Madam President," he responded, pointing to her heart. "After all, without them, YOU wouldn't be standing here right now. They helped make this happen!"

In the days following Kalyssa's pronouncements, groups of American white supremacists scattered across the deep South, skinheads in the northwest, and Aryan congregations along other areas in between were seen on television building mountains of Confederate flags, protest signs, wooden clubs, large white crosses, and KKK costumes of long white robes and pointy hoods. Fires were set to these piles of hatred. "We were wrong," a man identified as a former Grand Master of a local KKK group in Mississippi told a live TV broadcaster. "Our arrogance and short-sightedness got the better of us. We didn't try hard enough to get along. We didn't know. We know now."

"Reunification" parades took place not only in dozens of American cities, but in many other cities and towns around the world. Blacks, whites, Latinos and Hispanics, Asians, Native Americans, gays, Jews and Arabs, Catholics, Muslims, Hindus, Africans, and Aboriginals all walked arm in arm, hand in hand, young and old, elderly in wheelchairs and infants rolling in strollers. All marched down the main streets of their communities, smiling and clearly enjoying the experience.

Making a grand gesture, President Winfield, VP Schoenberg, and Cheryl Schoenberg returned days later to the site in Alabama that had originally prompted JT's call to action by the aliens. Posing for photographers along with those who had, just weeks earlier, shouted out horrendous racial slurs and held signs of bigotry and hatred, the two leaders of the United States of America now felt only a sense of peaceful rapture.

The president spoke before a bank of microphones. "In this time, on this day, in this new world of ours," she declared in a commanding voice, "all of us, everywhere, have definitive proof, for the very first time in the history of our civilization, that now, without question of any kind, all men, women and children who have ever lived, and who ever will live in the future, WERE TRULY CREATED EQUAL by the INFINITE GOD OF ALL LIVING THINGS!

Today, thanks to our friends from the sky and our hero Jonathan Tuckerman, we can confirm that TOGETHER, WE FINALLY HAVE THE ABILITY TO WALK THROUGH THE FRONT DOOR AND ACHIEVE WHAT DR. MARTIN LUTHER KING PREDICTED FOR US SO LONG AGO:

WE HAVE ARRIVED AT THE PROMISED LAND!"

CHAPTER SIXTEEN

Next up for the JT squad: the World's Overpopulation Crisis. The Tuckerman team, with the wind at their backs and the world at their feet, studied the epidemic of human beings reproducing themselves at an unacceptable rate. With the world's current population at over eight billion, the group learned there was a global increase every day of 250,000 more people born than those who died. Mankind's population was exceeding that of any other primate species by over 10,000-fold. The mere presence of too many humans on Earth had continued to cause the extinction of other primates, as the over-abundance of humans was crowding them off the face of the planet.

Meghan arranged a long, intense meeting for Jon and his staff with the World Population Balance Organization. Through them, the team was informed that overpopulation can theoretically not only be stopped but easily reversed, if only every male and female that wished to procreate could somehow contain their "offspring output" to no more than two children in total. By averaging one or two children per human adult, the total world population would decline by the year 2150 to about five billion, less than half the eleven billion that was currently being projected. Within the next 115 years, the overall global population would be stabilized, indefinitely.

"How can Jorthon and Kalyssa possibly ensure that every adult human only procreates twice during his or her lifetime?" JT asked the group. "Who are *we* to control the number of children that our fellow human beings create in the future?"

Lauren stepped up to the plate. "Dad, we have no RIGHT to do this, but we do have the NEED to do SOMETHING... so that future generations don't consume more resources than the Earth can provide. We're the most selfish group of animals on the planet, and at the rate we're going, we're going to screw ourselves out of enough sustainable land and food to survive. And I'm using the word 'screw' quite literally."

August 22nd arrived. JT again floated through the sky again and reappeared inside the huge craft.

"Greetings once more, friend, what have you learned?" Kalyssa asked.

Jon began to explain to his fellows the latest conundrum he'd been pondering.

"We understand that the act of sexual intercourse for humans is highly enjoyable," Jorthon stated. "However, humans have been unable to control their sexual lust and desires. They have been seeding too many new births at too high a rate to ensure long-term sustainability."

"The act of sexual intercourse is more than highly enjoyable," Jon interjected. "When it's done with someone you love, it's as close to a religious, God-like experience as we are able to achieve."

"We can only comprehend that concept intellectually," Kalyssa said, "As we do not procreate ourselves through sexual contact. What you call 'sex' is not within our nature. We procreate solely through genetic implantation. Each pair of us may create just one new being every fifty Earth years."

Jon fell silent. "Your species doesn't experience physical pleasure?" he asked.

"Our contentment comes from the peace and tranquility we have achieved from being at one with our surroundings—our 'nature.' Our souls all belong to the same Infinite Creator. Through him, we experience a sense of fulfillment and joy," Jorthon explained.

"That's very interesting," JT said, pausing. "So might you have any ideas how my people can address our overpopulation situation?"

Kalyssa left the room and returned quickly. She placed into Jon's hand a small, clear-pink capsule. "May I see your screen?" she asked.

JT gave her his iPad. She placed her hands on either side and closed her eyes. "Take this pill and your screen to your laboratories," she said. "When ingested only once by a female at the age of 12 years or older, this compound will ensure that her reproductive system will allow her the ability to conceive no more than twice. The chemical interaction from this capsule will attach to her DNA and 'instruct' her uterus, ovaries, and fallopian tubes to recognize only two live births. And just two placentas may be generated. After that, her reproductive system will become inoperable.

"The effects of this drug will neither endanger any woman's health nor the life of any current fetus. You might think of this as a reproductive roadblock. Each female body will recognize just two pregnancies, and thereafter, will allow none. Also, after a second birth, each woman will no longer ovulate—what your females call 'periods' will cease."

Jon went silent for a minute. "How can I possibly ask every woman or young girl on the planet to take these?" he whispered.

"We cannot help you with that part of this situation. This must be pursued strictly on a voluntary basis," Jorthon instructed. "Surely with the powers of persuasion that exist on Earth through your media and your advertising, telling humans what to eat, what car to drive, what clothes to wear, the benefits to all of mankind by every woman's commitment to this new request can be conveyed convincingly?"

Back at his desk, Jon called out, "Meghan, please get me a meeting with the head of every top ad agency in town, as soon as possible!"

Two days later, Team Tuckerman met with all the most powerful advertising executives in Manhattan in one large meeting. Jon explained to them that, collectively, they had a chance to use their creative abilities to change the world. They could play a role in establishing a harmonious balance for mankind during the next century by convincing all females of child-bearing age to commit to having no more than two children during their lives with just one pill.

"I ask each of you to come back to us, one week from today, and present an advertising campaign you and your people feel would persuade and inspire every girl over 12 and ever woman in the world to take this new pill. What we are requesting here is not frivolous. It is critically important to ensuring the future survival of our entire species."

A week later, Jon and staff met again with the same advertising industry titans. Each presented a possible name for the pill, a campaign theme and slogan, and a holographic video pitch on how to convey this remarkably unprecedented "ask" into a simplified yet powerful suggestion. Several of the pitches Team Tuckerman were shown were deemed too sexually inappropriate or suggestive... others felt too "corny" or downright frightening.

Team Tuckerman decided that the final presentation, entitled "Two 4 U," had the right tone, substance, and message. In the pitch, an average-looking young woman in her early 20s is shown walking through New York's Times Square. As she walks, she must do her best to avoid being bumped into—and colliding with—the tens of thousands of other pedestrians who are overwhelming the sidewalks through their overabundant presence. She clearly feels like the ball inside a pinball machine as she makes her way through the crowd. She then gets onto an overstuffed subway car, and, clearly miserable, can barely breathe as she's being squished alive.

Arriving at her modest apartment building in the Bronx, she goes into her bedroom, looks at her iPhone and sits on her bed. She is upset. Her mother enters the room and says, "Cindy, darling, are you okay?"

The young woman replies, "Mom, Tim keeps asking me to marry him. I know I'm not ready yet, but I don't want to upset him. He wants kids. What should I do?"

Obviously a warm, loving and concerned parent, the mother says, "There is no rush to get married now. When you're ready, you'll just know it, in your heart. Your dad and I trust you. However, before you *do* decide to go that way, and you want to have kids, be sure to take one of these." The mom holds up a small package that looks like a box of allergy pills.

"What's that, mom?"

"'Two 4 U,' Cindy! It's a little pink pill that will allow your body to make two—and only two—beautiful babies in the future."

"But why just two?" asks Cindy.

"Because our Alien Friends have told us that if men and women continue making too many children—as we've been doing for hundreds of years—soon there won't be enough room on our planet for everyone to live. We need to make our planet safe for all the new people yet to be born, right?" the mom states happily.

Cindy takes the package from her mom's hand and reads it. "'Two 4 U.' This sounds really important, huh?"

The mom adds, "And the best part is that ONLY WOMEN HAVE THE POWER to make the world a better place. WE ALONE ARE IN CHARGE OF THE WORLD'S FUTURE!"

Cindy works the small pink pill out of the package and reaches over to her nightstand to get a glass of water. She swallows the pill, then looks at the camera. "Two for Me. Two for You. Two for Us All!" She smiles and the mom gives her a hug. The spot ends with a close-up of the packet containing the magical pink pill.

"Very sweet," Lauren said at the conclusion of the two-minute-long piece. "I like the mother-daughter rapport. I think teen girls and young women and their moms could actually have that kind of a conversation in real life."

Jon stood. "Congratulations, Mr. Sanders, you've impressed our toughest critic—my daughter! Your agency is now in charge of spearheading a global advertising media blitz. 'Two For You' is a great name for this product. Please have your people produce multiple versions of this concept, tailored for the forty-two overpopulated markets around the world we've identified, in their languages. Meghan will give you that list. Send me a budget for a global campaign. I'll speak with the president and my friends at the UN and put the funds together for you."

Three weeks later, a global advertising blitz entitled "Two For Us All!" promoting the 'Two 4 U' pill, hit the world like a rocket. The holographic videos, print ads, and giant billboards promoting the pill—customized to the individual markets they appeared in—were so well received, online demand for the drug overwhelmed the manufacturers. There was an immediate six month long waiting list for 'Two 4 U' during just the first week alone.

"We have never, ever, in all our years supplying pharmaceuticals to Wal-Mart, seen advance numbers like this —not even for Viagra!" one drug rep told Tuckerman. "More than forty-four million women around the globe have already gone online to place their names on the 'Two 4 U' waiting list. While this new pill might help keep the world's population from exploding, demand for this product already has."

By the time 'Two 4 U' pills were ready to be sold in brick-and-mortar stores, lines of women, quite literally millions around the world, stood for hours at their neighborhood pharmacies, supermarkets, drugstores, and mass merchandise retailers. Media coverage of women standing in lines was global and intense. Crowds in New York, Los Angeles, Chicago, Miami, London, Paris, Rome, Athens, Tokyo, Moscow, Mexico City, Cape Town, Berlin, and many other large metropolitan centers, were estimated to be nearly 100,000 in each.

Airplanes carrying thousands of cartons of the 'Two 4 U' pills were shown on television landing at airstrips large and small across the continent of Africa. Humanitarian aid workers were seen throughout the dark continent greeting local townspeople, explaining to the women there, adults and teens alike, the benefits of the new wonder drug. Not only did untold millions of young African women nod their heads in approval, swallowing the pills on television without hesitation, but they followed those actions by performing colorful tribal songs and dances about it in their remote villages.

Most of the world's media heralded 'Two 4 U' as a literal godsend: "Perhaps the most significant gift to date Jonathan Tuckerman's 'Friends from the Sky' have bestowed upon humanity, 'Two 4 U'—a little pink pill—represents a truly enormous milestone. It's the gift of a sustainable Planet Earth for all of mankind, well into the future."

However, numerous religious groups and even the Pope himself were dubious and critical of the "Aliens Playing God" with the future of the human race —and many of their leaders made their abhorrence known. Realizing this, Team Tuckerman quickly commissioned a follow-up series of advertisements that reinforced the facts that taking the Two 4 U tablet was wholly optional, that it would entirely prevent miscarriages and abortions, that birth control pills would continue to prevent births, even if one took a Two 4 U pill, and that if any girl or woman accidentally took a second (or more) Two 4 U tablet in the future, the effects of any such tablet beyond the first one would be negated.

President Winfield invited the Pope and Jon Tuckerman to a private meeting at the White House to help further ebb the growing controversy.

Following that gathering, the Pope delivered a speech, citing that "while the Catholic religion has long held that conception of any kind was an act against God, we must also become realists and recognize the scientific fact that continuing new births at the current rate of human population would have dramatic negative effects on our tiny planet in the not so-distant future. Therefore, it is with a heavy heart that I can neither endorse this new opportunity that our Alien Friends have presented to mankind, nor can I discourage it."

CHAPTER SEVENTEEN

Jon and Susan were once again at the White House having lunch with their favorite president when a young man JT did not recognize approached the trio. "Oh, Jon, I wanted you to meet Clarence Connors. He's our new Administrator for the EPA. He wanted to say hi."

Jon stood and the two men shook hands. "Mr. Tuckerman, such an honor," Clarence said.

"That's very sweet of you, Mr. Connors but, really, I'm just getting by with a little help from my friends. They're the ones doing the heavy lifting."

Susan and the president smiled at each other. "Don't listen to him, he always says that," the two women said in tandem, laughing.

"Mr. Tuckerman," Clarence continued, "do you think it might be possible to ask your friends if they can share with us their technology so we might develop our own clean energy systems, as they use?"

"That's a great question, Clarence," JT answered. "Why do you ask?"

"My siblings and I lived with our parents in Pittsburgh. We were poor and our house was near an old oil refinery there. When we were growing up, we were sick almost all the time. My sister had asthma that was so bad my dad had to take her to the hospital twice a month. I promised myself then, if there ever was some way for me to make the air cleaner so my sister could breathe, I would.

She passed away at the age of fourteen."

Jon stood silent.

"I know you've got the weight of the world on your shoulders, Mr. Tuckerman," the young man continued, "but you are truly in a unique position. The president invited me here to meet you. I hope you don't think I'm being too bold."

"No, not at all," JT responded. "Thank you for telling me about your sister. I wish I had one. Actually, I did—a twin, I was told—but she died just after birth. It would have been nice…"

He paused. "I have an idea." Jon turned to face President Winfield. "Can I steal him?" JT asked, pointing to Clarence. "Can I bring him with me to New York? I'd like to work up a plan of attack with him when we get back there."

The president smiled. "What do you think, Clarence? Want to go change the world?"

Clarence was thrilled. "Yes of course... thank you so much! Unbelievably cool... me hangin' with the Wonder Man!"

At the UN suite the next day, Clarence Connors became an immediate hit with Team Tuckerman—not to mention an instant "love connection" with the lovely and talented super aide Meghan Marx, who appeared to become tongue-tied in his presence.

"Check them out," Lauren whispered to her brother when the two were clearly flirting with each other. "Now, *that's* what chemistry looks like!"

JT assigned Clarence, Meghan, and Team Tuckerman to compile data that listed the worst oil refinery polluters across the United States, as well as all other major industrial sites that were spewing the largest levels of carbon dioxide, pesticides, and chemical waste into the sky, the water, and the earth. Beyond that list, JT suggested the team meet with representatives from around the world to learn which companies and locations in their countries were also the most blatant and significant environmental offenders.

September 22 and the great airship arrived on schedule, suspended above the still waters of the East River. Having never before seen the craft up close, Clarence rose from his desk to peer through the window. Oh, my good freakin' God," he said.

Quite unexpectedly, JT walked up to him and grabbed his shoulder. "Hey kid, wanna go for a ride?" Clarence was shocked. "What? Who ME? You want ME to go out there onto that enormous THING?"

Jon actually found a great deal of humor in his terror. "Sure, why not? They never told me I couldn't bring a friend along. Come on, let's go find out." JT scooped up his iPad, handed the device to Clarence, and then led the terrified young man through the suite, down the hall, up the elevator and onto the roof. "Maybe you should hold my hand," Jon told the man, who was literally shaking in his boots. Clarence reached out for dear life, and seconds later the beam shot down. A flash, and the two men were now inside the mightiest vessel in the known universe.

Onboard, it was quite obvious that Clarence Connors, the Head of the Environmental Protection Agency for the United States of America, was scared shitless. "Who is your new friend, Jonathan?" Jorthon asked.

Kalyssa approached the frightened fellow, and peered lovingly into his eyes. "You have lost a loved one," she said. "It is the reason you are here."

"Guys, this is Clarence Connors. He's the head of our Environmental Protection Agency," JT explained. "I hope you don't mind my bringing him along. He's our leading advocate for finding a way to end the pollution in our skies caused by the giant oil refineries and fossil fuel industries that have been destroying our air quality for far too many decades." JT turned to his friend. "Clarence, go ahead... tell them about your sister."

Trembling, Clarence spoke firmly. "My sister Jamie—her name was Jamie. Her entire childhood, she never asked for toys or games or any of the things a young girl would ask parents for. She only used to pray that one day she could breathe like everybody else. She had asthma, terrible, terrible asthma. We grew up a few blocks from a huge oil refinery. The sky above our house was so polluted, you rarely saw blue. I used to promise her that one day, when we were both grown-ups, we'd work together to change the air quality in the world. She never got that chance. When I met Mr. Tuckerman, I had to ask him if he'd speak to you about this. But it looks like now I'm doing too much talking... sorry!" The man's body contracted sheepishly.

"A sister's love is strong," Kalyssa said.

"And important." Pointing to the iPad, Jorthon asked, "What can you show us?"

JT had to nearly pry the device out from Clarence's death-gripped hands. He then presented to his comrades the data his team had compiled on the location of disgusting refineries, smokestacks, and manufacturing sites around the world belching smoke and filth into the sky and spilling refuse into the water and the soil.

Drawing up courage from the tips of his toes, Clarence continued, "There have long been rumors that if and when extra-terrestrials came to Earth, they would have the technology to provide mankind with clean energy. Cost free, renewable, clean energy—enough for every living human being. Can you do that?"

Jon was a bit shocked by his colleague's brazenness. At the same time, he more than admired his tenacity and ability to speak eloquently, given his nervous state.

"How well do you know your history, Mr. Clarence?" Jorthon asked. "Have you ever heard of Nikola Tesla?"

"Yes, sir, of course," Clarence replied. "Genius inventor. He created free, wireless electricity and also said that one day people would be able to communicate with each other through wireless devices."

"He was one of our friends," the Tall White said. "Our people helped him develop several of those ideas, and more. Unfortunately, dark forces within your government murdered him. He did not live long enough to fulfill them."

"You knew Tesla?" Clarence was dumbfounded. "That's just way cool!"

"Give me a moment, please," Jorthon said as he left the room.

"Your loving commitment to your sister is clearly apparent," Kalyssa said, touching Clarence lightly on the shoulder. "Family bonds are like no other. One's relatives are always the most significant."

Jorthon returned, holding a small item, which he placed in Clarence's hand. To JT and Clarence, the object looked like a clear glass golf ball with a piece of metal inside that spun wildly. The metal, shaped like an "X," was half red and half black.

"This simple machine has the ability to extract significant amounts of power from preexisting energy reservoirs... what your scientists have long hypothesized as 'quantum vacuum zero-point energy.' Just one of these devices can provide enough free power to run the home of a family of ten, indefinitely. And not just provide electricity to the home, but also power its machines, devices, and automobiles. No pollution results from their use. They can be mass produced quite inexpensively," Jorthon told them.

Kalyssa added, "This item can end all need on your planet for coal, oil, gasoline, and nuclear power." She touched the iPad for a moment with both of her hands. "Give this technology to your manufacturers. Have them mass produced. Provide them to every human, every family, every business, every school around the world. They shall forever end the dependence by your species on fossil fuels. This machine is the nightmare of every person who has made a fortune from those industries, giving nothing back to man in return. The time has come for your people to end reliance on fossil fuels and nuclear energy forever."

Clarence's face lit up. He was ecstatic. "Thank you SO Much!" he exclaimed. "One question... what about the existing refineries operating right now that are still spitting death into our air?"

"We will eliminate them, swiftly," Kalyssa promised, smiling. "Earth is about to experience a most dramatic change, Mr. Clarence.

An unprecedented and monumental shift in your macro-economy. Free power for all will soon become plentiful," she said.

"Large companies that have made billions of dollars spoiling your resources and your climate shall wind up and dissolve. They will become obsolete. Human consumers will now have the ability to use their funds for other basic items important to maintaining life," Jorthon added.

Almost instantaneously, JT and Clarence found themselves back at the UN. Jon whistled as he sat at his desk, then turned around to see Clarence, sobbing, in Meghan's arms. "It's going to change!" he said between tears. "It's all just going to goddamn change! Just like I promised Jamie!"

Meghan embraced Clarence tenderly. It was apparent to the rest of Team Tuckerman that she had found her soulmate. She shot Jon a look and he winked back at her with love. Whenever Meghan smiled at him, he always felt as though he could almost hear her heart beating.

In the days that followed, Jon provided the alien technology to enormous manufacturing plants around the world. Stunned CEOs, realizing that the aliens could destroy their operations if they refused, reluctantly committed to the massive global economic shift this simple new product represented.

A few weeks later, President Winfield, JT, and Clarence Connors posed with the heads of many of the world's top manufacturing companies, holding the samples of the new free energy products. "With this powerful gift given to us by our remarkable alien friends," the president told the media, "our children and their children and *their* children will enjoy a world in which every breath they take will be guaranteed to keep their bodies healthy, happy, and most importantly, alive!" JT asked Clarence to name the clean energy "golf balls." They were instantly christened "Magic Jamies."

And once enough Magic Jamies had been globally distributed weeks later, the Dodger Stadium Special was seen on television destroying every oil refinery, filth-producing smokestack, nuclear power plant, and chemical waste dump around the world. Using bright orange beams of light, these plants were rendered inoperable and no longer toxic.

Notably, not a single human being was harmed at any point during this realignment process.

CHAPTER EIGHTEEN

The president had permanently reassigned Clarence to the UN, where he quickly became a power player within Team Tuckerman. Days later, he asked Meghan Marx to marry him... a move that surprised no one.

Clarence's passion for helping to alleviate the massive problems facing the environment inspired all the other members of the team, most notably Isak, whose guilt over working for a huge oil company for many years had finally taken its toll on his conscience. With Clarence now spearheading future meetings, the team decided to tackle Global Warming next, and soon heard presentations from the Sierra Club, Greenpeace, the Union of Concerned Scientists, the Next Gen Climate Organization, iMatter, 350.org, and the Citizens Climate Lobby about the extent of damage the Earth had been saddled with for too long.

The group was informed about the massive holes within the ozone layer, how the polar ice caps and glaciers were melting far too quickly, how the temperatures of the world's oceans were too high, and how the deforestation of Brazil's rainforest was adversely affecting the world's oxygen output. They also learned a great deal about acid rain and were thrilled when they realized that the aliens' recent help in destroying smokestacks had already begun making an impact on their detrimental environmental effects.

Jon took extensive notes during these sessions yet could not wrap his mind around the enormity of the problems. While he never once doubted the quite literally supernatural powers of his friends, here now, with the challenge of revising the Earth's environment on a planetary scale, he became panicked. JT felt as though perhaps he'd come to the limits of his influence.

"Why are you so bummed out tonight?" Susan asked him at dinner at the penthouse. "They've never let you down, not once. True, these environmental issues are huge... they've been evolving for hundreds of years. So what if Kalyssa and Jorthon can't fix *all* of these problems? They're not magicians. They're scientists. All you can do is ask, Jon. Just ask. I'm sure they'll come up with some solutions far beyond our imagination."

Jon smiled at his partner... his beloved Dr. Parks. He glanced at Russell, whose omnipresence in his home gave him constant reassurance. "Yes... of course, you're right," he said. "We've done so much in such a short time. I just think fixing the environment is *The Big One*... the real prize. When I was a kid, I was fascinated by stories about President Kennedy. He once said, 'Our most basic common link is that we all inhabit this same small planet. We all breathe the same air. We all cherish our children's future. And we are all mortal.'"

"Oh! You and your beloved President Kennedy!" Susan snickered. "What's the fascination there?"

Jon replied, "Sometimes I think maybe I inherited a piece of his spirit. After all, I was born on the day of his assassination."

"Oh my god, I never realized that before!" Susan replied, a truly surprised look on her face.

On October 22, Jon and Clarence once again caught the "A" train to the Dodger Stadium Special. Clarence, now a new man—his self-confidence almost bursting from his body following his initial success with Jon and the aliens, along with the excitement of his newfound love with Meghan—stood strong and proud alongside his mentor. "Hello again, Jonathan and Mr. Clarence," Kalyssa said. "What have you learned?"

"Show them, Clarence," JT said.

Clarence proudly opened the iPad and began detailing for the wondrous aliens the enormity of the environmental hazards confronting the Earth. Kalyssa and Jorthon listened intently, occasionally eyeing each other during the young man's talk. Clearly far more knowledgeable than their visitors, the Great Aliens played along, seemingly rather pleased by the innocence of Clarence's thoughtful and passionate presentation.

Following their viewing of countless screens filled with data on the iPad, the aliens responded. "We have many technologies at our disposal that can help your Earth reverse these challenges... all of them," Jorthon said. "Tell your fellow men that in the coming weeks, we shall be touring your globe, and the atmosphere surrounding it, and we will begin making the necessary repairs. Inform them that they may witness our efforts through sprays, rays of light, and sonic manipulations that will appear and sound completely foreign to them. Possibly even frightening. Be sure to let them know that our methods are noble... that we have only the best intentions in our minds and hearts for improving the living conditions of every member of your race on this planet."

In the days following, back at UN headquarters, Jon and Clarence were awed by remarkable television news footage from around the globe as the airship was seen hovering over the great oceans, the North and South Poles, the Brazilian rainforest, and many other locations, emitting beautifully colored smoke, lights, sprays, and noises that defied description with human words.

JT and Clarence were now receiving phone calls—hundreds of them—from scientists across every nook and cranny on Earth. They were hearing that the ocean temperatures had begun cooling dramatically in just a few days, that the ice caps had not only stopped melting but had begun expanding, that the holes in the ozone layers, most notably over Antarctica and over the Arctic on the Asian side, were becoming "filled in," as though by magic.

Environmental activists from South America were phoning to tell the team the trees in Brazil's rainforest, which had for so long been cut down by illegal logging companies, were now releasing powerful chemical compounds as soon as a first cut was made—these chemicals causing any human being attempting to cut them down to fall asleep for days. The entire deforestation process there was now no longer tenable.

"Mr. Tuckerman, YOU ARE THE MAN!" Clarence said, rushing up to his new best friend and giving him a giant bear hug. "The Hero of the Environment! *My* Hero!" Clarence declared, while everyone else smiled in delight. Jon glanced around the room at his hugely thrilled team members—most notably, his children applauding him—and a tear or two trickled down his cheek.

The only thing that would have made Jonathan even happier was if, at that moment in time, Clarence would just simply stop squeezing him to death.

CHAPTER NINETEEN

The mayhem taking place in Jon Tuckerman's office was even more overwhelming than normal, following the pronouncements by scientists and researchers around the world that the oceans had cooled more than six degrees on average, that the ozone layer had been completely repaired, and that smog conditions had been resolved across Mexico City, Beijing, Ahwaz/Iran, New Delhi, Cairo, Moscow, Mongolia, Pakistan, Saudi Arabia, and Bangladesh. Polluted air had also receded into history across New York, Dallas, Las Vegas, Phoenix, Los Angeles, Bakersfield, Sacramento, and numerous other cities throughout the United States.

Now dubbed "Hero of Earth," JT's renown continued to propel him. He'd become, without question, the most discussed human being in the world.

On the morning of October 8, 2034, hubbub ensued when a TV camera crew, quite unexpectedly, burst into JT's office, having successfully evaded Meghan's normally protective arms at the reception area. The crew and its reporter, a very striking blonde woman with bright red glasses, ran straight to Jon's desk and thrust a microphone into his face. "Mr. Tuckerman! What is your reaction to the news?" the woman asked him.

A bit embarrassed, JT looked up and into the camera lens and said, "I am thrilled and delighted that our extra-terrestrial friends have been able to accomplish so very much in such a short time."

"No, no!" the reporter interjected. "What's your reaction to the Nobel Prize announcement?"

Jon shot a look at Meghan, who appeared equally shocked. The rest of Team Tuckerman stood up from their desks and approached the camera crew. "What are you saying?" Jon asked, stunned.

The phone rang. "She's on two!" Meghan shouted.

JT pressed a button on his upgraded console so the president's call could be projected into the room as a hologram. The TV camera crew recorded everything.

"Johnny boy, you did it! As I predicted almost a year ago, you were just named the winner of this year's Nobel Peace Prize... an honor you clearly deserve. They just called to ask me to inform you directly. Isn't this exciting news?"

Jon sat silent on the phone. The blonde reporter continued to smile at the befuddled man who simply did not have the ability—at that moment—to put together any English words.

The president continued, clearly reading, "'For his untiring efforts to find peaceful solutions to international conflicts, to advance basic human rights and dignity, and to promote economic and social development around the world, we bestow the 2034 Nobel Prize for Peace to Mr. Jonathan Michael Tuckerman of New York City.' Jon, you still there?"

JT began to cry. "Yes, thank you Madam President. That's very nice," he said, then gently hung up.

The reporter again thrust her microphone into his face. "Any words for your fans around the world?"

Jon just stared at the woman.

Lauren, realizing her dad was in trouble, interjected herself into the situation. "Listen, ah, can we talk?" she said to the reporter and the camera crew, forcefully turning them away from her distraught father so they now faced into the center of the room. "Interview us instead," Lauren said, indicating herself and her brother Isak. Realizing that his kids were playing interference for him, JT stood and quickly raced out of the suite.

Meghan ran after him in the hall. "Mr. T! Go home! Get drunk! Take a nap! Read a book! Kiss your wife! Do something FOR YOURSELF! Go see a movie! Get the hell out of here! Spend some time alone with your thoughts. We'll cover for you."

Jon turned back, hugged his assistant, and then raced toward the elevators. Instead of heeding her advice, however, he decided to go up to the roof of the UN building, alone. Outside, the sun was shining on a beautiful fall Manhattan day. A slight breeze blew through his silver hair as he began walking around in a large circle on the roof, completely lost in thought.

He stared up into the beautiful blue sky—the sky that had so changed his life—and realized just then that this was the very first time he'd ever been on the roof without the enormous spaceship hovering above it. Here was the same sky that had delivered him from death... that had reunited him with his children... that had enabled him to befriend the President of the United States.

The sky that had chosen him—HIM alone, among all of mankind—to solve those problems that had previously been considered insurmountable. The sky that had so enriched his life by bringing Dr. Susan Parks into it, and Russell, and Meghan, and Clarence, and all of the other wonderful men and women he'd met during the nearly one year since aliens from another world had plucked him out of the sea, wet, cold, and dead, and nurtured him along to where he now stood... atop the United Nations building—the most distinguished and beloved man on Earth.

Jon sat on the rooftop on his butt with his legs crossed. He placed his head into his hands and began to weep. Softly at first, then harder and harder, until he was now sobbing uncontrollably. He began making noises from the deepest depths of his soul... sounds he'd never heard before in his life.

Lauren appeared on the roof, having sensed intuitively that her father would be there. She found the man who'd given her life sitting on the ground, crying as though he were in mourning, and gasped. Without saying a word, she approached her dad, kneeled next to him, and held him tightly. She began sobbing as well. No words were spoken. The love between this father and his beloved daughter was profound and all-consuming.

Perhaps, for the first time in their lives, these two human beings, who shared DNA and decades of history, had become "two parts of the same one."

CHAPTER TWENTY

It was now November 2034. Magazines and newspapers around the world ran cover stories commemorating the "One Year Anniversary of Their Arrival" and of the world's introduction to Jon Tuckerman and his miracles.

Behind his back, President Winfield and Susan had been working with Lauren, Isak, Meghan, and Russell to plan a 71st birthday party for their favorite fellow. It was determined that the Plaza Hotel, on Fifth Avenue in Manhattan, would be the venue. The group had put together a hand-selected invitation list of the people with whom Jon had become closest during his previous eleven months at the UN.

Susan informed Jon of the event just a few hours before it was to begin, and he was quite pleasantly surprised. "Really? Wow, that's so nice," he said. The pair dressed in formal attire... Susan never looked more radiant in her life. Lauren and Isak showed up at the penthouse, and the foursome took a stretch limousine to the hotel, which was only six blocks away.

Standing on the red carpet in front of the hotel, the media was respectful and excited. This was Jon's first big "social" engagement since he'd been thrust upon the world's stage overnight. When the president arrived, she posed for photos with Jon and Susan, and also with the two younger Tuckermans—much to the delight of the photographers present, who realized the value these pictures would add to their bank accounts in the morning.

The food and drink during the gala was beyond reproach, the music from a not-too-loud pop/rock band was strong, and virtually every one of the 400 people in attendance danced joyously. Clearly the biggest celebrity there, JT was besieged by virtually every woman in the room for a dance, but he gracefully declined, wishing to remain solely by Susan's side.

At 10:00 pm, President Winfield approached the microphone on the stage, clinking a tall glass of champagne with a spoon. "Hello, ladies and gentleman," she beamed. "Thank you all for coming out tonight to help me honor not only the man of the hour, but the man of our generation! Johnny, can you please come up here a minute?" Susan kissed her man seated beside her at their table, and helped propel him up from his seat, so he could then approach the stage.

"One year ago today, a man we never heard of, and never even knew existed, came into my life... the lives of everyone here (besides Isak and Lauren)... and the lives of everyone else in the world. When I first met him, he was disoriented, angry, tired, and alone. Well, look at him now!" Everyone applauded. "Johnny, we wish you the healthiest and happiest seventy-first birthday anyone ever had! And isn't *this* party a little better than the one you threw for yourself a year ago tonight?" Everyone laughed. "Come on up here and say a few words."

An apprehensive JT walked up to the president, who hugged him and led him to the mic. Everyone in the room stood for a heartfelt ovation.

When it finally ended, he said, "Thank you all so very much for coming out tonight. That was very kind of you," Jon began. He glanced at his daughter and saw that she was crying. It touched him deeply. "President Winfield, Isak and Lauren, Susan, Meghan, Russell, Clarence, and my newfound friends who are sitting here in this room right now, all I can say is that not only has this last year been one helluva ride, but this birthday is without a doubt the best fucking party I've ever had!" Riotous applause and smiles abounded.

"We love you JT!" someone screamed from the floor. "I love you back," Jon responded.

The band began to play the '70s ballad "You Light Up My Life." "May I have this dance?" the President of the United States asked the World's Most Famous Man. As the two began a slow dance atop the stage, dozens of other couples beneath them also hit the dance floor. Jon whispered into his partner's ear, "I never, ever, could have imagined this moment when I was drowning."

"And aren't we all glad you didn't?" the president responded.

In the course of just 365 days, Jonathan Michael Tuckerman's world had turned inside out and upside down, somehow miraculously landing right side up.

Following the birthday bash, Jon and Susan returned to the penthouse. Too tired for sex, the couple collapsed into a heap on the bed. Jonathan tossed and turned for much of the night. Finally falling asleep about 3:30 am, he had a nightmare. He dreamed he was in a car, behind the wheel, with his late wife Janice, just moments before the horrific accident that was to take her life. They were arguing in the dream. She was yelling at him that he was about to kill her. That she didn't want to die. During the encounter, Jon realized that he had truly loved Janice, and that he was profoundly sorry... not only that the marriage had ended, but that it did so in such a traumatic and sudden manner.

"No, God, no!" Jon screamed in his sleep. Even in his dream, he could not avoid the fatal collision—he bolted upright, panting.

"What is it?" Susan asked, now awake and concerned.

He leaned against her. "Janice... in the car. I just killed her! Again!" he cried, trembling.

Susan, topless, in just a pair of white silk panties, shot out of the bed. "I'll be right back," she said and left the room. Jon placed his face into his hands, shaking his head no. A few minutes later, the lovely doctor reappeared. "Well, I just gave poor old Russell quite a peep show," she joked. "Here take this," she handed JT a tranquilizer. "And drink this," she added, handing him a cup of hot chocolate.

Jon did as instructed.

"Everything's fine, okay? I'm here for you. I'm here and I'm not leaving. That's a promise! After all you've been through this past year, it's no wonder those terrible old memories are coming back up. Especially after tonight." "Thanks Suze, I really appreciate it—I really appreciate *you!*" JT whispered. "I just wish there was a way I could go back somehow and undo that night."

A moment of silence.

"Maybe your friends could help?" Susan suggested.

Jon looked up at her in surprise. "I wonder?" he replied.

CHAPTER TWENTY-ONE

The planning for the Nobel Prize ceremonies in Oslo, Norway, was extensive. President Winfield had instructed her staff to work directly with Susan, Meghan, Isak, and Lauren to coordinate all the details and logistics involved. The Tuckerman family and guests were to be flown, housed, and fed for the bulk of the week prior to the event. The president, vice president, and various members of their families, as well as an assortment of U.S. Senators, Congressmen, and members of the UN, including General Secretary Kim, were also to be in attendance on the big day.

Jon was informed that he could bring to Oslo a "reasonable number" of those closest to him. Of course, Meghan, Russell, and Clarence were added into the mix. Isak requested that his partner, Harold, be invited, and JT instantly agreed. Lauren also asked that her most recent boyfriend,

Charles, a poet and performance artist she had left behind in Paris, be invited as well, and he was.

JT had been an only child. His father was dead, and his mother had long been in a coma in a nursing facility. He racked his brain to think of any other relatives he might be able bring along to the prize ceremony. No one else came to mind.

The entourage took to the skies on December 5, 2034, five days prior to the December 10 ceremonies. The flight was filled with great joy and humor. The president served as hostess—as though those assembled were amidst a private party for which she was the grand dame. Susan and Lauren spent a good deal of time in private talks with each other and with the president, making Jon feel pleased that "his three best girls" had all become so remarkably close.

Upon their arrival in Oslo, the group made its way by ground caravan to the Lysebu Hotel. The president had requested that the entire hotel be bought out for the Tuckerman entourage for the entire length of their stay. The unprecedented request was honored, giving JT and his family and friends ultra-VIP status. The staff of the hotel were beyond honored to be attending to this remarkable American. (His fame in Europe was perhaps higher than anywhere else in the world, save for Africa.) Several hotel employees—desk clerks, bellmen, concierges, maids, etc.—wept as they shook Jon Tuckerman's hand. Many others cried when merely standing a few feet away. The adulation, which JT had never asked for nor enjoyed, was simply something he now had to endure on a daily basis.

The president had requested lavish banquet style dining for her and her guests each night of their stay at the Lysebu. That first night, much fuss was made over Harold and Charles, who had arrived separately earlier that day from Iceland and France, respectively. Reunited with their significant others, Jon, Susan, and the president made a big fuss over each man, much to the delight of Isak and Lauren. It filled JT's heart with joy to see how important these two strange men seemed to be to his beloved children. In all the years he'd known them previously, he'd never gotten to see either of them in love.

During the afternoons, Jon and his family would take walks throughout the magical city of Oslo, sightseeing and taking photographs, as would any normal group of tourists on vacation. Not wanting to interfere with the well-deserved quality time the savior of mankind was spending with Susan and his kids, the president gave Jon plenty of distance during the daytime.

Of course, everywhere they went, the locals of Oslo were speechless when they saw Jonathan Tuckerman, a true living legend, simply walking through their streets, as though he were a normal human being. While no one had the audacity to approach him for a handshake or an autograph, many shot pictures of him from afar with their phones. Adult men and women shed tears as he neared them, teenagers gave him "thumbs up" gestures, and small children seemed to know, instinctively, that hearing their parents whisper "that's the Wonder Man" was a moment in their young lives that they would always remember.

On the evening before the big event, the president knocked on the door of JT's suite. Susan opened it and ushered her into the room. Jon sat at a desk, reviewing his speech.

"How are you holding up, my dear man?" the president asked.

"This is all just too much," Jon whispered. "I don't deserve the Nobel Prize."

"There he goes again, Madam President," Susan said. "Wallowing in his own mire."

The president pulled up a chair and sat next to Jon. "Because of you, Jon, this past year has been one of the most significant in all civilized history. The work that you've been able to spearhead through your relationship with those friends of yours has made the lives of billions of people better. I know you still have mixed feelings about all this acclaim, and I understand that. But my dear Jon, without you, and you alone, the remarkable accomplishments that have taken place during these past twelve months would never have happened."

Smiling at the most powerful woman in the world, Jon leaned over and patted her gently on the arm. "You were there with me, Madam

President. You were with me every single step of the way. It wasn't anything I did in a vacuum. You were my guiding light."

The radiant woman became teary. "Friends for life?" she asked.

"Friends for life," he answered.

The morning of December 10, Nobel Prize day, Jon Tuckerman made wild and crazy passionate love to Susan, as though in a frenzy. After the two of them climaxed together, they fell into a tangle of arms and legs on the bed, laughing hysterically. "Well, Mister Tuckerman! Where on earth did that volcano come from?" Susan joked.

"That, my dear, is what you might call mania. Sheer nervous energy, panic, and all-consuming terror," JT replied.

The pair walked naked into the bathroom and Susan turned on the water to the shower. "Tonight's going to be the most singularly important night of my life, Susan. The whole world will be watching me... ME!... being handed the Nobel Prize for Peace. You might say I'm just a tad nervous, my darling angel face and head."

Susan hugged him. Jon, so extraordinarily attracted to this woman, who was as beautiful on the inside as on the outside, was still truly amazed that she was involved with him at all, despite his global acclaim.

"Hey, I've got an idea!" Susan joked as she turned off the water for the shower. "Let's go downstairs together, right now, and have a great big naked breakfast!"

Jon laughed. "Sure! Why not? Let's do it! Let's eat naked next to my children and the President of the United States and pretend nothing's unusual. I love that!"

"You think we'd get their attention?" Susan added.

Jon gently stroked her long, perfect brown hair. "I love you, Susan Parks," he whispered. "You are the woman I've waited to meet my entire life. And it only took my suicide and aliens from outer space to make that happen!"

Jon got down on one bare knee. "Wanna marry me, kid?"

Susan got down on one bare knee as well. "You know it, my angel face and head," she replied.

CHAPTER TWENTY-TWO

The president, the vice president, Jon, Susan, Isak and Lauren and their respective partners, were all decked out in fantastic formal wear... the men in black tuxedos, the Tuckerman women in color-coordinated designer evening gowns, the president in her signature magenta. The entourage was taken in one large stretch limousine to the entranceway to Ullevaal Stadium, the largest venue in all of Oslo. Due to the unprecedented demand for tickets for that year's Nobel Peace Prize ceremonies, the organizers of the annual event had to change the normal venue for the prize to a stadium, Oslo's largest venue, which could accommodate 28,000 people. The organizing committee had also initiated a lottery system for tickets after having received more than 24.5 million requests from around the world.

As the president, vice president, JT, Susan, the Tuckerman kids and their dates left their car, paparazzi flashbulbs began to virtually blind them. The group had to walk a red carpet gauntlet at least 40 feet long, with hordes of media members standing along both sides, five or six people deep. "Jon, I've been to a lot of big events during my career," the president shouted into JT's ear above the chaos, "but never in my life have I seen anything like this! You sure know how to draw a crowd."

The lights that illuminated the carpet from the video cameras as well as the pops of flash from the still photographers, made breathing difficult for the entourage. Countless microphones were stuck into the faces of the president and JT—reporters screaming questions. "Just keep walking, kid," the president said to her star. "Don't say a word to anyone. Save it all for our speeches."

Jon turned to Susan, "Can we go home now?" he said, not even joking.

"It'll all be over soon, my poor baby boy," his new fiancée said, beaming.

Following the successful procession through the media gauntlet, the president and JT walked together, arm in arm, into the stadium and onto the stage platform that had been specially designed and constructed for this occasion. (Susan, the VP, the young Tuckermans, and the rest of their group took their seats in the front row.)

Once the audience realized Jon Tuckerman was on stage, a standing ovation, the likes of which Europe had rarely if ever seen before, erupted. Shrieks, cheers, thunderous applause, shouts of "Bravo" and "Jeg Elsker Deg" (Norwegian for "I love you") filled the open-air stadium and the sky above it.

JT squeezed the hand of the President of the United States so tightly, she'd later tell a number of interviewers she thought he'd broken a few fingers. The two took their seats on a raised dais table. These new "friends for life" had to await the end of the deafening roar of the crowd, before the ceremony itself could actually begin.

Dr. Franz Sternheim, himself a renowned research scientist who'd won the Nobel Prize in Science and Medicine the previous year, was to serve as the MC for the evening. He walked up to the podium and motioned for the audience members to sit down, but they did not adhere to his wishes.

Jon's standing ovation lasted for eighteen minutes... a world record, eclipsing by one full minute the ovation Robert F. Kennedy received during the 1964 Democratic Convention in Atlantic City, New Jersey... as a tribute to his fallen brother, the late President John F. Kennedy.

Finally, after what seemed an eternity, Dr. Sternheim was able to address the crowd. "Thank you very much, ladies and gentlemen," he began, "for attending the 2034 Nobel Peace Prize ceremony. This year, we honor a man whose accomplishments, after just twelve months in the public eye, have already been chiseled into stone, and will appear inside every history book to be published in the future. Before we proceed, please watch the screens on either side of the stage."

For the next twenty minutes, a documentary film was shown compiled from news footage shot around the world, chronicling each of the extraordinary accomplishments the world had enjoyed due to Jon Tuckerman's influence. The film began with his initial "appearance" along with Jorthon and Kalyssa at Dodger Stadium, and was followed by diverse video clips of his successes... the giant UFO hovering above major military installations around the world and neutering the globe's nuclear arsenal—and the looks on the faces of the military personnel watching, helpless, as well as the huge "NO NUKES!" headline in the *New York Times*; the manna from heaven with the recipients from around the world eating the substance and smiling; the ginormous water silos descending to Earth and the globally iconic video of the young African boy getting sprayed by the fresh water and dancing in the stream, along with the opening of TWPs around the world; newborn children receiving life altering injections; mentally disabled people 'waking up' after having been fitted with Harmony Buds; the burnings of guns in huge piles; the massive cartons of gold descending from the great ship at Yankee Stadium and the construction of new housing developments around the world; Kalyssa's admonishment to mankind in the sky atop the UN building, followed by Ku Klux Klansmen burning Confederate flags; tremendous lines of people, in cities around the world, waiting to retrieve their "Magic Jamies" and their "Two 4 U" pills; smokestacks being snuffed out by light beams from the Dodger Stadium Special; and scientific TV news reports of the ocean's cooling temperatures, the halt of the Brazilian rainforest destruction, the healing of the ozone layer, and the thriving polar ice caps in the Arctic Circle and Antarctica.

Jon watched the film in silence, his chest heaving up and down rapidly, his palms sweating. He had no idea a documentary was going to be shown... or that it even existed in the first place. "Meghan and your kids," the president whispered into his ear. "A special surprise gift." She winked. As he viewed the movie now being shown to the 28,000 people in the stadium, and to the hundreds of millions more watching the live broadcast from their homes around the world, he realized, for the first time, that perhaps he truly HAD helped make a real difference after all.

Another standing ovation took place following the end of the film... this one only lasting a couple of minutes. Dr. Sternheim again made hand motions for everyone to sit back down so the event could continue. When calm was finally restored, he announced, "Tonight, ladies and gentlemen, we have a most special guest who would like to introduce the recipient of this year's Nobel Prize for Peace. Please welcome now, from the United States of America, President Tameka Winfield."

The president walked up to the podium to the third standing ovation of the night. As Sternheim had done before her, she kept saying, "Sit, sit! Come on now!" and clearly laughing while she did so.

When those sitting on the stage could once again hear their own thoughts, the president spoke. "Good evening, Oslo! Thank you so much for welcoming us here tonight. And to all of you watching at home, 'God Kvelt'! Hello to you as well!" More applause embraced her thoughtful use of Norwegian.

"We'd like to thank the Nobel Prize committee, and everyone involved in getting us here tonight, for extending such wonderful encouragement and warmth." She paused for a few seconds. "I've had many, many remarkable moments during my lifetime… watching as a child when my father would come home from work at night and kiss my mother in the kitchen; attending a great college and getting a degree—the first in the history of my family to do so; falling in love with my late husband and making my two wonderful daughters, Patrice and Annie; spending time with my three beloved grandchildren, Kylie, Katie, and Kevin; getting elected as the first woman—and the first African American woman—to become President of the United States.

"All of these life moments have meant the world to me. I truly thought I had already accomplished everything a person could ever accomplish in her life. And then I met this man," she said, pointing to Jon, sitting several feet behind her and to her right on the stage. "Mister Jonathan Michael Tuckerman came into my office on the evening of November 22, 2033—his 70th birthday," the president continued. "Earlier that night, he had tried to drown himself in the Pacific Ocean, feeling that his very existence held no purpose, that no one loved him, that life itself had betrayed him."

Isak and Lauren gave each other looks as if to say, "God, we really fucked that up, didn't we?"

The president continued, "When I first met Jon, he was shivering cold, he was angry, and he was upset. He was in a state of shock. After all, aliens from an advanced civilization far beyond our own had just plucked his naked ass up from the sea and flown him in a UFO the size of *Big Ben*. They had chosen him—HIM, above all other human beings on the Earth, to serve as a conduit between themselves and the rest of us.

"During the course of just this past year, working closely with our benevolent friends, Jon Tuckerman has helped the world overcome hurdles that had long been considered without solution. In combination with the wisdom, abilities, and technologies of our visitors from the sky, Jon has deftly managed to end the nuclear age; feed the hungry; provide water to those without; heal the sick; cure the mentally challenged; end racial, religious, and sexual-orientation intolerance; stop gun violence; house the impoverished; end our reliance on the fossil fuel industry;

address the issue of global overpopulation; and heal many of Planet Earth's greatest environmental catastrophes. I think he deserves an A-plus on his report card, wouldn't you agree?" Big applause.

She paused for dramatic effect. "I can proudly say that now, just a bit over one year exactly from the moment we first met, that having had Jon Tuckerman intersect with my presidency—and with my life—and becoming close personal friends with him, his brilliant children, and the lovely Dr. Susan Parks has been, without question, the most joyous, the most profound, the most awe-inspiring, and the most remarkable experience of my entire life.

"So, without further ado, it is with the utmost pride, friendship, and crazy-ass love that I have the honor to present the 2034 Nobel Prize for Peace to my dear, sweet 'Friend for Life,' the Hero of Earth, the Wonder Man himself, Mr. Jonathan Michael Tuckerman!"

Pandemonium in the stadium. Ear splitting applause. Not only was every single person in the arena clapping, they were doing so WHILE STANDING ON THEIR CHAIRS!

JT arose from his seat, sweating profusely. He approached the president at the podium and they embraced. She handed him his award. The flashes from cameras—both from the media covering the event, as well as from the tens of thousands of cell phones being held aloft by audience members—were like bolts of lightning illuminating a massive thunderstorm.

Standing alone at the podium, Jon Tuckerman, now a "Certified Living Legend," could hardly breathe. Waiting for the ovation to settle down, he looked at the front row to see his son, his daughter, and his fiancée—along with his three closest friends, Meghan, Clarence, and Russell—all weeping, as they cheered him along with the other 27,994 people in the sold-out stadium. He turned around to see, on the podium behind him, the president, the vice president, Secretary General Kim, Dr. Sternheim, and at least half a dozen Nobel Prize committee officials also clapping their hands raw.

Trying to quell the acclaim, JT mimicked Dr. Sternheim's hand motions to illustrate to everyone that it was time to stop applauding and *just sit the fuck down already*. After an interminably long time, they finally did.

Now complete and utter silence filled the space as Jon surveyed the massive crowd with his eyes. Feeling faint and trembling noticeably, he realized that THIS MOMENT IN HISTORY was the most important he would ever experience in his life. Standing there, RIGHT THEN, was the reason he'd been born, the reason he'd survived drowning, the reason he'd been chosen by Jorthon and Kalyssa to help save the world.

He knew he *had* to give this speech… that he had to say SOMETHING, ANYTHING… that he could NOT choke or faint or vomit or drop dead from fright. With the whole world watching, Jon Tuckerman knew that he simply had to force himself RIGHT FUCKING NOW to rise to this truly fantastic, and quite literally supernatural, occasion.

"I'm just a man," he began , his words echoing across the massive stadium's PA system. "An ordinary man who was lost and alone, who'd given up all hope. And then one night, without advance notice or any idea why, I was chosen by incredible beings from another galaxy none of us even knew existed, to help the world solve its herculean problems. Why I was chosen, I still do not know. I'd been a very unhappy man for many, many years. I'd experienced many profoundly sad times and felt unworthy of love. But today…" he began to get choked up and paused. The crowd stayed mute for nearly a minute.

"But today," he continued, summoning up courage he never knew he had, "I realize that I am an incredibly fortunate guy. I've regained the love of my two beautiful children, Isak and Lauren. I've met the woman of my dreams, Dr. Susan Parks. And I have the respect and support of the greatest leader in the history of the United States, my best friend, President Tameka Winfield." More wild cheering.

"I've also had the honor and the trust bestowed upon me as a gift— the most spectacular gift any one human being has ever received—by two members of an advanced race of extra-terrestrials. For those of you who may not know their names, they are Jorthon and Kalyssa. Thanks to their confidence in me, I am here today, standing before you now, to accept this incredible award—this Nobel Prize for Peace—a remarkable honor I can leave to my children as my legacy."

He paused again for a moment and took a sip of water. Dozens of people from the stadium shouted out "We love you, Jonathan!"

"I love you back," he answered.

He looked across the stadium from left to right, top to bottom. The venue was enormous. He felt like an ant under a magnifying glass. "This past year, I have been blessed far beyond any one man's wildest dreams. This prize is an honor far more prestigious than any one person could ever earn alone. The accomplishments we've made around the world this past year were all solutions—otherworldly, yes—but scientific solutions to problems that humankind created... yet, alone, humankind could not resolve.

Tonight, I share this prize with the many others who worked with me to get us here. First of all, thank you, again President Winfield, for your guidance and love and support every step of the way." Wild applause. "Thank you Isak and Lauren, my wonderful, talented children, for your work at the UN, and accepting your flawed father back into your lives." More clapping. "Thanks to my amazing staff at Team Tuckerman, led by my superstar colleague Meghan Marx. Thanks also to Clarence Connors, our environmental guru and the real hero of the Earth. And a personal thank you to Russell Chimelong, without whom I would not be fed, and therefore would not be standing here tonight!" Laughter.

"Thank you, Secretary General Kim and all of my wonderful friends and colleagues at the United Nations, as well as the great supporters we've had in the United States Congress." Applause. "And to all of the other hundreds and hundreds of doctors, scientists, researchers, humanitarian aid workers, advertising creatives, teachers, professors, ministers, rabbis, clergymen, volunteers, CEOs, pharmaceutical executives, manufacturers, technical advisors, and various other geniuses who've worked with Team Tuckerman to help us make our world truly a better place for everyone— to all of you, my thanks are without end." More applause.

"Thank you so very much, my dear, sweet, Dr. Susan Parks, for literally saving my life, by teaching me that the long dead heart of a broken man can actually come back to life." Susan blew Jon a kiss.

Jon took another moment of silence, and then a deep breath. "Of course, I would be remiss, if I didn't thank the two most important members of Team Tuckerman... without whom none of this would have been possible." He looked skyward. "Thank you, thank you, so very much Jorthon and Kalyssa from the interdimensional Pleiades star system, for lifting me up in every way a man can be lifted up, and bestowing upon me your trust—a gift that I could never possibly repay." Great applause.

Pause. Then, fighting back an emotional outburst of tears, JT soldiered on, his voice noticeably cracking repeatedly. "I'd like to say thank you to my mother, who is near the end of her journey, in a coma in a hospital bed back in New Jersey. Mom, I wish you could have been here with us tonight. You would have really enjoyed this. Thank you for everything... I miss you and I love you."

Silence. Now weeping, Jon took one last deep breath. "And finally, to my late father, Jack Robert Tuckerman, who passed away back in 2017, and who I think about—and miss—every single day of my life, I'd like to say..." Jon thrusted the Nobel Prize up into the air.

"DAD, THIS IS FOR YOU!"

As Jon's knees began to buckle. The president ran up to him in time and steadied her highly emotional hero just before he would have stumbled to the ground. The crowd was on its feet one last time, with a final ovation nearly equivalent to the one that greeted JT when he first entered the stadium.

Just then, something quite unexpected happened. The Dodger Stadium Special made a surprise guest appearance. Swirling wildly and projecting colors, textures, and patterns from another place and time across the sky right above Ullevaal Stadium and bathing the huge crowd of 28,000 in dazzling lights beneath it, the massive UFO put on an indescribably enthralling light show.

Moments later, however, a huge, dark-purple-colored V-shaped flying craft appeared from behind the clouds and began firing short powerful bursts of orange-flared laser lights at Jorthon and Kalyssa's ship. Massive sparks bounced off the Dodger Stadium Special as it hurriedly zigzagged across the sky and away in efforts to evade this unprovoked attack.

JT instantly knew something was wrong. But the 28,000 audience members sitting below this spectacular air show "ooed" and "aahhed," applauding the action taking place just above their heads, believing the theatrical presentation in the sky was the planned closing portion of the evening's ceremonies.

It wasn't!

PART TWO

Second Chances

"I wanna go back and do it all over. But I can't go back, I know."
—Eddie Money

CHAPTER TWENTY-THREE

It took a good week for the Tuckerman clan to settle back down in Manhattan following the adrenaline rush of Oslo. JT told no one, not even the president, that he feared the "light show" in the sky above the stadium in Norway might have been a bad omen. He began worrying about his alien friends—a part of him feeling that perhaps they might even be gone forever. He did his best, however, to keep any signs of this stress from the others in his closest orbit.

Susan began to notice that Jon's physical appearance had changed a bit after the prize ceremony. His face now appeared softer and his eyes warmer, the lines in his forehead and the dark circles under his eyes seemed to have vanished. Deeply touched by the events of the year just past, he was becoming more mellow.

"Dad are you actually happy?" Lauren teased repeatedly during their frequent dinners back at the penthouse.

Jon would smile gently and reply, "I suppose some old dogs *can* learn new tricks, kiddo."

JT and Susan continued to have world-class sex. She had introduced him to fun new fantasies like role-playing. Jon loved every sticky-sweet moment of his new bedroom adventures with the woman of his dreams.

The Tuckermans spent the 2034/2035 holiday season in New York, shopping, taking in a number of Broadway shows, and eating at the finest restaurants in town, the tabs almost always "on the house." On New Year's Eve, the four Tuckermans were asked to announce the countdown to the dropping of the huge ball in Times Square on live television.

The family truly had The Big Apple at its feet.

Finally returning to his office at the UN in early January, Jon and his children received a hero's welcome. The well-wishers and fans kept coming and coming, wanting to shake Jon's hand, get an autograph, or pose for a selfie with the superstar. JT had entered a new tier of celebrity... a stratospheric distinction previously enjoyed only by a few martyred leaders, popes, Elvis, The Beatles, and maybe a handful of other movie or rock music stars from the previous decades.

Many began treating Jon with a self-imposed "distance," as quite often people approaching him were now suddenly overwhelmed by his stature, some unable to get within a few feet of him. On rare occasion, a woman or two would faint in his presence, which not only embarrassed JT, but began to make him feel like something of a leper. His fame both drew the attention of many like a magnet and repelled others like a rare and fragile jewel that was too valuable to be touched.

Jonathan Michael Tuckerman had become Above Human.

Team Tuckerman eventually resumed its activities when JT erased the whiteboard, and he and his colleagues replaced those missions already accomplished with problems they'd not yet tackled: Drunk Driving, Second-Hand Cigarette Smoke, Religious Fanaticism, Emotional Trauma, Falsely Convicted Prisoners, Missing Children, Automobile

Safety, and other issues were now destined for positive interference by the Great Aliens.

Collectively, the group was committed to taking advantage of their "Heavenly Connections" for as long as possible, as they realized that Kalyssa and Jorthon could easily just leave at any time. "Let's knock out as many of these items as we can," Jon said. "Tomorrow, the unexpected could happen. They might take off for some reason and never come back." JT knew this better than anyone else.

During lunch breaks, and often after work in the evenings, Jon and his children would walk the streets of New York, just to enjoy the marvelous sights and smells of the city that never sleeps, and to ingest the ambiance of its hustle and bustle. Of course, starstruck New Yorkers continued to be in awe of their most celebrated resident, but they mostly remained at a respectful distance from Jon and his kids as they passed by.

Lauren was constantly amused by the looks on the faces of their fellow walkers when they realized who the man in between the two much younger people actually was. "Dad, I think if Jesus Christ himself was walking naked behind you right now, no one would even notice," Lauren joked.

Isak described the feeling as if the three of them were moving inside a *giant plastic bubble with feet*. "All these people can look in and observe, and feel like they know us," he said. "To them, we're like tropical fish inside a mobile aquarium."

Jon spoke sparingly during these walks. He relished taking in the sights and sounds of his newly adopted hometown. "I love this city," he'd whisper to his kids as they ate hot dogs and pretzels from corner food carts. "It's all here. Life. All of it. Anything you could ever think of, want, or need. The greatest show on Earth."

President Winfield and Secretary General Kim began encouraging Jon to become more well known to the general public on a personal level, so that the myth and legend of "Being Jon Tuckerman" would become less burdensome. The president secured for JT a personal publicist who began booking him for appearances on nearly every major television and radio talk show in America. He was also greatly in demand by print journalists, bloggers, and podcast hosts for his insights on the state of mankind and its future. His newly hired press agent, Heather Burg, was given a desk at the UN suite, and was kept extremely busy both arranging for—and accompanying Jon to—interviews with these various media outlets.

One night during a live television interview in New York on CNN, JT was unexpectedly ambushed by his interviewer, Don Rinehold, with a question his publicist Heather had not prepared him for. Toward the very end of a fifteen-minute talk, primarily on Jon's thoughts about the Infinite Creator and the seemingly limitless abilities of his aliens, Rinehold said, "Mr. Tuckerman, of course we're all very grateful to you for the progress that's been achieved through your efforts with your alien friends. But there is one question that you've never answered for us... and I'm sure it's a question that millions of our viewers would really love to know the answer to."

JT shot a glance over to Heather, who was standing in the wings at the side of the stage. "I have no idea... sorry!" she mouthed in response.

"Why *you*? Why did this alien race come from wherever it is they really come from and pluck *you* out of the Pacific Ocean to become our hero? Why are *you* the savior of our planet? What did *you* ever do in your life to deserve such an unprecedented honor?" Rinehold had pulled a fast one.

JT's face went pale. "Don, I honestly don't know. I've never known. They never told me. I assumed they were nearby, saw me drowning, and were kind enough to save my life by pure coincidence. They probably felt sorry for me. That's all I can think of."

"So you've never just come out and asked them directly... why me?" Rinehold challenged. "Don't you think it's time to do that, Mr. Tuckerman? Wouldn't *you* like to know the truth? Don't you think the *entire world* is entitled to know the answer to that question?"

JT felt defeated. He nodded his head. "Don, you're right. We *should* know. I'll ask them the next time I'm onboard. I promise."

"And will you come back on my show to give me that exclusive?" Don pressured.

Completely backed into a corner, Jon answered, "Yes, okay. I will."

Rinehold turned his head to the camera: "We'll be right back after this short commercial break."

The phone in JT's limousine rang incessantly on his ride back home. "Johnny, he really nailed you there, didn't he?" President Winfield consoled. "If you recall, I asked you that same question the night we met. I think he's right. I think you owe it to yourself to find out. *Screw* the rest of the world, Jon. YOU need to know! I'm just sorry it had to happen this way."

Isak phoned next. "Pretty brutal, Dad. I don't think you can stall any longer. You're going to have to ask your little friends what the deal is."

Lauren's call: "Daddy, I'd like to know too! I'll bet it's some amazing reason, like you're the reincarnation of Buddha or something like that. Ask them! Love ya," she said, hanging up as quickly as her call had begun.

Susan met JT at the penthouse, where Russell had prepared a virtuoso meal of lasagna with sausage and peppers. "Tough day at the office, dear?" she frowned, mocking him in a most loving manner.

"You could say that," Jon answered, trying to smile.

Susan continued, "You know, it's been a hair over a year since they dragged you out of the sea and plopped you onto the world's stage to make you the 'Hero of Earth.' I agree with Don—I think they owe it to you to tell you the why."

"You're right," JT said. "The fact that I never asked them that question doesn't make sense, even to me."

"Of course, I'm sure they have a reason, and it's probably a great one," Susan said, handing Jon a large glass of chardonnay. "You weren't plucked up at random. They revealed themselves to the whole world right after they saved you. Seems to me that was something they were planning to do anyway. And… it's almost like they *knew* where you were going to be that night. No way that was a coincidence… I believe it was predestined. Right Russell?"

The kindly man smiled with his eyes and nodded. "Predestined, yes," he agreed.

Susan continued, "They knew you were going to be in trouble. They were waiting for you. They not only saved your life, but they elected to save the rest of us too. Perhaps your karmic destiny was designed by a higher power, lover boy!"

Jon nodded, then drank his wine quickly, desperately trying to forget the Rinehold interview entirely. He sat at the table, eyes wide, salivating over Russell's latest savory delight.

CHAPTER TWENTY-FOUR

Over the next several days, as his UN duties continued at their usual hectic pace, JT was distracted. The Rinehold interview had troubled him more deeply than anyone imagined. Meghan and the rest of his staff could see that their boss appeared greatly distracted and they moved with extra caution in his presence.

Jon and Team Tuckerman had studied the problem of Drunk Driving and had assembled a wealth of statistics when the Dodger Stadium Special swung by for its meeting with JT on January 22, 2035. Rising from his desk, and clutching his iPad, Jon left his suite mumbling to himself, "Today's the day... the Big Ask."

Beamed onboard the craft again, the Benevolents approached their favorite human. "Hello dear Jonathan, what have you learned?" Kalyssa asked.

Jon was clearly not acting himself and said nothing.

"You seem troubled, friend," Jorthon said. "What is the matter?"

"Well… for starters… your little 'airshow' in Oslo—what was that all about? I've been worried sick about you two. That didn't look… right," JT said.

"You will learn of these matters in time," the Great White replied. "A situation we must discuss with the Great Creator first."

Then, sucking up courage from his deepest depths, JT added, "Also, I'd like to know... No. I NEED to know... WHY you selected *me*. Why did you make ME your voice on Earth? How did you know the perfect time to save my life? Why *me* above all others?"

"Jonathan, your questions are reasonable, and we knew the time would come when you would ask them," Jorthon said. "To give you a quick answer... we have been protecting you since the day of your conception. Your father…"

"MY FATHER?" JT interrupted, stunned. "YOU knew my Father?" he asked.

"Yes, of course," Jorthon answered. "Both of your parents are the link between us."

Jon felt lightheaded. He hopped up onto the table of light and sat on it. "I don't understand."

Jorthon left the room, and Kalyssa gently touched JT's shoulder. "Do not be alarmed, Jonathan. All will be explained."

When Jorthon returned, he held a rectangular-shaped object, about the size of a shoebox. It looked like a picture frame. In its center was a rotating, amber-colored block of clear plastic. Jorthon held it aloft. "There is much for you to see here," he offered. "With this device, you will be shown select recorded moments from the lives of your father and your mother. Your people would likely call these 'home movies.' We will leave you to view the start of this story."

The Tall Whites left the room.

Jon Tuckerman's full attention was now focused on the beautiful framed amber block in his hands... its cool, pleasing glow both hypnotizing and calming him as it sprang to life with imagery the man could never in a million years have expected.

Jon watched in awe as his father, Jack Tuckerman, a bespectacled, nerdy-looking man in his early thirties, stood outdoors on the tarmac of a military airfield in the early evening. JT could clearly read a nearby sign: "Edwards Air Force Base." He knew right away this moment must have taken place during one of his dad's regular trips to California during the late 1950s and early '60s. His father had worked with the U.S. Army and members of the aerospace industry to implement the designs of his drone-based, intelligence gathering, photographic technology. A group of men in military uniforms surrounded his father. They were all shielding their eyes as they watched a small rocket blast off, straight into the sky.

"Looking good, Jack," a general said to Tuckerman Senior. "Let's see what kind of pictures your $4-million flying garbage can is able to get of these goddamn flying saucers."

Jack smiled, seemingly pleased with the launch. "I'll speak with you gentlemen later. I'm going to track my baby on radar," he said. Walking toward a small group of bungalow offices, JT's father entered a building filled with electronics gear—dials and switches and oscilloscopes that would have been featured in any popular sci-fi movie during that time period. Standing over the shoulder of a young radar operator, he observed the movements of his just-launched new invention on the scope.

During his reverie, JT could see a *Playboy* magazine calendar pin-up girl tacked to the wall in the radar room. It read "February 1963." Suddenly, the prominent, dark green blip that had been so prevalent on the radar screen in front of the two men became *two* blips for a few seconds, then both blips disappeared. Tuckerman Senior leaned in. "What happened?" he asked the confounded operator. "Where's my little lady?"

The group of military officers from outside came rushing into the room, troubled looks on their faces. "We just saw another one, Jack," the general said, both frightened and annoyed. "A silver craft covered in bright blue light. Looked like it was going to collide with our launch, but then it just vanished. We were watching with binoculars, and then... just gone! No smoke, no explosion, just suddenly nothing!"

"Yes, sir, that's what our radar reading seems to indicate as well," the young tech told his commanding officer.

"Odd. Very odd," Jack Tuckerman said. "If it didn't explode, and it didn't crash…"

Jon, watching his father's dilemma, was astounded by the man's appearance. He hadn't seen his dad since saying goodbye to him on his deathbed back in 2017, some 18 years earlier. Jon was completely mesmerized by this viewing experience.

The next scene JT was shown seemed to be a few hours after the first... later that same night. His father was driving a car, alone, through the surrounding high desert encompassing Edwards Air Force Base. As though viewing the activity from the passenger seat, JT could see the look of concern on his father's face, and noticed that the older man's ever-present pocket protector, yellow Bic pen, and orange mechanical pencil were just as prominent as they'd always been in his everyday life. He also noticed his dad's military access clearance badge attached to his winter coat lapel. Jack, listening to big band music on the radio, would occasionally poke his head out the driver's side window to gaze up at the sky. It was a clear, crisp winter's night... the stars were plentiful and magnificent.

"Where *are* you?" he said aloud. Suddenly, what appeared to be a shooting star fell from the sky and began hurtling toward his car. Tuckerman Senior was blinded by the light coming through his windshield, and began to steer the car erratically, zigging and zagging on the desolate highway. When a loud "whoosing" noise overwhelmed him, the man lost control of the steering wheel and involuntarily drove his car a few feet into a sandy, tumbleweed-filled embankment.

Jack's hands were shaking... his breathing heavy. He looked ahead through the windshield to see a marvelous, glowing, oval-shaped object, about twelve feet long, perhaps twenty yards from his impacted car. "Can't be!" he whispered out loud to himself, making his way out of the vehicle. As he walked toward the craft, he glanced up once again at the sky, then in every direction around him. All else was normal and calm— all but this fairly small, luminescent object that drew him like a magnet.

Now, just a few feet from the orb, Jack stopped in his tracks. A beautiful being, about four feet tall, with long, white-blond hair and wearing a glowing white uniform was crawling out and away from the craft, which, upon closer inspection, looked like a giant egg. Glancing up at Jack Tuckerman, the alien, who appeared to be a rather young Male, grimaced, as though in pain. Jack, with no one else around for miles in any direction, realized that it would be up to him to either help this creature or flee for dear life.

JT, immersed within this viewing experience, realized that his father's alien was clearly a Nordic... a member of the same race as Kalyssa and Jorthon.

Jack knelt to the ground, then scooted himself forward on his knees, a few inches at a time, to get a closer look at the distressed being. "Who are you?" he whispered.

The alien lay on its back, retaining direct eye contact with the scientist. "We study your planet," he said, telepathically, to the curious man. "We have been coming here for longer than your species has existed. We have been following your work, Jack Tuckerman, and have enjoyed the clever methods you have employed in your sky-based detection systems."

JT watched his dad's interaction with pure fascination. Entranced by this private "home movie" of his father's activities from seventy-two years previous, his mind raced, trying its best to process this startling newfound information.

"My drone device... earlier tonight... vanished. Was that you?" Jack asked the creature.

"I was sent to capture your photographic system to study it for our observational purposes," the alien communicated. "To gauge man's advancements in the technology during your time frame. We have been most impressed by your inventive methods and were hoping to research them further. However..." the little alien winced in pain, holding the side of his body with one of his hands, "my craft accidentally skimmed the surface of your rocket too closely. It burned a small hole in my ship."

Tuckerman Senior glanced at the alien's orb and noted an opening on its side about the size of a basketball. He also saw his captured drone system inside the hole, still "beeping" inside the craft.

"So, YOUR spaceship collided with MY rocket?" Jack asked, astonished. "I am so sorry this happened. Here, let me help you." The scientist bent down next to the alien's side and saw a three-inch-wide wound in his abdomen. Jack slid one arm under the creature's neck and his other hand beneath his waist. The scientist, expecting to have to perform a herculean move to lift the being, was completely surprised that the alien's weight was minimal. He was as light as a sofa cushion.

"The air base hospital is only about fifteen minutes from here," Jack said. "I'll take you there. I'm sure they can patch you up."

The alien became extremely alarmed. "NO, Mister Tuckerman! That must not take place at all! Your people are not ready for the reality of my existence! Your military will capture me, study me, and put me on display for your political leaders for years to come. We are not here to interfere with your human history. We only come to check on your latest scientific developments. This was my very first mission. I must get back to my Father... the Infinite Creator. He will be most worried about my disappearance."

Jack was stymied. "Well, looking at your ship there, I don't think it's going to get you anywhere any time soon." The alien again grimaced in pain. "Plus, you're really hurt. Someone needs to patch you up." The scientist in Jack Tuckerman felt, of course, that taking the creature to the base made the most sense. The human being inside the man, however, pitied the small, downed alien and felt he should heed this special being's warning.

Carrying the alien to his car, Jack said, "I'll take you to my motel. I'll find some way to help you there."

The creature replied, "I must do something first." He raised his hands to the sides of his head and, seconds later, his orb was incinerated.

"Your ship!" Jack said, aghast. "Why did you do that? And how will you get back?"

The being responded, "It is not yet time for your people to have proof of our existence. My people will find me soon... tomorrow night, as you count time."

Tuckerman Senior, back at his car, managed to open the rear door on the passenger side, then laid this magical alien from outer space across the backseat. Quickly racing to the driver's door, the scientist hopped in and frantically turned the key. As he dislodged the vehicle from the sandbank, he hit the highway with a fervor. "You have my word," he told his guest, who lay in agony behind him, "As long as I'm alive, no harm will come to you."

CHAPTER TWENTY-FIVE

The next scene JT was shown through the amber swirl quite literally blew his mind. His father had driven the creature to a motel, obviously not too far from the air base. After parking, Jack removed his winter coat, opened the back door, draped his coat over the alien, and carried him to the front door of room #217. Jack knocked on the door. Jon was amazed to then see HIS MOTHER, JANE, open that door!

"Honey, I've brought some work home," Jack said.

"Oh, my good God," Jane said, "Who's your new friend?"

Jack gingerly entered the room and gently lay the alien down on one of the two beds. Now in terrible pain, the creature could barely speak, but did convey to the couple, through facial expressions, a feeling of warmth and love. He then closed his eyes and appeared to have fallen asleep.

"He's hurt," Jack said.

"What happened? What is this, this…" Perhaps for the first time in her life, Jane was at a loss for words.

"Proof, honey," Jack said. "He's proof that they exist! He fell from the sky! His craft collided with our launch tonight. I need to help him."

Jane went into the bathroom, wet a washcloth, and brought it over to the creature. She sat beside him on the bed, and gently placed it across his forehead.

From the distance of many decades, JT continued to observe his long-deceased father and comatose mother in a California desert, giving aid to a living, breathing extra-terrestrial, way back in February 1963… nine months before Jon was even born.

The Tuckermans sat on the other bed and watched as the creature, clearly in pain, struggled to breathe. Confused and conflicted, the pair, speaking in whispers, weren't sure what to do next.

"He begged me not to bring him to the base," Jack told his wife. "So, I can't do that… I SHOULD do that, but I promised him I wouldn't."

"This is historic, Jack," Jane said. "We definitely should respect his wishes… but he really *is* injured. God, I hope he doesn't die here. I wish we knew how to help him."

The alien awoke and turned his head toward the conversation. Staring at the couple intensely, he telepathically said, "Zinc. Must bathe in zinc," before falling back to sleep.

Jack and Jane looked at each other in surprise. "Did he just say zinc?" Jack asked his wife.

"Yes, that's what I heard too," Jane replied. "Where are we going to get zinc at this hour?"

Jack put on his scientist brain. "Vitamins!" he said. "Zinc is in multiple vitamins. We need to find a drugstore!"

"We're in Lancaster, the middle of a desert," Jane answered. "There aren't any drugstores here."

"But Los Angeles is only ninety minutes away," Jack replied. "And I know they have a drugstore there—a famous one, in fact. Where that old-time actress Lana Turner was discovered… Schwans? Schwins?"

"You're thinking of Schwab's," Jane answered. "Lana Turner was actually discovered at a nearby soda shop. I saw a documentary once about her life. But Schwab's *is* in L.A. On Sunset Boulevard."

"Well, that's where I'll be first thing in the morning," Jack answered. The Tuckermans did their best to catch some sleep that night, but with an alien from the sky moaning in the next bed over, theirs was a tenuous sleep at best.

When 6:00 am arrived, Tuckerman Senior hopped in the shower, threw on his clothes, and pecked his wife on the cheek. "In search of zinc," the scientist whispered boldly. "As much as I can find."

In the bitter cold of the high desert on a dark and early February morning, Jack Tuckerman got into his car and began the interminable drive down Route 14 from Lancaster to the Sunset Strip in Los Angeles. JT was shown only snippets of his father's heinously long drive as he continued to watch this lost moment in time on the alien "home movie" view screen.

Arriving at Schwab's just minutes before it was scheduled to open at 9 am, Jack parked his car and ran up to the front door, knocking wildly. A young attractive redhead approached from the other side. "Sir," she replied through the glass. "We open in 10 minutes."

"Please! I need to get inside NOW!" Jack yelled, a bit frantically. "It's very, very important!"

Realizing the depth of the man's insistence, the young woman relented, unlocking the door.

"Vitamins?" Jack asked, breathless. "Please, for God's sake, tell me you sell multivitamins?"

"Yes, of course," the woman answered, "Right this way." The redhead led Jack down the main aisle of the store to the back wall. "Just got a fresh batch in yesterday. Here you go... but why the emergency? What's so urgent about needing vitamin pills?" she asked.

Taking just a few seconds to scan the labels on the various vitamin jars before him, Jack said, "For a friend. A very special friend. He must have them as soon as possible. It's truly urgent. Perhaps one day you'll read about him in a history book."

Jack began to load up his arms with as many bottles of multivitamins as he could hold. "Can you please bring me a few bags?" he asked the woman. She quickly returned with several. "Here, help me fill these," Jack instructed. "I'll take as many as possible, as long as they have zinc in them."

"Jeez, mister, sounds like your friend has a zinc addiction, huh?" the confounded woman said as she reviewed each label to ensure that the coveted ingredient was present.

Finally filling up four large shopping bags to the brim, Jack said, "okay, that should do it. I hope. I really, truly hope."

The duo walked the parcels up to the cash register, where the woman counted them up. "Sir, you're looking at a fortune here," she said. "104 bottles of vitamin pills are going to cost you $96!"

Tuckerman Senior was a bit stunned. "You're right, that is a lot. Can you accept this?" He removed an American Express credit card from his wallet.

The woman replied, "Wow, don't see many of these around. But yes, I can charge it." The woman ran the card through a hand-held metal device, then handed Jack his card back and a carbon. "Please sign here," she instructed.

He did so. "Can you help me out to my car, miss?" Jack asked.

"Sure," she replied. "We wouldn't want to keep your zinc-hungry friend waiting too long now, would we?"

The next scene JT was shown was his father returning to his motel room carrying the bags filled with vitamin bottles.

"He's not looking too good," Jane told her husband. The duo rushed into the bathroom, where the alien was curled into a fetal position inside the bathtub. He'd begun to turn a sickly shade of brown —a color Jane instinctively knew was not a good sign.

"I have your zinc!" Jack announced. "Lots of it! What now?"

The being smiled weakly. "Powder. Zinc powder. Cold water and zinc powder," the creature communicated.

"These are *pills*," Jack said to Jane. "We've got to smash them into powder. I have an idea." The scientist raced out of the room and ran to the motel's office. "A hammer!" he shouted at the desk clerk. "My kingdom for a hammer!"

The lethargic man behind the desk said, "okay, calm down, buddy. Give me a sec." He walked through some beaded curtains behind him and returned a few moments later with the tool. "Here ya go, enjoy yourself, have a party," the sarcastic clerk said. "Just don't forget to return it later today."

In a flash, Tuckerman Senior returned to his room. He grabbed a Gideon's Bible out of a dresser drawer, then got on his knees on the bathroom floor and began spilling out bottle after bottle of vitamins atop the book. "We need to smash these up," he instructed his wife. As Jane began to pulverize the vitamins, Jack made another trip to and from his car, bringing in the other bags of vitamins he'd purchased at Schwab's. The scientist looked around his room, found a yellow pages phonebook, unplugged a lamp with a heavy round base, and brought both items into the bathroom. Jack began smashing vitamins with the lamp base atop the phone book, while Jane continued using the hammer atop the bible.

Over the course of the next two hours, the Tuckermans crushed and pulverized more than 15,000 vitamin pills, while sitting on their butts astride a bathtub containing a dying being from outer space. Jane filled the tub with cold water and began sweeping the vitamin powder into the water with her hands as quickly as she could. It was now just after 12:30 pm. All the pill bottles had been emptied, and both Jack and Jane were quite exhausted.

They kneeled now and looked the troubled young alien in the eyes. "It's all the zinc they had," Jack said, apologizing. "I hope it was enough."

The creature faced the couple. "Thank you," he whispered telepathically. "I could have asked for nothing more."

Noticing that the alien was still an unhealthy color, Jane became distraught. "It wasn't enough," she said. "It isn't right. We're gonna lose him!" Jack reached out to his wife and put his arm around her.

"Leave me now, please," the being said. "Must rest. Rest is best. Close the door and allow me to sleep."

The Tuckermans rose and left, obeying his wishes.

JT continued watching his heroic parents as they tried to save this foreign lifeform. Extremely proud, yet at the same time rather nervous, Jon had no idea what the outcome of this situation was going to be.

The next scene: Jack and Jane were asleep on their bed when the phone rang, jarring them awake. Jack answered. "Hello? General Charles? Yes, oh sorry. You need me there *now* for a post-mortem on the launch? Oh, ah, uhm… no, I'm not too busy doing other things. It's just that, I, ah, err, ahm, my wife had a medical situation this morning. No, no, not an emergency. She needed some medication. But she's doing better now, thanks, thanks for asking. Yes, I can be there within the hour. Yes, okay general. Fine. See you then. Okay, goodbye." He hung up and sighed.

"Janey, I've gotta get back to the base," Jack said. "Regardless of how our friend in there is doing, I have GOT to get back for this meeting and finish up my report."

"I know, I know," Jane said. "I'll keep my eye on the little guy. Go do what you need to do."

Resigned and saddened, Jack decided to check in on the creature before he left. Fully expecting to find an alien corpse floating atop the bathtub, a notable shade of chartreuse, Jack instead found the small, wondrous being standing up in the middle of the room, glowing his normal, bright white color again.

He smiled at the scientist. "Zinc and rest are best!" he declared wordlessly.

"Janey!" Jack shouted.

JT's mom entered the bathroom and was overjoyed to see the young alien had healed. "Oh, thank the good Lord," she said.

"The base!" the alien said. "I must return to the base now! There, they will come for me."

Jane's maternal instincts kicked in. She grabbed a large towel and began drying off her guest. "Well, now that you're fixed, there's no reason for you to be all wet and cold," she said. The woman tenderly dried the being's long white hair, and patted down his arms, chest and legs, and tapped at his face. "There, good as new!" she smiled. "All shiny and bright and magnificent!"

Deeply touched by the woman's kindness, the creature appeared almost teary-eyed. His facial expression became quite serious. He lowered his body so that he was now kneeling before Jane. He raised his hands and gently placed them both just over her belly. He closed his eyes. Suddenly, a powerful, bluish-white light emanated from his hands, making Jane's entire abdomen glow brightly. Jack and Jane stared at each other intensely.

"Your son shall become our 'Chosen One,'" the creature said dramatically. "My people will watch over him and ensure his safety for the length of his life. In this manner, we shall repay the kindness you have presented to me."

"She's… she's pregnant?" Jack, truly surprised, asked the alien, who nodded as though to say "yes." Jane and Jack were virtually frozen during this tender ceremony.

"Thank you," Jane finally whispered to the creature.

"Please Mister Tuckerman, now I must go back to the base!" the alien urged the scientist, as he stood up.

"Holy shit!" Jon said out loud as he continued watching the alien home movies device on the Dodger Stadium Special. "Jorthon and Kalyssa saved *my* life because my parents saved one of *their* fellow aliens!"

The next scene JT was shown presented his father once again driving his car, now with the little alien sitting up in the backseat. Next to him was one of Jack's suitcases, opened and clearly empty. "You must disguise me," the creature told Jack. "I will hide inside this," he said, pointing to the large piece of luggage. "You must wheel me inside, into your radar room. There, I can do the rest."

Pulling off to the side of the road, the air base within sight, Tuckerman Senior opened the passenger door and helped his alien friend position himself inside the suitcase. "Zip, zip," the being requested, and Jack obliged.

Moments later, Jack approached the front gate at Edwards. Flashing his all-access badge, he was quickly allowed onto the base. Jack was obviously nervous; his hands were shaking. He parked, then extracted the suitcase from the backseat. He placed it upright, extended its handle, and began to wheel it forward.

Arriving moments later inside the radar control room, Jack was greeted by the general and others. "Looks like you just can't wait to get the hell back to New Jersey, eh, Tuckerman?" the general joked. "What's the matter, you think my men are going to steal your dirty underwear out from your car?"

Thinking fast, Jack responded, "Oh, ah, sorry, General Charles, of course not. It's just that I have a special gift inside here for my wife. It's a surprise. It's very valuable and I'd rather not take any chances that something might happen to it. Thanks for understanding." Without a moment's hesitation, Jack wheeled the suitcase over to the side of the room and propped it up against a wall, just underneath the February 1963 *Playboy* magazine calendar.

"Gentlemen, now that our special guest star is back," General Charles quipped a bit sarcastically, "we can discuss the anomaly that was observed interfering with our launch last night. Please follow me into the conference room." The radar room cleared out, with Jack Tuckerman the last to follow. As he left, he quickly glanced back at the suitcase. Fortunately, he was the only one in the room to notice that the zipper had begun "unzipping itself" from the inside.

With the general, Jack Tuckerman, and their team now in another part of the building, the creature managed to extract himself. He crawled out from the suitcase and walked toward the radar control board. The being smiled to himself, realizing how primitive these ancient technologies were to him. "Wonderful," he whispered out loud while smiling. "Brilliant." The alien sat at a desk, atop which appeared a very early computer keyboard of some kind, connected to an enormous bank of reel-to-reel data tape machines revolving in all directions. Closing his eyes, he began to type on the keyboard, and then flipped switches, spun dials, and slid the gizmos embedded across the primitive instrument panel in every direction.

Quite unexpectedly, an armed soldier entered the room, a rifle slung over his shoulder. Noticing what simply could not be—a small, brilliant, alien being with long flowing white hair, sitting at the control board inside a top-secret military base—the soldier swung his rifle into firing position. "You there! Who are you? Step away now! Stop what you're doing, do you understand me? I need you to step away RIGHT FUCKING NOW!" The solider, terrified, spoke into a small walkie-talkie mic on his lapel. "Command, this is Mahoney. Need backup immediately. Building 4. Intruder alert. Send backup. Building 4 NOW!"

A bright, red-swirling alarm light went off and loud airhorns began piercing the silence. "I'm not ready yet," the alien communicated to the man, matter-of-factly. He waved his left hand in a counter-clockwise direction, many feet from the soldier's face. The man fell to the floor, sound asleep. The being continued his work at the control panel, seemingly without a care in the world.

A burst of soldiers now exploded into the radar room—most standing, some kneeling, all with weapons drawn. Concurrent with the commotion, General Charles, Jack Tuckerman, and the others who'd been meeting in the adjacent conference room hurried back into the radar room as well.

"What the fuck?" the general shouted when he noticed an obvious alien creature had entered his inner sanctum. Now realizing Jack's suitcase was opened and empty, General Charles screamed, "Tuckerman! Does this 'valuable' fucking Martian belong to *you*?"

Jack ran up to the alien, placing himself in harm's way and spreading his arms out in a protective stance. "He comes in peace! It was an accident. He's only here to study us. He simply needs to get back to his own kind!"

The general was livid. "Not on my watch is a *goddamned alien* going to screw with the USA!" The leader turned to his soldiers. "Arrest this hideous creature immediately!" he ordered.

At that moment, brilliant white light—so bright it felt to all present as though the roof of the building had been removed during a hot July day—filled the radar room. Every human being assembled gasped... the light made breathing difficult. The alien leaned into Jack. "Your son," he conveyed into the scientist's ear, "our 'Chosen One.'" The being then vanished into the shaft of light.

Crippled by the brightness, the soldiers could only try to shield their eyes from the pain. After perhaps 30 seconds, sudden, overwhelming, and complete darkness befell Building 4. The light, and its obvious spacecraft of origin, were gone in a flash. Then the men in the room and, in fact, every man located within the perimeter of the entire Edwards Air Force Base itself, suddenly and inexplicably fell sound asleep. Even Jack Tuckerman. They would all remain asleep for many hours.

The "home movie" JT had been watching for the past hour came to an end. Still onboard the great craft hovering above the UN building, Jon was speechless. Jorthon and Kalyssa returned to greet him.

"Do you have questions?" Jorthon asked the rattled Hero of Earth.

"Where do I even begin?" JT gasped. "That young alien, the one my parents helped, do you know him?"

The Nordics laughed heartily. "Jonathan, my friend," Jorthon said, "that young alien WAS ME!"

JT fainted.

When Jon awoke, he was back at the penthouse, in bed, fully dressed, under the covers. It was only 3:00 pm. Russell, who had entered the room just moments after JT's return (to change the bed sheets) found his boss inside and jumped six inches in fright. "Mr. T!" he shrieked. "How did you get home without me knowing? Are you a *magician?*"

Jon raised his head from his pillow. "Russell, my good man, believe me when I tell you, I'm more like the *rabbit* inside a magician's *hat.*"

CHAPTER TWENTY-SIX

A few days after JT's "viewing experience," the President, JT, and Susan were having lunch at the White House. The trio were sitting in silence as they ate when Susan broke the ice... "Madam President, perhaps you can talk to him. He's barely spoken to me, or to anyone, since they showed him that 'home movie' of his parents."

The president, who'd been informed about the event, looked over at Jon. "Clearly that was heavy stuff. You know, I meant to tell you, Johnny, I asked the Air Force to go through their 'Project Blue Book' files from the early 1960s, especially cases of UFOs recorded over California back then. I told them to set aside boxes of that material for you. They're over at the National Archives building on Pennsylvania Avenue, if you wanna take a look."

"Project Blue Book?" Susan asked.

The president explained, "Project Blue Book was a series of studies of unidentified flying objects conducted by the Air Force, starting in 1952 that ended in 1970. Thousands of reports of flying saucers around the world were recorded during that time. Many of those reports were explained to be natural causes or man-made objects, but many others remained unexplained. It seems that, perhaps, some of those cases may have involved Jon's friends."

Intrigued about Project Blue Book, JT's face registered intrigue. "He never told me," Jon said to the women. "My dad never told me anything about saving the life of an extra-terrestrial creature back in 1963, and how that alien promised him I'd be their 'chosen one.' I just can't wrap my head around it!"

"You have to remember, Jon," the president continued, "back then, our military officers, Air Force pilots, aerospace engineers, and outside contractors working on our national defense systems in the sky would have been ridiculed, fired, or possibly even arrested for letting the public know that 'little green men' really did exist. Your father could have lost his job, his reputation, even his pension, had he let anyone know about that encounter. I'm not surprised he kept it under wraps."

"I think it's also odd that Jon's mother never said a word either," Susan added.

After lunch, JT and Susan walked outside the White House and toward their awaiting limousine. "Honey, would you mind if I went over to the archives building now?" Jon asked sheepishly. "I'm dying to see what's in those files."

"No, of course not," Susan replied. "I'll head back to the City. Just come home whenever you're ready." She kissed him tenderly and the two got into the limo.

"Mully, please drop me at the National Archives," Jon requested, "and then take Susan to the airport."

"You got it," the ever-reliable Mully replied.

Upon his arrival, gasps from tourists visiting the National Archives greeted JT. He approached the front desk and spoke to an older woman who appeared to be in charge. "The President sent me," he whispered.

"Why yes, of course, Mr. Tuckerman, we've been expecting you!" the woman gleefully replied. "Please follow me."

Jon and the woman walked toward the rear of the main hall and down a staircase. There, they caught an elevator down to a subterranean level where massive aisles of shelving held countless cartons of all shapes, sizes, and colors. They walked toward the furthest corner of the floor, finally arriving at a darkened area. The woman flipped on the lights and pointed out a series of large metal shelves, four tiers high, fifteen feet across, and stacked with dozens of file boxes marked "PROJECT BLUE BOOK Case Studies: 1960-1970."

"These were shipped over here back in 2015," she told Jon. "Our government's investigation into ridiculous flying saucer nonsense." She looked into JT's face. "That is, until *you* proved it wasn't ridiculous nonsense after all!" She smiled at him

Jon nodded back in silent acknowledgement.

"Please let me know if you need any help, Mr. Tuckerman," she said. "Maybe you'll learn something more about your special friends." She winked and left the area.

Jon pulled a box labeled "Blue Book: Origins" off a shelf, set it on top of a table, put on his reading glasses (a new accoutrement of late), and sat on a chair. He began reading the first file folder he discovered inside the box, and quickly learned that Project Blue Book was the third in a series of government-commissioned studies of unidentified flying objects over the United States (and elsewhere) conducted by the U.S. Air Force.

The first study, which began in 1947, was named "Project Sign" and was followed by "Project Grudge" in 1949. "Project Blue Book" was launched in 1952 and remained in effect until January 1970. The studies of all three projects were to determine if UFOs were a true threat to U.S. national security, and to scientifically analyze UFO-related data to determine if those incidents were, in fact, "other-worldly" events or simply unexplained natural or man-made phenomenon.

JT spent the next eight hours sitting in that corner, pulling various file folders out of assorted, smelly old boxes that had been lingering for eons.

During his research, he learned that over the course of its eighteen years in existence, Blue Book had collected more than 12,600 UFO reports, concluding that most of the sightings had been misidentifications of natural phenomena (such as clouds, stars, planets, or "swamp gas") and conventional aircraft. However, even after intense analysis, there were another 700 UFO reports within the files before him that remained classified as "inexplicable."

Jon read that in March 1952, U.S. Air Force General Charles Cabell had become dissatisfied with the state of the Air Force UFO investigations going on since 1947—the year of the legendary Roswell crash, and became head of the new Project Blue Book effort. Another military officer, General William Garland, also believed the UFO question deserved serious study since he, himself, had witnessed a UFO in flight. He joined forces with Cabell.

Cabell and Garland gave birth to the newly incentivized 'Blue Book' initiative and assigned Captain Edward Ruppelt to head it. Ruppelt coined the term "unidentified flying objects" to replace the phrase "flying saucers" (which had caught on with the general public around the world following the sighting of nine strangely shaped flying silver aircraft by American pilot Kenneth Arnold, during a flight Arnold had made in his private plane over the skies of Washington State in June 1947).

Ruppelt streamlined the way in which UFOs would be reported to and by military officials, in hopes of alleviating the ridicule usually associated with UFO witnesses. He ordered the development of a standard questionnaire for UFO observers, in hopes of accumulating data that could be used to chart statistical analysis. During his tenure with Blue Book, Ruppelt sought the advice and participation of many hundreds of scientists and experts from across the United States. Each U.S. Air Force Base had a Blue Book officer to collect UFO reports and forward them along to Ruppelt.

Along the way, Ruppelt enlisted the assistance of renowned astronomer Dr. J. Allen Hynek as the lead scientific consultant to the project. Hynek would later become quite famous for having created the term "Close Encounters of the First, Second, and Third Kinds." A vocal skeptic when he began working with the Blue Book project, Hynek's feelings changed after he encountered a number of highly problematic UFO reports he personally deemed inexplicable.

Scattered within the boxes Jon dug through were dozens of photographs, most in black and white—a few in color—of "flying saucers" of all shapes, sizes and colors. "They've been here with us, all this time, all along," Jon said out loud to no one. "And we were never told they were real. What did the government think was going to happen? We were going to freak out in the streets?"

Clearly ashamed over the lack of truth in leadership that had preceded his event at Dodger Stadium, it was right then JT realized the librarian was right. HE was the singular human being who'd finally proven, without question, that other races of beings from elsewhere were not only a hypothetical possibility, but a true, hard fact of reality.

JT read on. Ruppelt and Hynek had enlisted the aid of hundreds of specialists across the country to evaluate each UFO report that was submitted to Blue Book. This team of experts (comprised of astronomers, meteorologists, psychiatrists and psychologists, physicists, and electronics engineers) collected, collated, evaluated, and distributed their findings to all interested government agencies and contractors. Their reports detailed all pertinent information concerning unexplained sightings of phenomena in the atmosphere which might potentially be of concern to the national security of the United States.

Upon its conclusion, Project Blue Book determined there was no evidence of any kind that atmospheric sightings reported as "unidentified" were of extra-terrestrial origins. "Well, you guys got that one wrong. Wouldn't you say?" Jon said out loud to the box, quite pissed off.

JT then reread the phrase "electronics engineers," and his whole body perked up. That was his father's profession! He stood from the table, stretched his back, then perused additional boxes still sitting on the shelves. After several minutes, he found one labeled "Blue Book Personnel: 1960-1970." He lifted the box off the shelf and placed it atop his reading table. He dug through the files nervously. Finding a folder labeled "Contributing Scientists," he sat and continued poring over the yellowing pages.

At the very bottom of the carton, Jon found the gold he had come looking for. There, he discovered a file listing over 450 scientists, engineers, and other specialists who had worked in tandem with the military to compile data on unexplained Blue Book sightings during that decade. Listed alphabetically between "Professor Corey Trenton, University of Chicago" and "Dr. James Ulmer, Yale University," Jon saw "Jack R. Tuckerman, Electronics, Fort Monmouth, New Jersey." Next to his father's name were the dates of the forty-two UFO sightings he'd investigated. The first was February 10, 1963 at Edwards Air Force Base, and the last, October 7, 1969, over a farm in Maine.

Jon shot up from his chair. "Holy fuck!" he shouted. "There it is! My father was a UFO hunter! I cannot fucking believe this!"

He grabbed the document with both hands, ran through the room, caught the elevator, and hurried up to the front desk. A different woman was now seated there. "I've gotta have a copy of this!" he said excitedly, waving the papers in his hand.

This new woman, who somehow did not realize who Jon was, reviewed the papers, and said, "Sir, I'm sorry, this document is not to be copied or removed from the premises."

Jon was incredulous. For the very first time since he'd become a living legend, he played the fame card. "Ma'am, do you have any effing idea who I am?" he demanded.

The woman became hostile. "Sir, would you like me to call security?"

"Yes, I really would," Jon replied, incredibly annoyed. "Please do that."

The woman pressed a button on her desk and, moments later, two burly security men ran up to her. When they arrived, they both realized that JONATHAN TUCKERMAN was standing before them!

"Mister Tuckerman?" one said in disbelief. "Is that really you?"

The other man simply stood open-mouthed. The first man turned to the woman and said, "Shirley, do you know who this is?"

Clearly baffled, she shook her head no.

"This is Mr. Jon Tuckerman, the Wonder Man! Hero of Earth! Friend of the Great Aliens who came to save us!"

The woman leaned forward and took a closer look into Jon's face. "Oh my dear God, I'm so sorry!" she exclaimed, turning bright red. "You ARE him! Sorry! Damn these new glasses. Here, let me see this," she added, taking the papers from Jon's hand. "I'll make you some copies right away!"

❧

JT arrived back home at the penthouse about 2:00 am that morning. He quietly entered the abode, expecting that Susan and Russell would be sound asleep. However, much to his pleasant surprise, Russell was seated in the living room, reading a book, and sipping a brandy. Upon seeing JT enter, he hopped up excitedly to greet his boss. "You're home! The great gladiator has returned from the war!" he joked. "Dr. Susan said not to expect you until tomorrow morning. Are you hungry?"

Jon, always grateful for Russell's extraordinary kindness, said, "No, that's okay, Russell, thanks anyway. I'm so tired. Is she asleep?" "Yes, sir, since midnight," Russell replied. "We watched some TV together —a special report about your Nobel Prize event. It was the first time we had a chance to watch it."

"That really was something, wasn't it?" JT agreed. "I'm so glad you were able to share that night with me." For the first and only time in his life, Jon approached Russell and hugged the man warmly. Unexpectedly, JT started to cry. Russell patted him on the back, as would a father whose son had just told him the girl he'd asked out for a date had rejected him.

"There, there, Mr. Tuckerman, sir, everything is just fine, just fine," Russell reassured him. "It's all good, you see. So much pressure on you, I understand. Many, many people rely on you. You have too much pressure."

Jon extracted himself. "Thanks, my good friend," he said. "Thank you for being in my life."

Jon walked off into the bedroom and disappeared behind the door. Not wishing to disturb his sleeping lover, he moved as quietly as a mouse, removing his clothes and slipping under the covers. Still clutching the pages in his hand that proved his father had been involved in UFO research for many years during the 1960s, he lay his head on the pillow, eyes wide open. The reality of his discovery blew his mind. He simply could not believe it.

JT tossed and turned for hours, desperately trying to get a handle on this newfound, life-altering information. Finally asleep, he began to dream. The images were ragged and jumpy at first, bits and pieces of everything and nothing. The president's face. Jon's kids when they were small. Sex with Susan. The streets of Manhattan. All of the scattered images were cut and pasted together in a patch quilt of abstraction, all without rhyme or reason.

And then HE appeared. Jack Tuckerman, Jon's long deceased father. In the dream, which was in vivid black and white, Jon was a young boy, perhaps 7 or 8 years old, outdoors at night, in his pajamas, walking through the backyard of his childhood home. As he walked, he saw before him his dad, now in his early 40s, looking up into the sky through a telescope and smoking a pipe. Jack was making notes in a small book as he continued to observe the heavens. "Hiya, boy," the older man said to JT. "Can't sleep?"

Little Jon replied, "Daddy, what are you doing?"

"Just watching the skies," Jack answered. "Keeping an eye out for an old friend."

"Your friend lives in the sky?" JT asked.

"Actually, yes, JT. He's just one of many who live there. Your mom and I met him years ago, before you were born. He was a wonderful little fellow, so warm and friendly. Filled with good light. He was not much older than you are right now. *He still comes to visit me every once in a while.*"

Jon bolted upright in bed, panting hard. His eyes now wide open, he appeared to be having a panic attack. He could barely catch his breath.

Susan abruptly left slumberland when Jon grabbed her right arm in a death grip.

"What's wrong?" she asked, startled. JT was sweating and couldn't respond. Susan got up on her knees, leaned over to her partner, and held him tightly. "Please Johnny, it's okay. I love you. It's all going to be alright. I'm here for you."

JT placed his head onto Susan's shoulder and began to sob. "My dad," he whimpered. "I just saw him —just now. In a dream."

"He's still in here, Jon," Susan said, touching his chest. "He's still in your heart and always will be. He's in your DNA."

Jon reached over to his nightstand and grabbed the copied document. He turned on the light and handed it to Susan. She read it. "Oh my God," she cried. "He knew about them for years!"

"And he never, ever told me," JT replied softly as he now lay his troubled head against his lover's warm, comforting chest.

CHAPTER TWENTY-SEVEN

Team Tuckerman spent the next few weeks meeting with members of the American Lung Association and other groups committed to eliminating cigarettes and promoting the dangers of second-hand smoke. However, Jon no longer came into his office every day, so Isak had stepped up in his place as the team's de facto leader. Susan had even fashioned a disguise for Jon (wig, hat, fake moustache) so he could stroll the streets of New York incognito, without having to endure the constant stares and "oohs and ahs" that had accompanied his public life for over a year. For the first time in decades, JT began going to the movies during the daytime, to escape the constraints of his heavy position. When Isak had compiled the required data, he texted Jon to come to the UN to get briefed. JT, who walked into the building forgetting he was in disguise, was stopped at the security desk when the guards there didn't recognize him. It actually made Jon laugh when they had to apologize after he revealed his true identity to the bewildered men.

Feb. 22, 2035, the beautiful "unidentified flying object" returned over the East River once more. Isak handed his dad the infamous iPad, filled with information about the hazards of cigarettes and second-hand smoke. "Come with me," JT said, gently grabbing his son's shoulder. "Let's do this together."

Isak was truly surprised. "Yeah, sure... okay, I guess," he said. The two men made their way silently onto the UN roof.

Onboard the craft, Jon was noticeably sullen. Isak was ecstatic. "Hello again, great friend," Kalyssa said. "So nice to meet your son!"

"Thank you," Isak whispered.

"So, Jon, what have you learned?" Jorthon asked.

JT did not reply. "Dad, say something!" Isak said, nudging his father with his elbow.

Jon finally spoke. "My father knew all about you and your people, and he never told me—his only son. I feel like I was betrayed. All those years—all the times we were together, alone, he never once said a word to me. I can't understand why."

The Great Nordics glanced at each other. "You must realize," Jorthon explained, "that while the leaders of your government, and the leaders of governments of many other Earth nations, knew much about our existence during that time, they felt, not without reason, that the general public would panic if informed of the truth. Their fear of civil unrest was not unfounded. Are you aware of the famous radio broadcast by Orson Welles?"

"No," Jon answered.

Jorthon continued, "On October 30, 1938, actor Orson Welles performed a radio play from New York called *The War of the Worlds*. The play was extremely realistic and described a hostile invasion by Martians. Over a million radio listeners believed that a *real* Martian invasion was underway. Panic broke out across the country. In New Jersey, terrified civilians jammed highways seeking to escape the mayhem. People begged police for gas masks to save them from toxic gas and asked electric companies to turn off their power so Martians wouldn't see their lights. One woman ran into an Indianapolis church and yelled, 'New York has been destroyed! It's the end of the world! Go home and prepare to die!'

"It was also said that the broadcast triggered a number of suicides. When news of the panic made its way back to Welles at his New York radio studio, he went on the air as himself to assure his listeners that his show was just fiction."

Jon's heaviness lifted a bit. "Well, that does explain a lot, I guess. I just wish my father would have confided in me." He paused. "I had a dream about him the other night... God, it felt so real. I miss him so much. I wish I could see him again just once." Turning to Isak, Jon added, "I so wish you could have met your grandpa."

"Dreams are man's connection to the Infinite Creator," Kalyssa said. "They are how the human brain processes the data of life, melding both the real and imagined, synthesizing the two into creative solutions. They are the Creator's communication channel to each of you. Each dream has meaning and purpose. None should be ignored."

She left the room and returned in a moment holding two small, glass triangles. In the middle of each object, a bright, dark red spot pulsated. "May I have your screen?" she asked. JT held forth his iPad, and she placed her hands on either side. Then she handed one triangle to Jon and the other to Isak.

Jon stared into the pulsing red light. "What does this do?" he asked.

"Your request, fulfilled," Jorthon said. "This item can record your dreams while you sleep and play them back to you when you are awake."

"Are you serious?" JT asked, the implications of what he'd just heard stunning him.

"Dad, this is beyond amazing," Isak added.

"Yes, of course," Kalyssa said. She then pressed a small, oval shaped piece of what appeared to be black rubber into the center of Jon's forehead. He looked like an observant Catholic on Ash Wednesday.

"You must wear this transmitter when you are sleeping," Kalyssa explained. "It will translate the electrical impulses running through the circuits that travel from the brainstem to the thalamus to the cortex. These signals will then be sent to the recorder."

Pointing to the glass triangle, she continued, "This must be kept at most three feet from your head at night. It will record all of the imagery and audio data your brain produces while you are sleeping. When you wish to view your dreams the next day, just remove this," she peeled the small black dot from Jon's forehead, "and place it here," she pressed the dot onto the bottom of the glass triangle's base. "Your dream sessions can then be projected as three-dimensional holograms. This device will display as many of your dreams as you have the patience to watch."

Jon held the triangle and the dot up to his face to study them. "This is wonderful. Thank you. God, I hope I'll be able to see my dad again."

"You will see him and much, much more, dear friend," Jorthon said. "Feel free to share this technology with your people. The schematics are on your computer. Perhaps this gift will alleviate your sadness, and we hope it may bring joy to your fellows."

Following the aliens' bestowing of the device to the two Tuckerman men, Isak proceeded to inform Jorthon and Kalyssa about the dangers of cigarettes, presenting them with a good amount of data on the famous Tuckerman iPad.

The aliens told Isak and Jon that they could develop a chemical spray to be used on all tobacco fields, rendering the plants limp and useless.

"Do it," Jon said. "Let's make that happen. No one should be smoking cigarettes in this day and age. It's a stupid habit, long past its expiration date."

Back at the UN, while Isak regaled Lauren and his cohorts with tales of his onboard experience, Jon asked Meghan to assemble the giants of the tech industry as soon as possible.

She quickly reached out to the heads of several old school legacy tech companies—Apple, Microsoft, Samsung, Sony, Google, Facebook, Oracle, Intel, Cisco, IBM, and Tesla, along with several of the bigger modern day tech firms like FutureInk, CyberView, HoloDig, and DynaDisc, among others—informing them all that "Mr. Jonathan Tuckerman of the UN needs to see you right away."

Two days later, JT found himself standing before the men and women whose companies had ruled how human beings lived, worked, and communicated with each other for decades. The triangle and the black dot were on his desk. "Thank you all for coming," he began. "My alien friends have presented us with a dramatic gift. It was given to me purely as a personal matter, but they gave me permission to share it with the rest of the world."

He lifted the triangle and the dot. "Isak, what should we call this contraption?" Jon asked his son.

"Say hello to 'Dream TV' everyone," Isak responded, adding, "believe it or not, this device can record your dreams while you sleep, and play them back to you the next day."

A moment of silence was followed by cheering and applause. The executives stood. "Marvelous!" "Wonderful!" "Amazing!" they declared. "We should have thought of that ourselves," the CEO of HoloDig noted.

"The schematics are in here," Jon said, lifting his iPad. He then went on to explain how the system worked. "I'd like to make this technology available to everyone at an affordable price. I am bestowing upon each of your companies these blueprints so you can build your own versions. You are free to manufacture and sell them as you choose, but I must insist that half of all profits after costs and shipping be donated to a notable charity that my team here will approve." Every CEO in the room readily agreed to Jon's terms. The meeting was adjourned, with each executive then awaiting his or her turn in line to pose for a photo with Jon while holding the triangle and the dot. Isak downloaded the schematics for "Dream TV" onto a number of portable flash drives so that each CEO could leave the meeting with the technology in hand.

Within weeks, "Dream TV Mania" had gripped the United States. The major manufacturers had each moved the new item to the top of their product offerings list and had flooded the marketplace with their own versions of compelling advertising campaigns, after receiving Team Tuckerman's "blessings to go forward." President Winfield was given the first manufactured Dream TV unit, which was presented to her by Jon and the CEO of HoloDig. The trio posed for a photo in the Oval Office... the picture appeared in virtually every business and tech media outlet in the world. Many of those news outlets declared the new invention "Technology's First Intergalactic App."

After having the Dream TV system in her bedroom for only one week, President Winfield declared the product "an incredibly powerful means of self-expression and self-awareness." In an interview with the *New York Times*, she described the moments she'd had with the system as "the most intensely personal experience anyone could ever imagine. I've had the chance to visit again with all my departed loved ones... my parents, my sister, and my husband... in dreams that I did not even remember when I woke up.

"I've been shown solutions to legislative issues that seemed to have no positive course of action. I've had eye-opening conversations with world leaders. Of course, many of my dreams were silly or nonsensical or cartoon-like, but even *they* were highly entertaining. For me, personally, I believe that anyone fortunate enough to have this experience will find it highly rewarding. Once again, I'd like to thank Jon Tuckerman and the Benevolents for this most wonderful gift."

Not to be outdone by HoloDig having beaten all others to market, the CEO of DynaDisc offered a one-million-dollar bonus to any of its engineers who could develop a system whereby a person's recorded dreams could be disseminated digitally to television or the Internet. Akiko Tayaka, a young computer genius from Japan, came up with the solution.

DynaDisc then teamed up with an enterprising media distribution company in New York to launch the "Dream Television Network." Following in the footsteps of its ancestors, radio in the '30s, TV in the late '40s/early '50s, Music Television (MTV) in the '80s, and YouTube in the early 2000s, "DTV" quickly became the most watched broadcast and streaming content channel on the planet.

"DTV" unleashed upon pop culture a new cast of instantly famous characters who merely had to upload their digitally recorded dreams via the DynaDisc "Dream Adaptor" to the new TV network's website. Quickly famous were the twin nineteen-year-old boys in Minnesota who rode exotic roller coasters in their dreams, and the forty-year-old housewife in Florida in whose dreams she spoke with her dead cat... especially hilarious, since the cat talked back!

Other newly minted DTV stars were the voluptuous twenty-three year old red-haired model in Texas whose dreams about ballet dancing on the Moon, Mars, and other planets triggered a new wave of dance lessons for young girls; the ten-year-old African American boy in Georgia who had the ability to "go back in time" and visit with his great-great-grandfather, a slave during the Civil War era, whose death had preceded the young boy's birth by more than 150 years; and dozens more equally idiosyncratic personalities scattered across the USA.

And within months DTV caught the attention of users from around the world as well.

President Winfrey, perhaps the biggest advocate of dream recording, had her security team establish a protocol for the digital storage of her dream sessions. "I'd prefer these not get out into the public at this time," she told her staff. "However, I think they should be archived for my presidential library for after I die."

In similar fashion, over the course of months, virtually every world leader, enjoying their own love affairs with the Dream TV systems, also developed protocols to ensure that their private dreams—containing their deepest secrets and darkest fears—would similarly be archived in private security vaults.

Following the Dream TV explosion—and during one of the regular White House lunches in which the president, Jon, and Susan ate quietly—the president noted that Jon was clearly more upbeat than he had been in the recent past. Having now "seen" his father numerous times in his own DTV dreams, it seemed Jon had made some peace with the man.

President Winfrey said, "You know, Johnny boy, had you applied for the patent for Dream TV, you'd be extremely wealthy today."

"I suppose," the Hero of Earth said, half smiling. "But I didn't invent it. I only mentioned the dream about my father to them. They offered it to me. I can't cash in on my relationship with Jorthon and Kalyssa—it wouldn't be right. Right?" he asked uncertainly.

"Too modest, kid." The president laughed. "Johnny dear, you are just far too modest!"

CHAPTER TWENTY-EIGHT

As promised, Jon had his publicist Heather book him for a second appearance on Don Rinehold's CNN program. The serious yet affable host first began discussing with his guest how much he was enjoying his Dream TV system. "It's crazy stuff, Mr. Tuckerman. Really wacky but incredibly enjoyable. It's a real kick in the pants."

JT smiled, "I'm glad you're enjoying it, Don. You should talk to the president sometime and compare notes."

The interview then moved to the real reason Tuckerman was there. "I really do want to thank you for coming here again," Rinehold said. "We were told by your publicist that your alien friends revealed to you something all of us around the world have been dying to know—the 'why'—the reason they chose you to represent them on our planet."

Rinehold turned his face to the camera, "For those of you watching tonight and around the world, here now, as promised, is a true exclusive. Mr. Tuckerman, please take it away... the show is all yours."

Jon took a sip of water and glanced over at Heather, who gave him a "thumbs up" sign from the wings of the TV studio. Then, as calmly and coolly as possible, he described for Rinehold and his massive viewing audience the history behind his having become the Wonder Man.

In a very orderly and methodical fashion, JT explained to viewers who his father had been, and the history of Project Blue Book. He talked about how he'd been shown, through an alien "home movie" viewing screen, the night back in February 1963 when his dad had been testing a drone device of his own invention at Edwards Air Force Base in California. He described how that drone and a small UFO had accidentally collided, causing the small orb, containing a young Nordic alien, to crash land on Earth.

Jon recounted how the alien, who'd been badly injured in the crash, had been discovered by his father, who rescued him and brought him to a nearby motel, where Jon's mother had also been staying. He relayed how the couple had spent the rest of that night and the next morning caring for the suffering creature. Jon explained to the audience how his dad had driven for hours to get to the famous Schwab's Drug Store in Hollywood for a tremendous supply of vitamins, and how, upon his return to the motel, his parents spent hours crushing those pills into zinc powder, which cured the remarkable being in the bathtub.

"Schwab's? Really?" Rinehold interjected, chuckling. "Lana Turner! That's wild. Sorry to interrupt... please continue Mr. Tuckerman."

Jon went on to describe how the alien had illuminated his mother's belly, turning it a bright white-blue color, then telling his parents that the little alien's people would always protect their unborn son. That he, Jon, would become their "Chosen One" as a means by which to repay the kindness his parents had extended to the extra-terrestrial creature.

JT continued the story... relaying how, following the alien's recovery from his wound, his father had snuck him back onto the military base, from where the creature was able to contact his 'people' and arrange for a successful, and dramatic, rescue mission.

Jon stopped talking, took another sip of water, and then let out the big reveal. "And that young alien, Don? Turned out to be my friend Jorthon!"

Rinehold gasped. "Are you kidding me?" the host said. "The Tall White alien that rescued you from the Pacific Ocean the night you were drowning is the SAME FREAKIN' ALIEN that your parents saved seventy-two years ago in California?"

Perhaps for the only time in his broadcasting career, the CNN host was speechless. He stared at Jon for a few moments in utter amazement. Then, turning to the camera, Rinehold said, "Folks, I need a minute here. We'll be back after this break."

Returning to the air after a few commercials (including one promoting Two 4 You,) Rinehold had regained his composure. "Mr. Tuckerman, that is truly a fascinating story, and yes, it really does explain the 'Why you?' I asked about a month ago. Can you please tell us more about that 'home movie' screen you mentioned?"

JT went on to talk about what the device looked like and how it presented scenes that were so "real" to him he almost felt like he was there, watching those long-ago moments as they were being projected.

"Did the aliens tell you how they just happened to have recorded all those scenes of your parents?" Rinehold asked. "I wonder if they have 'home movies' of all of us? If they do, I'd sure love to see mine... and I know my audience would like to see theirs, too. Can you please ask them the next time you're with them? And if that view screen can be made available, like you did with Dream TV, I'd bet millions out there would love to get their hands on one of those, too!"

In the limo ride back to the penthouse, JT said to Heather, "I just love how this guy keeps giving me homework assignments."

The harried publicist shrugged and said, "I know, I know, but he raised a good question there, Mr. Tuckerman. What if your aliens DO have home movies of all of us? Can you imagine the demand there would be for everyone to watch them?"

☙

The next time Jon was onboard the Dodger Stadium Special, he did not hesitate to ask his Great Hosts the questions Rinehold had raised during the interview.

"Greetings again Earth friend," Jorthon smiled.

"What have you learned?" Kalyssa asked.

"Before I discuss with you the issue of wrongfully detained prisoners that my team has been researching, I have a bunch of questions I'd really appreciate if you could answer for me," Jon began.

"Of course, Jonathan," Jorthon said. "We have always been honest with you. What do you wish to know?"

JT let fly a string of questions like the rat-tat-tat of a Tommy gun. "How is it that you just happened to have movies of my parents the night you crashed, Jorthon? You told my parents your people would always protect me my entire life... how did you know where I was going to be every moment back then? Do you have 'home movies' of me, too? Are there movies of everyone in the world? And if so, how is that even possible?"

"Please sit," Kalyssa said.

Jon hopped up, once again, onto the now legendary "table of light."

"This may sound difficult for you to comprehend, Jonathan, but as you may or may not know, there are eleven dimensions within space-time," Kalyssa said. "Each of these dimensions is parallel to the others. In one of these dimensions, the Infinite Creator blanketed, over your entire planet, what your brain might call a 'grid of watchful eyes.' These are not cameras as your people have come to know, but they are apertures through which He is able to quite literally 'keep an eye' on his creations on the Earth. Every moment of every life of every human being is constantly surveyed and recorded by Him... from birth to death.

The 'home movies' we showed you of your mother and father and Jorthon were downloaded from the watchful eye-lens dimension by the viewing device you held in your hand. So, yes, there are home movies of your entire life, as well as the lives of every human being who has ever lived."

Jorthon spoke next. He approached Jon and lifted the small glass vial attached to the silver necklace around JT's neck that Susan had given him as a gift a year and a half earlier. "In addition to the watching of mankind by Our Creator, Kalyssa and I have also kept a special eye on you. This piece of metal, here, was our way of tracking your every movement. I implanted this device inside your mother's womb the morning she and your father saved my life. We always knew where you were, and as each and every time danger approached you, it 'pinged' us, like an alarm, so we would have the ability to prevent you from becoming harmed or killed."

The Great White paused. "I suppose I should tell you now, Jonathan, that my Father, the Infinite Creator, allowed me to make a rare exception in your case. To date, you are one of very few human beings on Earth whose 'predestined death date' has been altered by us. He agreed to allow me to delay your death. In fact, you otherwise would have died earlier any number of times during your life."

Jon was shocked beyond all measure. "The car accident... with Janice?" he asked.

"Yes, of course," Jorthon said. "You would have been destroyed that night along with her, had it not been for this arrangement with Him. And several additional times, as well, when you were younger, and a few other times more recently. You have expressed concern to us about 'playing God'—well, you might say that Kalyssa and I *have actually 'played God' with your life*... quite often to preserve and protect it. Only a handful of your predecessors have ever been so closely guarded by my people."

JT didn't know what to think. "Thank you, then," he whispered, "for without you, I guess Isak and Lauren would never have been born."

"Yes, that is quite true," Kalyssa said. "And today you would not be the 'Wonder Man.'" She chuckled.

"Can I see them?" Jon asked. "*My* home movies? Can I see them?"

"The next time we see you," Kalyssa said, "we will hand you a customized unit which will allow you to do so."

"And not just watch," Jorthon interjected. "We will devise a new system whereby you will also have the ability to speak to and be seen by others within the 'scenes' of the movies, and to interact with them in the moment. However, you must know, and this is very, very important Jonathan, nothing you might say or do while visiting those lost moments in time will cause any change to historical facts. Things that have happened in the past cannot 'un-happen.' Also, you can only revisit each of those events just once.

We will implement this novelty for you, solely as a means to allow you the ability to express new thoughts and emotions, and even physically change the nature of those events while they re-happen—but, only during your viewing experience. In this way, you can redo those things you may have regretted ever since those events originally took place. Again, nothing you might say or do while visiting those lost moments in time will cause any change to historical facts after your viewing experience ends."

"I understand," Jon said softly. "Sounds like some of those 'home movies' may resolve a bunch of unanswered questions I still have about my past. I'm sure everyone in the world would like to see their own 'home movies' as well. Thank you so very much... once again. Your contributions to my life... and the lives of everyone on Earth continue to amaze me."

Jon then went on to discuss with Jorthon and Kalyssa the troubling issue of prisoners—based around the world—who had been incorrectly or falsely accused and convicted of major crimes.

Kalyssa handed JT a small, blue, egg-shaped object—about the size of a hardball. "Have any human male or female hold this object in one hand while testifying on a witness stand in any courtroom," she instructed. "They will be compelled to testify ONLY to true facts—they will not have the option to tell a falsehood. Your people might equate this to 'truth serum'—yet it works without any harmful side effects."

During the following days and weeks back at his UN office, JT discussed with the president her ideas as to how best to have this new "legal aid" admitted into the nation's judicial system. Discussions were begun with leading technology companies to prepare to mass market this new product, following its positive review by the Supreme Court and approval by the U.S. Congress.

President Winfield named the incredible blue egg "The Truth Will Out."

CHAPTER TWENTY-NINE

Another month passed, and Jon was becoming less and less engaged from the daily proceedings at the UN, with more and more of his thoughts on introspection. Now spending much of his time at the penthouse, he remained in close contact with his children and Meghan, hoping that the trio would continue to identify and spearhead the research on major world problems. Jon's new plan was just to present those issues in person to Jorthon and Kalyssa each month on behalf of Team Tuckerman, without really having studied them in advance.

However, the next time he was beamed aboard the giant starship, JT was unprepared to discuss any issue of global significance. His mind was clearly elsewhere. The aliens greeted him warmly as always. Jon smiled apprehensively.

"As we promised," Jorthon said, presenting him a hand-sized, golden-colored instrument that reminded Jon of the transistor radio he'd received for his tenth birthday and cherished as a child. Along the side of the device were three digital dials, indicating day, month, and year. Its center featured a rippling glass ball that revolved in a most hypnotic fashion. Kalyssa and Jorthon explained to their guest how to adjust the dials to specific requested calendar dates. They told Jon that the scenes would be projected, in a similar fashion to Dream TV, as high definition, 3D, full-color holograms. To begin any home movie "presentation," the viewer merely had to press his/her thumbprint onto the ball. To end the experience, the three dials on the side of the machine needed to be clicked into the "zero" position.

Jorthon told the bewildered man, "We've preset the first selections for you here, so you may see the moments in your life when we interceded on your behalf. We'd like you to view them, first. After that, you are free to select any date from the history of your life, and view what you were doing that day."

"To join into the action of a scene you are watching," Kalyssa added, "say 'Take Me Back' out loud while pressing your thumb against the ball."

Jon held the miraculous object in his hands and looked up into the warm glowing faces of his benefactors. "Can my movies be seen by others? And may I share this technology with the world?" he asked meekly.

"Whomever is sitting close to you will have the ability to concurrently view your life moments," Jorthon replied. The Great White then placed his finger atop Jon's iPad screen. "And if you believe this machine is of benefit to you, feel free to have it manufactured to the masses. The schematics are inside your little machine," he added.

"And what would you like us to address next?" Kalyssa asked.

Jon went silent for a moment. "Can we talk about Project Blue Book? I find it fascinating that my government studied the UFO phenomenon for decades, but the general public never knew anything about it."

Jorthon went on to explain to Jon that his people were well aware of this effort by the U.S. Air Force and were careful to continue their

observations of Earth and humankind from a respectable distance—
enough to avoid concrete detection by America's primitive technology
systems during the 1940s and beyond.

~

When Jon returned home to the penthouse, Susan cried with delight, "Is
that it? Let me see!" The doctor, wearing a tank top, a pair of short shorts,
and flip-flops, embraced Jon, kissed him, and placed her hands atop his.
"My good God in heaven, have you tried it yet?" she asked.

"No," Jon replied, trembling. "I'm afraid to. This thing overwhelms
me. If it does what they say it can do, millions and millions of people
are going to have the chance to 'rewrite' moments in their lives that they
really fucked up the first time. The idea of that is just completely mind-
boggling."

"I have an idea!" Susan said. She ran into the bedroom for a moment,
and then came back into the living room, motioning for Jon to sit on
the couch. "I think we should get high first, and then watch your home
movies all night."   ugh!

Jon was taken aback. "I haven't gotten high since the Clinton
administration." Susan chuckled. "And where's Russell?" he asked.

"I gave him the night off," Susan replied. "He went to visit his son in
Philadelphia. I wanted tonight to be just about you and your life story.
I'm here for you, baby. Every step of the way... good, bad, or ugly." She
lit up a thick joint and took a hit, then passed it to Jon.

"Well, there goes my weed abstinence," he joked, inhaling the joint
and then choking for a full fifteen seconds. The duo repeated the process
a number of times, until they both looked at each other, and burst into
hysterical laughter.

"Oh Johnny boy, my hero man," Susan mocked. "Let's fire this thing
up and see where it leads us!"

Jon pressed his right thumb onto the rippling ball in the center of
the view device, and it quickly came to life. Over the course of the next

several hours, he and Susan, sitting side by side on the couch, witnessed a series of moments from Jon Tuckerman's life.

First scene: Five-year-old JT is seen playing jump rope with two adorable young girls in the driveway of the home next door to the Tuckerman family's 1960s New Jersey residence. Jon's childhood neighbors Cathy and Lizzie are standing at each end of the rope, swinging it, while JT is hopping up and down, over and over again.

"22, 23, 24, 25," counts Cathy as Jon continues to successfully hop above the rope.

"26, 27, 28, ahh, too bad," adds Lizzie when Jon's lucky jumping streak ends.

"I don't wanna jump anymore," JT says.

"Wanna climb?" Lizzie asks.

"Sure!" Jon answers.

The three children are next seen walking to the corner of their block. There stands a large billboard sign, promoting the local drugstore just around the corner. The kids walk inside the sign's interior structure... a lattice of long wooden beams that serve as the sign's skeleton. The girls begin climbing up the left side of the billboard, while JT climbs up the right.

The three youngsters are having a fun time, obviously having done this before. When they reach a point of about twenty-feet high, Lizzie calls out, "Hey, JT! You know what?"

Jon answers, "What?"

"I love you!" She blows him a kiss.

Startled by this display of affection, JT loses his grip on one of the wooden beams and begins to fall backwards through the air, facing up. Lizzie and Cathy react in horror. Jon descends as though in slow motion, his arms and legs flailing in all directions.

A bright white light illuminates the scene. From nowhere, Jorthon appears and catches the flying youngster in his outstretched arms before he crash lands onto the hard soil. JT is out cold. The girls flee, terrified. Jorthon carries JT across the street to a neighbor's house. No one is home. He gently places Jon on a couch, then turns to leave. As Jorthon is about to beam out of the house, JT wakes up and sees just the back of the alien's glowing body and his long white hair. Jon's face clearly registers great surprise. He has no idea what had just happened nor who (or what) his Savior had been. Jon sits up on the couch and scans the room. Not recognizing his surroundings, he stands up and leaves, shutting the door behind him.

Next Scene: Jon and Susan watch as nine-year-old JT is running around the playground at his elementary schoolyard. He and his best friend Ronnie are chasing each other. Ronnie calls out, "Let's chase the girls!"

JT answers, "Yeah!" The two youngsters set their eyes on Wendy and Robin, identical twin sisters.

"I'll get Robin," Ronnie says. "You get Wendy."

Giggling joyfully, the two young girls play along as JT and Ronnie chase them around and around in circles on the blacktop. The girls, obviously faster than the boys, taunt their pursuers. "You'll never catch me, JT!" Wendy shouts teasingly, looking over her left shoulder.

Jon, just a few feet behind her, looks ahead and notices that there is a break in the metal pole that holds up the metallic fence on the border of the playground. The broken pole appears to be sharply jagged and menacing. As his potential little girlfriend continues to mock him, Jon cries out, "Wendy! Stop! The fence!"

"Ya can't fool me, JT," Wendy calls back.

With a remarkable burst of adrenaline, Jon manages to run IN FRONT of Wendy, pushing her to the ground so that she avoids the broken fence post. She falls, skinning her knees. However, due to the momentum of his speed, JT knows that he is going to collide with the razor-sharp pole, face first. He closes his eyes, preparing himself for impact.

Bright white light. All activity on the playground stops. The light beam bends the entire length of the metal fence, pressing it flush to the ground. The light vanishes. When the activity of the children starts up again, JT is standing on *the other side* of the crushed fence.

Wendy, horrified, screams at Jon, "Look what you did to me!" Her knees are bleeding badly.

Her sister, Robin, kneels at her side. "We're gonna tell Mrs. Kaufman what you did, JT!" the defiant sister reprimands. "You're gonna get in so much trouble!"

JT watches in guilt as Robin places her injured sister's arm around her neck and helps her limp back into the school building.

His friend, Ronnie, howls with laughter. "Ooh, Jon Tuckerman," he mocks. "You're in the shit can now!"

A clear illustration of the phrase "no good deed goes unpunished," JT walks over to the steps just outside the schoolhouse building and becomes teary-eyed. Shame and guilt overwhelm him.

CHAPTER THIRTY

"How traumatic!" Susan whispers, hugging Jon. "It's no wonder you had 'girl problems' later in life." She kisses JT's head. "I need to pee, hold on a sec." As Susan walks off, Jon continues to sit on the couch in somewhat of a daze. Susan quickly returns and settles back in next to Jon. "Alright, let's check out what's next," she says.

The couple are now shown the next chunk of Jon's early life. They see JT playing softball at school. He appears to be about fourteen. He approaches the batter's box, holding an aluminum bat. At his far-right side, the coach calls out mocking encouragement. "Come on, JT, you retarded peckerhead! Do something decent this time, okay? You struck out your last two ups... try not to be a total loser today alright?"

JT glances at his coach and manages a weak smile. He swings and misses the first two pitches, and is now convinced he will, once again, strike out in front of his classmates.

"Hit the stupid ball, JT!" his friend Ronnie screams from the dugout. "Don't be a peckerhead!"

Wanting desperately to impress both his coach and his best friend, Jon promises himself under his breath that he is going to hit the fuck out of the next pitch that crosses his path. He does! He hits the ball so hard its cover flies off. The ball makes its way well over most of center field.

"Run, you idiot, run!" the coach screams. "That might be the best hit you'll ever have in your whole life!"

JT, beaming with pride, runs the bases. Easily speeding past first, he hones all of his attention now on second. He knows he can get there, and possibly even make it to third. Just as he is a few feet from second base, the center fielder throws the ball, fast and hard, to the second baseman. However, the ball was not thrown in the direction of the second baseman's glove. Instead, it's now heading directly toward JT's face. Focused solely on the bag at second, Jon does not realize he is microseconds away from a serious concussion.

Bright light—all action stops. The ball "plops" straight to the ground. The light vanishes. Action resumes. Jon is well past second base and continues running to third. The second baseman, befuddled, picks up the ball and throws it to the catcher at home plate.

"Nice triple!" the coach hollers at Jon. "Maybe you aren't a total loser after all, 'Peckerman!'"

Next Scene: Jon and Susan watch a moment from JT's senior year in high school. His rock band "Eclipse" is rehearsing for a student variety show. A decent lead singer in his day, Jon fronts the band, which includes his lifelong friends Steve on guitar, Scott on bass, Mitch on drums, and Richie—whom everyone calls "Johann"—on organ. Eclipse is rehearsing a song made famous by the '80s band REO Speedwagon called "Time for Me to Fly."

Each member of the band stands in position on the stage, with Jon at the center, just in front of a microphone on a stand. Mr. Post, a portly physics teacher, approaches them, clipboard in hand. "Alright, boys, remember your act must be no more than five minutes... no long drum solos or anything. Make the most of it. Enjoy yourselves. But, for God's sake, don't play so goddamn loud!" He walks off into the wings of the stage.

The lights go down, then we hear the guitar introduction to the song. The stage lights come up... a vibrant, powerful red color blankets the musicians. Jon, standing just inches from the microphone, sings the first two verses. Then, just as he begins to sing the words in the chorus—"I believe it's time for me to fly"—he leans in closer toward the mic, his lips accidentally touching it. He receives an electric shock so powerful he gets knocked back four feet through the air, landing onto the floor of the stage... his head just in front of Mitch's bass drum. His eyes roll up into his head and his mouth starts foaming. The band stops playing.

Mr. Post races over to Jon, kneeling beside him. "Tuckerman? You okay?"

No response.

The stage becomes illuminated in bright white light—so bright everyone on the stage, and even those in the auditorium watching the rehearsal, begin shrieking in pain. When the light vanishes, JT is sitting up, rubbing his eyes, but obviously no longer greeting death.

"Dude, what the fuck?" Steve the guitarist asks him.

Mr. Post shoots the teen a nasty look for the language, then turns back to Jon. "Tuckerman, you had us worried. You alright now?"

JT looks up at his teacher. "What happened?"

Mr. Post responds. "About 40 milliamps."

Jon stands with a helping hand from Mr. Post. "I'm good, it's all good. Let's try this again." He walks back to the mic, quickly touches it with his hand, receives no shock, then nods to his bandmates to begin performing the song a second time.

Next Scene: Jon's in college in Boston. He's twenty years old. He and his roommate, Brad, are smoking a joint at a party. There are at least another fifty to sixty college students in attendance. Music fills the air and the lights are darkened for a party ambience.

"Dude, too bad you couldn't ask her to come here," Brad says to Jon.

"Yeah, I know. I tried. I stood outside her door for 15 minutes, but I couldn't even knock," Jon said.

"Why are you so afraid of her? She's just a girl," Brad says.

"She's THE girl, man," JT replies. "I've got a crush on her that won't quit." Just then, the girl Jon was discussing, Marissa, enters the party, arm in arm with a tall, blond, good-looking guy.

Brad nudges his buddy. "Dude! She's here!"

"Oh, fuck, no," Jon says.

Marissa and her date are walking right past JT and Brad when the beautiful girl with long red hair winks at JT, as though to taunt him.

"Goddamn! She's hot, Jon," Brad says.

JT, obviously crushed, can barely speak. "Get me outta here, man," he laments. "I can't watch this."

The two students leave the party and walk outside the building. They enter a side alley. "I know what you need, buddy," Brad says. He takes out two small sugar cubes and tastes one. "Here, lick this," he says, offering Jon a tab of LSD.

"Acid? Ah, uhm, I'm not sure…"

"Come on, Johnny, you need this," Brad advises. "It'll cure what ails ya." JT hesitates, then licks the cube. He and Brad then begin to walk along Commonwealth Avenue in Boston on this bitter cold, wintery night.

As they walk, it begins to snow. The two young men, wrapped in coats, hats, scarves, and gloves, are obviously freezing… the night's air becoming smoke from their breaths. Suddenly, Jon notices that the scenery around him is becoming brightly colored and wildly distorted. The buildings bend and weave like rubber, the lamps in the streetlights turning into rainbows. The snowflakes falling before him begin to feel like bird seed pellets against his eyelashes.

"Fuck, dude, I'm fucking high, too fucking high!" Jon tells his buddy.

"Isn't this cool?" Brad answers.

A group of young female college students pass the two men. To Jon, *every one of them resembles Marissa*! "Fuck no," he whispers.

Continuing to walk, Jon starts hearing his innermost voices out loud. "Loser! You should have asked her out! What's wrong with you? She should be YOUR girlfriend, not that other guy's... you pathetic fuck!"

An MBTA trolley car comes barreling down the middle of Commonwealth Avenue. Jon's inner demons are now screaming at him. "You don't deserve to live, Jon! Do it. Fucking do it. Kill yourself. You'll never get the girl. You will always be alone!"

Jon bolts away from Brad and runs toward the middle of Commonwealth Ave. "Dude!" Brad screams.

JT is committed to ending his life. The trolley is speeding along at forty miles per hour. Jon stands on the tracks in the path of the mass transit vehicle just sixty feet away... its bright headlights aimed squarely at his torso.

Suddenly, intense bright light from above. Jon is lifted straight up into the air and hangs there, suspended in time. The trolley races past where he'd stood just seconds before. Brad, watching from the sidewalk, believes he is hallucinating. "Jesus and Mary H. Christ," he says. "Fuckin' intense!"

With the trolley car now passed, Jon is gently replaced by the light beam back down onto the sidewalk beside his friend. He and Brad continue to walk.

"Dude, I just had a dream about you!" Brad declares. "It was so fucking real!"

CHAPTER THIRTY-ONE

"My God, they really have been watching out for you your whole life!" Susan cried.

"I had no idea," Jon responded. "I always knew something about my life was 'off,' but I never could put my finger on it. If someone had told me that God-like extra-terrestrial beings have been my guardian angels all this time, I never would have believed them," he laments.

Next Scene: Newlyweds Jon and Janice, both in their late twenties, are asleep in bed. A sudden, terrible loud cry pierces the air—it sounds like an animal, perhaps a dog, is being tortured to death. JT sits bolt upright, the hairs standing up on the back of his neck. A second cry, even worse than the first, is heard. Now Janice also sits up. "What on Earth is that God-awful sound?" she asks.

JT replies, "I think it's a neighbor's dog. Maybe he got his head caught in something."

"Go see," Janice says, volunteering her husband. "Go check it out. Whatever the hell that is, it's definitely *not right*."

JT puts on a bathrobe and pokes his head outside the front door of their small, one bedroom apartment. It's silent, until it isn't. A third ear-piercing scream, now clearly from a dog, echoes down the hallway. Following the source of the noise, Jon makes a series of two sharp right-hand turns until he comes upon the door of a neighbor five units away.

"What the hell am I doing right now?" he says out loud to himself as he knocks. A few seconds go by, and Jon knocks again.

Suddenly, a short, squat, hefty man, about fifty, wearing only undershorts and sweating profusely, answers. "What do YOU want, JEW?" he snarls at Jon.

"We heard a noise—it was horrible! Sounded like a dog in trouble. Do you have a dog?"

Just then, Jon can see two German shepherds in the background behind the angry neighbor. "They're just fine, see," the man points. "Both of my dogs are fine. Why don't you mind your own business, *You Fucking Jew Kike!*"

JT, stunned by the insult, studies the man and realizes that not only is he sweating, but his face and chest are bright red, and much of his upper torso appears to be covered in claw marks. OMG, what? - Like, what.

A light bulb. "Are you SCREWING your DOG, mister?" Jon asks.

"Fuck you, cocksucker!" the man screams at Jon. "Who the fuck are YOU to question ME?"

The neighbor dashes away from the front door for a moment and returns with a large butcher knife. "Son of a bitch, cocksucker," the man shouts, leaping on top of Jon and knocking him to the ground. "Couldn't mind your own fucking business, huh?" he screams, threatening to plunge the knife deep into Jon's chest.

Bright light. The neighbor, knife held high above JT, begins to turn purple. He drops the knife onto the hallway carpet and clutches his chest.

He cannot breathe. He falls off to the side of Jon's body, and curls into a fetal position on the hallway floor. The light vanishes. Seconds later, two police officers—a man and a woman—arrive. They draw their guns. "You on the floor, what's going on here?"

JT quickly sits up and explains the situation. His neighbor, panting and purple, writhing on the floor, cannot speak. The cops position the neighbor so he's now also sitting up and his purple color begins to subside. "Get me away from HIM!" the man says, scared to death of the light that protected Jon and caused his near heart attack. "Get me the hell outta here!

The cops lift the man off the ground and handcuff him. They take the knife as well.

"Looks like your wife called us just in time," the male cop says to JT.

"We'll send animal services in the morning to come get those dogs," the female cop says, noting the canines inside the madman's apartment. The officers close the apartment door and walk the neighbor to their squad car.

Jon, sweating and confused, has no idea where the mysterious bright light that just saved his life came from.

CHAPTER THIRTY-TWO

Susan bolts off the couch. "How come you never told me about that horrific neighbor? That nutjob could have ended your life back then!"

Jon shrugs. "I've been working hard, for so many decades, to just 'bury' the darkness from my past, Suze," he says. "So much pain. So many problems. So much unhappiness. I did my best to shove it all into a ball, roll it up, and stuff it inside a mental lock box in the deepest part of my brain."

"Well, you should probably have worked through these things over the years," Jon's lover responds. "Serious therapy. Hypnosis even. Lots of people live through trauma, but the best way to move forward is to embrace it—confront it head on. You never did. And now I know why you tried to 'off' yourself on your big birthday."

"More?" Jon asks.

"Yes, of course. How can we not watch the next hidden chapter of my boyfriend's supernatural life story?"

Next Scene: Jon and his two children, Isak, age 10, and Lauren, age 8, are sitting atop a jet ski, careening through the Pacific Ocean just off the coast of Catalina Island. It's a bright, beautiful summer day. Isak sits at the front of the craft and is handling the speed controls on the handlebar. JT sits in the middle, Lauren just behind him, holding on to her dad's waist. "Slow down, boy, easy!" Jon shouts to Isak, whose maniacal look of mischief is painted across his adorable face. In the nearby waters, a number of yachts and sailboats, large and small, are lazily floating in the sea. However, the bobbing of the waves from other boats passing by creates a series of wakes through which the Tuckerman family is having to navigate.

"Watch out, Isak, and slow down!" Jon screams to his son, but, unfortunately, it's too late. The trio smacks into a larger than anticipated wave, instantly flipping the jet ski—and the three Tuckermans—over and upside down into the water. Isak and Lauren are wearing life vests... Jon is not. The young children begin laughing, safely floating, and they start swimming toward the nearest yacht about twenty yards away. Jon begins sinking rather quickly. He'd been dumped into the ocean so fast his brain has not yet registered his predicament. He is breathless and disoriented.

Trying desperately to "right" the jet ski and climb back on it, Jon is unable to do so. He clings to the upside-down craft, panicking, his heart beating much too quickly. He is very grateful, though, to see that his two kids are calmly making their way toward the nearby boat.

"Please help me," Jon says out loud to no one. "Please don't let my children watch me drown."

Bright light. All action stops. The light vanishes. Jon suddenly finds himself standing onboard the nearby yacht, beating his two children there by just a few seconds.

Isak looks up at JT from the water. "How'd you do that, Dad?" he asks.

"I have no idea, boy," Jon replies, as he kneels at the edge of the luxurious boat and reaches for Isak and then Lauren, successfully heaving both of them onto the vessel's wooden deck.

"That was fun, Daddy!" Lauren shouts excitedly. "Can we do it again?"

Next Scene: Jon, in his fifties, is working late at night at his office. We see a sign in the background: "Tanner & Tuckerman Events." Jon is pouring over his financial records on his computer screen, shaking his head and obviously distressed. "Fucking, fuck, fucker," he mutters. "That son of a bitch stiffed me out of seven grand. I hope he chokes on a chicken bone and dies very painfully."

A single desk lamp lights the room, which contains filing cabinets and shelves filled with paper goods, party favors, costumes, masks, silver balloons, dried flowers, and other memorabilia collected from years of JT's party productions.

Jon pours himself another bourbon in a small glass and sips it. He picks up a photo on his desk and sees himself, Janice, Isak, and Lauren all together, appearing happy and carefree. "Sorry, kids," he says to the photo. "Daddy's going down. Daddy's going down to the ground."

Jon gets up from his desk and stretches his back. He begins walking around the office. A clock on the wall reads 2:00 am. Jon pulls a box off one of the shelves and pulls out a rubber chicken and a false nose with attached moustache and glasses. He puts on the nose and holds the chicken aloft.

"Hello boys and girls," he says to an imaginary audience as though the host of a kiddie TV show. "My name is Jon Tuckerman. Would you all like to watch me fuck over a five-million-dollar-a-year business single-handedly? Come on! I'll show you how!" He makes the chicken "dance" in mid-air, mocking himself for all to see. "Hello everyone, I'm just a great big chicken man who can't do anything right! Isn't it fun to be me? I owe everyone in the world lots and lots of money! Woo hoo!"

Disgusted with himself, he tosses the chicken and fake nose back into the box. He then walks down a hallway and enters a small kitchen area. He opens the fridge, retrieves two pieces of bread and a few slices of cheese, and places those items inside a toaster oven. He sets the machine to 250 degrees, then sits at a small kitchen table. While the sandwich is baking, Jon sets his head down atop the table and falls asleep.

Moments later, smoke begins pouring from the toaster oven. Flames leap forth from the machine and run up the wire that extends into the electrical outlet on the wall. The wall then bursts into flames as well... the kitchen is on fire.

Jon is still asleep—until he hears the smoke alarm going off. He rubs his eyes—he is surrounded by smoke and flames.

"Fucking shit! Fucker!" he screams. Realizing the windows in the kitchen are too small for an escape, he makes a run for it, dashing into the nearby hallway. Flames and smoke are rapidly spreading and are now exceeding the kitchen. Jon pulls his shirt up to his face and begins to breathe through it. He can barely see now; the smoke is so thick it thwarts his path to the front door. As he feels his way toward safety, he trips over an extension cord on the floor, falling face-down onto the ground.

Smashing his right knee into the cement floor with a bang as he falls, he screams "Goddamn, cocksucker!" Tears start to trickle down his face, both from the smoke inhalation and the crippling pain from his leg. "Well, I guess this is goodbye, gang," he says out loud. "The 'Johnny Tuckerman Show' has been cancelled. At least NOW the IRS can't come after me... so that's good."

An outside light appears, so bright it bursts open an exit door and blows it off its hinges. A powerful spray of cooling powder blasts through the office space, rapidly extinguishing the fire. As though being sucked up with a giant straw, the smoke dissipates very quickly.

Jon sits up, massages his damaged knee, and shakes his head in bewilderment. "Well, I guess *somebody up there* must like me," he whispers.

CHAPTER THIRTY-THREE

"My dear God," said Susan, now almost crying. "What a shit show. I'm surprised you lasted as long as you did BEFORE your little 70th birthday suicide swim!"

"It's been unpleasant," JT replied. "Lots and lots of obstacles; an endless series of torment and frustration." The two stared into each other's eyes for a moment.

"More?" Susan asked.

"I must, but I'm not looking forward to the next bit," JT responded. "I'm pretty sure I know what's coming up next."

The final scene Jon and Susan watched that night was the one he'd most been dreading. He and his lover reviewed the moment in which Jon and Janice were driving from San Diego to Los Angeles through the pouring rain on the last night of Janice's life. With the distance of decades behind him, Jon, while watching the worst moment of his life, realized how incredibly tired he was that night... and how he NEVER should have been behind a steering wheel in the first place.

Janice is glaring at Jon. "We just don't love each other anymore, Jon," she says. "We have no passion. No romance. We don't even have sex," she scolds him. "I want lust in my life. I want a man who can please me... who can make me feel like a real woman. You've lost it! Our love is long gone. The man I met and married years ago isn't there anymore. I'm just not 'into you,' as the kids say." — ugh! No one talks like this

Susan elbows Jon in the present. "Say something to her!" she urged. "Tell her how you feel. Apologize! Change it up! Now's your chance!"

Jon gazes again at the alien view screen, takes a deep breath, presses his thumb against the rippling ball, and says "Take Me Back!" Miraculously, he next finds his present-day self inside the car, driving. "Holy shit! Janice!" he cries, "I came back for you!" He quickly pulls the speeding car over to the shoulder of the road and turns off the engine.

"Get out of the car RIGHT NOW!" he shouts at her.

"Are you a complete lunatic?" Janice answers. "It's pouring rain!"

Jon bolts out of the driver's side of the car, runs around its rear end, and approaches the passenger door. He opens it, screaming, "Janice I need you out of the car RIGHT FUCKING NOW!"

Janice gives Jon a look of complete shock and anger. "What on earth is wrong with you?" she says as she reluctantly gets out of the vehicle. Jon slams her door shut, then takes her forcefully by the hand and runs away from the freeway's shoulder. They stand under some tall trees... the leaves deflecting some of the rainfall that is pounding down all around them.

"I loved you very much, Janice!" Jon screams. "I'm so sorry I wasn't man enough for you. I got distracted with work and didn't have enough energy to give you what you needed. But we did make two great kids, right? That's something we can always be proud of. That's the real reason we met. And you should know, by the way, they turn out really great when they're older!"

Janice, holding her purse over her head to shield the rain, is taken aback by Jon's conciliatory tone and baffled by his "older" remark. "I don't know WHY we're having this conversation here, now, in the rain, but YES, you're right, I agree. Making our kids *was* the reason we met, Jon. But what do you mean by 'when they're older'?'" she asks.

Jon, knowing the death of his wife is just moments away, continues, "Janice, I am so, so sorry our marriage and our lives didn't work out. I never meant to hurt you in any way. We won't see each other again after tonight, so I need to apologize to you right now, for everything. I'm very, very sorry, honey. I need to know you forgive me. Please, I'm begging you. Can you forgive me for ruining our marriage and ending our lives together?"

In spite of the rain, Janice can see tears running down Jon's face, and realizes the depth of his sorrow. "Yes, I forgive you, Jon. It's alright. We tried. It just wasn't meant to last. We gave it a good shot. And we'll always have the kids. I accept your apology." She pauses. Then, like a delayed reaction, asks, "But why won't we see each other again after tonight?"

A car racing down the freeway at 65 mph slams on its brakes and, due to the rain-soaked pavement, skids into the back of the Tuckermans' car on the shoulder. The car is plowed—hard—into its predestined collision with a large telephone pole. Janice sees the crash and shoots Jon a look of astonishment. "How did you know, Jon?" she asks her husband in true awe.

"I came back for you," he repeats. "I came to see you again, from the future in 2035. Tonight was the night you died. I'm so very sorry, Janice," he says softly. "I hope you can rest in peace now."

Intense bright light, and Janice simply disappears. Jon looks at his car, and notices that Janice's now lifeless body is once again sitting in the passenger seat. Her side of the car had been slammed full force into the pole on the right shoulder of the freeway. The left side of the car—where Jon had been sitting—is cushioned in light. The car has almost literally split in half. The vehicle behind Jon's—the one that crashed into it—is also severely damaged. However, the driver, a young woman in her early twenties, apparently only has minor cuts and bruises.

An ambulance pulls up to the scene a short time later. Two paramedics hop out and see Jon, standing alone under the trees, off to the side on the shoulder. "Hey buddy, you okay?" one calls out.

Jon looks at the men in despair, not really knowing how to answer that question.

༄

The alien projector went dark. The home movie show was over. Jon was ashen. Susan held him closely, whispering into his ear, "That was truly awful, Johnny. I'm so sorry that you had to go through that."

"I lived. She died," he said, guilt-ridden.

"But at least you had the chance this time to apologize to her first, right? Thanks to this machine, the aliens gave you the opportunity to apologize to Janice. And she accepted your apology. There's a lot to be said for that. You should realize that experience was a real gift."

Jon looked up. "You're right, I guess," he said. "There was no way I could have prevented Janice from dying that night. Jorthon and Kalyssa told me that everyone has a predestined death date... and that was hers. At least, this time, I was able to say I'm sorry. She knew I felt bad about how things stood between us... and she understood. I actually got a 'do-over.'"

"You got a second chance," Susan agreed. "Through this magical theater machine thingy."

"That's it... 'Second Chance Theater,'" Jon said. "I'm going to get this out to everyone. I'm sure lots of other people out there need another shot at second chances in their lives too."

The following morning JT, back at his UN office and for the second time in four months, had Meghan assemble the greatest minds from the world's leading technology companies. He presented to them the premise behind "Second Chance Theater." The CEOs were once again astonished by the features of the new system, with the head of FutureInk remarking that the "idea of not only viewing your previous adventures, but actually having the ability to interact within them, more than boggles the mind. It's a total game changer."

Jon allowed each executive to hold and inspect the viewer and, again, each man and woman posed for a photograph with JT and the device in hand. However, a slightly different opportunity than the Dream TV offer was presented to the CEOs this time. They were each free to produce and market these systems, but one half of all profits after manufacturing costs and shipping had to be paid into the newly launched Jonathan M. Tuckerman Family Trust. He figured with *this* device, which had been created specifically for *him,* he was entitled to generate future profits, so his children would be financially comfortable the rest of their lives.

In just a few months after its introduction to the general public, the Second Chance Theater viewing system had become the biggest and most historic new product launch in world history. Lines at retail outlets were tens of blocks long, online orders overwhelmed every major e-commerce retail website, and media coverage detailing the ramifications of the remarkable new machine was nearly ubiquitous and overwhelmingly positive.

Therapists and psychiatrists around the world quickly realized the therapeutic benefits of Second Chance Theater, suggesting to their patients that they could sit together, watch, and "re-write" moments from those patients' pasts that had caused them great trauma, conflict, guilt, shame, and anguish. Rape victims could become empowered by confronting their abusers; those who'd watched loved ones die now had another chance to tell those leaving this world how much they were loved, and to spend a few more final moments with them; bad decisions about financial investments, hostile arguments, regrettable sexual indiscretions, problematic political decisions, accidental killings... all these moments— and more—could now be dissected and revised by those involved, often after many decades of time had passed.

The device was also globally used within jails and prisons... as those convicted of particularly heinous crimes but who had since become remorseful over their horrific actions, could now at least virtually apologize to their victims.

The Dream TV Network launched another cable television channel, and "Second Chance Theater TV" quickly filled its airwaves. People from around the world were able to upload fascinating moments of their lives so that others could view them. The new TV network offered content far more interesting, compelling, and remarkable than anything even the most creative of Hollywood's minds could ever have envisioned or imagined.

CHAPTER THIRTY-FOUR

Jonathan and Susan decided to get married on June 17, 2035—her 40th birthday. The news thrilled Isak, Lauren, and the president. Heather Burg sent out a press release making the announcement to the world. The global media ran photos of JT and Susan from his 71st birthday party and the Nobel Prize ceremony to accompany the story.

Having so enjoyed Jon's party at the Plaza Hotel, the couple chose that same venue to be the site of their upcoming nuptials. JT told his fiancée to invite whoever she thought best, as the idea of sending out invitations to the world overwhelmed him. Susan, Lauren, Meghan, and President Winfield worked as a team, routing their suggested invitation lists to each other through email, until it was pared down to 500 people.

May 22, 2035 came around, and once again Jon and Isak boarded the flying marvel from the Pleiades dimension. Isak had prepared himself to discuss the fact that more than a dozen scientists from around the world had recently identified three large comets in outer space with trajectories that included direct pathways toward Earth. The iPad, which JT had literally handed off to his son as a rite of passage, was on the craft once more.

"Hello again, Tuckerman-men," Kalyssa said.

"What do you bring us today?" Jorthon asked.

Jon was a bit hesitant as to how to proceed. "Before we begin our problem du jour," he began, "I wanted to let you know that Susan Parks and I are getting married in a few weeks. I've decided to take off five months for our honeymoon, as we'd like to take a long, leisurely trip around the world for fun and relaxation. I hope the two of you don't mind? I'm not trying to shirk my responsibilities. And if it's okay with you, I'd like Isak to take my place while I'm gone... I just need some quality time alone with my new bride."

"That is marvelous news," Kalyssa said. "Congratulations. She seems like a lovely, intelligent woman... and we know the sex you make with her provides you with great happiness!" — ugh, why?

JT shot a quick glance at Isak, as his son turned his head the other way in an attempt to avoid the embarrassing remark entirely. — Same!

"Yes, that will be fine," Jorthon added. "We will accept Isak as your ambassador in your absence. We understand your need for some time to yourself. We have challenged you with quite a lot these past eighteen months. May I make a suggestion?"

"Sure, of course."

Jorthon continued: "May I see your screen?" Isak handed him the iPad. Jorthon held it for a few seconds, then returned it to the elder Tuckerman. "I have placed into your computer, Jonathan, fourteen ancient sites around the Earth that I believe might be of great interest to you. They are all comprised of structural remains that *my* ancestors built with the help of *your* ancestors, thousands of years ago." — ancient aliens without the

"Wow, that's great! Thank you!" Jon said, truly excited. "I've always wanted to visit the pyramids in Egypt. Is that one of the sites?" Racism!

"Yes, of course," Kalyssa said. "We are quite certain you will greatly enjoy these locations, given your newly discovered knowledge of the expanded universe. They remain some of the largest and most enigmatic constructions on your planet to this day."

At that point, Isak and Kalyssa began to discuss options for the destruction of the three recently discovered errant comets.

Concurrently, JT and Jorthon viewed, together, the various locales on the iPad screen that depicted the structural artifacts Jorthon was recommending.

కొ

With a jam-packed schedule that continued propelling him forward, Jon's next few weeks whizzed by, and before he knew it, June 17th had arrived. JT, Isak, and Russell took a short limo ride from the penthouse to the Plaza Hotel. Susan and Lauren had spent the night there, with Lauren helping her soon-to-be stepmother primp for her big day. Susan's parents, Dr. Raymond Parks, a noted brain surgeon, and his wife, Debra, a teacher at an art school, had also arrived twenty-four hours earlier from their home in Brooklyn to assist their only child.

The entourage from Washington, D.C. had arrived that morning on Air Force One, and took a series of limousines to the Plaza. Susan had asked both President Winfield and Lauren to be her "maids" of honor. Isak, of course, was JT's selection as best man.

Throngs of media stood, respectfully, along the red carpet laid out from the hotel's lobby and down the front outdoor staircase. There was no hysteria this time in getting their coverage, as the reporters and still photographers wished to show some decorum for this important day in the Wonder Man's life.

Russell had been placed in charge of the Plaza's kitchen, a role he was more than willing to play. He carefully inspected every morsel of food that was being prepared for the wedding reception, diligently informing each of the chefs that "Mr. Tuckerman does not like it 'too salty'... so, please, don't do 'too salty.'" The chefs begrudgingly obliged the famed cook's requests.

Jon's children had once again invited their partners, so Harold and Charles each made their first trips to the United States to join in the festivities.

Although Jon had been born and raised in the Jewish faith, he no longer held the tenets of that religion in high esteem. Susan, raised a Protestant, also had little interest in formalized religion. As a result, the pair requested that former New York City Mayor John Sheffield, now a much-in-demand Justice of the Peace, perform a civil ceremony.

Hundreds were already seated when the Tuckerman entourage peeked into the ceremonial room. "Dad, I'm so proud of you," Lauren said, kissing her father on the cheek. "You finally found The One! I know you and Susan will always be very happy together."

"Thanks kid," JT responded, deeply touched. Lauren then excused herself to help her future stepmother apply her finishing touches.

"Dad! Oh, fuck!" Isak said. "I forgot the ring!"

Jon's face went cold. "Please tell me you're kidding, boy!" he replied.

"Gotcha! Didn't I?" the younger Tuckerman said. "Of course, I have it. Would I really do something like that to you?"

JT shook his head in mock dismay, then grabbed his son and squeezed him tight. "I love you, son-shine," he said. "Please don't ever, ever forget that." Mayor Sheffield met Jon and Isak outside the doors to the main room. "Ready, men?" he asked.

"Absolutely," Jon replied. "Let's fire this rocket!"

The three men entered the room, walking as a triangle down the long white carpet toward the dais. Everyone inside stood to applaud their hero, Jonathan Tuckerman, Friend of Aliens. Jon and Isak waved and nodded at the hordes in attendance... each and every one of them seemingly thrilled at having been invited.

The former mayor, Jon, and Isak took their places at the front of the room. Then, just moments later, President Winfield and Lauren Tuckerman, walking arm in arm, strolled down the aisle to great applause.

When they reached their posts, the mayor nodded to the organist. As she began to play Mendelssohn's classic "Wedding March," all heads turned to the doors behind them. Dr. Susan Parks, bedazzling in a custom-made wedding dress by one of Italy's foremost fashion designers, began walking arm in arm with her father, a distinguished looking man with salt and pepper hair and a broad, beaming smile on his face.

Jon's heart was racing as he saw this vision—this goddess—walking down the aisle to marry him. HIM! "In what universe did I earn the privilege of marrying the most brilliant and beautiful woman that ever lived?" he whispered to his son.

Isak nudged his dad with his elbow. "You did pretty good, old man," he joked. "She's not too shabby."

Heartfelt applause accompanied Susan and Dr. Park's walk down the aisle. When they arrived at the front of the room, Dr. Parks lifted his daughter's veil, kissed her cheek, and gave her a warm hug. Then he shook Jon's hand before he joined his wife, sitting in the front row. Susan positioned herself in between the president and Lauren. The organist stopped playing. The room went silent.

"Hello everyone," Mayor Sheffield began. "Thank you all for coming today to celebrate in the joyous coupling of this truly extraordinary man and his truly extraordinary bride. I've been asked to make this ceremony short and sweet, so I'd like to now ask our bride, Dr. Susan Elizabeth Parks, to recite her vows."

Susan reached out to Jon and took hold of his hands. "My hero," she said. "I knew the first moment we met that you were different. A man 'above' the norm. Of course, neither I nor anyone else in the world knew, that night, just how 'high above the norm' you really were!" Scattered laughter. "While supernatural circumstances may have led to us meeting, there's nothing supernatural about the love I feel for you—the very real love I've come to cherish and enjoy, every single day of my life. Thank you, Jonathan Michael Tuckerman, for beaming down from a giant flying saucer and into my arms. And just so you know, I'm never going to let you go!"

Applause.

Jon's reached his shaky hand into his jacket pocket, and pulled out a small piece of paper. "Before I met you, I had only experienced truly unquestioned love twice in my entire life," he read—his voice breaking. "When I first looked into Isak's eyes and cut his umbilical cord, and the first time I held Lauren in my arms. Now, every single time I kiss *you* I get to experience unquestioned love again and again. Susan, you are the woman of my dreams... the woman I never thought I'd meet... the woman who repaired my black and blue heart. Thank you so very much for being in my life. I can't wait to see what the rest of our adventure together will bring to us!"

The long applause was finally broken by the mayor. "May we see the ring?"

Isak patted down his various pockets, pretending he couldn't find it. The audience laughed politely. He pulled it out and handed it to his emotional dad. — this is a lame clichéd trope —

"Jon, please place the ring on Susan's finger and repeat after me: *With this ring I thee wed.*"

Jon did so.

Next, the mayor said, "Susan, may we see the ring?" Lauren handed Susan her ring for Jon. "Please place the ring on Jonathan's finger and repeat after me: *With this ring I thee wed.*" Susan did so.

"And now by the authority invested in me by the State of New York," Mayor Sheffield intoned, "I proudly pronounce you man and wife. Jonathan, you may kiss your beautiful bride." Jon lifted Susan's veil and they kissed.

A standing ovation greeted them. Jon turned to hug Isak, Susan hugged Lauren then the president. The newly married couple then quickly ran hand in hand down the aisle... hurtling themselves into the massive ballroom next door.

The Plaza ballroom was gorgeous, bedecked in colorful flowers from around the world. Speeches extolling the new man and wife were made, food was eaten, the cake was cut and smushed into the newlyweds' faces, and the band played joyous music for the dozens of dancing couples.

As Jon and Susan danced in the center of the floor, surrounded by their hundreds of guests, Lauren approached the couple. "Hey, Dad? Ahh, is it my imagination, or is that woman over there who I think she is?" she said.

Jon glanced over at one of the large round banquet tables and saw, sitting in the very furthest chair from him in the entire room, a woman with long, curly black hair and large, dark-rimmed glasses. "Barbara?" he said to his daughter in true amazement.

"Your second wife is here?" Susan said, stunned. "Who invited her?"

"Not me!" Jon said. "I haven't seen or spoken to her once in fifteen years."

Lauren added, "I wonder why that bitch is here."

"I suppose I should go find out," Jon replied. "Be right back."

Susan and Lauren decided to dance together, while Jon strolled over to Barbara's table. She glanced up at him and gave him a perfunctory smile. Jon sat beside her. "Hello, I guess. How've you been?" he said.

"Well, I'm not the rich and famous alien cult figure that you are," Barbara replied in her usual haughty manner. "But, all things considered, I'm doing quite well."

"May I ask who invited you?" Jon said, truly annoyed.

"I'm actually covering your wedding for the *New York Post,*" she answered. "I'm their new gossip columnist. I was credentialed as media through your publicist, Heather Burg."

"Really?" JT said. "I'm surprised she didn't tell me."

"Well, I have a new last name," Barbara answered. "I'm no longer Barbara Tuckerman... it's Gardener now. I remarried eight years ago."

"Well, good for you, I suppose," Jon said, standing. "Nice to see you again."

As he began to walk away, Barbara stood. "Oh, uhm, Jonathan, there's something we need to talk about—it's important."

That got his attention. Jon turned and sat back down. "And what might that be?" he asked, hugely annoyed.

"I want the rights to your life story—for a book I plan to write. With your new status around the world, I'm sure it will be a best-seller. I already know a great deal about you from the two years we were married, and you know I'm an excellent writer. What do you say?"

Jon was stunned. "Why would I give MY life story rights to YOU? You were a cold, distant wife to me. All we did was argue and disagree about pretty much everything. You weren't particularly kind to my children. I'm not too happy with your request, Barbara, to be honest." He stood again.

"I was hoping not to have to play the 'secrets' card with you, Jon, but I will if I have to," she added.

Jon's blood froze. He sat back down. "Would you really do that to me?" he asked.

"Jon, you are now the most famous man in the world. Do you know how much money I could make selling a story about the embarrassing sexual encounters you had as a teenager? Remember how drunk you were when you told me those deep dark secrets from your past?"

"Not really," JT said, "but I do seem to remember you swearing to me that you'd never tell anyone—ever!"

"Times have changed, my darling ex," Barbara replied. "Circumstances have changed. I truly believe I'm the logical writer to acquire your life story for a book. If you sign those rights over to me, I swear to you—on my life—I will not include your adolescent secrets within it."

Jon was stone.

"I have a contract right here," Barbara said, pulling out a thick packet of legal papers from her oversized pocketbook.

"You came to MY wedding to BLACKMAIL ME and make me SIGN a LEGAL DOCUMENT RIGHT NOW for MY LIFE STORY? Barbara, you really have some balls on you!" JT shouted, completely disgusted.

"Oh, another thing. I also want the rights to merchandise products and services based on your experience with the aliens and related to outer space, flying saucers, and all things out of this world. I figure I can make millions of dollars on those items alone, along with the royalties I'll see from 'our' book."

"You suck," Jon said, standing for the third time. "Stay here. I'll have my lawyer come work out the details with you." Jon walked away from his heinous ex-wife and approached the table where Vice President Bradley Schoenberg and his transgender daughter Cheryl were sitting.

The VP stood. "Congrats, Johnny, boy," he said, warmly shaking JT's hand. "Susan's such a great gal. I know you two will be very happy together!"

"Thanks very much, that's very kind of you," Jon said.

Turning to Cheryl, Jon said, "May I speak to you, privately, for a moment?"

"Yes, of course, Mr. Tuckerman," Cheryl said standing. The two walked away to a private corner of the room.

Cheryl Schoenberg was a highly successful, Manhattan-based business affairs attorney with a shark-like reputation, before and after the surgical transformation. Jon explained his predicament to Cheryl, including the fact that Barbara had a great deal of "extremely embarrassing, sexual information" about his past that he would do anything to avoid ever seeing the light of day. He also told Cheryl about his ex's request for his life rights for a book, and for other products and merchandise that would solely benefit a woman he could not stomach.

"You've come to the right girl," Cheryl replied. "But first, you need to pay me a dollar—my retainer fee, so I can officially be your lawyer." Jon pulled out a bill and handed it to her. She tucked it in between her cleavage. "Alright, Mr. Tuckerman, you are now my most important client. So where is this bitch from hell? I'm going to tear her a new one."

Jon pointed out Barbara.

"Don't worry. I'll get the best deal possible out of that wicked witch. Trust me," Cheryl said.

"Thank you," Jon answered. They hugged. "I appreciate your help."

As Cheryl walked over to Barbara's table, JT reapproached Susan and Lauren, who had been working up a sweat on the dance floor, having become the center of attention for all.

"What was that all about, baby?" Susan asked.

"Yeah, Dad, what did that whore want?" Lauren added.

"Just some old business that had to be taken care of," JT answered. "But it'll all work out. I'm pretty sure everything's going to be just fine. You'll see."

CHAPTER THIRTY-FIVE

Susan had loved Jorthon's idea of her and JT traveling around the world to visit ancient, alien-inspired sites during their honeymoon. Tapping into the four million dollars in gold that Jorthon had gifted him, Jon asked Meghan to set up all the five-star hotels, first class airline seats, and luxury ground transportation logistics for their five-month, multi-continent tour. While he knew, of course, that he could have requested, and likely received, complimentary accommodations from every airline and hotel on the planet, Jon did not wish to take advantage of his fame in that manner.

Jon and Susan's first stop was England, where they spent several days in the English countryside outside of Salisbury. There, they marveled at Stonehenge, the Neolithic monument that had inspired Erich von Däniken to suggest the site was a model of the solar system that also may have functioned as an alien UFO landing pad. After all, how else could those massive stones have ended up hundreds of miles from their original home quarries with the technology of the day, their tour guide posed.

From the UK, the Tuckermans flew to Delphi in Greece, a place often referred to as one of the "navels of the world." There, they saw artistic, carefully placed stone monuments depicting deities descending from the sky. Among the artifacts was a replica of the "Omphalous," a cone-shaped stone object that legend says began human life at Delphi after it fell from the sky. According to legend, two large metallic birds emerged from the stone and flew around the world, eventually deciding that Delphi was where human civilization would begin.

Derinkuyu, Turkey was next on the Tuckerman's list, where JT and Susan spent a day exploring that site's underground city carved entirely out of bedrock. There, they saw giant, disc-shaped doors that could only be closed from the inside, suggesting that there was an exterior enemy prevalent during their construction. Legend suggests that those who took refuge in this underground city were hiding from an aerial-based enemy.

From Turkey, Susan and Jon next flew to Lebanon, where they took countless photographs of the Jupiter temple and the trilithons... gigantic, megalithic blocks of stone found at the base of a large platform around the city of Baalbek. The stones were so large they dwarfed average human beings, with archeologists estimating the weight of many of those blocks at over three million pounds apiece!

Egypt was next up and, of course, Jon and Susan were thrilled to the point of tears when they were able to stand beside—and touch—the Great Pyramids of Giza. Built more than 4,500 years ago, the Pyramids at Giza are monumental tombs where ancient queens and pharaohs were buried. The structures were crafted by the perfect placement of millions of precisely hewn stones weighing at least two tons each. Jon learned from a tour guide that even using the modern technology of 2035, human beings today would be hard pressed to construct a pyramid as large. Susan was also awed by the fact that the three great pyramids were built to align perfectly with the stars in Orion's belt, legend suggesting they pointed to the faraway home of their designers.

Also in Egypt, the Tuckermans spent time at the Hathor Temple in Dendera, where a giant, stone art engraving on a wall depicted what appeared to be a light bulb. Due to the fact that no soot on the ceilings inside the temple from torches used to light the way during construction was ever found, von Däniken believed the ancient Egyptians may well have had access to electric lights.

From Egypt, JT and Susan were off to India, visiting Mahabalipuram, a magical place near the water, where many carved objects depicting Hindu mythology brought to life could be seen in the rock carvings. In those rocks, Nagas—mystical Hindu creatures—and their epic battles in the sky were featured. The artistry there brought Hindu history to life, as though the images were a picture book made of stone.

While not on Jorthon's list of sites to experience, Susan and Jon's next journey was to China, where they spent days at the Great Wall. The couple was surprised by how many Chinese natives, not to mention other tourists, were respectful of the Hero of Earth and his new bride by keeping their distance and not asking for autographs or to pose for photos.

Next on their itinerary was the very long flight from China to Easter Island in the middle of the South Pacific. Onboard their plane, Jon and Susan entered the "mile high club," making love in a tiny bathroom while two flight attendants, fully aware of their shenanigans, looked the other way. Upon arriving on the island—one of the most remote places on Earth—Jon became teary-eyed when he saw the nearly 1,000 enormous "Moai"—large stone figures depicting exaggerated human faces scattered across the landscape. According to von Däniken, the Moai represented people who had "descended from the sky." The Tuckermans learned that these stone monuments were each about thirteen feet tall and weighed fourteen tons. Their tour guide suggested that the carvings were likely sculpted for religious or ritual purposes, theorizing that the ancient civilization may have perished as the result of an environmental disaster of its own making.

Following their adventure in the South Pacific, Jon and Susan next made their way to Bolivia, South America. There, they strolled through

Puma Punku, part of a giant Bolivian site known as Tiwanaku, which offered remarkable views and included truly unique archeological finds. Remnants of gigantic monuments that stood thousands of years ago were scattered all around the site, with many of the stones weighing more than one hundred fifty tons apiece. Archeologists believed the site predated the Mayan period, and that the area was a flourishing center for pre-Columbian culture and commerce as early as 600 A.D. Under the surface of nearby Lake Titicaca, which the Tuckermans also toured, were recently discovered monolithic structures fifteen to twenty meters under the water. According to estimates, that placed the site of this early civilization between 11,700 to 10,800 B.C., making it the oldest site of a past civilization known to modern man.

A quick trip north to Peru was the next stop on the "Tuckerman Tour of Ancient Alien Artifacts." There, the couple spent days visiting Machu Picchu, a fifteenth century Inca town located atop a mountain ridge, at nearly eight thousand feet above sea level. The site included the Temple of the Sun, considered one of the Seven Wonders of the World. From there, Susan and Jon chartered a small airplane and flew over the famed Nazca lines... enormous geoglyph formations best seen from the sky that depict animals, insects, and birds, and include what many have considered airstrips for the landing of flying aircraft. Scientists have long believed the Nazca lines were more than two thousand years old, with many theories about their creation, including that they had been "drawn by aliens." Otherwise, how would an ancient culture of men been able to craft such huge designs in a desert without the ability to fly, their pilot pondered.

Other sites in Peru for Jon and Susan included Cusco, where massive stones fit together so precisely a single dollar bill could not fit between them, and a fortress called Sacsayhuaman, where terraces of giant stones, some weighing as much as 360 tons each, were chiseled and stacked together like a jigsaw puzzle.

Further north, the pair visited Teotihuacan in Mexico. The site, whose name means "City of the Gods," was a sprawling ancient city known for its pyramidal temples and astronomical alignments. Well over two thousand years old, the city was said to have housed more than a hundred thousand people and was considered to be much more technologically developed than should have been possible in the pre-Aztec era of Mexican history.

For a considerable change of scene, the Tuckermans next headed to the "Last Frontier"—Alaska—where they spent two weeks on an extensive cruise of the state's southeastern coast. They met their ship in Ketchikan, then sailed past Sitka, along Juneau and Glacier Bay, then past Valdez, Anchorage, and the Kenai Peninsula, before circumventing Kodiak Island.

As the final stop on their honeymoon tour, Susan and JT went off to Maui. With no further "alien sightseeing items" left to check off the agenda, there, in Hawaii, they were able to eat, drink, swim, sunbathe, and finally just relax.

They also made love on the world's most romantic beaches, for hours on end. —Please Aliens save us from this Horny Athor!

CHAPTER THIRTY-SIX

Upon returning to the contiguous United States, JT and Susan went first to Los Angeles to shut down his vacant apartment there, which the U.S. Government had been maintaining for him since November 2033. Susan felt sorrow for the "old Jon Tuckerman," who'd resided in that seedy, dark and depressing apartment in a questionable neighborhood for far too long.

Next, the pair went straight to the White House, as President Winfield had been regularly texting with them for months to get their latest tourist photos and gossip and telling them how much she couldn't wait for their reunion. "You two look GREAT!" the president said, delighted to see her favorite, well-tanned newlyweds back again as they sat for another of their traditional lunches. While Susan shared with the president the most recent photos of Hawaii on *her* phone, *Jon's* phone rang.

"Hello?" he answered. "What? Are you sure?" he said, now standing and clearly concerned. "How long? Alright, thanks for letting me know. Goodbye."

"Johnny, what's wrong?" Susan asked, seeing that Jon's face had gone pale.

"That was the home—where my mother is," he said, robotically. "She only has a few more hours left."

The president bolted straight up from the table. "Let's go!" she stated.

"What?" Jon said.

"We're going to visit your mother RIGHT NOW, Jon! Let's move that famous ass of yours. You're a globetrotter now. It's time to take a trip up to New Jersey. You don't have much time to spare," Winfield said.

The president made a quick phone call, grabbed something out from a drawer from the legendary 'Resolute Desk,' then led her guests through the front of the White House and into a limousine. "Airport, Mully," she ordered, "as quickly as possible."

Jon was pleased to see Mully again. It had been a while since their last encounter, and he'd always trusted the man to ensure his safety. Arriving at Obama International a short time later, the trio was driven right up to the stairs of Air Force One, the magnificent, sky-blue plane always kept at the ready for any last-minute presidential adventure.

Landing just over an hour later at Philadelphia International, the president, Jon and Susan Tuckerman, and Mully were met by another limousine, along with an escort of local area police cars and motorcycles. Mully, who now replaced the original limo driver, asked JT the name of his mother's facility.

"Manchester Gardens," JT answered.

Punching the info into his GPS, Mully replied, "Got it. We should be there within the hour."

Jon had last seen his mother in October 2030, on her 90th birthday, when he had placed her in the Manchester Gardens nursing home for the aged. At the time, his mother's Alzheimer's disease had completely erased her memory, and she was no longer able to remain living at her home with her long-time caretaker, Tina.

Now 95, Jane Tuckerman's spine had curved to the point where she had become an immobile hunchback. It had broken his heart to see his mother so deteriorated. But, as an only child living 3,000 miles away, it was all he could do to make her comfortable in a facility where she could be closely monitored—not to mention the fact that the cost of her monthly expenses had been extremely difficult for him to maintain, given his previously spectacular financial failures.

As their car pulled into the circular gravel driveway outside the facility, Jon said, "Don't expect much of anything, you guys. She's lost. She's been lost for years. She won't know you, Madam President, and she won't know me. This is going to be a very difficult experience."

Susan patted Jon's shoulder. "She's your mother, Jon," she whispered. "We've come to pay our respects and to say goodbye. Nothing more."

An excited gaggle of both male and female nurses gathered quickly inside the lobby of the building—which resembled an old hotel—when the president, Jon, Susan, and Mully walked inside. "Mr. Tuckerman! So wonderful to see you again!" shouted Mrs. Marion Cohn, Executive Director of the center. "And I see you've brought some special friends along with you!" Jon quickly shook the woman's hand, and then introduced her to the President of the United States as well as his new wife.

"Mrs. Cohn, can you please take us to Mrs. Tuckerman's room immediately?" the president requested. "Jon needs to see his mother right away."

"Of course, please follow me," the woman said, leading the world-famous trio plus their bodyguard down a series of hallways, past a cafeteria, a library and a rec room, where several white-haired men were shooting billiards. Then the four made their way down a long corridor to the very last room on the left... #57A.

"Please don't be frightened, Mr. Tuckerman," Mrs. Cohn said. "You're not going to like what you see. She won't know you're here, but perhaps somewhere deep down inside she *will sense* your presence, regardless."

The woman opened the door and Jon looked like a deer in the headlights. The president took one of his arms, Susan the other, and the three walked into the room, with Mully bringing up the rear. On a hospital bed, in the middle of the room, a small, hunched woman, curled into a fetal position, was hooked up to a number of electrical wires with a breathing tube in her nose, laying in silence. A seated male attendant who was observing Jane's heart monitor, rose when the president and her entourage entered the room. He saluted the president—she smiled back at him warmly.

Jon's face said it all... utter and complete sorrow. His mother no longer even resembled a human being. She looked more like a gnarled white pumpkin.

"Jane? Jane dear," Mrs. Cohn said, "Your son is here! Jon! Jonathan Tuckerman! I've been telling you about him, remember? He made friends with those wonderful aliens from outer space, and he's been helping people all over the world solve their problems. He's here, Janey, he's really here! Your son, the hero, has come to visit you!"

Jon stopped dead in his tracks, about three feet from the bed.

"Come on, Jon, you have to do this," Susan said, trying to drag the stubborn mule.

"She doesn't have much longer Jon," the president interjected, trying to pull him closer to the bed. "You must go make your peace with your mother right now, kid. Come on. Don't waste time."

The women let go of Jon's arms. He quietly shuffled toward his mom's deathbed, horrified at the sight. He leaned over the guardrail on the bed, kissed the old woman on her forehead, and gently patted what little silver hair she still had left on her head. "Mom? It's JT. I'm here, Mom. I came to see you."

Of course, the woman did not respond. The male attendant offered Jon his chair, which Jon pulled up next to the bed and sat. "Mom, I wish you could hear me," he whispered. "I have so much to tell you... so many incredible things have happened these last two years. It would have been so great to share them with you." He reached out and began stroking his mother's outstretched right hand, then looked up at Susan and the president. Both women were holding back tears.

Then, from out of nowhere, a loud "beeping" noise startled everyone in the room. "Jon!" Susan exclaimed. "Your necklace!"

JT looked down at his silver necklace and saw that the glass vial containing the alien metal sliver was now suspended in mid-air and glowing bright blue. It was also the source of the unfamiliar sound. Jon, Susan, the president, Mrs. Cohn, Mully, and the attendant all looked at each other in shocked silence.

"JT?" The group heard a quiet, yet clearly distinguishable elderly female voice. "Johnny, dear, is that you?" They turned to see that Jane Tuckerman, the ancient 'vegetable' of a woman, was suddenly sitting straight up, and seemed completely coherent and aware of her surroundings!

"Holy FUCK!" Jon said, shooting up out of his chair. "Mom? You can hear me?"

"Of course, I can hear you. I can see you too, JT. That's usually how it works, right?" she said, laughing. The others in the room were incredulous.

"My good God," Mrs. Cohn said to Jon. "That's the first time she's spoken since the day you brought her here!

"Johnny come closer, dear," Jane said. "I see you have the charm with you." The 95-year-old woman reached out her hand and pointed at the glowing, glass vial, still suspended in the air. "I never thought I'd see this again," she said, touching it gently. "Isn't that just something."

"Mom, you *know* what this *is*?" Jon asked.

"Yes, of course, dear. The tracker. The tracker our little friend embedded into your hand when you were inside me. Your dad told me about it."

"Mrs. Tuckerman, you remember the alien you met in 1963? You actually remember that?" the president asked, astounded.

"Why yes, of course, dear. His name was Jorthon. We named our son 'Jonathan' in his honor. Would YOU ever forget meeting an alien from outer space?" Jane replied.

Jane glanced over at Susan, her eyes growing wide. "Johnny, who is this stunning young woman?"

Susan approached the bed, "I'm Susan, Mrs. Tuckerman, Dr. Susan Parks, err, I mean Dr. Susan Tuckerman. I'm Jon's new wife. He's the love of my life."

"Mine too," Jane said. She looked over at her son and winked. "She's a keeper, JT." She smiled. "Whatever you do, be sure you don't fuck this one up!"

The president and Susan chuckled. Jon did not.

"Mom, I didn't introduce you yet to someone else. Another very important woman in my life." He took the president's arm, ushering her closer to his mom's bed. "Mom, this is Tameka Winfield. She's the President of the United States."

Jane peered deeply into the president's eyes and beamed. "Well, of course she is, Jon," the woman said proudly. "Who else could she possibly be? She's magnificent."

The president, for one of the few times in her life, began to blush.

"Mom, I need to ask you about Dad—about you and Dad. Why didn't you ever tell me about his work on Project Blue Book? Why didn't you guys let me know about Jorthon and how you saved him?"

The woman looked startled. "You've met Jorthon? Oh my, isn't that nice," she declared. "Such a lovely little fellow. How is he doing these days?"

"He's just fine, Mom—and not so little anymore," Jon answered. "He's been helping us save mankind from every imaginable problem and disaster."

"Oh, that's so nice, such a special little boy," the woman said again.

The president nodded her head at Mully, and her bodyguard pulled out from his coat pocket a long, slender, black velvet box and opened it. The president lifted the object it contained into the air. "Mrs. Jane Tuckerman," the president said as she walked over to the elderly woman's bed. "On behalf of your historic heroism in a moment of unprecedented adversity, and for your efforts to save the life of an injured creature from another land who came to Earth to benefit mankind, I would like now to bestow upon you the Presidential Medal of Freedom. Mrs. Cohn, can you please help me?"

The executive director of the facility and the President of the United States each leaned forward over opposite sides of the bed and installed the distinctly beautiful medal, held on a long, dark blue ribbon, around Jane Tuckerman's neck. Jon sat back down on his chair, speechless.

Jane touched the medal around her neck and smiled. "Well, isn't that nice. Thank you, dear." She turned to Jon and whispered, "Can you imagine, a *woman president!*"

The president and Mrs. Cohn took a few steps back from the bed. Jon stood and hugged his leader. "Thank you so much," he whispered into the president's ear. "She'll never realize what you did here today, but I'll never forget. And I'll be sure Isak and Lauren know too." President Winfield hugged her favorite hero right back.

"Johnny?" Jane called out. He returned to her bedside.

"Yes Mom?"

"Is Karen here with you? Have you found her yet?"

JT turned to look at the others in the room, making a facial expression that read, "Huh?"

"Your sister, Karen, JT," the woman continued. "Is she here too?"

"Mom, I don't have a sister," Jon answered.

"Your twin," Jane continued. "Your twin sister, Karen."

"Mom," JT said, now realizing what his mother was referencing. "My sister died at birth. Dad told me so when I was a young boy."

"No, no, no!" the woman said, becoming surprisingly agitated. "That was a lie! Just a cover story. Karen was stolen. Taken from us at the hospital just minutes after she was born."

Jane then leaned closer to Jon and stared deeply into his face. "She's STILL ALIVE, JOHNNY! I've seen her in my dreams. You must find her." Jane reached out and pulled Jon toward her. "PROMISE ME! SWEAR IT TO ME, BEFORE I DIE!"

"Alright, Mom, alright," JT agreed reluctantly. "I promise. I swear. I will find my sister. I will find Karen."

"That's a good boy, Johnny," Jane whispered and smiled. "I could always count on you... my only son. Now I can rest."

The glass vial around Jon's neck stopped glowing, and quickly fell back into its normal resting place against his upper chest.

Jane stopped talking or moving, her body re-contorting into a fetal position. The heart monitor she was attached to flatlined, making a terrible, and quite obviously final, beeping noise.

Mrs. Cohn reached over the bed, felt for a pulse, turned off the machine, and shook her head. "Mr. Tuckerman, I am so, so sorry for your loss," the woman told JT and his comrades. "She's gone."

"Rest in peace, dear, sweet Jane," the president whispered.

&

Jane Tuckerman's funeral was televised globally on November 22, 2035—which normally would have been Jon's next date aboard the Dodger Stadium Special. However, a few nights before, he'd watched a dream on his DTV system in which Jorthon spoke to him, informing him that he and Kalyssa had to return to the Pleiades interdimensional star cluster for several "Earth months." They needed to touch base at home with the Infinite Creator before "Kalyssa could begin the next chapter of her life." Jorthon conveyed to Jon that the duo would return on June 22. Jon had no idea what any of that information meant, but he knew he would miss them.

President Winfield had arranged for Jane to be buried in Arlington National Cemetery, even going so far as to have Jack Tuckerman's body exhumed from its resting place in La Jolla, California (with JT's permission, of course) so he could lay side by side with his now deceased wife, in a place of national honor and recognition. The president had also posthumously awarded Jack Tuckerman the Presidential Medal of Freedom.

The small burial service, seen by billions around the world, was attended only by JT, Susan, Isak and Lauren, plus the president, the vice president, Secretary General Kim, Meghan, Russell, Clarence, and Mully. It took place at the grave site at Arlington. After a rabbi finished chanting the "Mourner's Kaddish," the Hebrew prayer said at funerals, the president spoke.

"I only met this woman for a few minutes, just at the very end of her life," Winfield began. "From her, however, I received a feeling of warmth, of compassion, of love, all of which she clearly invested in our friend, Jonathan Tuckerman to make him the hero he's become to us all.

The actions by this woman, and her husband, Jack Robert Tuckerman, on a cold California night more than seven decades ago were unique in the history of the world. Through sheer compassion for another in trouble, these two people assisted a creature from another world—a small, injured alien being—helping him to heal and return to his own people. Had it not been for the efforts of Jane and Jack Tuckerman on that night—February 10, 1963—we may never have received the help for our nearly insurmountable problems, nor the wonderful gifts transforming our lives which have been secured for us by their son, Jonathan, through his extraordinary friends, Jorthon and Kalyssa from the Pleiades dimension."

Deeply moved, Jon, with tears streaming down his face, held hands with Susan and Lauren, while Isak, now standing behind his father, patted him on the shoulder.

"Jane, dear, we wish you peace and love and rest," the president said. "Thank you for your heroism. Thank you for your son. And thank you for your service, not only to your country, but to your planet, and to all of mankind."

The rabbi began to sing another prayer in Hebrew, "Etz Chaim Chi" ("It is a Tree of Life for Those Who Grasp It"), as JT, Susan, Isak, Lauren, and the president each took a shovel, scooped up a bit of freshly dug dirt, and gently tossed it into the open grave, atop the coffin inside. "Goodbye, Mom," JT said. "Thank you for being my mother."

With Susan on one of JT's arms and Lauren on the other, and with the president arm in arm with Isak, the five, all under Mully's protective watch, began their contemplative walk back toward their awaiting limousine.

"So, Johnny boy, what now?" the president asked. "What's next?"

"Karen," he quickly replied. "I need to look for my sister."

Jane Tuckerman's funeral fell on Jon's 72nd birthday.

- Bestie, were almost where you should be wrapping up the story not giving us side Quests

PART THREE

Tomorrow's Calling

"What Heaven Brought You and Me Cannot be Forgotten."
—Stephen Stills

CHAPTER THIRTY-SEVEN

Jon spent virtually the entire 2035/2036 holiday season in bed, deeply depressed, both by his mother's passing and the fact that he'd made a deathbed promise to her that he would find his sister who, if even alive, would now be a 72-year-old woman living only-God-knows where. The president, Isak, Lauren, and Russell did everything they could do to cheer him up, and Susan would parade around their bedroom in new, sexy lingerie. All of which had no effect on lifting his sour mood. — *That sentence gave us a sour mood!*

Even the aliens' Harmony Bud ear plugs—unfortunately and for reasons entirely unknown—made no difference in lifting JT's spirits. He was committed to being morose.

Jon told the president and Team Tuckerman that the aliens had put a "pause" on their helpful activities for a while. He had already handed the reins of 'power' at the UN to Isak, certain he would step up in his father's absence. The group continued to meet with advocates from around the world on a diverse variety of problematic topics concerning mankind, adding them to the giant whiteboard. Everyone remained hopeful the aliens would return in the near future.

"My father told me they'll be back," Isak told his colleagues at the UN. And while he honestly wasn't sure if that would indeed be the case, he meant those words sincerely when he said them.

Jon did leave the penthouse once during this time period. Clarence had arranged for a very small, intimate wedding to Meghan, to be held in a private meeting room at the UN. Jon managed to get out of bed to attend the ceremony, as Clarence had asked him to be his best man. It was only JT's extreme fondness for both of these marvelous people who had so impacted his life that not only did he make an exception of getting dressed and shaving, he even wore a suit and tie.

Clarence, aware that Jon had been "under the weather," as Susan had informed everyone, was truly thrilled he'd made the effort to attend his wedding. "I really love you, man," Clarence said, when Jon walked into the room. "I know you haven't been feeling well. It means the absolute world to me that you would show up here tonight."

"I wouldn't have missed it," Jon replied through a strained smile. "I wish you two happiness together forever."

President Winfield had also become concerned about Jon's well being. She and Susan spent that New Year's Eve at the penthouse with Jon, in his pajamas, watching the giant ball drop on TV, marking the launch of 2036. "Jon, things *are* going to pick back up for you," the president said as the trio shared a bottle of wine and ate a huge bowl of popcorn. "When I lost my mother, I couldn't talk for three weeks. I know where you're at. But we're here for you—all of us. Whatever we can do to help you, just name it."

"How am I supposed to find my so-called sister?" Jon lamented. "*Why* did I make that promise to my mother? My father told me she was dead. My mother was delusional. I'm so conflicted, I can't think."

The president hugged him. "I've been thinking about that—a lot actually," she said. "In my gut, I believe your mother must have had a reason to extract that promise from you. I'm going to do everything in my power to help you, Johnny dear," she said. "Give me a few days. You'll see."

On Monday, January 5, 2036, Russell responded to a knock on the front door of the penthouse. Two men introduced themselves, and Russell ushered them into the living room, asking them to wait there.

He knocked on the bedroom door. "Mr. Tuckerman, sir?"

"Yes, Russell?" Jon answered from bed. It was 2:00 pm.

"There are some gentlemen here to see you. Should I send them away? They are from the FBI and CIA."

This got Jon's attention and he sat up. "No, no, it's alright," he announced. "Tell them I'll be right out. Give me a minute."

Jon put on his robe and entered the living room. There he saw two men he'd never officially met, but who had been present during his very first meeting with the president just hours after the big "event" at Dodger Stadium. "Hello, Mr. Tuckerman, sir, I'm Kerry Wade," said one. "I'm the Director of the FBI."

"Nice to officially meet you, Mr. Tuckerman," said the other man. "I'm Walt Stevens, head of the CIA. May we sit down?"

"Yes, of course," Jon said. "Would you guys like something to drink?" "Coffee would be great," they said in unison.

"Be right back," Russell said.

The three men sat. "Mr. Tuckerman, the president informed us about your dilemma... the possibility that you have a twin sister, that your father told you she'd died at birth, and that your mother, on her deathbed, told you that she was still alive. That's quite a story, and we understand your concern," Stevens said.

Added Wade, "We're here to help you, Mr. Tuckerman. The president has assigned both of our departments to assist you in your search, wherever it may lead. First things first—we did find this." The man handed Jon a piece of paper.

He saw that it said "Live Birth Registration Certificate—Office of Registrar of Vital Statistics" from the Township of Neptune, County of

Monmouth, State of New Jersey. Name: Karen Lisa Tuckerman. Sex: Female. Place of Birth: Fitkin Hospital, Neptune, N.J. Date of Birth: November 22, 1963.

Said Wade, "You *did* have a twin sister, Mr. Tuckerman. In fact, we spoke to an archivist at that hospital who told us your sister was ten minutes younger than you. She *did* exist."

"But then, the intriguing part," Stevens added, "is that there was no record of her after that—zero. No police reports of her abduction. No death certificate stating that she became deceased. No ransom notes, no kidnappers' threats, no adoption papers anywhere. She quite literally just disappeared right after her birth. According to our research, both of your parents may have been correct. She may have died and it was never verified, or she may have been taken, and that was never reported either. The case of your sister Karen is a true mystery."

Jon sat back in silence. "If you had been there—if you could have seen my mom's face," he said softly, "you would've been convinced that she was right—that my sister is still alive—out there, someplace. I swore to my mother that I would find her. What am I supposed to do now?" Jon became teary-eyed.

Russell returned with coffee for the three men.

"Please take a look at this, Mr. Tuckerman," Wade said, offering him a large photograph. Jon inspected it... the photo was of a very attractive woman, clearly in her early 70s, with long dark brown hair, brown eyes, and a brilliant smile.

"We had our best FBI artist create this sketch of what your sister might look like, if she is still alive today," Wade continued. "He based this sketch on the physical characteristics of yourself, your children, and photos of your parents and crafted an amalgamated family resemblance. Based on this artist's track record of having drawn hundreds of 'wanted' posters for us over the past twenty-five years, with very successful 'capture' results, we are fairly certain that *if* your sister still exists, she might very well look something like this."

Jon stared at the photo for quite some time. "She's really beautiful, huh?" he muttered. "I wish I'd had the chance to know her during my life. She seems like a special girl—woman." He sort of smiled. "Do you think, is it even *possible,* she might still be around somewhere?" His eyes twinkled with hope.

"Mr. Tuckerman, you introduced the world to magical aliens from outer space, so clearly, in your universe, *anything* is possible," Stevens said, chuckling. "I give you my word that if your sister is alive, through the power of the CIA, the FBI, and the orders of the President of the United States, we are going to goddamn find her—if it's the last thing we ever do."

Jon stood. The two men also stood. They shook hands. "This is terrific news, thank you so very much," JT said. "I imagine you're going to send this photo out there?"

"This sketch will be routed to every media outlet, police station, federal office, post office, bank, shopping mall, grocery store, and restaurant in the United States. And we'll be reaching out to all of our international ambassadors for worldwide distribution as well," Wade said.

"Is there anything I can do?" Jon asked.

"Yes," Stevens replied. "You can appear on as many media outlets as you can, discussing your missing sister and presenting this sketch. We have established an 800 phone number and a dedicated website for any information that can help us locate Karen Tuckerman. Also, the president has posted a $150,000 reward for any information leading up to your sister's discovery... as a personal gift to you."

The next day, Jon woke up early, got dressed, and returned to the UN. He received a warm welcome from everyone, from the guards in the lobby to the passengers on the elevator to, of course, all members of Team Tuckerman. Everyone was thrilled that the Hero of Earth had returned to the civilized world.

Jon showed Isak and Lauren the sketch. "Meet your Aunt Karen," he said, mournfully.

"She's stunning, Dad," Isak said.

"She's hot! I hope she's still among the living," Lauren said. "It would be pretty cool to have another Tuckerman woman to hang out with—if we find her, of course."

JT asked his publicist Heather to set up another interview for him on the Don Rinehold show on CNN. She did so, and Jon appeared on the program the next evening.

"Mr. Tuckerman, so, so great to have you back again," Rinehold said to his special guest. "I've been meaning to thank you so much for the Second Chance Theater system. My God, I've learned so many things about myself these past months, as I'm sure my viewers at home have as well." He continued without pausing, "I understand there's a very important, very personal matter you need to tell the world about. Please take it away... the show's all yours."

Jon took a sip of water. He then held up the FBI sketch of Karen. The camera zoomed in to get a tight shot. "I need your help," JT began methodically. "To everyone out there... everyone watching this program tonight, and to your friends, and to their friends—this is a sketch of the woman who may well be my long-lost twin sister, Karen Lisa Tuckerman. I was born a twin on November 22, 1963, in Neptune, New Jersey. My sister vanished moments later and has never been seen or heard from again. My father told me she died at birth, and that's what I was led to believe my entire life. However, as many of you know, I lost my mother recently. On her deathbed, she told me that my sister was still alive. She was absolutely convinced of that fact. She made me promise I would do everything possible to find her."

Jon took another sip of water. "So, if anything I've ever done for you or your family or your friends, through my work with the aliens these past two years, has touched you or affected your life in any positive way, I'd appreciate your assistance. If you can find it in your hearts to please help me and my children locate this woman—my sister—my only sibling... I would be most grateful to you.

"Also, I should probably mention, President Winfield has kindly offered a $150,000 reward to anyone who provides solid information leading to finding Karen or her location. If you think you might know who or where this woman is today, or if you think *YOU might be* this woman, please visit www.Find_Karen_Tuckerman.com, or phone

1-800-RU-KAREN. Thank you very much, and thank you, Don, for this opportunity."

Don appeared touched and moved. "Mr. Tuckerman, for all you've done for us, for all you've contributed to our world, for all the good deeds you've helped us achieve, you are certainly deserving of an answer here." He turned and spoke straight to the camera. "To my audience in the U.S. and around the world, you've just heard a plea from our Wonder Man. He needs our help. Every one of you now has the opportunity to pay something back to Mr. Tuckerman. I urge all of you to do your best, put on your detective goggles, and try to find this long lost woman. Let's give this remarkable story a happy ending. We'll be right back after this commercial break."

Jon Tuckerman's appearance on the Don Rinehold show was replayed the next day on CNN and virtually every other major news broadcast in America. The FBI had disseminated the sketch of "Karen Tuckerman" across the USA, while the CIA enlisted the help of UN-based ambassadors and the heads of intelligence units from dozens of other governments around the world in coordinating a global search for this important, long-missing woman.

Over the coming days, Jon became more uplifted and upbeat than he'd been in a very long while. With the ongoing encouragement of his family, Russell, Meghan, Clarence, and the President of the United States, he was convinced that, at some point in the very near future, he would be getting a definitive answer about the status of Karen Lisa Tuckerman—one way or another.

Following the Don Rinehold broadcast and the distribution of the FBI's sketch, over 227,000 women across the United States responded to the plea, either by calling in or submitting their information through the website. While most of these "applicants" came in from the Eastern portion of the country, many others were scattered across the South, the Midwest, and along the West Coast.

The FBI had set up dozens of DNA testing sites coast to coast to handle the influx of would-be "Tuckerman sisters," with the media reporting long lines of women waiting patiently for their turns at those field offices. Jon and Susan often watched the TV news for updates, but at the end of each day, FBI Director Wade would phone them to say "sorry, nothing yet."

JT felt confident that the FBI had the situation well in hand in America. However, he was less assured that the search for Karen was being handled as aggressively as it could be internationally. He discussed this with CIA Director Stevens, who suggested perhaps Jon take a global tour of major media markets. That way, he could make personal pleas for help on the top television shows around the world. JT thought this was a solid plan and asked his son if he would accompany him on such an undertaking. Isak readily agreed.

Vice President Schoenberg, eternally grateful to Jon for his help in eliminating sexual gender bias against his daughter, Cheryl, volunteered Air Force Two to fly JT and Isak to as many far off lands as they deemed necessary. "If *my* sister was missing," the VP told Jon, "there would be nothing stopping me from finding her either. Best of luck to you."

Susan and Lauren accompanied Jon and Isak to the airport, for the start of their international "Must Find Karen Tuckerman" Tour. President Winfield had assigned Mully to travel along with the men as their personal protector and bodyguard. As the five approached the beautiful, sky-blue airplane, Susan said, "Before you guys take off, I have an announcement to make." Lauren smiled, having already been informed of the upcoming surprise. Susan looked at Jon. "Love, I'm pregnant! Twins! What were the odds on that?"

Jon was, of course, shocked but not completely surprised. "But, how?" he asked rather foolishly.

"Ah, Dad, you know that's what happens when you screw without protection, right?" Lauren joked.

Isak chuckled.

Susan beamed. "Hawaii, Johnny," she replied. "Maui. I'm pretty sure it happened in Maui."

CHAPTER THIRTY-EIGHT

Meghan and Team Tuckerman had arranged for JT and Isak to speak on top television news programs in thirty-four countries over the course of the next three months, with Mully accompanying the men everywhere to ensure their safety. All the logical cities were included on the itinerary: London, Paris, Madrid, Rome, Hamburg, and Moscow, of course, along with other stops including cities in Poland, Greece, Turkey, Iraq, Egypt, Libya, South Africa, India, China, South Korea, Australia, Peru, Brazil, Argentina, Venezuela, Mexico City, Vancouver, Montreal, and winding up in Toronto. Then back to New York.

While Jon was apprehensive about leaving Susan behind, she had reassured him that all would be well. "I'm a doctor, Johnny," she reminded him. "And it's early. I have a staff full of other great doctors. I'll be just fine. You go out there and find your sister. That's the only thing you need to worry about right now."

After JT and Isak kissed Lauren and Susan goodbye, Mully escorted the Tuckerman men onto the vice presidential plane. Jon turned back to look into Susan's eyes. He felt her overwhelming love... an honor he wasn't sure he really deserved.

∞

While Jon, Isak, and Mully were busy traveling abroad, a great number of developments were taking place back in the USA. First, Susan gave Heather Burg permission to announce the pregnancy via press release. News of the impending joy was reported by countless media outlets around the world.

As JT's lawyer, Cheryl Schoenberg held a "Come to Jesus" meeting with Jon's ex-wife, Barbara, having negotiated far more favorable terms with her than JT had been expecting. (Cheryl had cleverly employed a private investigator to dig up some juicy dirt on Barbara, which helped level the playing field.) In exchange for the full rights to Jon Tuckerman's life story, and endorsements of no more than twelve "products or services" that would be "alien" or "flying saucer" or "outer space" themed, Barbara agreed that half of all profits from her proposed book and the merchandise she planned to get into the marketplace would go to the Jonathan Michael Tuckerman Family Trust. Cheryl had also updated the Trust so that it made provisions for any of JT's and Susan's as yet unborn children as well.

With the ink barely dry on the deal, Barbara began her book research by requesting interviews with Lauren, Meghan, and Clarence. "The woman's a fucking pig," Lauren lamented to Cheryl over the phone. "I want nothing to do with her."

"Unfortunately," the lawyer responded, "your father needs you to cooperate here. This 'pig' has some dirt on your dad he does not want her to reveal. If you love him as much as I know you do, you'll do your best to suck it up."

"Yeah, okay, I understand," Lauren replied, none too happy about the fucked position she'd been placed in.

Barbara was relentless in seeking to interview virtually anyone and everyone who'd ever known Jonathan Michael Tuckerman. She tracked down his earliest childhood friends, Cathy, Lizzie, and Ronnie; his fellow high school band mates in "Eclipse;" Brad, his best friend from college; his former co-workers and employees at Tanner & Tuckerman along with the late Tanner's relatives; past clients; and so on.

She interviewed Secretary Kim and each member of Team Tuckerman, and spent two painfully long evenings with Susan and Russell at the penthouse (with Susan also having to "suck it up" for the sake of her beloved Jon). Barbara also managed to wrangle long talks with Mrs. Cohn in New Jersey, and even President Winfield who, well aware of Barbara's threats and Jon's distain of her, cooperated fully, hiding her repulsion.

Of course, no book of JT's life would be complete without interviews with the man himself and his son Isak. Barbara knew, of course, that those sessions would have to wait until the men returned from their global search for Jon's lost sister.

Concurrent with her book research, Barbara quickly managed to introduce a number of "flying saucer" toys and board games to the general public, having earlier befriended several major novelty manufacturers following JT's initial burst into fame. (Barbara's plan had long been in the works.) The first toys and games that hit store shelves across America sold out quickly. The general public neither knew about her blackmail scheme, nor would have likely cared had they known. The novelties, which all featured photos of Jon with Jorthon and Kalyssa from the Dodger Stadium Event (with Jon's exposed genitals obscured), ensured that they would all become highly profitable.

☙

President Winfield and Secretary General Kim were having lunch one day at the UN when the secretary said, "I wish there was some other way we could honor Mr. Tuckerman's heroism... some permanent 'mark' we could make so that future generations will come to know and remember that this man really did once live on the Earth, interacted with alien creatures from an advanced race, and through his noble efforts, helped make a permanent, global impact to better all of mankind."

A lightbulb apparently went off in the president's head. "I've got it!" she replied. "What if we changed the 'A.D.' on our calendars? What if 2036 A.D. became a new number with a new eponym?" Kim shot back an equally quick response: "A.T.C.... After They Came! They've been here for three years now. What if we changed *this* year to the *new* year of '3 A.T.C.'?"

"Fabulous, I love that," the president responded. "But how can we make a request of this magnitude to every country on the planet?"

"Let's introduce a joint proposal at the next UN General Assembly meeting," Kim said. "Let's make this suggestion to the world together."

"Yes," the president said. "Let's see if we can give life to this fantastic idea."

During the General Assembly gathering that Friday, the President of the United States and the Secretary General of the United Nations made a joint pitch to every country in the world about changing "A.D" to "A.T.C.," in honor of Jonathan Michael Tuckerman and the aliens that worked through him to better the plight of the human race. The idea was adopted on a voluntary basis, with 177 countries voting "yes" and only sixteen voting "no." For all concerned, the plan was to continue using both monikers, the current A.D. attribution for calendar years along with the new A.T.C. moniker, for the next five years until such time as the general public could make the final determination which designation they preferred.

It was also decided that on November 22, 2036, the Third Year Anniversary of the public arrival of Jorthon and Kalyssa to Planet Earth, "A.T.C." would make its first official appearance.

Meanwhile, the mayor and city council of Malibu, California, had acquired possession of Jon's old car and the discarded clothing, suicide note, and empty vodka and pill bottles he'd left on the beach the night of November 22, 2033. Upon unanimous vote by the city, the entire area of the bluff and the beach where Jon had attempted to drown himself on his 70th birthday—the same site where the aliens had come to save his life—had been cordoned off with permanent barriers. People from around the world now came to pay $5 apiece to spend a few minutes looking at this now historic location and to read the "unsuccessful" suicide note—now mounted on a plaque—he'd left behind there. The site drew the morbidly curious—as had been the case with the balcony in Ford's Theatre where President Lincoln was shot in 1865 and Dealey Plaza in Dallas, Texas where JFK was assassinated—with each site long drawing a crowd of history buffs to the present day.

୧୬

A truly unanticipated development took root in various countries around the world during Jon and Isak's "Seeking Karen Tuckerman" adventures. A surprising number of new "religions" sprang up, initiated and launched by charismatic local leaders who felt that proof of the existence of extra-terrestrial life had convinced them that what all of mankind felt they "knew about God" was wrong and incomplete. ~Here comes the ~Focults!

Since the initial appearance of Jorthon and Kalyssa and their enormous airship, the fantastic notion of God as an "old man with a long white beard sitting on a chair in Heaven" was becoming more and more disparaged. Young people felt the traditional "hand-me-down" religions they'd inherited from their parents were no longer valid or meaningful. While the leaders of these new "cults" were well-aware, by Kalyssa's own global announcement, that the two aliens themselves were "not Gods," these leaders nevertheless informed their followers to begin praying to the "God-like beings from the interdimensional Pleiades Star System" who, they felt, were far more "God like" in the modern age than any other entity that had come before.

TV news shows, newspapers, magazines and radio programs, podcasts, bloggers, and holographic content providers around the world began to cover reports of these new cults of people, worshipping Jorthon, Kalyssa, and sometimes even Jonathan, as "New Gods," crafted by their own imaginations, needs, and purposes.

Virtually every one of the chapels, homes, hotel rooms, and other meeting venues where these congregations were gathering to pray posted various photographs of Jon Tuckerman, his family, and "his aliens" on their walls and pulpits, and as standing artworks on easels.

Clearly "no God," JT—as mankind's "conduit" to extra-terrestrial life—surely must have an inside track to the Almighty Infinite Creator himself, many believed.

By praying to (and for) Jon, Jorthon and Kalyssa, members of these new cults were hoping to ensure that the Infinite Creator might "bless" their everyday lives with His miracles and wonders as well.

CHAPTER THIRTY-NINE

As they hopped around the world in search of Karen, Jon and Isak were treated as royalty wherever they went. Not surprisingly, the reactions to JT's personal appearances at top TV news stations brought out thousands upon thousands of people who stood in line in the snow, the rain, the blistering wind, just hoping for a glimpse of the Wonder Man in person... even from afar. Team Tuckerman had arranged for those TV stations to work with local area medical clinics to set up DNA testing sites nearby, so that women believing they may, themselves, "be" Karen Tuckerman could get tested. Jon and Isak, following their pleas on television and showing the FBI sketch, would then make their way to those testing centers in hopes of somehow stumbling into "Karen."

JT was besieged by autograph seekers and those who wished to take selfie photos with him and his son. It was the last thing on earth Jon wanted to do, but he usually obliged silently. Isak was far more personable and charming.

"Dad, we're famous, it's part of the job," Isak would joke to his father over and over again. But fame was never something the Hero of Earth had ever sought or desired. He simply wished he could be at home making love to his beautiful wife, eating Russell's amazing dishes, and relaxing, instead of fulfilling the dopey promise he'd made to his mother on her deathbed.

It wasn't all torture for Jon, though. He, Isak, and their ever-faithful bodyguard Mully were treated to first class flights, five-star hotels, room service, incredible meals, stretch limousines, and every other amenity fit to pamper the most important and legendary man on the planet. The food was so luscious—and plentiful—in fact, all three men gained about ten pounds each during their trip abroad.

The tour was not without its "moments"—both hilarious and nerve-racking, for sure. In Paris, a group of twelve women stood topless outside Jon's hotel with the words "WE ARE KAREN TUCKERMAN" painted in red across their bare bosoms. In Rome, police had to erect dozens of barricades to keep protestors—people who had never forgiven JT for allowing the aliens to eliminate nuclear weapons—from getting too close to the Tuckermans while they traveled within the city limits. When they appeared on Russian television, Jon and Isak were surprised by the appearance of the country's president, who, unexpectedly, joined them on the news to make his own, impassioned plea for his people to help the men find Karen. The big bear of a man hugged JT before the broadcast ended.

Elsewhere around the world, similar events took place. In Cairo, 115,000 women stood in line at the DNA testing site... one of the larger such international crowds. In South Africa, musicians banded together to perform a "Let's Find Karen Tuckerman" concert in Soccer City Stadium, at which Jon and Isak were special guests. The crowd of nearly 95,000, sang, danced, and cheered when they first saw JT walk onto the stage.

In Beijing and Shanghai, China, Jon and his son were embraced by the local militaries with parades in their honor and government officials having invited the men to wine and dine with them in splendor at their most elaborate, government-run venues. Residents of Sydney, Australia, also presented the Tuckermans with a special concert by The Kings, the hottest rock band in their nation, at the Sydney Opera House. The 6,000 available tickets—with all proceeds dedicated to UNICEF—sold out within minutes!

In Buenos Aires, three extremely attractive women managed to make their way into JT's hotel suite, surprising him—naked—in his bed when he got back from the TV news station broadcast. In similar fashion, a number of muscular, clean-shaven, well-tanned men were making sexual overtures to Isak—several blatantly propositioning him at the hotel bar and even at the DNA testing clinics.

While both of the Tuckerman men were highly flattered (and even, on occasion, slightly tempted to "partake"), they each politely declined the offers of groupie sex. It was the last thing on JT's mind, and Isak, who regularly communicated with Harold back in Iceland, knew better than to tempt the fates by tasting any of the forbidden fruits that were now so freely staring him in the face. Mully, however, who was single, often took advantage of his unique status as bodyguard to the world's most famous man. A smile rarely left his face!

Jon's luck took an unexpected, and very shitty turn, however, when he, Isak, and Mully were feted by the president of Bulgaria in Sofia City Province. The president and his fellow elected officials presented a massive, ornate banquet for the men, and everyone ate, drank, and danced for many hours. Later that night, however, while Jon was sound asleep in his room at the InterContinental Sofia Hotel, a trio of men in dark clothing managed to slip into his suite, drugging Isak and Mully so they would fall into a deep slumber. The men then burst into JT's room, scaring him nearly to death, and hurled him onto the floor. Two men bound his hands behind his back, gagged his mouth, and blindfolded him, while the third man accidentally broke the clasp on Jon's famous necklace—Jorthon's tracking device—which dropped to the floor without notice.

The kidnappers lifted Jon by his elbows and raced down the hotel's corridor into an awaiting service elevator. Jon's heart was pounding so hard he could barely breathe. A million thoughts raced through his brain: "Who are these people? What do they want with me? Is this my death? Don't they know I'm the 'Hero of Earth'?"

Seconds later, Jon found himself outside in a dark alley behind the hotel's parking lot. From nowhere, a massive deep-purple-colored flying V spacecraft appeared in the night sky, directly overhead. While Jon, still blindfolded, could not see the great ship above, he could feel its ethereal presence and began to shudder—his skin raising goosebumps from head to toe.

A dark grey colored beam of light shot out of the craft's belly and lifted Jon off his feet and swiftly through the air of the very chilly night. The kidnappers beamed at their great accomplishment and applauded themselves once the spaceship had successfully elevated Tuckerman onboard. Then it just vanished.

In a mere timespan of six minutes, Jon Tuckerman had gone from fast asleep global iconic hero to an inter-galactic abductee and "missing person."

The next few days of Jon's life, while never fully revealed to the members of Earth at large, would merely add to his already unprecedented story.

CHAPTER FORTY

Before anyone learned of Jon's kidnapping, life for members of the Tuckerman family continued as usual in New York. When she wasn't busy with her medical practice, or shopping for baby clothes with her mother and Lauren at the trendiest of Manhattan's stores, Susan kept a close eye on the FBI's progress with the DNA testing across America. She spoke with Director Wade daily and was continually frustrated by his lack of results.

Back at the UN, Lauren, Clarence, and Meghan were keeping the Team Tuckerman fires alive, but on a very low flame. With her father and brother gone, and Jorthon and Kalyssa on "hiatus," the trio pared down their staff to a skeleton crew. Of course, there was always an unending river of cards, letters, telegrams, and emails arriving for Jon. The new influx of messages were coming from well-wishers around the world who wanted to tell him they were praying for him to find his vanished sister.

"For all you've given," a letter from an eighty-two-year-old woman in Kansas said, "you should receive back in kind. Give your sister a warm hug from me when you find her," she wrote.

With the world at peace, anger and discrimination at bay, hunger and thirst sated, and global warming quickly dissipating, President Winfield and Vice President Schoenberg turned their attention to more grassroots level matters. They toured every one of the fifty states, meeting with residents in the most populated areas and listening to their ideas about how to improve their local governments and living conditions. Citizens were also conveying to the two American leaders how grateful they were to be living in a time when "the future met the present."

The president and VP also quite often appeared on local television news programs as well, summarizing what they'd learned during their meetings with the locals, as well as reminding everyone that "Karen Tuckerman is still out there—somewhere. Surely *one* of you must know something! Please help us find her," the president urged each member of her viewing audiences.

Lauren, who'd been an artist her entire life, would now spend hours a day at her desk at the UN simply drawing and doodling various figures on her sketchpad—people, animals, cartoon characters, flying saucers— as the phones were ringing less often and the whiteboard had been momentarily "retired."

One day while sitting there, Lauren reread the very first *New York Times* article about the Dodger Stadium Event. The paper included a giant cover photograph of her father "floating" between Jorthon and Kalyssa. Standing up to sharpen her colored pencils, Lauren accidentally knocked over her mug and spilled some coffee onto the photograph. She turned and glanced over her shoulder at the now brown-stained image and made a face registering utter surprise.

Lauren then walked over to her father's desk, retrieved the old black and white photograph of her dad and her Grandma Jane together, and walked it back to her own desk. She picked up a dark brown colored pencil and began to draw something.

"Oh my dear fucking good God!" she gasped. "I can NOT fucking believe it!"

CHAPTER FORTY-ONE

Jorthon and Kalyssa had returned to their home in the Pleiades interdimensional star system just after JT's dream about them a few weeks previous. They'd parked the Dodger Stadium Special in its port, next to thousands of other ships of equal size and structure. The aliens had been called home by the Infinite Creator, as He'd wanted to meet with all of his children within Pleiades to discuss an important, upcoming series of events.

The Pleiades interdimensional planet was a visually wondrous place, with tall vast structures comprised of platinum, copper, diamonds, rubies, and glass, reflecting the sunlight of its two stars in vibrant colors. The flora on the planet appeared as floating flowers, gently wafting through the air in circles above the thousands of residential constructions. Office and governmental buildings appeared less "flashy," primarily towering as miles-high, stick-straight arrows piercing the sky, their tips becoming lost in the clouds.

Millions of Pleiadians had gathered from around the universe for this unique meeting, which was held under "The Dome," a fifty mile wide, open-topped, clear glass, semi-circular construct located in the middle of Kalnar, the central city of the Pleiadian civilization. While the Infinite Creator had directly spoken to Jorthon just three times during his lifetime, Kalyssa had not yet received that same honor. She was a bit nervous about this unprecedented meeting and, judging by the looks on the faces of her fellows also assembled there, realized quickly that something truly extraordinary was about to happen.

"My children of the Pleiades," the commanding, booming voice of the Infinite Creator shook The Dome. "It is wonderful, of course, to see all of you again, gathered here in the same place at the same time. As you know, I have been aware of all of your activities at all times, and I am so very pleased to say that I am proud of you and your accomplishments across my galaxy. The work that each and every one of you has done—and continues to do—on a daily basis warms my heart and continues to inspire me."

"Unfortunately," the Creator continued, "my humans on Planet Earth are soon to enter into a new age. The Alpha Draconians I delivered into the universe millennia ago have evolved to a point of military achievement that I neither foresaw nor wish to allow. They have become evil, in every sense of that word, showing no mercy, no compassion, no love for their fellow beings from other planets and dimensions."

"Kalyssa," the Great Voice boomed. "Your work on the Earth will soon become invaluable."

The look on Kalyssa's face was one of pure amazement... the Infinite Creator was speaking directly to her!

"You and Jorthon have done tremendous work in correcting mankind's mistakes there. I've been so very pleased by your progress. As you know, when Jorthon was young and observing humans for the first time, he had an unforeseen incident which necessitated the aid of human interaction—something that had never occurred previously. As many others of you do NOT know, Jorthon promised two humans that he would protect their son as an offering of thanks. You, Kalyssa, have long been part of that arrangement."

"Yes, I do know that, Great One," Kalyssa replied respectively.

"The Draconians have their minds set on disrupting Planet Earth's newly enjoyed homeostasis. In the near future, they plan to reveal their combat vessels from their various 'hiding places' so as to interfere with the significant accomplishments you and Jorthon have set in place. However, their actions will not be bold or obvious at first. A group of their military leaders have long been seeding themselves on Earth, in disguise as humans, to begin laying a foundation for human disharmony and chaos. Once they feel ready for further action, they will call for a full-out airborne attack by their troops from the sky.

Kalyssa, in a short span of time, I am going to ask you to live among the humans on Earth as though one of them. Your assignment will be to discover as many Draconians in human disguise as you are able, and then to 'tag' them. Speak with Euclid for more instructions on this. Your father, Jorthon, will concurrently assemble a fleet of vessels that will regularly patrol the skies just above Earth—just beyond sight of man.

As these Draconians are detected and identified, you, Kalyssa, will alert Jorthon and his team to their locations. Jorthon, you and your comrades will work quickly to extract these threats, beaming them up from the ground and onto your ships. You and your team will then bring those terrible creatures to me, so I may deal with them for punishment."

"Yes, of course, Great One," Jorthon responded.

"To the rest of you, I will convey my further instructions quite soon," the Infinite Creator continued. "The Draconians are making plans to dominate many other inhabited realms as well. I will need all of you in this effort to diminish their threat... hostilities I do not condone and wish to prevent from ever taking hold."

When the booming voice ended, the Pleiadians began to scatter.

*

So strong had been the drugs they were given, Isak and Mully didn't awake for a dozen hours after Jon's abduction. When the men realized JT was gone without a trace, Mully first called Bulgaria's President Radov Rumanski to inform him that his country had betrayed the great trust of the United States and that he would hold Rumanski personally responsible for this greatest of horrors.

While Mully was talking with Rumanski, Isak first phoned President Winfrey, and secondly Susan, who nearly fainted. During the conference call, the president reassured Jon's wife and son that "the Government of the United States of America, and I, personally, will do everything in our power to retrieve Jonathan, no matter what!"

In the meantime, Jonathan Michael Tuckerman had been stripped naked, tied to a bizarre looking light table, and denied food and water. He was surrounded by a truly hideous looking group of aliens resembling tall, slightly-hunched human-dinosaur hybrids. The leader, a heinous creature called Larpeen, was the only one who communicated— telepathically—with Jon.

Finally aware of his surroundings, Jon screamed, "Who are you people? Why am I here?" His body ached from the lack of nourishment and his tightly bound limbs. "Don't you know who I am? I have friends in very high places, by the way, you should know!"

"Yes, of course we know of the Wonder Man, Jonathan Tuckerman, Earth's Hero," Larpeen replied, snorting sarcastically while telepathically shooting his words deep into JT's cochlea. "You are the false prophet of mankind who was befriended by the Creator's Chosen One. But we both know you are truly nothing... a pissant. An insect who achieved glory through no words or deeds of his own. Merely the object of affection for he who we truly seek."

Jon was puzzled for a minute by this remark, finally realizing its implications. "Jorthon?" JT asked. "You want Jorthon? Why? What did he ever do to you?"

"Your friend Jorthon is my Great-Great-Great-Great-Great-Grandson," Larpeen answered, shocking Jon to his core. "He became the favorite of the Infinite Creator upon his birth and has never been informed of his true Draconian heritage. The Creator became displeased with my race a hundred thousand Earth years ago and worked to *redesign* His people so as to appear more to His liking. Thus, the Tall Whites.

My Draconian heritage, and the heritage of my people, displeased the Creator, and caused Him to banish us from his grace. We have been left alone to fend for ourselves these many millennia—with those of us who remain on your Planet Earth hiding deep within undersea caverns. But now that Jorthon has entered into the sphere of Earth, it is he who I must lure to this ship. I have no need for *you,* Tuckerman. It is Jorthon alone who I must confront, face to face."

Jon looked down onto his chest and realized, for the first time since his kidnapping, that he no longer had his interstellar tracking necklace. "I have no means of contacting Jorthon," JT said to the frightening Larpeen. "Your henchmen lost my tracking device. You've taken me for no apparent reason and no apparent gain."

"We have no need of your device," Larpeen snarled into Jon's ear. "We have a different plan. I'm sure the pleas of your United States President will have the ability to draw the elusive Tall White out of his hiding place."

"President Winfield?" Jon replied. "She would do anything to protect him—and me. She won't help you, you fucking scumbag."

"I suppose we shall see about that!" Larpeen countered with an evil leer and another truly obnoxious snort.

On the third day after Jon's abduction, President Winfield got a phone call she would never forget. A drone-like, mechanical voice gave her the following message, devoid of any inflection, emotion, or passion:

"If you wish to retrieve your 'Wonder Man' Tuckerman, you will send an urgent plea to the Tall White Jorthon. You must send the Tall White to rescue him. He and no other. Tell him Tuckerman is on our ship—the coordinates are Latitude 43.413029; Longitude: 34.299316; DMS Lat.

43-degrees, 24-minutes, 46.9044 seconds N; DMS Long 34-degrees 17 minutes, 57.5376 seconds E; UTM Easting 605,193.50; UTM Northing 4,807,502.42; Depth: 2,212 meters.

Drop no bombs, send no ships, gather no armies. Jorthon alone must attend to the gathering of your precious little Tuckerman. Anyone else will doom him to a painful, tortured death."

The President of the United States hurriedly scribbled down the data, her chest heaving deeply, her writing hand shaking, a few droplets of sweat trickling down her forehead. When the call ended, she hung up with a thud and screamed out to her secretary in the adjacent room, "Get me my Cabinet... NOW!!!"

"The Black Sea," announced Secretary of Defense Romano. "The coordinates you were given are the bottom of the Black Sea, Madam President."

It was the consensus of the U.S. Cabinet that the president should follow the kidnapper's demands "to the letter." It was then agreed upon that she should deliver a national address on television but disguise the message so as not to inform the globe that the Wonder Man was missing and inadvertently cause widespread panic. Her very delicate talk would gently reach out to Jorthon in a non-threatening quest to secure his aid.

That evening, President Tameka Winfield presented a primetime address on American television broadcast live from the White House. "My fellow Americans," she began, hiding her discomfort. "This has been a great season of change for us all. A time of new beginnings. Our wonderful friends from the Pleiades, Jorthon and Kalyssa, have ushered in the next chapter of human history through their wondrous efforts and technologies, while working hand in hand with our own 'Wonder Man,' Jon Tuckerman."

The president paused. The camera zoomed into her face. "Jorthon," President Winfield said calmly, now looking directly into the lens. "I have a personal matter I am in a great hurry to discuss with you." She paused again. "I'm not sure if you 'watch' American television or if this message will even reach you, but, again, I have a VERY important personal matter that I simply MUST discuss with you in person. And soon, please. Please. As soon as possible, in fact!"

Winfield paused again, taking a sip of water. "Forgive me if I am speaking out of turn, Jorthon, as I know you have clearly stated that you would only work through Mr. Tuckerman. But I am facing a personal dilemma, and I truly need your help to resolve this matter. So if you somehow hear this message and have the ability, please contact me at the White House at any hour, day or night. I will be most appreciative of your response to this urgent matter!"

One final pause, then the president again looked into the camera. "Separately—to my fellow citizens—I wish you all the best of everything as we move further into our new future together. I remain eternally grateful to have been your president through this new era. Good night and may God bless the United States of America."

CHAPTER FORTY-TWO

It was 3:15 am the morning after the president's broadcast when the Dodger Stadium Special suddenly appeared above the White House, bathing the iconic building in an intense beam of soft white-blue light.

Seven secret service men raced into President Winfield's bedroom to find Jorthon, also bathed in the same bright light, suspended a few feet from the floor. Instead of his usual calm, beatific face, however, he seemed a bit perturbed.

Tameka Winfield bolted upright in bed. "Jorthon! Oh my God! It's really you! You heard my plea?"

"Yes, Madame American President, I apologize for my delay. I have been distracted by an urgent new instruction from the Great Creator on Pleiades and have been 'out of touch' as you might say as to the newest developments on Earth. One of my fellows who was traversing your solar system happened upon your message and relayed it to me. I assume this concerns Jonathan?"

Winfield turned to her left side and retrieved a piece of paper laying on her nightstand. "Yes," she said, pointing to the note. "Jon's been taken—kidnapped apparently—and I was told that you are the only one who has permission to retrieve him. These are the coordinates where he is located, I believe." She handed the paper to Jorthon.

He took a quick glance. "The bottom of the Black Sea. Interesting. I believe I might know what this means…"

The president stood before the Tall White. "Can you do it? Can you bring him back to me? To us?"

Jorthon's face changed from annoyance to true concern. "I made a vow to his parents that I would always protect him. So protect him now, I must. And I will."

The bright beam of light suddenly disappeared, and Jorthon, along with his great airship, vanished into the night sky.

Less than two minutes later, Jorthon's massive ship was hovering above the dead-center point of the Black Sea. The same white-blue light appeared once more, and Jorthon beamed himself down into the dark waters below.

Jonathan, still tied to the disgusting light table, was momentarily blinded by Jorthon's dramatic appearance inside Larpeen's demonic vessel.

"Aha! The Great Jorthon! You've arrived at last!" the horrific Draconian leader shouted in glee.

Jorthon glided over to Jonathan and said, "I'm sorry, dear friend. This is something that should never have taken place. I was attending to some urgent business at my home and neglected to keep my vigil for your safety. I hope you can forgive me."

"This is SO not your fault, Jorthon," JT answered. "This prick over here used me to lure you inside this ship. I was hoping you would have stayed away. I could never stomach it if any harm every came to you!"

Jorthon silently untied Jonathan's bonds and JT hopped off the table. He was now standing upright, naked, teeth chattering.

"This is no way to treat my friend," Jorthon said to his new opponent. "And who are you, by the way?"

Larpeen leaned against a side wall of his ship. "My name is Larpeen. I am the leader of a long-scattered civilization that once ruled this small planet. We are called 'Draconians.' I am 10,000 years old, Jorthon, and in fact, I am your great-great-great-great-great-grandfather."

Jorthon was truly surprised. "Why am I first learning of you now?"

Larpeen continued, "The Great Creator designed my people long ago to first shepherd order on this Earth when the large beasts known as 'dinosaurs' roamed this planet freely. But over eons of time, He abandoned us. We had to fend for ourselves by building up our own power. Wars among factions of my brothers broke out across the continents. The Creator became displeased and scattered my kind across the galaxy, leaving very few of us still here on Earth to lurk in deep underwater hiding places. It has taken me several millennia to regroup and regain contact with my people who remain.

My dream today is to restore our original mandate," Larpeen droned on. "We Draconians were originally meant to oversee weak humans. But when we learned that you had come to Earth to play games with this 'Tuckerman insect,' I knew my time was getting closer to make my presence known. I cannot allow you and your Tall Whites to ruin my perfectly beautiful plan for chaos and neglect, bloodshed and ruin."

Jorthon placed his hands on Jonathan's shoulders and closed his eyes. A second later, the white-blue beam of light reappeared, and JT was lifted skyward. He appeared back inside the Dodger Stadium Special, collapsing to the floor. A loving Kalyssa covered him with a blanket and gently lifted him upon the nurturing light table—the same surface that had brought JT back to life after his suicide attempt.

JT looked into Kalyssa's face: "Jorthon! Is he here?"

"Not yet," she responded. "We must continue to wait."

With the release of JT, Jorthon understood his sole focus now was to confront Larpeen. "The Infinite Creator, the Father to us all, is greatly concerned about your kind," the Tall White explained to his new foe.

"Regardless of our shared ancestry, I have come to Earth to aid mankind in his forward momentum per the Creator's request. To teach and use our technology to evolve these simple beings into the future, so that love, compassion, warmth, and kindness are the order of the day. Your plans for Earthlings do NOT coincide with the Creator's wishes, Larpeen," Jorthon said. "I must inform Him of your plans. My people and I will do whatever it takes to thwart your negative efforts."

Larpeen lifted a small device resembling a "Second Chance Theatre" projector from a shelf and handed it to Jorthon. "Here, you must learn from whence we came. You must realize how your beloved 'Infinite Creator' treated his earliest creations. Watch this."

Jorthon held the device in his hands and was shown a series of truly horrific scenes: Dozens of Draconians fleeing for their lives, running from a stampede of T-Rex dinosaurs clearly intent on eating them; volcanic eruptions pouring massive quantities of molten lava down mountainsides, destroying the makeshift, tent-like homes of Larpeen and his fellow citizens; tidal waves crashing onto beachfronts, drowning thousands of Draconians in a horrible fashion; frigid snowstorms burying Larpeen and his followers inside twelve-foot-high snowdrifts. Each scene Jorthon saw depicted extraordinary cruelty and hardship for the entire Draconian Race on ancient Earth.

Jorthon knew, from just moments of watching these terrible "home movies" that Larpeen had indeed proven his point. The Infinite Creator had, in fact, neglected and forsaken his "mistake" of a race, without mercy.

When the "movies" ended, Jorthon said, "This history was not taught to us."

"Well, maybe this will teach you now!" With this pronouncement, Larpeen opened his mouth wide and sprayed Jorthon's face. With a terrible "hissing" noise, a thick, dark yellow substance shot out of the Draconian's mouth and into Jorthon's eyes, blinding him.

"As YOUR people have become blind to the plight of mine, so shall YOU yourself now become EQUALLY BLIND!"

Jorthon stumbled a bit, reaching his hand to his eyes and covering them with his palm. Then he stood perfectly still and meditated for a moment. Quickly, a bright, white-blue light reappeared and zapped him skyward.

As Kalyssa had continued to comfort Jonathan, Jorthon suddenly materialized inside the Dodger Stadium Special.

She quickly realized that Jorthon could not see and was highly distressed. "What happened, Father? What have they done to You?" she asked. Jorthon reached into his shirt pocket and retrieved a glittery object. "Kalyssa, place this new tracking device around Jonathan's neck. His original is no longer available."

Kalyssa did as her father requested.

Just then, the huge spaceship darted off over Eastern, then Western Europe, the Atlantic Ocean, and finally Washington, D.C., all in just two minutes, streaking the international night sky with a burst of brilliant, bright red lights.

At precisely 4:00 am Eastern Time, the Dodger Stadium Special returned to its previous position above the White House. Jonathan, now wearing a silver blanket as though an outer coat, was beamed onto the White House lawn. Secret service men rushed outside to retrieve him, while President Winfield, in a lavender bathrobe, joined them.

"Thank goodness you're okay!" the president cried. "I was worried sick about you!"

Jon was only semi-aware of his surroundings. "Madam President is that you?" Jon asked, weakly.

"Yes, dear," the president answered.

"Could I possibly trouble you for a BLT sandwich on sourdough toast with a pickle on the side?" JT asked.

She laughed. "Yes, Jon. I believe that can be arranged."

The President of the United States, on her knees on the White House lawn in the middle of the night, gently rocked the head of the Hero of Earth in her arms as he dozed off to sleep.

She then began to weep quietly.

CHAPTER FORTY-THREE

Returning to the Pleiades, Jorthon and Kalyssa walked over to what humans would describe as a "park bench," and sat down. "Why did I not learn about these Draconians while being schooled?" Kalyssa asked her father.

"I only rarely heard of their existence in passing from others," Jorthon replied. "They were not discussed—they were clearly an embarrassment to Our Father, and it was obvious to all He did not wish to talk about them or share their story with us."

"It appears now is the time to address this," Kalyssa said.

"Yes, agreed," Jorthon replied. "But before I meet with the Great One, I must bring you to Euclid."

Euclid's Great Library was a stunning four-mile-tall structure designed to contain the data of the ages. Euclid, long renowned as the

"Knower of All Things," greeted Jorthon warmly. "My old friend, so nice to see you again!" the ancient alien said. "So sorry to hear of your recent, ah, recent 'condition.' And surely this must be your daughter, the infamous Kalyssa?"

"Hello, dear Euclid," Kalyssa responded. "Nice to meet you as well."

"Kalyssa, I leave you now in good hands," Jorthon said before gliding off into the distance, leaving Euclid and Kalyssa alone.

"Of course, you wish to know more about our nemeses—the Draconians, I assume?" the old alien asked.

"You assume correctly," Kalyssa replied.

Euclid stroked his chin, released a deep sigh, and began. "The Alpha Draconians are the Infinite Creator's very first test subjects… the oldest known sentient, non-animal race in our galaxy. They are reptilian-human hybrids with leathery scales, Y-shaped tongues, and claws, as well as multiple abdomens. Through the course of millennia, they have managed to assemble the first great military might—yet today, their technology lags far behind ours. Organically angry creatures, they fight for the glory of their clan and for the legacy of their lineage. The Creator originally placed them on the Earth, where they originally ruled the dinosaurs. Eventually, they advanced their race to a point where they could leave the planet via spacecraft.

They breathe hydrogen, exhale nitrogen, and have three spinal columns, which meet to form long, powerful tails. Many of them fled from the Earth long ago—with their mission in life being to one day return… to reclaim their original habitat and eliminate all of mankind—all humans who have flourished there during the interim years. Their agenda today is to covertly consume Earth through political, financial, and social immersion, then greatly disrupt the human population through wars and diseases. All this from a series of undersea bases.

We Pleiadians have been designed by the Infinite Creator as benevolent beings. We have been blessed with receiving the 'best' of His remarkable wisdom and grace. Unfortunately, while He was still experimenting with the launch of intelligent lifeforms, He seeded upon the Earth those dreadful Draconian reptiles. Today, they have evolved and now have the uncanny ability to transform their appearance—they have mastered the ability to appear to others as human."

"Men on Earth are fragile creatures," Kalyssa said. "They mean well, but for too long have lost their way. They are capable of great love and affection. But before Jorthon and I came to meet them, they were also long prone to great violence against each other. However, even with their best defenses, they'd never stand a chance of survival against such a hideous Draconian race as you describe."

"The Creator's request for you, Kalyssa, is to monitor the Earth for the impending Draconian revolution. It is critically important to His legacy," Euclid added. "He is well-aware of how you have—during your recent years of Earth-time—become emotionally invested in the fate of man. That is why He selected you for this task. I'm sure you will not let Him down."

Euclid then handed Kalyssa a box of rings, another box filled with vials of liquid, and a third box with dozens of small metallic objects. "Sit, child, while I explain these very important materials to you," the legendary being told her.

శ్రీ

An exhausted Jonathan Tuckerman finally returned home to New York in early May, embracing his family—and Mully—in a much-welcomed reunion at the Tuckerman condo. During the course of his globe-trotting adventures seeking Karen, JT had begun to grow a beard... frizzy, curly, and bright white. After recounting the horrors of captivity to his family, JT asked those gathered if, during his absence, there had been any "update" in the quest to find his sister. Isak told him that by the end of the abruptly-concluded Tuckerman Tour, over 2.4 million women... in the thirty countries they had visited... had been DNA tested to determine if they were related to the Tuckerman bloodline. Much to everyone's dismay, not one of the women even came close to being a match.

Lauren and Susan—her forward-thrusting belly now noticeable—began calling Jonathan Santa Claus. Clearly, the women had missed their "main man" a great deal, and vice versa. Jon was quite teary-eyed when he hugged his glowing wife and his beautiful daughter.

One evening, while Susan gathered the family into the dining room for a meal, Lauren pulled her father aside. "Dad, when will you be speaking with your friends next?" she asked.

"June 22nd," he replied. "Not sure why they like the 22nd of each month so much. But that's what they said. Why do you ask?"

"Can you take me onboard with you then? There's something I'd like to ask them myself—in person. Would that be cool?" Lauren asked.

JT was surprised. This was the first time his daughter had expressed any kind of interest in meeting Jorthon and Kalyssa face to face.

"Sure, of course," he answered. "I've taken Isak and Clarence up there. It's certainly your turn next, no problem." He reached for his beloved daughter and put his arm around her shoulder. "Kiddo, I really missed you," he said, kissing her on the cheek.

Over the course of the next six weeks, things were calm and relatively happy for the Tuckerman family, despite the fact that, through DNA testing, over 3.2 million women globally had now been eliminated as being "Karen." The directors of the FBI and CIA no longer even phoned Susan every day. Their calls had dwindled down to once a week. The two men were truly baffled. Director Stevens told Susan most recently, "It's remarkable, that with all the media exposure, all of the appearances by Mr. Tuckerman and Isak around the world, and all of the efforts of our manpower on the ground, we've been unable to make a discovery for you. We're so very sorry to have let your family down. Our search continues, however. We don't give up easily," he added.

In private, JT and Susan discussed the most logical answer to the "where is Karen Tuckerman" riddle.

"Johnny, she probably passed away decades ago, someplace God awful," Susan suggested. "I know it's a terrible thing to say, but I think your mother was wrong. As she said, she was 'dreaming' about Karen on her deathbed. Clearly, those dreams were so strong she became convinced that your sister was still out there someplace. My theory is that she was kidnapped from the hospital, maybe by a barren woman pretending to be a nurse, taken far away, and was never told her true identity. Her abductors probably raised her poorly. Perhaps she even made attempts to escape and was killed, or died in poverty, sometime during her youth.

I think we need to move on, dear," she added. "The odds of us ever tracking down a living, breathing Karen Tuckerman are just not good. I believe it's best for us all if we moved forward with our lives and stopped holding our breaths for another miracle to come along."

Jon nodded his head in agreement. "You're right, of course," he said. "She's long gone. My mother was hallucinating. Let's give Wade and Stevens until the end of the month, and if they still haven't found a match, we can tell them 'Thank you' and to wrap it all up." He smiled, leaned against his wife, and gently patted her protruding stomach. "Besides," he added, "with these two little characters coming our way soon, we'll have more than enough to keep our attention focused for a long time!"

Susan was very appreciative of Jon's interest in his new twins. She had feared that her pregnancy would scare him terribly and drive him further into his deep state of depression. Thankfully, it did just the opposite.

He was steadily becoming more and more elated each day.

While Isak and Lauren continued to check in with Team Tuckerman at the UN, Jon, Susan, and quite often Susan's mother Debra, went "baby shopping." The trio was greeted with great fanfare everywhere they went, with JT—whom the media had re-nicknamed "Saint Nick"—quietly and politely refusing to sign autographs or pose for photographs. He merely wanted to hold Susan's hand, walk around each store methodically inspecting the goods, bond with his mother-in-law, and just enjoy the long-forgotten role of being an expectant new parent.

On the morning of June 22nd, after not having been there in many months, JT, with Isak and Lauren at his side, returned to the UN building. As always, he was welcomed with applause, smiles, and warm wishes. This time—with his new Santa Claus beard—also with laughter and chuckles as well. He greatly enjoyed the beard... feeling as though it was a form of "disguise"—allowing him to hide his true self from the world through the now thick white forest of a mess sprouting forth from his face.

At the Team Tuckerman suite, Secretary General Kim, Clarence, and Meghan were all thrilled to see their idol once again. His desk had been covered in gloriously colorful flowers and his chair was replaced by a replica "throne" (which had been provided by a local Broadway theater producer). Jon got great joy from the gestures and, when he sat on the throne for the first time, everyone in the room took photos (which ran all over social media channels the following day).

Late morning arrived, and the prominent hum of the returning Dodger Stadium Special once again signaled to all inside the UN that the aliens had returned to New York to meet once again with the Wonder Man. Lauren glanced at her father from across the room... clearly apprehensive. JT couldn't remember a previous time, ever in her life, that his daughter had appeared nervous about anything.

Jon stood from the throne and took both of Lauren's hands. "Kiddo, are you ready to do this thing?"

She smiled weakly at her old man. "Yep, for sure. There's something I need to discuss with them... and today's gotta be the day."

Hand in hand, JT and Lauren left the suite, rode the elevator up to the top of the building, and strode across the roof, stopping dead center. The giant airship beamed its powerful ray of light at the pair—Lauren hyperventilating; her dad squeezing her hand tightly.

"It'll be fine, kid," he whispered to her. "It's weird and strange, but I promise you, it's painless."

Onboard the Dodger Stadium Special, Jorthon and Kalyssa were greatly overjoyed to see Lauren. "The famous Lauren Tuckerman!" Kalyssa said. "I am so very pleased to see your father has finally brought you here to meet us."

"Greetings, dear Lauren, I am Jorthon." Jon's heart broke when he realized that the Tall White's eyes were now sealed shut—a result of the evil Larpeen. Apparently, however, Jorthon was still able to "see" and "recognize" his surroundings—an ability Jon assumed must be telepathic.

Lauren, noticeably shaking and voice quivering, said, "Yes, of course, Jorthon. I know who you are." Turning, she added, "And the beautiful Kalyssa. Thank you both for saving my father's life."

"My daughter asked me to bring her onboard to meet you guys," Jon said. "She has something important to discuss with you." He looked at the younger woman with great pride and smiled. "She didn't tell me what it is, so I'm just as curious as you are to hear what she has to say. Lauren, take it away, kid."

Lauren grabbed hold of the table of light to steady herself. A few noticeable beads of sweat dripping from her forehead down the sides of her face. "I have a theory," she began quietly. "A disturbing theory that I need to ask the two of you about," she said.

Lauren looked deeply into Kalyssa's eyes—the incredibly beautiful glowing Nordic with the ability to hypnotize all of mankind and a smile to break human hearts. Lauren took a deep breath. "Kalyssa... ARE YOU KAREN TUCKERMAN?"

JT's knees buckled. "What did you just say?" he asked his daughter, completely taken aback. He let out a nervous chuckle and returned his glance at the aliens. "Sorry about that," he offered. "You see, we've all been looking for my so-called 'twin sister' ever since my mother, on her deathbed, told me Karen was still alive. We've looked all over the Earth, but haven't been able to find any trace of her. Clearly, she's long gone—most likely dead. We're all just a bit obsessed in trying to find her."

"Yes," Kalyssa said, having moved closer to both Jon and Lauren and looking them deep in the eyes. "My given birth name was Karen Lisa Tuckerman. I am your sister, Jonathan."

Jon fainted. His daughter and Jorthon lifted him up and placed him upon the table of light.

"Daddy?" Lauren said, leaning over the man. "Are you okay?"

Jon resuscitated quickly. "Oh, ah, yeah, sure, I'm fine." He sat up and stared at Kalyssa.

"Huh? How? What are you talking about?" he said, clearly upset and shaken.

"My father will explain it all to you," Kalyssa said as she took hold of one of Jon's shoulders with one hand and held Lauren's hand with her other one.

"Jonathan," Jorthon began, "the day your parents saved my life, your mother had just become pregnant with twins—a male and a female—as your parents had made love the morning of the night I crashed into Earth. I was so grateful to them for saving me that I rewarded them in two ways. As you know, I implanted a metal tracking device into the right hand of your fetus so that we would always know exactly where you would be—to keep you safe from harm throughout your life.

At the same time, I *also embedded a healthy dose of Nordic DNA* into that female fetus while touching Jane's stomach. In this manner, I could ensure that your twin would have great Pleiadian abilities. I crafted her so that she and I could, together, always observe and protect you, as I had promised your parents at that moment. A moment you yourself observed through our 'home movie' device."

"This is just too much," Jon said. Then, looking at his daughter, asked, "How did *you* figure this out?"

"I accidently spilled coffee on a photo of the three of you from Dodger Stadium while you were in Europe, Dad. Then, when I saw Kalyssa with dark brown hair instead of white, I compared her face to the picture on your desk of you and Grandma Jane together coming home from the hospital after you were born. I had chills up my spine. I saw your mother's face in Kalyssa's! It became crystal clear to me all at once."

"But why didn't you say anything to me all this time?" JT asked.

"I didn't want to be wrong, Daddy. I didn't want to get your hopes up or disappoint you. That's why I asked you to bring me here today. I needed to ask them face to face if my instincts were correct or way off base."

"Your instincts are perfect," Kalyssa said, smiling. "We are sorry to have caused you any concern or anguish, Jon. As you know, we have been absent these past Earth months—having to deal with some extraordinary news from our home dimension. But now that we have returned, we will do our best to make this slight up to you."

"Karen Lisa… Kalyssa! I get it now," Jon said, proudly making the connection.

"Your father handed baby Karen to me through an open window at the hospital, Jonathan," Jorthon explained. "She had been born just moments earlier. It was our secret—he knew she was special and that she would thrive best by living with me. He told your mother a lie to best protect the baby's life."

"Another major news bulletin my father never told me." Jon sighed.

"I took her immediately up to my home base so her initiation into our culture could start right away," Jorthon continued. "As a tribute to the name your parents gave her, I simply embellished it a bit by blending the words Karen and Lisa together, as you deduced, then giving it a little Pleiadian flourish!" He smiled.

"We did not mean to keep this from you, Jon," he added. "But, as Kalyssa is Earth's very first alien-human hybrid, the Great Creator asked us specifically not to reveal this information to humans unless absolutely necessary. We did not know how your people or your president might react to these facts. This was a detail we had hoped to tell you at some point in the future—but apparently that 'future' was today."

Jorthon turned his head towards Lauren and said, "However, the fact that your daughter is a brilliant detective, Jonathan, just made this information too appropriate to resist sharing."

Jon and Lauren looked at each other, and then repeated, in unison, "ALIEN-HUMAN HYBRID?" At first appearing frightened, they then began to laugh, harder and harder, until they were howling so loudly they had to hold each other bodily, tears of laughter streaming from their eyes. "That's the funniest thing I've ever heard in my life!" Lauren said.

Hopping off the light table and approaching Kalyssa, Jon asked, "May I hug you, sis?"

Kalyssa smiled. "Yes, I suppose so, dear brother. I have never been 'hugged' by a human." The two embraced warmly. "I am most happy to see your acceptance of this fact. We feared you would be most displeased with our decision to keep this from you."

"There is other news, Jon," Jorthon said. "I have been called upon by the Infinite Creator—reassigned, you might say—to another mission that will keep me in the skies for some time. It concerns our 'friend' Larpeen and his like. I am afraid this is the last I will see you on Earth for a while." The alien extended his hand to JT.

The Great White and the Hero of Earth smiled warmly at each other while they shook. "I'll miss you, wonderful friend," JT said.

"Also, Kalyssa has something more to tell you," Jorthon added.

"I've been instructed by the Infinite Creator to now spend all of my time living on Earth," the wondrous Kalyssa stated. "He wishes me to 'embrace' the human side of my heritage." Looking at both JT and Lauren, she added, "I will need your help... both of you... with this transition."

"Holy shit, that's amazing!" Lauren squealed. "Welcome to the Tuckerman family, Aunt Karen!" Lauren gently approached her new aunt and gave her a touching and warm embrace.

While Jorthon from the Pleiades star cluster—the Great White Alien who'd changed the lives of all on Earth in less than three years—stood aside, Jon, Lauren, and Karen Lisa Tuckerman, aka 'Kalyssa,' smiled, laughed, and hugged for a good, long while.

It even appeared to Lauren—for one brief flashing moment—that her new aunt may have had a tear in her eye.

The three Tuckermans clearly rejoiced in this long overdue, and completely unprecedented, family reunion.

CHAPTER FORTY-FOUR

The next big step for JT and his family, of course, was to tell President Winfield the stunning news. At the conclusion of their most recent Dodger Stadium Special meeting, Jorthon flew off into space, while Kalyssa began her adventure of living on Earth—she'd accompanied JT and Lauren back to the UN, where her highly dramatic surprise appearance caused virtual chaos throughout the building. The Team Tuckerman suite became standing room only, with the curious waiting in long lines to say hello to the lovely and infamous Nordic Woman.

Isak was overjoyed to learn that Kalyssa was his aunt. He, JT, and Lauren accompanied Kalyssa in their limo back to the penthouse. Back at the condo, the look on Susan's face when she learned the news was priceless. She burst into tears. Russell's face was equally impressive... his mouth formed a shape as if to say, "Oh my!"

"How marvelous!" Susan said once the news settled in. Hugging her new alien sister-in-law, she said, "Never in our wildest dreams would we have guessed that YOU, of all people, errr, beings, would wind up as our long-lost Karen Tuckerman. Thank God our search is over!"

"You can thank Lauren and the Infinite Creator," Kalyssa corrected Susan, "as *she* made the connection, and *He* requested that I now live on Earth amongst you."

The Nordic turned to Jon. "So, brother, do you think you might be able to find me a place to live?"

"Shouldn't be a problem, sis," Jon answered, smiling.

Russell prepared a dinner banquet that night fit for royalty. While Kalyssa did not "eat food" like humans (she kept her nutritional intake a secret), she greatly enjoyed sitting at the table with her relatives. She could smell the wondrous smells that Russell's meal presented. To everyone's utter surprise including her own, she *was* able to drink, and enjoyed Chardonnay immensely.

After dinner, Jon went into the living room and made a phone call. "Madam President?"

"Yes, dear Johnny, how are you?" the woman replied.

"Err, ahh, uhm, we have some news for you. It's pretty big, like *really fucking big*!" he said.

"What new news could you *possibly* have to tell me?" the president joked.

"Ahh, I think it would be best done in person. In fact, my entire family would like to tell you together, all at once."

"Well, now I'm more than intrigued," President Winfrey said. "Don't tell me—your kids are getting married?"

"Uhm, no, far bigger than that," Jon replied.

"Something I should be nervous about hearing?" she countered.

"No, I don't think so," JT said. "But it's *so huge* it may require a meeting with your Cabinet, after we tell you." The president invited Jon and his family to come to the White House the next day.

The short flight from New York to Washington, D.C. the next morning was notable for the looks on the faces of all others at the two airports when they saw not only JT and the entire Tuckerman family strolling through, but also Kalyssa, one of the two Great Aliens whose role in transforming mankind had become far beyond legendary. All of the lookie-loos who spotted her were not only startled, they were a bit frightened as well. They moved several feet back as the Tuckerman clan walked past them.

Arriving at the White House, the family left their limo and headed toward the front doors. The always reliable Mully, standing there to greet them, began to stutter when he realized that Kalyssa was among them.

"Mr. Tuck-tuckerman," he said, "I see you've brought one of your fr-fr-fr-friends with you today."

"It's alright, Mully," Jon said, "She's one of us now. Long story. Everything's just fine."

Mully led the procession further into the building, and directly into the Oval Office. "Madam President, the Tuckermans plus guest are here to see you," he announced, having half-opened the door into the president's inner sanctum.

"Well don't keep them waiting, Mully," the president said, "Bring 'em on in here!"

When President Winfield, one of the world's calmest, warmest, most level-headed women, realized that Kalyssa—the stunning alien—was entering her office along with JT, et al., she was overwhelmed with surprise.

"Kalyssa!" she said, breathlessly, approaching the beauty. "I can't believe this! It's such an honor to finally meet you." She extended her hand

Kalyssa accepted it and the two women shook. The president looked over at Jon. "So, JT, I guess your surprise is that Kalyssa really *IS* one of your friends now?"

"Ah, Madam President," Jon said, "it's a bit more complicated. I think we should all sit down."

Over the course of the next hour and a half, Jon, Susan, Isak, Lauren, and Kalyssa each took turns explaining to the President of the United

States the backstory to everything... all of it. The other half of "why" the Great Aliens from the Pleiades dimension had come to Earth to rescue Jon from the sea and help him become the Hero of the Planet. *was that unexp! ian*

While listening, President Winfrey would often place her hand up to *slip* her mouth, stifling the wonder, especially when it was revealed, by Kalyssa herself, that SHE was Karen Lisa Tuckerman! At that point, the president clutched her heart and literally jumped two inches off the couch.

"ARE YOU SERIOUS?" the president shrieked. Her eyes said it all... complete and utter shock. "Johnny, your mother was right! Karen IS STILL ALIVE! She knew it all along. She just didn't know the specifics. What a story!" she said, becoming more and more excited about the possibilities this new information presented.

"Madam President," Jon continued, "given the fact that Kalyssa is the first ever alien-human hybrid in the history of the world, and that she is now going to be living as a 'human' here on Earth, we wanted you to know first, before the news that she will now be walking amongst us permanently, got out there. We aren't sure how to let anyone else know —or even IF we should let anyone else know the full story? Or if, maybe, it should remain just our little secret?"

The president stood, walked over to Kalyssa and sat next to her. "Kalyssa, dear," she said. "Your very existence is a true miracle! You are the only one of your kind anywhere in the universe. You should be the cause of great celebration. People everywhere should be told the entire story... your story. I don't think this is something to be hidden in the dark. I believe this information should be cherished and embraced and announced to the world."

Kalyssa took the president's hand and together they stood. "Madam President," the alien said, "there is something I need to further discuss with you, but in private."

"Even from your family?" Lauren questioned, only half-kidding.

"Yes, dear niece, I'm afraid so," Kalyssa replied. "May we go somewhere quiet to complete this conversation?" the Nordic asked.

"Yes, of course, dear, follow me," the president answered.

The two women left the Oval Office through a side door and disappeared into a private alcove. The Tuckerman family remained behind, practically dying of curiosity, while luxuriating in the incredible comfort of the president's office.

"You look very concerned, Kalyssa," the president said. "You're making me nervous. Is the situation so secretive you can't even discuss it in front of your new brother?"

Kalyssa revealed to the President of the United States the Great Creator's news of the impending threat by the Draconians. How the Creator had revealed to her that a number of their military leaders had already made inroads within the human race, in disguise, to prepare for an upcoming invasion of Earth in the near future. "The Creator has placed me here now to uncover these Draconian leaders, so that my people—including Jorthon and many others of his kind flying in their airships above—can extract them from the Earth and thwart the start of their takeover of mankind.

We do not wish Jon to know yet. In fact, we do not wish to alarm any member of the human race. However, as a world leader and Jon's closest friend, you have been approved to learn of this news. I wish to enlist the aid of your intelligence agencies to work with me to track down and locate these evil creatures. Believe it or not, their highly primitive stealth technology interferes with our much more sophisticated location technologies, providing unreliable data."

President Winfield, a woman with a fairly dark-skinned complexion, turned a new shade of pale. She leaned against a wall as though the wind had been knocked out of her. "Of course, Kalyssa dear," she said. "I will share this information only with those most trusted within my cabinet, and with a few other leaders who I believe have a right to know. We will not announce this news to the world, for fear of panic. I will classify what you've just told me as 'Above Top Secret'. Only those with a true need to know will know. You have my word."

The two women shook hands... the president's hand, for perhaps the only time in her adult life, was a bit wet and clammy.

That night, President Winfield gave a one of a kind speech to the nation and the world, from behind her desk in the Oval Office. It was carried by every television, radio, and online news site on the globe. "My fellow Americans, and my fellow members of the human race," she began, once again her charming and commanding self, "I come to you all tonight with a truly incredible announcement—one so dramatic and unexpected, it took my breath away when I first heard it myself. Now that I've had a few hours to digest the information I am about to share with you, I have not only embraced it, I have come to realize that what you are about to learn will enhance all our lives."

She continued. "As everyone knows, Jonathan Tuckerman was saved and helped by two magnanimous aliens from the Pleiades star dimension—Jorthon and Kalyssa. We've all known that for more than two years. However, what none of us knew before now, even Jon Tuckerman himself, was the fact that the beautiful, Nordic female alien known as Kalyssa was, in reality, KAREN LISA TUCKERMAN, JON TUCKERMAN'S LONG-LOST TWIN SISTER!"

The White House cameraman shooting the president's speech was so started by this revelation that even *he* momentarily shook the camera up and down, causing a rare "technical glitch" during a live presidential broadcast.

"Kalyssa has informed us that she is the world's first ever alien/human hybrid! As such, she has decided she would like to live here on Earth side by side with the rest of us to experience her 'human' heritage and to better embrace the 'human' experience.

So now, without further ado, I'd like to present Kalyssa, aka Karen Lisa Tuckerman. She'd like to say a few words to you all." The president stood and left her seat behind her desk.

Kalyssa walked behind the desk, remained standing, and began to once again speak telepathically. "Human beings are a wonderful race," she said. "You all have so much to offer now that war and violence and hunger and disease and petty conflicts have been resolved. Your capacity for love, your enjoyment of art and music and culture, your ability to spend time together just talking, having a meal, or drinking Chardonnay are all lovely and magnificent. These are pleasures we from the Pleiades do not experience in the same ways.

Now that my brother, Jonathan Michael Tuckerman, and his lovely family have been informed of my true identity, we have decided, as a group, to share this information with all of you. While the story of my genesis was not something we wished to hide, Jorthon and I were originally instructed by the Great Creator Himself to keep these facts from mankind until the time was exactly right to make such a revelation.

With the truth of my existence now revealed, I choose to live amongst you, as one of you, if you'll have me. During the coming days, months, and years ahead, I look forward to getting to know many of you and learning of your life experiences. Thank you very much for your acceptance, and I wish each of you a good evening."

The giant headline in the *New York Post* the following day said it all: "Holy Pleiades, Batman! Nordic Beauty Kalyssa is Karen Tuckerman! Gorgeous Alien to Now Live on Planet Earth!" The byline read: As Reported by Barbara Gardner (aka Jon Tuckerman's ex-wife).

President Winfield arranged for Kalyssa to move into a penthouse apartment, equal in splendor to the one she'd given JT, atop a building just two blocks north of Jon and Susan's residence. The president went out of her way financially, so as to keep that upscale Manhattan neighborhood "all in the intergalactic family."

CHAPTER FORTY-FIVE

When the news broke that Kalyssa, aka Karen Tuckerman, would be living as a "regular human being" in modern-day Manhattan, the public's interest in her, not to mention that of the media, skyrocketed. While her public persona would be as a novelty—a stunning single woman from outer space, now living among her "fellow man"—Kalyssa's real mission on Earth was to seek out, confront, and "tag" as many Draconian military leaders currently residing on the planet as she could discover, so that Jorthon could remove them, permanently.

As Kalyssa would privately reveal to President Winfield, the Draconian race, living as they did deep inside undersea caverns, were immune to the various sprays, lights, sounds, and other technologies Jorthon and Kalyssa had used on human beings when they eliminated anger, violence, hatred, and intolerance. Kalyssa also made the president aware that while

Draconian technology was far inferior to those of her fellows from the Pleiades, human military leaders would still remain essentially helpless to fight back against the Draconian war machine, even with the latest detection equipment and exploding missiles and bombs made in the good old USA.

With the work of Team Tuckerman now indefinitely "on hold," the president and Secretary General Kim gave Kalyssa the same UN suite to serve as a base of covert operations. A number of FBI and CIA agents had been assigned to work directly with her, being told by the president to "do whatever it is she asks you to do. And don't ask questions."

While the "alien half" of Kalyssa was compelled to spend most of her time working to sniff out her nefarious enemies, the "human half" of the beautiful creature longed to spend as much time as possible with her new family. To that end, both Susan and Lauren insisted on taking Kalyssa clothes shopping—the trio causing near riots everywhere they went throughout Manhattan's finest women's stores. Paparazzi photographers followed Kalyssa's every move, especially after she'd dyed her hair red and began wearing the most cutting edge styles and hottest fashions this side of Italy.

The rights to one photo—that of Kalyssa wearing a very short, bright pink sundress, with revealing cleavage—had been acquired by Barbara Gardner. Barbara turned the utterly sexy picture into the biggest selling print poster in history, eclipsing poster sales of such earlier American sex symbols as Betty Grable, Rita Hayworth, Marilyn Monroe, Raquel Welch, and Farrah Fawcett. _Must we mreadelly sexualke the alien?_

Kalyssa was bemused and entertained by the chaos her mere presence caused. Even men and women of great wealth, fame, and social status became almost completely flustered when trying to speak with her. Susan and Lauren did their best to introduce their new relative to all of the most powerful, and influential "movers and shakers" in town. A few very brave men worked up the courage to ask Kalyssa out for dinner dates. She did her best not to offend them when she turned them all down, replying simply, "Sorry, I do not eat human food."

June, July, and August, 2036 in Manhattan, New York became known across the country as "The Summer of Kalyssa."

Barbara finally managed to corral Isak into a long, sit down, audio-taped interview about his life and his relationship with his father. Fiercely defending his parent, and having never once enjoyed being in Barbara's vicinity, the interview was "like pulling wisdom teeth," the writer would later tell her publisher. Knowing, however, that his cooperation was important, and not wishing to cause his father any embarrassment whatsoever, the young man eventually phoned Barbara to say that he'd "re-considered his behavior" and asked her to give him another chance.

The second and third interviews were much more forthcoming.

Jon, meantime, had been bitching and moaning for weeks about his impending solo time with his second wife. As he himself had now become Barbara's final interview subject, he met with Susan and Cheryl Schoenberg at the lawyer's office to go over the ground rules.

"She sucks... I hate her," Cheryl told the Tuckermans. "But she is a good writer. I've seen a number of her efforts in a variety of newspapers and magazines. We have an ironclad agreement with her, Jon, that she is *not* to discuss with you ANY topics regarding your sexual history or proclivities, past, present, or future."

Susan turned to Jon. "When are you going to tell *me* the naughty things you used to do, you bad boy?" She laughed. — Hopefully Never?

"Ah, uhm, someday, maybe," JT said. "But you'll have to get me drunker than drunk first!"

"Deal," Susan agreed.

Turning to Susan, the attorney continued, "Between us, she is DYING of jealousy about you, Suzie Q. You are everything she's not... beautiful, far more accomplished, famous, and the woman who was able to find true love and happiness with the friend of aliens."

Susan laughed.

"What was it about that creature that ever interested you in the first place?" Cheryl asked Jon.

"Lust... plain and simple," JT replied. "We were set up through mutual friends. On our first date, we went to dinner, drank far too much, and ended up having sex on the grass outside her apartment building. I was never even attracted to her." He looked at Susan. "Honestly, not at all. She was so into the sex with *me* I became addicted to it. But when it came to living together, and especially when it came to interacting with my kids, she was hostile, angry, and bitter. She couldn't have any children of her own and had zero interest in being a 'step-mommy.'"

"That explains a lot. I'm surprised you lasted two years with her," Susan said.

"You and me both, baby doll." Jon sighed.

The meeting place for the long-delayed "Tuckerman vs. Gardner" onslaught took place on the 4th of July, 2036 at a private suite inside the Plaza Hotel... Jon's comfort zone. Following a Tuckerman family breakfast, Susan, Isak, Lauren, and Cheryl all waited for Jon downstairs in the hotel lobby, after reassuring him that "everything will be just fine. Relax. Take a breath. Get your ass up there and it'll be over before you know it."

Jon arrived at the suite first. He tried to make himself comfortable on the couch, then went to the chair—couch to chair to couch to chair a number of times, never deciding which POV spot in the room would be best. A knock on the door brought Barbara, who was not wearing her mannish glasses this time ("contacts," she said), and had slimmed down significantly since the last time JT had seen her... at his wedding.

Jon so hated admitting to himself that he suddenly found her incredibly attractive, in a "sexy librarian" kind of way. — NO', جداً!

"Hey Johnny, are you ready for me?" she joked, smiling, a large, portable, tape recorder suspended from her shoulder.

"Ready as I'll ever be." He sighed reluctantly.

She patted his arm. "I'm not the dentist, you know," the writer said, realizing the extent of her subject's advanced agony. "This won't hurt as much as you think. I'm not out to 'get you,' JT," she offered. "My goal is to tell the world your story, your whole, entire story, so that everyone will know, long after you're gone, who you really were, what you really did, and why you are so very, very important today." She smiled at him. Much to his surprise and instant regret, Jon smiled back.

The pair sat down (Jon finally decided on the chair; Barbara took the couch), and the writer pressed "play" on her recorder. She began talking to her ex-husband calmly, and in a remarkably soothing manner. Within just the first few minutes, Jon felt at ease, and loosened up. While he wanted to detest this woman with every fiber of his being, she was being so uncharacteristically charming to him that his long-prepared game plan—to remain as aloof and unresponsive as possible—quickly lost its merit.

The interview lasted eleven hours... far longer than the three hours each "side" had agreed upon legally. Jon had had to phone downstairs to tell his awaiting family to "go home." Everything was going "fine" and he'd fill them all in on the details later that evening. A twinge of jealousy coursed through Susan's veins... surprising the shit out of herself. She knew full well how much Jon loved her, and how he loathed Barbara, but the fact that he was spending so many hours—alone—in a magnificent hotel room suite with his ex-wife, with whom Jon had had countless sexual romps in years past, made her question—only briefly—his loyalty for the first and only time in their lives together.

When all was said and done, the JT/Barbara interview was relatively painless. They'd covered his childhood, his lonely/sexually frustrating teen years (in broad terms—no specifics), his relationship with his parents and friends, his college days in Boston, his early years in Los Angeles, and meeting Janice. They discussed an overview of that marriage, his kids, his company (high points and low), the car accident, of course, and its aftermath.

Barbara knew full well, obviously, how *she* and JT had met, romanced, and parted, so she shared her side of that tale with him. Much to his surprise, he agreed wholeheartedly... that their relationship had been built solely and fundamentally on fucking. "When you started to have real money problems, you lost all interest in sex—the one thing we had in common," Barbara noted. "After that, it was game over," she said.

"You're absolutely right, I agree," Jon replied, appreciating her honesty.

Although sex talk had been removed from the arrangement legally, Barbara did ask him about his "love life" during the years between their divorce and when he met Susan.

"An endless series of one-night stands, an occasional call girl or two, but mostly a tremendous amount of porn," Jon answered. "If you're going to write my story—the whole story—you might as well keep things honest. You have my permission to add that in."

"Well, I'm glad you at least had those outlets," she joked. "A man with your sexual appetite has needs. Susan must be one lucky lady."

As Jon's time since becoming instantly world famous had previously been well-chronicled... starting with his attempted suicide, his rescue, Jorthon and Kalyssa at Dodger Stadium, meeting the president the first time, setting up Team Tuckerman at the UN, his miracles and inventions, his Nobel Prize, the death of his mother, and his search for—and ultimate discovery of—Karen/Kalyssa, Barbara spent the next hours simply "fact checking" what she already knew.

"You've got it all right, Barb," Jon said. "Every bit of it. Clearly, you've done your homework. Nice job."

Barbara polished off the interview with a simple question about his future. "So, Jon, with all that you've accomplished, with two healthy children that adore you, with a stunning, pregnant wife at your side and babies on the way, with all of your wealth and acclaim, a Nobel Prize, and your legendary status, what's next for you? Where does the story of the 'Wonder Man' go from here?"

Jon took a long pause. "Joy," he answered simply. "Love. Happiness. Susan, Isak, Lauren. The new twins. My sister. Family. Friends. Life. Everything I never knew how to enjoy or embrace before my 70th birthday. I want to gobble all of that up now, for as long as I can. I'm going to squeeze every last moment out of the piece of coal that was most of my life.

And hopefully I'll get to join my parents in the great beyond when it all ends."

CHAPTER FORTY-SIX

Susan Elizabeth Parks Tuckerman gave birth to perfect, beautiful, healthy twins... a boy and a girl... on August 22, 2036. JT and his ecstatic wife named their son Jacob Dodger Tuckerman ("Jake" for short), and their daughter Jane Maui Tuckerman ("Maui" for short). Photos of the four, along with Isak, Lauren, Kalyssa, Susan's parents, and the President of the United States, taken inside Susan's hospital room, showed the entire gang all bursting with pride.

The President (who'd been named the "Honorary Grandmother" of the twins), was quoted as telling the world's press: "It's never a bad day when a brand new TUCKERMAN—or TWO—join the rest of the human race! Now, I'm just waiting for the day when Isak and Lauren are going to bring me some more little Tuckermans to play with too!!"

Soon after the birth of the twins, President Winfield held a special session in the White House situation room so Kalyssa could present the top military leaders with details about the Draconian presence on Earth. When the beautiful alien walked into the room, even five-star generals—grown men who'd earned their honors from fierce and heroic combat during skirmishes around the world in earlier years—became a bit tongue-tied.

"Our great friend Kalyssa has brought to our attention an ugly and frightening situation," the president began. "One that we must not make known to the general public for fear of terrible panic. After all she and her father Jorthon have done for us, it is time for us to repay those kindnesses with our aid to her and her people. Kalyssa, it's all yours."

Kalyssa stood before the room... her commanding presence mesmerizing. "Unfortunately, an evil race of beings known as 'Alpha Draconians' have been methodically melding themselves in amongst you—us—'humans'—so they may eventually take command of governments, armies, businesses, and schools," she declared. "Their goal is to dominate mankind, eliminate billions of human beings, and rule the planet Earth—the planet upon which they were regretfully created eons ago by the Great Creator, and now wish to reclaim.

The Infinite Creator has informed me that several dozen of their military leaders—at least fifty or more—have already entrenched themselves into positions of power around the Earth, in disguise. A very highly advanced race of reptilian Creatures—far older than any other race that now exists—they have the ability to appear and behave as human men, having removed their own tails to do so."

A number of America's top brass gasped.

Kalyssa continued, "Jorthon and a number of his colleagues are patrolling the skies above Earth in their airships. They will remain vigilant indefinitely to ensure that the Draconians do not begin sending warcraft here from other points within your solar system for a full-scale invasion. In the meantime, I've been tasked with locating those already embedded on this planet, confirming their identities, disabling them temporarily, and then 'tagging' them with a tracking device so that Jorthon and his squad can beam them up onto their ships and deliver them to our Creator for punishment."

General Curtis raised his hand. Kalyssa acknowledged him as having a question. "Are these, these, 'Draconians' more powerful than you or Jorthon?" he asked. "How will you be able to identify them? And disable them? And what do you mean 'tag' them? Seems incredibly dangerous to me."

Kalyssa showed everyone in the room one of the rings that Euclid had given her in the Pleiades dimension. "Draconians exhale pure nitrogen," she explained. "My device here changes color from clear to deep red when exposed to pure nitrogen. When I encounter a Draconian, he will need to be injected with this." She held up one of the vials of liquid that Euclid had also given her. "Once he is drugged, I will have time to implant one of these." She next held up a small piece of metal resembling a large thumbtack, another of Euclid's gifts. "I will attach it to the stub of his removed tail. I am told he will be unable to feel it there. This is a beacon that will send a powerful signal, undetectable by their technologies, to Jorthon and his fleet. They will then have the ability to extract those so tagged, lift them from the ground, and place them inside their ships."

Secretary of Defense Romano spoke next. "It appears you have this plan well thought out, Kalyssa. How is it that we can help?"

"We believe most strongly that the Draconians who have recently begun to emerge from their underwater lairs are working in close contact with many world leaders... either within governments or as advisors to presidents, kings, queens, and dictators," the beautiful Nordic continued. "As the world now believes I wish to present as 'human,' it would be best if the president and those of you here now can arrange for me a conventional 'world tour,' by which I might have the opportunity to meet as many of those leaders in person as possible. The premise will be that I am doing research on the various cultures, customs, and ethnicities of Earthlings, yet the reality shall be that I am working to draw out these heinous Draconian creatures who, most likely, will be equally interested in meeting me."

The president stood. "Well, then, we have our assignment." She turned to the Secretary of State. "Jim, I want you and your people to collaborate with everyone here to arrange a comprehensive global tour for Kalyssa with our major world leaders. And as soon as possible." Turning to the alien, the president added, "Would you mind if I tagged along?"

Kalyssa, having not previously considered that option, and clearly intrigued, replied instantly, "Why, yes. That would be most helpful... as your British people say, 'quite lovely.'"

As the president was about to adjourn the top-secret meeting, Kalyssa's Draconian "detection ring" suddenly turned dark red. Completely startled by the notification, she looked closely into the face of James Franklin, the Secretary of State, sitting just a few feet away, and noticed he was sweating.

"You?" she said, pointing out one of President Winfrey's key advisors. Franklin stood quickly and made for the door. "Stop him!" Kalyssa shouted. The security men inside the room did so.

The president was astonished. "I trusted you for YEARS!" she said, inches from the Draconian's face. "Kalyssa, what do we do with him now?" the president asked, almost shaking with anger.

Kalyssa turned to General Curtis. "Take this," she said, handing the man the vial of fluid. "Have this hideous thing drugged. Then stick this into the stub of his tail," she added, handing the military officer the large metal tack. "Within a few seconds after this is accomplished, stand back. My father will send down his shaft of light to carry this creature away."

ↄⱸ

Following the president's announcement to the media that "Secretary of State James Franklin had, unfortunately, died of a heart attack during a Cabinet meeting," she and the remainder of her team (following Kalyssa's having "cleared" all the other members) went to work setting up a massive world tour agenda, mirroring many of the same locations JT and Isak had visited just months earlier. They also added a number of other, more remote, cities. The president told the media that she and Kalyssa would soon leave to visit with over one hundred world leaders—"in their capital cities"—to help the magnificent alien make their acquaintance, "so she may better understand all facets of the human experience here on Earth."

That cover story was never broken for the entire length of the tour. President Winfrey and Kalyssa were wined and dined, honored and entertained, by kings and queens, presidents and prime ministers, princes, dictators, and great leaders everywhere. The two women had established a modus operandi during these giant receptions and events... if and when Kalyssa's ring turned red while she was talking to someone, she would wink at the president. The president would then walk over to Kalyssa's location and distract the Draconian with small talk while two members of the president's Secret Service force would walk behind the Draconian subject, stealthily inject him with Euclid's sleeping fluid, then subtly extract the suspect to a nearby, pre-selected "quiet room."

There, Kalyssa would attach Euclid's "thumbtack" tracking monitor into the tail stump of each evil creature. The security men would next quietly take the "prisoner" to a nearby secluded outdoor location, where they would await Jorthon's colossal beam of light to come and lift him aboard the Dodger Stadium Special.

While the first few attempts at this process were a bit hairy (a Draconian "mayor" in Ireland being a particularly large fellow who required a double dose of serum), Kalyssa, President Winfrey and her security men worked out the kinks fairly quickly. Kalyssa's hunch—that embedded Draconian leaders would be as curious about her as she was about them—turned out to be absolutely true. Her massive global celebrity had lured them out into the open like starving flies to the richest, sweetest honey.

During the course of the four-month tour, Kalyssa and President Winfield conversed with, identified, and "tagged" (and Jorthon and his mates had extracted from the ground) forty-four members of the dreaded Draconian race from seventy-seven countries. Most of the snagged Draconians had been posing as members of the military; advisors to presidents, kings, and queens; wealthy businessmen; cabinet members;

scientists; teachers; and notable artists, musicians, and social media influencers.

By the time the "Welcome to Earth Kalyssa Tuckerman" tour finally ended, she and the President of the United States had, essentially, neutered the impending threat by the dreaded Draconians on Earth—the heinous creators the Infinite Creator had feared would soon eclipse humanity.

Unfortunately, though, Kalyssa and President Winfield hadn't found them all.

CHAPTER FORTY-SEVEN

A few weeks before Jon's 73rd birthday, while he and Susan were holding the twins (JT with Jake, Susan with Maui), and with Russell ever rising to the occasion by warming up baby bottles and dealing with the couple's diaper service, the phone rang at the penthouse. Announced the phone's overhead robotic answering voice: "Hello, Mister Tuckerman. The Governor of New York would like to speak to you. Shall you take the call?"

"Yes, I will, Candida," JT responded.

Next, the Hero of Earth heard, "Mr. Tuckerman? This is Governor Perry, I just got off the phone with Mayor Blythe and we discussed, in great detail, an idea we'd like to offer you. Do you have a minute?"

Little Jake started to cry, so JT motioned for his wife to "switch babies" with him. "Yes, alright, what's going on?" Jon replied, intrigued yet a bit skeptical.

"We'd like to celebrate your impending birthday on November 22 with a parade... a large, special parade through Manhattan, to honor your contributions to New York, the United States, and the world," the governor stated. "Would that be of interest to you at all?"

Jon cupped his hand over the phone and spoke to Susan. "They want to throw me a birthday parade through New York. What do you think?"

"Duh, yes, of course, you goose," she replied. "That sounds like fun. Tell him 'yes.'"

"Hey Governor, the 'boss' says 'yes.' So sure, that's fine. Count me in."

"Terrific! I'll have my people and the mayor's people coordinate with your assistant Meghan at the UN. Will that work for you?"

"Sounds good. Thanks... that's very cool, actually. I had no plans for my birthday this year, other than burping babies and changing dirty diapers."

The governor laughed. "Stay tuned, Mr. Tuckerman. More details to come."

No one was more excited about the birthday parade than Meghan. She immediately involved Isak and Lauren, and the trio worked very closely with the event's organizers to ensure that every single detail—no matter how small—would be carefully considered and implemented.

The mayor told Meghan that "our goal is to draw more people to this event than have ever been assembled at one time in the history of Manhattan. We want to show Mr. Tuckerman just how much New Yorkers value his contributions to society, and how grateful we all are that he was chosen by the Benevolents to better the story of man."

Meghan, Isak, and Lauren wanted the parade to be highly inventive visually, so they came up with the idea that their father would ride atop an enormous float designed as a traditional silvery "flying saucer." It would have a large perimeter and an open air "bubble top" at its center, within which JT could sit or stand and wave to the crowds. The trio, of course, invited President Winfield to participate, and, although exhausted as she was by the recently concluded world tour with Kalyssa, she readily agreed.

Realizing that the date of the parade would also be her alien aunt's birthday, Lauren asked Kalyssa if she would like to ride in the parade as well. Surprisingly, Jon's sister declined, telling her niece that she had "another commitment—a date with history" that would prevent her attendance at that time.

As the date of the birthday parade approached, Jon yet again became highly introspective and ambivalent about all that he'd achieved. "I don't deserve a *parade*," he moaned to Russell one day while Susan was out shopping for baby supplies. "Russell, my *parents* did something truly remarkable a very long time ago—why should *I* be the one reaping all these honors? It's enough already, don't you think? I don't deserve any of this. My parents were the heroes, not me!"

Russell stood directly in front of his boss and smiled. "Mr. T," he spoke clearly and firmly, "your parents' heroism was so that YOU, and you alone, would be selected by aliens to improve life for all of us. Think of this parade as a tribute to your parents and the culmination of their life's work. I'm sure if they were still alive, they would have been most proud and happy to see you being so honored."

Russell continued, "You deserve this honor.. perhaps more than any other person who has ever received one. How could you possibly walk away from such a rare and wonderful thing? Your children will remember this for the rest of their lives—even the little ones."

JT smiled. "What would I do without you, Russell? I can always count on you for your wisdom and your sensibility. One of the biggest honors of my life has been having you in it." For the second time ever, Jon hugged his loving aide.

Organizers of the parade deemed it best for the event to begin at the UN building. There, the Tuckerman family members, the president, and all the other notables asked to ride in the parade would gather and enter into their vehicles. From the UN, the parade route would travel west for a few blocks onto 42nd Street, and then proceed north on 5th Avenue all the way through Midtown, ending up at Marcus Garvey Park at East 124th Street.

Parade officials had secured the services of virtually every single available police officer across all five of New York City's boroughs to maintain decorum and prevent any of JT's fans from getting too physically close to their hero. It was estimated that more than five million people would attend the parade—breaking Manhattan's record crowd of four million for famed aviator Charles Lindbergh in 1927, and easily eclipsing such other record-breaking turnouts as those for Teddy Roosevelt, Amelia Earhart, Douglas MacArthur, the Apollo 11 astronauts, and Nelson Mandela.

Russell prepared an extraordinary breakfast for the Tuckerman clan on the morning of November 22, 2036. JT, Susan, Isak, and Lauren stuffed their faces with the most remarkable huckleberry flapjacks in the history of life, along with extra crispy bacon, farm fresh scrambled eggs, and the best coffee money could buy. Jake and Maui were surprisingly subdued while Susan, sitting at the table, took turns nursing each of them behind a carefully placed baby blanket.Mully had been assigned the task of retrieving the Tuckermans and driving them down to the UN. Lines of people had already begun to gather, many hours before the scheduled 1:00 pm start time of the parade. As their car made its way down Fifth Avenue, everyone inside, including Mully himself, marveled. "Mr. Tuckerman, it's too bad nobody cares about your birthday," he joked.

"Yeah, I know, right? It's gonna be a 'wash.' We should probably just turn around and head back home," JT replied with heartfelt good humor.

"Daddy, dare I say you're happy again?" Lauren remarked.

Jon looked deep into the eyes of each of his beloved adult children, his cherished new ones, and his beloved Susan. "All of my life, all I ever wanted to be was happy... just truly happy," he said softly. "And right now, yes, Lauren, I can tell you, without any doubt whatsoever, that I have never been happier in my entire life than I am right now."

CHAPTER FORTY-EIGHT

The morning couldn't have been brighter, warmer, or more filled with promise, given that it was late November in Manhattan. The Tuckermans arrived at the UN at noon. Throngs of people were standing outside, respectfully behind the police barricades, with hordes of media members setting up their gear in the bleachers specifically erected for their cameras. The giant flying-saucer-shaped float was parked in front and was immediately deemed by all four adult Tuckermans to be hilarious and quite impressive. JT and his family left their car and began to mingle with the crowd—Mully serving as bodyguard.

"There they are—America's Royal Family!" shouted President Winfield, who had arrived simultaneously in her limo. She approached JT and hugged him, then proceeded to do the same with Susan, Isak, Lauren, and even Susan's mother, Debra. She gently kissed the foreheads of each of the infant twins and beamed. "They're going to be trouble, you guys." She smiled at JT and Susan. "They're going to break hearts and take names!"

Governor Perry and Mayor Blythe joined in with the president and the Tuckerman gang. "You know, Mr. Tuckerman," the mayor said as he shook Jon's hand, "New York City always honors its own. And even though you're originally from *New Jersey,*" he chuckled, "you represent what New York's all about. You've become synonymous with watching out for the 'little guy.' Well today, Jon, we're all here to let you know there's nothing 'little' about you!"

"That's very kind. Thank you," JT replied sincerely.

Members of the Brooklyn High School marching band arrived, as did flag twirlers from a variety of high schools based across the five boroughs. The sun was shining, the weather was glorious, and the excited looks on everyone's faces was infectious.

"*You* did this, Daddy," Lauren said to her pop. "You made all of this happen. Just look around. All this is just for you!" She pecked her dad on the cheek.

"Alright everyone! Let's please get started!" Secretary General Kim shouted to the assembled through a megaphone. "Please take your places!"

The flag twirlers were arranged at the very front of the parade, the marching band lined up next. The special guest cars in order behind the marchers were the mayor's limo, the governor's limo, the president's limo, and then Jon's UFO float. Behind Jon was the stretch limousine containing the six members of the Tuckerman family, and behind it, the final vehicle carrying Secretary Kim.

JT entered the giant flying saucer float through a side door, took three short steps up inside, then sat on the tall chair placed there. He watched the hubbub all around him from his truly unique perch at the dead center of the spectacle, and suddenly found the whole predicament hilariously funny. He turned back and shouted out to Isak and Lauren, "Hey kids! Check it out! Your dad's an alien from outer space!" All within earshot laughed. Mully, who'd been assigned to drive the "UFO," perhaps laughed the hardest.

Jon, smiling from ear to ear, realized at that moment the real honor for him just then was sharing this hilarious and exciting moment with all of the people he most loved and cherished in his life.

The planned one o'clock start time for the parade ran a little late. Finally, at 1:30, the marching band launched the parade, playing the Stephen Stills song "Love the One You're With." Trumpets were blaring, trombones were belching, and drummers were drumming, as the adorable young flag twirlers began to perform as well.

Suddenly a large, dark cloud appeared, blocking the sun for just a few moments. Jon shuddered as it passed just as quickly.

Tens of thousands appeared on both sides of 42nd Street, cheering the entourage as it proceeded past them. Large signs reading "We Love You Jon!" and "JT for President!" and even "Jonathan Tuckerman! I Want to Have Your Babies!" were spotted interspersed throughout the crowd.

Isak leaned over his shoulder to Susan, shouting, "Hey! Didja ever think that YOU would marry a global sex symbol?"

Susan laughed out loud. "Yeah, you know I only married your Dad *for his looks, right?*"

The adult Tuckermans laughed so hard they started to cry. (Debra Parks played along.)

The parade took a sharp right turn onto 5th Avenue, and there the riders were confronted with what could only be described as an overwhelming sea of humanity. Jon was overcome with emotion when he realized that literally millions of people from around the world had gathered, at this time, on this date, in this place, to say "thank you" to HIM... one man, one simple lost soul, whose supernatural twist of fate could never have been anticipated and would never be repeated.

Tears began to trickle down his cheeks. "Mom," he whispered up into the sky, "THIS ONE'S FOR YOU!"

In addition to the massive hordes on the streets, countless more fans were watching through the windows of the high-rise apartments and office buildings running along 5th Avenue as well. Tickertape was being thrown from the tops of buildings onto the flying saucer float below... while an assortment of panties, garter belts, and bras of all sizes, along with large daisies, red roses, and other objects of affection, were tossed directly at the "UFO" from the crowds on the sidewalks.

The drivers of all the parade vehicles (including Mully inside the float) were so engaged and emotionally involved with the overwhelming enthusiasm of the crowds that they drove at a lesser pace than, perhaps, they would have normally done. Men, women, and children of every nationality, religion, shape, and color stood dozens of people deep behind the barricades on each side of the street.

From his perch high atop the other vehicles and even above the height of the tallest people in the parade, Jon could see everything... the smiles on the faces of his family, the president's famous beaming face, the occasional tear running down the cheek of Secretary General Kim— everyone, every single person involved in the event itself, was so joyous and ecstatic simply for being present. Jon, although completely isolated physically by his position inside the flying saucer, felt, for only perhaps the second time ever—the other being the Nobel Prize ceremony—that his life's purpose had been fulfilled, that he'd honored the memories of his beloved parents, and that he'd touched *so many people, so deeply,* that perhaps he should simply retire, move away from Manhattan with Susan, Jake, and Maui, and start life anew in some quiet, remote log cabin, somewhere out in the middle of Montana or New Mexico.

The magnificent St. Patrick's Cathedral was coming up on the right-hand side of the parade route. Jon had been meaning to go inside and inspect the famed interior ever since he'd first arrived in Manhattan. "I have got to get my ass in there," he told himself inside the UFO bubble. There were *so many* people all around him now, on both sides of the avenue, it was stunning. There were even a few teenagers who'd climbed onto the roof of the cathedral and were almost literally "hanging from the rafters." Jon turned around and pointed them out to his adult kids.

"That's just beyond amazing!" Isak shouted at his dad.

While Jon continued to wave, his arms aching, he wondered what all these people did with their daily lives. *What did they do for a living? Were they good providers for their families? Were these young people cheering him on good students? Were they helpful to their parents? Were they happy?* Then, for some reason, JT flashed back to the moment he was in the Pacific Ocean on his 70th birthday. He began thinking of all that had happened to him in the following three years... all the successes; all of the remarkable people he'd met, befriended and, in Susan's case, fallen in love with; all of the physical, mental, emotional, and environmental changes he'd helped make for his fellow human beings—all for the betterment of everyone.

For a few quick seconds, he also recalled his brief Draconian kidnapping experience and shuttered. "No, no, no," he said out loud to himself. "Not now!"

Jon saw a mother holding her young son in the crowd—the two were waving to him. He understood in that moment the world really did herald him as a hero. He knew he was truly beloved. He finally came to accept the fact that he had accomplished far more in just three short years than any other human being before him had ever done in any entire lifetime!

For a few moments—just a few fleeting moments—here, now, inside a fake UFO, while waving to over five-million cheering fans on his 73rd birthday, he truly felt alive.

Jonathan Michael Tuckerman was fully at peace with his lot in life.

CHAPTER FORTY-NINE

Three miles off the eastern shore of the Island of Manhattan, a single dark purple colored Flying V shaped UFO suddenly appeared in the sky, having emerged from behind the cloak of a massive black "raincloud." Seconds later, another sixteen similar craft quite unexpectedly shot straight up and into the air from their hidden perches beneath the Atlantic Ocean.

Seconds later, the Dodger Stadium Special seemingly materialized from nowhere, along with another five Nordic craft of similar size, shape, and colors.

Jorthon had anticipated this surprise attack by Larpeen and his followers and had assembled several of best fellow aviator pilots to join him in this air battle—the first ever of its kind—for the fate of the modern-day human race.

Laser beams of light began shooting out of the Flying Vs, bouncing off the ships of the Tall Whites. Jorthon's ship returned fire as did the ships of his teammates, and the display above the clouds drew as deadly as it was colorful. A number of Flying Vs began to disintegrate, falling from the sky and crashing back into the Atlantic in spectacular fashion. Several times, large schools of striped bass, bluefish, and/or perch were displaced by the crashes, hurtling flailing fish struggling to breathe high into the air before splashing back down into the sea.

At the helm of the Dodger Stadium Special, Jorthon quickly realized the largest of the Flying V ships—the one that had emerged from behind the giant raincloud—was Larpeen's. Although he'd been blinded by the hideous monster, he had since adapted to his situation, and had developed the ability to intuit where to fly his craft and how to outthink his opponent by melding his thought waves to synchronize with the robotic technologies of his craft. While the ships of the other Tall Whites continued to engage, and quite successfully shatter the defenses of the Draconian Flying Vs, causing damage or full-out destruction to virtually all of them, Larpeen's ship was larger and more powerful. The leader of the Draconian Race continued to resist Jorthon's anti-aircraft weapons through lightning-fast evasive maneuvers.

Larpeen's craft then suddenly shot across the sky, heading directly toward the Island of Manhattan. Jorthon knew that he had to follow in pursuit but was also well aware of the potential destruction that lay just ahead, not only for the residents of New York City, but also for the millions of participants attending Jonathan's parade.

JT's UFO float was now just a few blocks south of Fifth Avenue's Bezos Building (which had been formerly known as "Trump Tower" in previous decades.) Jon observed hundreds of people waving at him through the windows of the famed fifty-eight-story building. Having never before been inside that landmark, he'd long pondered visiting the Trump Presidential Museum, which was on its penthouse floor and honored the disgraced 45th President of the United States.

The Plaza Hotel and Central Park now loomed before the riders in the parade, above and at their sharp left. JT had always loved Central Park, having taken several private horse and carriage rides there with

Susan late at night to avoid any "fans" rushing him for autographs and photos. In fact, he and Susan had even tried to make love there once under a horse blanket, but it was too cold, and their raucous laughter killed any chance of a successful intercourse session taking place.

The parade, clearly a success far beyond anyone's wildest dreams, was about to enter its third and final leg when President Winfield turned around in her car and shouted back to Jon, "Hey Mr. Tuckerman! You can't say New York City doesn't love you today!" Jon smiled and waved, then looked at his watch.

It was 2:20 pm.

Suddenly, a horrendous noise similar to a sonic "boom" erupted in the sky above Fifth Avenue, and all movement of the vehicles within JT's parade came to a quick halt. Larpeen's massive purple Flying V craft had once again burst forth from its dark cloud hiding place and now positioned itself directly above JT's vehicle. Dozens of crowd members began applauding, thinking the strange ship's surprise appearance was part of the show—a repeat of the Oslo incident.

Jonathan Tuckerman, however, knew that it wasn't!

The Dodger Stadium Special next zapped itself above Jon's float as well, and began firing new and more intensely bright dark orange laser beams into Larpeen's craft. The V ship rocked back and forth from the blow, but then began to zigzag across the Manhattan skyline, firing its own purple beams of destruction at the tops of some of New York's most iconic buildings. The steeple-pointed tip of the Chrysler Building fell to the ground, along with the tops of the Empire State Building, the Flatiron Building, and even several top floors of the city's fabled Freedom Tower.

Miraculously, as virtually all of Manhattan was watching the parade, not a single human being standing below any of the destructive chaos was killed or even injured.

The Dodger Stadium Special kept itself in close pursuit of Larpeen's V. Jorthon realized the time had come for him to take an extraordinary measure. He purposely positioned his ship directly below the V craft.

Then, in an indescribably powerful flourish, he thrust his airship directly into the V's belly, propelling the V straight up into the sky for hundreds of miles in just seconds.

Larpeen's V, not having been designed to accelerate directly straight up that quickly, began to disintegrate. The Draconian spacecraft caught fire, and the evil Larpeen himself died instantly. As the flaming remnants of Larpeen's aircraft hurtled back down to Earth, Jorthon was able to "beam" those errant shards over the Atlantic, so they could return to Earth—and into the sea—without any further destruction to Manhattan.

The victorious Dodger Stadium Special now once again positioned itself directly above JT's UFO float vehicle. Jonathan looked up and realized that his dear friend Jorthon must have eliminated the dreaded Larpeen once and for all.

"And that, my friends, is how we do THAT!" JT said aloud to no one.

CHAPTER FIFTY

Seconds later: The first "bang" sounded like a car backfiring. Many of the people on either side of 5th Avenue stopped applauding and waving, while others continued to do so.

Another bang!" JT looked at his hands and saw blood. Lots of fresh blood!

In the car behind him, Isak and Lauren screamed "DAD!!!" while the President of the United States in the car ahead of Jon's stood up, hopped over the door of her car, and raced behind her—directly to the side of the flying saucer float where Jon had entered. Susan, quickly having handed Jake and Maui to her mother, left her vehicle too, as did Jon's two eldest children.

"JON/DAD!!!" the four screamed, as they tried desperately to open the side door of the float to gain access to where JT was situated. However, the handle on the door of the float appeared to be stuck.

The third "Bang!" was so loud, so prominent, so obviously awful, that now the entire crowd along 5th Avenue had begun shrieking in fright.

Susan managed to get the handle "unstuck" and opened the side door to the UFO float. There, she saw Jon, slumped over in the bubble top, a clear and horrific hole in the back of her husband's head. "NO!!!!!!!!!!!!" she screamed at the top of her lungs. She and the president, in tandem, managed to grab Jon and began to extract him from the float. Placing his arms on either of their shoulders, they pulled him out of the UFO and gently placed him onto the pavement of 5th Avenue itself, just across the street from the Plaza Hotel.

Isak and Lauren, shaking uncontrollably, kneeled alongside their stricken father, along with the President of the United States, Mully, New York's governor, and the City's mayor.

The stunned crowd remained behind the barricades in hushed reverence, simply not believing what they'd just seen.

Susan went into doctor mode, removing Jon's jacket and shirt and massaging his heart. His eyes were open wide and unresponsive. Blood gushed from his head wound.

"God, this is NOT happening!" screamed the president.

Suddenly, the sliver of metal inside Jon's tracking device necklace began "beeping" loudly, raised itself inches into the air, and then emitted a remarkably bright-blue light. The Dodger Stadium Special shot an intense beam of bright lemon-yellow light back down to his body, quickly beaming Jon back onboard the giant airship. When the light vanished, and the crowd could "see" again, they realized that *Kalyssa* now stood atop the giant UFO float. Her sudden and completely unexpected appearance shocked everyone.

With tears flowing down her face and speaking loudly—yet once again, as always, telepathically—Karen Lisa Tuckerman announced to all, "Unfortunately, this was Jonathan's time—his *Predestined End of Life Date*," she explained to the crowd. "Jorthon and I have delayed this event for as long as we could, but no one, not even your beloved Wonder Man, has the ability to postpone indefinitely the predestiny of his death. I am so very sorry to all of you for this tragic loss. My brother will be greatly missed."

A commotion was taking place a few blocks to the east, with members of the crowd screaming, "He's got a gun!' He's got a GUN!"

Kalyssa leapt off the top of the float and onto 5th Avenue. She then ran incredibly fast, and seconds later caught up with the large dark-skinned man who'd just fled from the Bezos Building while carrying a Remington 783 bolt-action rifle. Kalyssa tackled the assassin, thrusting him to the ground. The man, shocked to see the world-famous Kalyssa sitting atop him, acquiesced to her "citizen's arrest" and did not resist her restraint.

In a flash, a number of New York's boys in blue ran to Kalyssa's aid, quickly arresting the man and securing his gun as evidence.

✑

Jonathan Michael Tuckerman, the man of the hour, the man of the year, the man of a generation, the Hero of Earth, the Friend to Aliens, the Wonder Man, whose unprecedented efforts helped improve the lives of the impoverished and underprivileged, ended war and conflict and anger, healed the sick and fed the hungry, and repaired the health of the Earth itself, left his home planet at 2:30 pm Eastern Standard Time on November 22, 2036, 3 A.T.C., his 73rd and final birthday.

Jon's childhood hero, President John Fitzgerald Kennedy, had left *his* home planet in the same way—and on the same date—exactly 73 years earlier.

To the minute.

EPILOGUE

While the aliens' influence upon human beings had eliminated anger and stalled hatred, the emotions of sadness and sorrow remained. The world was consumed with grief after the Hero of Earth had been gunned down in broad daylight in the middle of New York City... on his birthday, no less. TV news clips of the shots fired, the frantic efforts of Susan and the President of the United States, Jon's disappearance into a beam of light, and Kalyssa's unexpected pronouncement about his predestined death date and dramatic capture of his assassin, were aired countless thousands of times on every news media outlet in existence.

Not since the mirror image assassination of President Kennedy in 1963 A.D. had grown men and women around the world wept openly in the streets, many falling to their knees, others holding onto each other to keep from collapse. Young children, dismissed for a week from schools had little more to do at home than try to console their sobbing parents. Crowds of ashen-faced citizens in public squares and sites around the world that Jon and Susan, as well as Jon and Isak, had visited, held candlelight vigils in giant parks, inside stadiums, and at other large venues.

Police charged David Ryan Hammond with the assassination of Jonathan Michael Tuckerman. Investigators inspecting the Bezos Building discovered that Hammond had somehow smashed (without getting noticed) a small hole through the glass of an office space on the 17th floor. Following his arraignment at the Supreme Court of New York, where the man was charged with first degree premeditated murder, his public defender requested of the court that Hammond be admitted to Lenox Hill Hospital for observation, as his actions following Jon's murder led them to believe he was intensely delusional.

On November 24, Dr. Arthur Sanders, president of Lenox Hill Hospital, gave a press conference before the world's media. He announced to the jam-packed crowd of reporters that "David Ryan Hammond, age 29, suffers from an extremely rare mental illness known as 'Capgras Syndrome.' People with this disease suffer from the delusion that a friend, family member, or someone else they have to come to know personally has been replaced by an evil twin imposter. Mr. Hammond had come to believe that Mr. Jonathan Tuckerman was Satan—the Devil himself on the Earth—and had to be eliminated. He has been examined by a team of four physicians and six psychiatrists, and it is our joint conclusion that, clearly, he was not affected by the aliens' pink spray that eliminated anger and violence from the rest of us. Due to this remarkably rare illness, he was simply immune to that process."

Kalyssa, however, knew the real reason that Hammond had killed Tuckerman. She was well-aware from the moment she captured him that he must have been a patsy within a Draconian plot to disrupt the harmonic balance of Earth. While sitting atop Hammond, Kalyssa looked into his eyes and knew that he'd been hypnotized. Kalyssa theorized that, most likely, a Draconian military leader, presenting as human and hiding out somewhere within the five boroughs of New York City, gained access to a rifle and had enlisted Hammond's help as soon as the parade route had been announced a few weeks earlier. Kalyssa was convinced that the Draconians had hypnotized Hammond, setting him up with both the idea to shoot at Jon and, afterwards, the inability to recall much of anything.

In lieu of a jury trial, Hammond's PD had him plead no contest to the murder charge. Hammond was instantly sentenced to spend the rest of his life at Bellevue Hospital.

☙

President Winfield, devastated beyond all words by the shocking death of her "friend for life," remained in office another seven weeks before deciding to voluntarily resign from her post. The woman had aged ten years during those weeks and had lost much of her zest for living. Handing over the reins of power to Vice President Schoenberg, Winfield retired to her massive estate in upstate New York. She brought Russell along with her. There, the gentle soul kept her fed and warm for the rest of her life.

Newly sworn President Bradley Schoenberg declared that November 22 of each future year hence would become a Day of Remembrance—a national holiday. The pronouncement, he declared, was "not to recall the horror of November 22, 3 A.T.C., but instead to celebrate the life and accomplishments of Mr. Jonathan Michael Tuckerman, a man whose heroism and forward-thinking ideas brought hope, light, and joy to billions. Let us all remember him fondly and continue to admire him for all he had the time to accomplish."

Early in January, Isak moved back to Iceland. Having long before left his previous job, he now devoted his time to both rekindling his relationship with Harold and launching a microgreens business, growing edible plants and herbs to be used as food for restaurants. While it was difficult for Harold to deal with the fact that Isak's mere presence was a constant reminder of his global fame—and all that came with that stigma—he did his best to combat all feelings of jealousy. The couple regained their balance with each other, even adopting several more dogs.

The moment she arrived back in Paris at Charles's apartment, Lauren immediately cut her long brown hair short and dyed it platinum blonde, hoping that by disguising her appearance she would no longer need to embrace the endless river of strangers coming up to her, reaching for her hand, and saying "I'm so sorry for your loss." The death of her father had devastated Lauren. She had completely stopped speaking for weeks afterwards. Charles was most kind and understanding, buying her new art supplies so she could just "paint her sorrows away."

Dr. Susan Parks Tuckerman, along with her infants Jake and Maui, relocated to a large estate in nearby Connecticut. She handed off her medical practice to her partners and decided to devote the rest of her life to just raising her children. Her property included a horse ranch, where the young Tuckermans would later learn to ride, and an adjacent farm, where the kids would bond with animals, milk cows, and collect chicken eggs. A few times a year, Susan and the twins were driven up to former President Winfield's estate, where the two women sat, drank Russell's wonderful cinnamon tea, and chatted quietly while watching the youngsters swim in Tameka's backyard pool.

Years in the future, Jake Tuckerman would become a world famous pop music singer.

Maui Tuckerman would become the second female President of the United States.

Secretary General Kim had commissioned a solid gold plaque be installed on the wall just outside the door of the Team Tuckerman office suite at the UN. The plaque read: "Here, on this site, from December 2033 A.D. until November 3 A.T.C., the United Nations held the Distinct Honor and Privilege of Serving as the Home Office for Mr. Jonathan Michael Tuckerman, Winner of the 2034 Nobel Prize for Peace. The World is a Better Place because of this Wonder Man."

Clarence and Meghan Connors relocated from New York to Washington, D.C., where they served as valued members of President

Schoenberg's new Cabinet. The duo was often sought by large groups and associations around the world for public speaking engagements, and by media outlets for interviews about their experiences with JT and Team Tuckerman. While eternally heartbroken along with everyone else, the two realized that the brief time they'd had with Jon and his aliens was the most extraordinary experience anyone could have ever asked for or imagined.

Fulfilling a promise she'd made to Jon three years earlier, Meghan privately met with both Isak and Lauren at Lauren's apartment during their initial period of quiet mourning. There, she relayed to them what their father had told her just before his second-ever ride on the Dodger Stadium Special. "Please tell my children I said 'thank you for letting me be their father again.'" The trio sat crying for a good while.

Barbara Gardner's book, entitled *After They Came*, was published just two weeks after Jon's assassination (she'd had to add a quick final chapter based on the events in New York,) and, of course, had instantly become a massive best seller, breaking every sales record in every country on the globe. Reviewers cited her tome as a "highly well-researched, fair, and balanced look at the life and times of one Mr. Jonathan Tuckerman, warts and all." The book, which had been translated into virtually every known language, became a cultural icon—a touchpoint for those who'd fallen in love with JT from afar during the last three years of his life and craved to know every possible detail of his existence, from birth to death. The book was assigned homework in high school English classes everywhere, becoming a classic "must read."

"He was a special man," parents would tell their children when passing along copies of their dog-eared copies of *After They Came* in later years. "He changed us all. And then he was taken too soon. Such a terrible tragedy."

Based on Jon's royalties from the sales of Second Chance Theater systems; the *After They Came* book; toys, games and other Jon Tuckerman-related merchandise hawked by Barbara—including the sexy poster of Kalyssa; as well as JT's $3.2 million in remaining gold from

Jorthon's nugget—Susan, Isak, Lauren, Jake, and Maui had all become multimillionaires. Each was set for life financially, to pursue any and all dreams they could imagine, once their sorrow finally subsided.

Kalyssa took up residence in Washington, D.C., where she became an ally to and friend with President Schoenberg. Before leaving office, President Winfield and Kalyssa had shared with the new president the fact that Draconians had embedded themselves in disguise around the world, in a calculated plan to overwhelm mankind. Truly horrified, President Schoenberg continued to make every resource at his disposal available to Kalyssa. While, of course, she didn't need any military might or weaponry—she had that well handled through her constant contact with Jorthon and the fleet of Plaedians who continued to patrol the skies above Earth, Kalyssa did regularly tap into the intelligence services of the FBI and CIA, as she continued her work to detect and track down the last suspected Draconian agents still left alive and carefully hidden around the world.

Kalyssa remained living on Earth for the rest of her life—another 1,240 years.

Much to everyone's surprise and consternation, both the Dream TV and Second Chance Theater systems completely stopped working just hours after Jon had been sucked back up into the great airship on November 22, 2036, 3 A.T.C. The heads of every major technology firm around the world were stymied—nothing could restore, repair, or replace those mediums that had provided so much to so many.

"It's as though Jon Tuckerman's passing took the lightbulbs out of their sockets," James Stayburn, CTO of Apple, was quoted as telling *WIRED* magazine.

After retrieving Jon's dying, blood-soaked body from the pavement of 5ᵗʰ Avenue, Jorthon had transported the Hero of Earth to the Plaeidas inter-dimensional planet. There, he placed JT on a massive light table inside the Library Building, asking his close friend Euclid to watch over the gravely "dead" man.

A quarter of Jon's head was missing—completely gone. His mouth was frozen open, and his eyes transfixed. He looked like a startled fish who'd just been unexpectedly pulled out of the sea on a fisherman's line. Naked and stiff, his body was now once again rotating on a horizontal table of light.

Obviously too far gone for any immediate help from Jorthon's "Life Juice," Jon was dead—good and gone. Deceased.

Jorthon and Euclid stood aside the man's body and smiled in stoic admiration. Euclid spoke first. "You did right by him—and fulfilled your promise to his parents. You did all that you could do. You put off his passing for as long as you possibly could. Predestiny is a bitch."

Jorthon touched the old alien on the shoulder. "Watch over him for me, will you?" he said.

"Of course, my dear friend, he'll be safe here with me, indefinitely," Euclid replied. "I give you my word."

Jorthon decided to take a short period of time off from his duties patrolling the skies above Earth. His battle against the Draconian fleet above Manhattan—which had quickly become legendary among his fellow Pleiadians—had taken a toll on his spirit. Also, the Infinite Creator had tasked Euclid with working closely with Jorthon in efforts to restore whatever vision might possibly be left for the Tall White to regain.

After three Earth months of rest and reflection, Jorthon finally did recapture a solid degree of sight. It was enough to sustain him for the next nine centuries of his life.

Exactly eleven years after Jon Tuckerman's assassination—on November 22, 14 A.T.C.—the slain man woke up inside the great Library Building within the Pleiades star system. He yawned, looked around, then realized he was sitting atop a massive light table—far brighter and more elegant than the one he'd become accustomed to inside the Dodger Stadium Special. After Jon hopped off the light table, the sight of Euclid and his surroundings startled him.

Jonathan Michael Tuckerman hadn't aged a day

"Hey Dad, here's a riddle for you. Find the answer.
There's a reason for the world - You and I."
—John Ondrasik

AFTERWORD

My father, Jack Robert Harary, worked for the U.S. Government's Department of Defense (U.S. Army) from summer 1951 until his retirement in the fall of 1996. He was an electronics engineer who helped design and invent new radar detection systems, guided missiles, and airborne drones that integrated the use of photographic spying equipment. (He once described one of his inventions to me as something that "looked like a flying garbage can").

Always highly secretive about his work, when asked what he did for a living, my father would only reply, "I helped the United States win the Cold War."

One night during the spring of 1970, my father and I were in his car approaching Dwight Drive in West Deal, New Jersey—the street we lived on from 1963 until 1978. He'd picked me up from a Hebrew school class—it was perhaps 6 pm and still daylight. As we turned onto Dwight Drive from the adjacent Deal Road, we saw through the windshield an enormous silver "Flying V" shaped UFO craft very, very slowly hovering over the homes of our neighbors. I recall it had three lights—one red, one blue, and one silver—on each of its tips.

I shouted, "Dad stop the car!" He did so and pulled the vehicle off to the side of the road. We got out and watched the giant craft glide directly above us—silently—perhaps 150 feet in the sky.

My dad said nothing. As though the sighting was commonplace, he was completely and totally nonplussed by the entire experience. I was hyperventilating, jumping up and down in amazement.

"Dad this is so cool! A UFO! We saw a UFO!"

My father simply winked at me and said, "Let's go home."

Now bouncing in my seat, I shouted, "Dad! I'm gonna put this in my diary!" To which my brilliant father coolly responded, "What? You have diarrhea?"

Upon returning home, I ran into the kitchen and picked up our (rotary) phone to call the *Asbury Park Press*—our local area newspaper. I distinctly remember the conversation.

A woman answered. I said, "Hi, my name is Danny Harary. I live on Dwight Drive in West Deal. I want to report a UFO! My dad and I just saw a big silver UFO flying over our street!"

The woman, sounding somewhat frantic, said, "Sonny, we're getting a LOT of phone calls about this right now! Sorry, but I have to go." She hung up. I looked in the paper the next day and was greatly disappointed to see no mention of my encounter anywhere.

No story ever ran.

My interest in UFOs was rekindled in 2007 when I was strolling through a bookstore in Los Angeles, simply killing time, and found an aisle of books about UFOs, aliens, and paranormal activity. I instantly flashed back to the UFO sighting I'd had with my father in 1970, having forgotten all about it, and began, that day collecting books on the subjects of unexplained flying craft and the possibility of extra-terrestrial life.

It's a passion that fascinates me still.

While reading Richard M. Dolan's 2002 book, *UFOs and the National Security State*, I was thrilled to discover, toward the back of the book, his chronological "Table of Military UFO Encounters." There were two entries within that table that blew my mind. The first on September 10, 1951, being a radar and visually-confirmed sighting of a metallic, disc-shaped object flying at 900 mph over the skies of Fort Monmouth, New Jersey. My father had begun working at the site just a few months earlier. Another sighting over Fort Monmouth is also listed in Dolan's book: July 1, 1952. On that date, Dolan notes that radar and visual contact occurred of two unidentified flying objects which hovered over the base, then sped away.

(Note: Renowned UFO researcher Richard Dolan provided a wonderful review quote for *After They Came*, which appears at the start of this book.)

I would very much like to believe that my father experienced one, if not both, of those Ft. Monmouth events—UFO encounters that had taken place just overhead at his then recently acquired place of employment.

And even further, I'd love to believe my Dad *actually knew* what UFO's really were!

❧

My father passed away in Boca Raton, Florida on April 17, 2017. Long before he developed dementia, I had asked him several times over the years if he had had *anything* at all to do with UFOs during his 45 years of service—inventing things that "fly and spy" for the U.S. Government. He consistently denied knowing anything about them whatsoever, but a few times I remember that he chuckled.

Later in his life, he did inform me that he and his second wife had seen some glowing, bright red flying objects over the Atlantic Ocean (off the coast of Belmar, N.J.) sometime in 1996, just before he relocated from New Jersey to Florida for his retirement.

"If UFOs really do exist," he told me at that time, "then that's what those red lights were."

On October 15, 2022, the night that I am writing these words, I phoned my mother, Joan, 88 at the time (my father's first wife), to ask her what, if anything, she might remember about my dad's work at the base. She told me a story I'd never heard before. "Very early on in your father's career at Fort Monmouth, they took him down into the vaults, spoke to him privately, and showed him something down there that they said was highly top secret. He was not to ever share what he saw down there with anyone. I remember he was really frightened when he came home that night—he was scared shitless. Your father was never the same after that."

Any knowledge of UFOs and/or aliens my beloved father may have had he took with him to his final resting place—the base of a beautiful tree in La Jolla Park in La Jolla, CA. There, my family and I scattered his ashes in May 2017.

I loved my father very much, and I miss him every day. Since he passed away, he has visited me and my two brothers, Bob and Mike, dozens of times in our dreams. The remarkable amount of love that this man had for his three sons and six grandchildren always was, and remains for us all, the indelible gift he left behind.

Thank you, Dad, for being my father.

You were *my* "Wonder Man"!